P9-DDS-511

Praise for Sophie Kinsella
and the *Shopaholic* novels:

"A hilarious tale . . . hijinks worthy of classic
I Love Lucy episodes . . . too good to pass up."
—*USA TODAY*

"Kinsella's Bloomwood is plucky and funny . . .
You won't have to shop around to find a more
winning protagonist."   —*PEOPLE*

"[Sophie Kinsella] gives chick-lit lovers a reason
to stay home from the mall."
—*ENTERTAINMENT WEEKLY*

"Don't wait for a sale to buy this hilarious book."
—*US WEEKLY*

"Perfect for anyone wishing that bank statements
came in more colours than just black and red."
—*THE MIRROR* (LONDON)

Also by Sophie Kinsella

SOPHIE KINSELLA

confessions

of

a

SHOPAHOLIC

A DELL BOOK

CONFESSIONS OF A SHOPAHOLIC
A Dell Book

PUBLISHING HISTORY
Transworld UK edition published 2000
Delta Trade Paperback edition published February 2001
Dell mass market edition / November 2003

Published by
Bantam Dell
A Division of Random House, Inc.
New York, New York

Book design by Karin Batten

Library of Congress Catalog Card Number: 00-060398

ISBN 0-440-24141-3

Manufactured in the United States of America
Published simultaneously in Canada

OPM 20 19 18 17 16 15 14 13 12

confessions

of

a

SHOPAHOLIC

1 Stallion Square
London W1 3HW

Ms. Rebecca Bloomwood
Flat 4
63 Jarvis Road
Bristol BS1 0DN

6 July 1997

Dear Ms. Bloomwood:
Congratulations! As a recent graduate of Bristol University
you are undoubtedly proud of your performance.

We at Endwich are also proud of our performance as a
flexible, caring bank with accounts to suit everyone. We
pride ourselves particularly in our farsighted approach
when it comes to customers of a caliber such as yours.

We are therefore offering you, Ms. Bloomwood—as a
graduate—a free extended overdraft facility of £2,000
during the first two years of your career. Should you
decide to open an account with Endwich, this facility will
be available immediately.* I do hope you decide to take
advantage of this unique offer and look forward to
receiving your completed form.

Once again, congratulations!

Yours sincerely,

Nigel Fairs
Graduate Marketing Manager

*(subject to status)

Ms. Rebecca Bloomwood
Flat 2
4 Burney Rd.
London SW6 8FD

10 September 1999

Dear Ms. Bloomwood:

Further to my letters of 3 May, 29 July, and 14 August, you will be aware that your free graduate overdraft facility is due to end on 19 September 1999. You will also be aware that you have substantially exceeded the agreed limit of £2,000.

The current balance stands at a debit of £3,794.56.

Perhaps you would be kind enough to telephone my assistant, Erica Parnell, at the above number to arrange a meeting concerning this matter.

Yours sincerely,

Derek Smeath
Manager

Ms. Rebecca Bloomwood
Flat 2
4 Burney Rd.
London SW6 8FD

22 September 1999

Dear Ms. Bloomwood:

I am sorry to hear that you have broken your leg.

When you have recovered, perhaps you would be kind
enough to ring my assistant, Erica Parnell, and arrange a
meeting to discuss your ongoing overdraft needs.

Yours sincerely,

Derek Smeath
Manager

One

OK. DON'T PANIC. Don't *panic*. It's only a VISA bill. It's a piece of paper; a few numbers. I mean, just how scary can a few numbers be?

I stare out of the office window at a bus driving down Oxford Street, willing myself to open the white envelope sitting on my cluttered desk. It's only a piece of paper, I tell myself for the thousandth time. And I'm not stupid, am I? I know exactly how much this VISA bill will be.

Sort of. Roughly.

It'll be about . . . £200. Three hundred, maybe. Yes, maybe £300. Three-fifty, max.

I casually close my eyes and start to tot up. There was that suit in Jigsaw. And there was dinner with Suze at Quaglinos. And there was that gorgeous red and yellow rug. The rug was £200, come to think of it. But it was definitely worth every penny—everyone's admired it. Or, at least, Suze has.

And the Jigsaw suit was on sale—30 percent off. So that was actually *saving* money.

I open my eyes and reach for the bill. As my fingers hit the paper I remember new contact lenses. Ninety-five pounds. Quite a lot. But, I mean, I had to get those, didn't I? What am I supposed to do, walk around in a blur?

And I had to buy some new solutions and a cute case and some hypoallergenic eyeliner. So that takes it up to . . . £400?

At the desk next to mine, Clare Edwards looks up from her post. She's sorting all her letters into neat piles, just like she does every morning. She puts rubber bands round them and puts labels on them saying things like "Answer immediately" and "Not urgent but respond." I loathe Clare Edwards.

"OK, Becky?" she says.

"Fine," I say lightly. "Just reading a letter."

I reach gaily into the envelope, but my fingers don't quite pull out the bill. They remain clutched around it while my mind is seized—as it is every month—by my secret dream.

Do you want to know about my secret dream? It's based on a story I once read in *The Daily World* about a mix-up at a bank. I loved this story so much, I cut it out and stuck it onto my wardrobe door. Two credit card bills were sent to the wrong people, and—get this— each person paid the wrong bill without realizing. They paid off each other's bills *without even checking them*.

And ever since I read that story, my secret fantasy has been that the same thing will happen to me. I mean, I know it sounds unlikely—but if it happened once, it can happen again, can't it? Some dotty old woman in Cornwall will be sent my humongous bill and will pay it without even looking at it. And I'll be sent her bill for three tins of cat food at fifty-nine pence each. Which, naturally, I'll pay without question. Fair's fair, after all.

A smile is plastered over my face as I gaze out of the window. I'm convinced that this month it'll happen—

my secret dream is about to come true. But when I eventually pull the bill out of the envelope—goaded by Clare's curious gaze—my smile falters, then disappears. Something hot is blocking my throat. I think it could be panic.

The page is black with type. A series of familiar names rushes past my eyes like a mini shopping mall. I try to take them in, but they're moving too fast. Thorntons, I manage to glimpse. Thorntons Chocolates? What was I doing in Thorntons Chocolates? I'm supposed to be on a diet. This bill *can't* be right. This can't be me. I can't possibly have spent all this money.

Don't panic! I yell internally. The key is not to panic. Just read each entry slowly, one by one. I take a deep breath and force myself to focus calmly, starting at the top.

> WHSmith (well, that's OK. Everyone needs
>   stationery.)
> Boots (everyone needs shampoo)
> Specsavers (essential)
> Oddbins (bottle of wine—essential)
> Our Price (Our Price? Oh yes. The new Charlatans
>   album. Well, I had to have that, didn't I?)
> Bella Pasta (supper with Caitlin)
> Oddbins (bottle of wine—essential)
> Esso (petrol doesn't count)
> Quaglinos (expensive—but it was a one-off)
> Pret à Manger (that time I ran out of cash)
> Oddbins (bottle of wine—essential)
> Rugs to Riches (what? Oh yes. Stupid rug.)
> La Senza (sexy underwear for date with James)
> Agent Provocateur (even sexier underwear for date
>   with James. Like I needed it.)

Body Shop (that skin brusher thing which I must use)
Next (fairly boring white shirt—but it was in the
*   sale)*
Millets . . .

I stop in my tracks. Millets? I never go into Millets. What would I be doing in Millets? I stare at the statement in puzzlement, wrinkling my brow and trying to think—and then suddenly, the truth dawns on me. It's obvious. Someone else has been using my card.

Oh my God. I, Rebecca Bloomwood, have been the victim of a crime.

Now it all makes sense. Some criminal's pinched my credit card and forged my signature. Who knows where else they've used it? No wonder my statement's so black with figures! Someone's gone on a spending spree round London with my card—and they thought they would just get away with it.

But how? I scrabble in my bag for my purse, open it—and there's my VISA card, staring up at me. I take it out and run my fingers over the glossy surface. Someone must have pinched it from my purse, used it—*and then put it back*. It must be someone I know. Oh my God. Who?

I look suspiciously round the office. Whoever it is, isn't very bright. Using my card at Millets! It's almost laughable. As if I'd ever shop there.

"I've never even been into Millets!" I say aloud.

"Yes you have," says Clare.

"What?" I turn to her. "No I haven't."

"You bought Michael's leaving present from Millets, didn't you?"

I feel my smile disappear. Oh, bugger. Of course. The blue anorak for Michael. The blue sodding anorak from Millets.

When Michael, our deputy editor, left three weeks ago, I volunteered to buy his present. I took the brown envelope full of coins and notes into the shop and picked out an anorak (take it from me, he's that kind of guy). And at the last minute, now I remember, I decided to pay on credit and keep all that handy cash for myself.

I can vividly remember fishing out the four £5 notes and carefully putting them in my wallet, sorting out the pound coins and putting them in my coin compartment, and pouring the rest of the change into the bottom of my bag. Oh good, I remember thinking. I won't have to go to the cash machine. I'd thought that sixty quid would last me for weeks.

So what happened to it? I can't have just *spent* sixty quid without realizing it, can I?

"Why are you asking, anyway?" says Clare, and she leans forward. I can see her beady little X-ray eyes gleaming behind her specs. She knows I'm looking at my VISA bill. "No reason," I say, briskly turning to the second page of my statement.

But I've been put off my stride. Instead of doing what I normally do—look at the minimum payment required and ignore the total completely—I find myself staring straight at the bottom figure.

Nine hundred and forty-nine pounds, sixty-three pence. In clear black and white.

For thirty seconds I am completely motionless. Then, without changing expression, I stuff the bill back into the envelope. I honestly feel as though this piece of paper has nothing to do with me. Perhaps, if I carelessly let it drop down on the floor behind my computer, it will disappear. The cleaners will sweep it up and I can claim I never got it. They can't charge me for a bill I never received, can they?

I'm already composing a letter in my head. "Dear

Managing Director of VISA. Your letter has confused me. What bill are you talking about, precisely? I never received any bill from your company. I did not care for your tone and should warn you, I am writing to Anne Robinson of *Watchdog*."

Or I could always move abroad.

"Becky?" My head jerks up and I see Clare holding this month's news list. "Have you finished the piece on Lloyds?"

"Nearly," I lie. As she's watching me, I feel forced to summon it up on my computer screen, just to show I'm willing.

"This high-yield, 60-day access account offers tiered rates of interest on investments of over £2,000," I type onto the screen, copying directly from a press release in front of me. "Long-term savers may also be interested in a new stepped-rate bond which requires a minimum of £5,000."

I type a full stop, take a sip of coffee, and turn to the second page of the press release.

This is what I do, by the way. I'm a journalist on a financial magazine. I'm paid to tell other people how to organize their money.

Of course, being a financial journalist is not the career I always wanted. No one who writes about personal finance ever meant to do it. People tell you they "fell into" personal finance. They're lying. What they mean is they couldn't get a job writing about anything more interesting. They mean they applied for jobs at *The Times* and *The Express* and *Marie-Claire* and *Vogue* and *GQ*, and all they got back was "Piss off."

So they started applying to *Metalwork Monthly* and *Cheesemakers Gazette* and *What Investment Plan?* And they were taken on as the crappiest editorial assistant possible on no money whatsoever and were grateful. And they've stayed on writing about metal, or cheese, or savings, ever since—because that's all they know. I myself started on the catchily titled *Personal Investment Periodical*. I learned how to copy out a press release and nod at press conferences and ask questions that sounded as though I knew what I was talking about. After a year and a half—believe it or not—I was head-hunted to *Successful Saving*.

Of course, I still know nothing about finance. People at the bus stop know more about finance than me. Schoolchildren know more than me. I've been doing this job for three years now, and I'm still expecting someone to catch me out.

That afternoon, Philip, the editor, calls my name, and I jump in fright.

"Rebecca?" he says. "A word." And he beckons me over to his desk. His voice seems lower all of a sudden, almost conspiratorial, and he's smiling at me, as though he's about to give me a piece of good news.

Promotion, I think. It must be. He read the piece I wrote on international equity securities last week (in which I likened the hunt for long-term growth to the hunt for the perfect pair of summer mules) and was bowled over by how exciting I made it all sound. He *knows* it's unfair I earn less than Clare, so he's going to promote me to her level. Or even above. And he's telling me discreetly so Clare won't get jealous.

A wide smile plasters itself over my face and I get up and walk the three yards or so to his desk, trying to stay calm but already planning what I'll buy with my raise. I'll get that swirly coat in Whistles. And some black high-heeled boots from Pied à Terre. Maybe I'll go on holiday. And I'll pay off that blasted VISA bill once and for all. I feel buoyant with relief. I *knew* everything would be OK . . .

"Rebecca?" He's thrusting a card at me. "I can't make this press conference," he says. "But it could be quite interesting. Will you go? It's at Brandon Communications."

I can feel the elated expression falling off my face like jelly. He's not promoting me. I'm not getting a raise. I feel betrayed. *Why* did he smile at me like that? He must have known he was lifting my hopes.

"Something wrong?" inquires Philip.

"No," I mutter. But I can't bring myself to smile. In front of me, my new swirly coat and high-heeled boots are disappearing into a puddle, like the Wicked Witch of the West. No promotion. Just a press conference about . . . I turn over the card. About a new unit trust. How could anyone *possibly* describe that as interesting?

Two

THERE'S JUST ONE essential purchase I have to make on the way to the press conference—and that's the *Financial Times*. The *FT* is by far the best accessory a girl can have. Its major advantages are:

1. It's a nice color.
2. It only costs eighty-five pence.
3. If you walk into a room with it tucked under your arm, people take you seriously. With an *FT* under your arm, you can talk about the most frivolous things in the world, and instead of thinking you're an airhead, people think you're a heavyweight intellectual who has broader interests, too.

At my interview for *Successful Saving*, I went in holding copies of the *Financial Times* and the *Investor's Chronicle*—and I didn't get asked about finance once. As I remember it, we spent the whole time talking about holiday villas and gossiping about other editors.

So I stop at a newsstand and buy a copy of the *FT*. There's some huge headline about Rutland Bank on the front page, and I'm thinking maybe I should at least skim it, when I catch my reflection in the window of Denny and George.

I don't look bad, I think. I'm wearing my black skirt from French Connection, and a plain white T-shirt from Knickerbox, and a little angora cardigan which I got from M&S but looks like it might be Agnès b. And my new square-toed shoes from Hobbs. Even better, although no one can see them, I know that underneath I'm wearing my gorgeous new matching knickers and bra with embroidered yellow rosebuds. They're the best bit of my entire outfit. In fact, I almost wish I could be run over so that the world would see them.

It's a habit of mine, itemizing all the clothes I'm wearing, as though for a fashion page. I've been doing it for years—ever since I used to read *Just Seventeen*. Every issue, they'd stop a girl on the street, take a picture of her, and list all her clothes. "T-Shirt: Chelsea Girl, Jeans: Top Shop, Shoes: borrowed from friend." I used to read those lists avidly, and to this day, if I buy something from a shop that's a bit uncool, I cut the label out. So that if I'm ever stopped in the street, I can pretend I don't know where it's from.

So anyway. There I am, with the *FT* tucked under my arm, thinking I look pretty good, and half wishing someone from *Just Seventeen* would pop up with a camera—when suddenly my eyes focus and snap to attention, and my heart stops. In the window of Denny and George is a discreet sign. It's dark green with cream lettering, and it says: SALE.

I stare at it, and my skin's all prickly. It can't be true. Denny and George can't be having a sale. They never have a sale. Their scarves and pashminas are so coveted, they could probably sell them at twice the price. Everyone I know in the entire world aspires to owning a Denny and George scarf. (Except my mum and dad, obviously. My mum thinks if you can't buy it at Bentalls of Kingston, you don't need it.)

I swallow, take a couple of steps forward, then push open the door of the tiny shop. The door pings, and the nice blond girl who works there looks up. I don't know her name but I've always liked her. Unlike some snotty cows in clothes shops, she doesn't mind if you stand for ages staring at clothes you really can't afford to buy. Usually what happens is, I spend half an hour lusting after scarves in Denny and George, then go off to Accessorize and buy something to cheer myself up. I've got a whole drawerful of Denny and George substitutes.

"Hi," I say, trying to stay calm. "You're . . . you're having a sale."

"Yes." The blond girl smiles. "Bit unusual for us."

My eyes sweep the room. I can see rows of scarves, neatly folded, with dark green "50 percent off" signs above them. Printed velvet, beaded silk, embroidered cashmere, all with the distinctive "Denny and George" signature. They're everywhere. I don't know where to start. I think I'm having a panic attack.

"You always liked this one, I think," says the nice blond girl, taking out a shimmering gray-blue scarf from the pile in front of her.

Oh God, yes. I remember this one. It's made of silky velvet, overprinted in a paler blue and dotted with iridescent beads. As I stare at it, I can feel little invisible strings, silently tugging me toward it. I have to touch it. I have to wear it. It's the most beautiful thing I've ever seen. The girl looks at the label. "Reduced from £340 to £120." She comes and drapes the scarf around my neck and I gape at my reflection.

There is no question. I have to have this scarf. I *have* to have it. It makes my eyes look bigger, it makes my haircut look more expensive, it makes me look like a different person. I'll be able to wear it with everything.

People will refer to me as the Girl in the Denny and George Scarf.

"I'd snap it up if I were you." The girl smiles at me. "There's only one of these left."

Involuntarily, I clutch at it.

"I'll have it," I gasp. "I'll have it."

As she's laying it out on tissue paper, I take out my purse, open it up, and reach for my VISA card in one seamless, automatic action—but my fingers hit bare leather. I stop in surprise and start to rummage through all the pockets of my purse, wondering if I stuffed my card back in somewhere with a receipt or if it's hidden underneath a business card . . . And then, with a sickening thud, I remember. It's on my desk.

How could I have been so stupid? How could I have left my VISA card on my desk? What was I *thinking*?

The nice blond girl is putting the wrapped scarf into a dark green Denny and George box. My mouth is dry with panic. What am I going to do?

"How would you like to pay?" she says pleasantly.

My face flames red and I swallow hard.

"I've just realized I've left my credit card at the office," I stutter.

"Oh," says the girl, and her hands pause.

"Can you hold it for me?" The girl looks dubious.

"For how long?"

"Until tomorrow?" I say desperately. Oh God. She's pulling a face. Doesn't she understand?

"I'm afraid not," she says. "We're not supposed to reserve sale stock."

"Just until later this afternoon, then," I say quickly. "What time do you close?"

"Six."

Six! I feel a combination of relief and adrenaline

sweeping through me. Challenge, Rebecca. I'll go to the press conference, leave as soon as I can, then take a taxi back to the office. I'll grab my VISA card, tell Philip I left my notebook behind, come here, and buy the scarf.

"Can you hold it until then?" I say beseechingly. "Please? *Please*?" The girl relents.

"OK. I'll put it behind the counter."

"Thanks," I gasp. I hurry out of the shop and down the road toward Brandon Communications. Please let the press conference be short, I pray. Please don't let the questions go on too long. Please God, *please* let me have that scarf.

As I arrive at Brandon Communications, I can feel myself begin to relax. I do have three whole hours, after all. And my scarf is safely behind the counter. No one's going to steal it from me.

There's a sign up in the foyer saying that the Foreland Exotic Opportunities press conference is happening in the Artemis Suite, and a man in uniform is directing everybody down the corridor. This means it must be quite big. Not television-cameras-CNN-world's-press-on-tenterhooks big, obviously. But fairly-good-turnout big. A relatively important event in our dull little world.

As I enter the room, there's already a buzz of people milling around, and waitresses circulating with canapés. The journalists are knocking back the champagne as if they've never seen it before; the PR girls are looking supercilious and sipping water. A waiter offers me a glass of champagne and I take two. One for now, one to put under my chair for the boring bits.

In the far corner of the room I can see Elly Granger from *Investor's Weekly News*. She's been pinned into a corner by two earnest men in suits and is nodding at them, with a glassy look in her eye. Elly's great. She's only been on *Investor's Weekly News* for six months, and already she's applied for forty-three other jobs. What she really wants to be is a beauty editor on a magazine, and I think she'd be really good at it. Every time I see her, she's got a new lipstick on—and she always wears really interesting clothes. Like today, she's wearing an orange chiffony shirt over a pair of white cotton trousers, espadrilles, and a big wooden necklace, the kind I could never wear in a million years.

What *I* really want to be is Fiona Phillips on *GMTV.* I could really see myself, sitting on that sofa, joshing with Eamonn every morning and interviewing lots of soap stars. Sometimes, when we're very drunk, we make pacts that if we're not somewhere more exciting in three months, we'll both leave our jobs. But then the thought of no money—even for a month—is almost more scary than the thought of writing about depository trust companies for the rest of my life.

"Rebecca. Glad you could make it."

I look up, and almost choke on my champagne. It's Luke Brandon, head honcho of Brandon Communications, staring straight at me as if he knows exactly what I'm thinking. Staring straight down at me, I should say. He must be well over six feet tall with dark hair and dark eyes and . . . wow. Isn't that suit nice? An expensive suit like that almost makes you want to be a man. It's inky blue with a faint purple stripe, single-breasted, with proper horn buttons. As I run my eyes over it I find myself wondering if it's by Oswald Boateng, and whether the jacket's got a silk lining in some stunning color. If this were someone else, I might ask—but not Luke Brandon, no way.

I've only met him a few times, and I've always felt

slightly uneasy around him. For a start, he's got such a scary reputation. Everyone talks all the time about what a genius he is, even Philip, my boss. He started Brandon Communications from nothing, and now it's the biggest financial PR company in London. A few months ago he was listed in *The Mail* as one of the cleverest entrepreneurs of his generation. It said his IQ was phenomenally high and he had a photographic memory.

But it's not just that. It's that he always seems to have a frown on his face when he's talking to me. It'll probably turn out that the famous Luke Brandon is not only a complete genius but he can read minds, too. He knows that when I'm staring up at some boring graph, nodding intelligently, I'm really thinking about a gorgeous black top I saw in Joseph and whether I can afford the trousers as well.

"You know Alicia, don't you?" Luke is saying, and he gestures to the immaculate blond girl beside him.

I don't know Alicia, as it happens. But I don't need to. They're all the same, the girls at Brandon C, as they call it. They're well dressed, well spoken, are married to bankers, and have zero sense of humor. Alicia falls into the identikit pattern exactly, with her baby-blue suit, silk Hermès scarf, and matching baby-blue shoes, which I've seen in Russell and Bromley, and they cost an absolute fortune. (I *bet* she's got the bag as well.) She's also got a suntan, which must mean she's just come back from Mauritius or somewhere, and suddenly I feel a bit pale and weedy in comparison.

"Rebecca," she says coolly, grasping my hand. "You're on *Successful Saving,* aren't you?"

"That's right," I say, equally coolly.

"It's very good of you to come today," says Alicia. "I know you journalists are terribly busy."

"No problem," I say. "We like to attend as many press

conferences as we can. Keep up with industry events." I feel pleased with my response. I'm almost fooling myself.

Alicia nods seriously, as though everything I say is incredibly important to her.

"So, tell me, Rebecca. What do you think about today's news?" She gestures to the *FT* under my arm. "Quite a surprise, didn't you think?"

Oh God. What's she talking about?

"It's certainly interesting," I say, still smiling, playing for time. I glance around the room for a clue, but there's nothing. What's she talking about? Have interest rates gone up or something?

"I have to say, I think it's bad news for the industry," says Alicia earnestly. "But of course, you must have your own views."

She's looking at me, waiting for an answer. I can feel my cheeks flaming bright red. How can I get out of this? After this, I promise myself, I'm going to read the papers every day. I'm never going to be caught out like this again.

"I agree with you," I say eventually. "I think it's very bad news." My voice feels strangled. I take a quick swig of champagne and pray for an earthquake.

"Were you expecting it?" Alicia says. "I know you journalists are always ahead of the game."

"I . . . I certainly saw it coming," I say, and I'm pretty sure I sound convincing.

"And now this rumor about Scottish Prime and Flagstaff Life going the same way!" She looks at me intently. "Do you think that's really on the cards?"

"It's . . . it's difficult to say," I reply, and take a gulp of champagne. What rumor? Why can't she leave me alone?

Then I make the mistake of glancing up at Luke Brandon. He's staring at me, his mouth twitching slightly. Oh shit. He *knows* I don't have a clue, doesn't he?

"Alicia," he says abruptly, "that's Maggie Stevens coming in. Could you—"

"Absolutely," she says, trained like a racehorse, and starts to move smoothly toward the door.

"And Alicia—" adds Luke, and she quickly turns back. "I want to know exactly who fucked up on those figures."

"Yes," gulps Alicia, and walks off.

God he's scary. And now we're on our own. I think I might quickly run away.

"Well," I say brightly. "I must just go and . . ."

But Luke Brandon is leaning toward me.

"SBG announced that they've taken over Rutland Bank this morning," he says quietly.

And of course, now that he says it, I remember that front-page headline.

"I know they did," I reply haughtily. "I read it in the *FT*." And before he can say anything else, I walk off, to talk to Elly.

As the press conference is about to start, Elly and I sidle toward the back and grab two seats together. We're in one of the bigger conference rooms and there must be about a hundred chairs arranged in rows, facing a podium and a large screen. I open my notebook, write "Brandon Communications" at the top of the page, and start doodling swirly flowers down the side. Beside me, Elly's dialing her telephone horoscope on her mobile phone.

I take a sip of champagne, lean back, and prepare to

relax. There's no point listening at press conferences. The information's always in the press pack, and you can work out what they were talking about later. In fact, I'm wondering whether anyone would notice if I took out a pot of Hard Candy and did my nails, when suddenly the awful Alicia ducks her head down to mine.

"Rebecca?"

"Yes?" I say lazily.

"Phone call for you. It's your editor."

"Philip?" I say stupidly. As though I've a whole array of editors to choose from.

"Yes." She looks at me as though I'm a moron and gestures to a phone on a table at the back. Elly gives me a questioning look and I shrug back. Philip's never phoned me at a press conference before.

I feel rather excited and important as I walk to the back of the room. Perhaps there's an emergency at the office. Perhaps he's scooped an incredible story and wants me to fly to New York to follow up a lead.

"Hello, Philip?" I say into the receiver—then immediately I wish I'd said something thrusting and impressive, like a simple "Yep."

"Rebecca, listen, sorry to be a bore," says Philip, "but I've got a migraine coming on. I'm going to head off home."

"Oh," I say puzzledly.

"And I wondered if you could run a small errand for me."

An errand? If he wants somebody to buy him Tylenol, he should get a secretary.

"I'm not sure," I say discouragingly. "I'm a bit tied up here."

"When you've finished there. The Social Security Select Committee is releasing its report at five o'clock.

Can you go and pick it up? You can go straight to Westminster from your press conference."

What? I stare at the phone in horror. No, I can't pick up a bloody report. I need to pick up my VISA card! I need to secure my scarf.

"Can't Clare go?" I say. "I was going to come back to the office and finish my research on . . ." What am I supposed to be writing about this month? "On mortgages."

"Clare's got a briefing in the City. And Westminster's on your way home to Trendy Fulham, isn't it?"

Philip *always* has to make a joke about me living in Fulham. Just because he lives in Harpenden and thinks anyone who doesn't live in lovely leafy suburbia is mad.

"You can just hop off the tube," he's saying, "pick it up, and hop back on again."

Oh God. I close my eyes and think quickly. An hour here. Rush back to the office, pick up my VISA card, back to Denny and George, get my scarf, rush to Westminster, pick up the report. I should just about make it.

"Fine," I say. "Leave it to me."

I sit back down, just as the lights dim and the words *Far Eastern Opportunities* appear on the screen in front of us. There is a colorful series of pictures from Hong Kong, Thailand, and other exotic places, which would usually have me thinking wistfully about going on holiday. But today I can't relax, or even feel sorry for the new girl from *Portfolio Week,* who's frantically trying to write everything down and will probably ask five questions because she thinks she should. I'm too concerned about my scarf. What if I don't make it back in time? What if someone puts in a higher offer? The very thought makes me panic.

Then, just as the pictures of Thailand disappear and the boring graphs begin, I have a flash of inspiration. Of course! I'll pay cash for the scarf. No one can argue with cash. I can get £100 out on my cash card, so all I need is another £20, and the scarf is mine.

I tear a piece of paper out of my notebook, write on it "Can you lend me twenty quid?" and pass it to Elly, who's still surreptitiously listening to her mobile phone. I wonder what she's listening to. It can't still be her horoscope, surely? She looks down, shakes her head, and writes, "No can do. Bloody machine swallowed my card. Living off luncheon vouchers at moment."

Damn. I hesitate, then write, "What about credit card? I'll pay you back, honest. And what are you listening to?"

I pass the page to her and suddenly the lights go up. The presentation has ended and I didn't hear a word of it. People shift around on their seats and a PR girl starts handing out glossy brochures. Elly finishes her call and grins at me.

"Love life prediction," she says, tapping in another number. "It's really accurate stuff."

"Load of old bullshit, more like." I shake my head disapprovingly. "I can't believe you go for all that rubbish. Call yourself a financial journalist?"

"No," says Elly. "Do you?" And we both start to giggle, until some old bag from one of the nationals turns round and gives us an angry glare.

"Ladies and gentlemen." A piercing voice interrupts us and I look up. It's Alicia, standing up at the front of the room. She's got very good legs, I note resentfully. "As you can see, the Foreland Exotic Opportunities Savings Plan represents an entirely new approach to investment." She looks around the room, meets my eye, and smiles coldly.

"Exotic Opportunities," I whisper scornfully to Elly and point to the leaflet. "Exotic prices, more like. Have you seen how much they're charging?"

(I always turn to the charges first. Just like I always look at the price tag first.)

Elly rolls her eyes sympathetically, still listening to the phone.

"Foreland Investments are all about adding value," Alicia is saying in her snooty voice. "Foreland Investments offer you more."

"They charge more, you lose more," I say aloud without thinking, and there's a laugh around the room. God, how embarrassing. And now Luke Brandon's lifting his head, too. Quickly I look down and pretend to be writing notes.

Although to be honest, I don't know why I even pretend to write notes. It's not as if we ever put anything in the magazine except the puff that comes on the press release. Foreland Investments takes out a whopping double-page spread advertisement every month, *and* they took Philip on some fantastic research (ha-ha) trip to Thailand last year—so we're never allowed to say anything except how wonderful they are. Like that's really any help to our readers.

As Alicia carries on speaking, I lean toward Elly.

"So, listen," I whisper. "Can I borrow your credit card?"

"All used up," hisses Elly apologetically. "I'm up to my limit. Why do you think I'm living off LVs?"

"But I need money!" I whisper. "I'm desperate! I need twenty quid!"

I've spoken more loudly than I intended and Alicia stops speaking.

"Perhaps you should have invested with Foreland Investments, Rebecca," says Alicia, and another titter goes round the room. A few faces turn round to gawk at me, and I stare back at them lividly. They're fellow journalists, for God's sake. They should be on my side. National Union of Journalists solidarity and all that.

Not that I've ever actually got round to joining the NUJ. But still.

"What do you need twenty quid for?" says Luke Brandon, from the front of the room.

"I . . . my aunt," I say defiantly. "She's in hospital and I wanted to get her a present."

The room is silent. Then, to my disbelief, Luke Brandon reaches into his pocket, takes out a £20 note, and gives it to a guy in the front row of journalists. He hesitates, then passes it back to the row behind. And so it goes on, a twenty-quid note being passed from hand to hand, making its way to me like a fan at a gig being passed over the crowd. As I take hold of it, a round of applause goes round the room and I blush.

"Thanks," I say awkwardly. "I'll pay you back, of course."

"My best wishes to your aunt," says Luke Brandon.

"Thanks," I say again. Then I glance at Alicia, and feel a little dart of triumph. She looks utterly deflated.

Toward the end of the question-and-answer session, people begin slipping out to get back to their offices. This is usually when I slip out to go and buy a cappuccino and browse in a few shops. But today I don't. Today I decide I will stick it out until the last dismal question about tax structures. Then I'll go up to the front and thank Luke Brandon in person for his kind, if embarrassing, gesture. And then I'll go and get my scarf. Yippee!

But to my surprise, after only a few questions, Luke

Brandon gets up, whispers something to Alicia, and heads for the door.

"Thanks," I mutter as he passes my chair, but I'm not sure he even hears me.

The tube stops in a tunnel for no apparent reason. Five minutes go by, then ten minutes. I can't believe my bad luck. Normally, of course, I long for the tube to break down—so I've got an excuse to stay out of the office for longer. But today I behave like a stressed businessman with an ulcer. I tap my fingers and sigh, and peer out of the window into the blackness.

Part of my brain knows that I've got plenty of time to get to Denny and George before it closes. Another part knows that even if I don't make it, it's unlikely the blond girl will sell my scarf to someone else. But the possibility is there. So until I've got that scarf in my hands I won't be able to relax.

As the train finally gets going again I sink into my seat with a dramatic sigh and look at the pale, silent man on my left. He's wearing jeans and sneakers, and I notice his shirt is on inside out. Gosh, I think in admiration, did he read the article on deconstructing fashion in last month's *Vogue*, too? I'm about to ask him—then I take another look at his jeans (really nasty fake 501s) and his sneakers (very new, very white)—and something tells me he didn't.

"Thank God!" I say instead. "I was getting desperate there."

"It's frustrating," he agrees quietly.

"They just don't think, do they?" I say. "I mean, some of us have got crucial things we need to be doing. I'm in a terrible hurry!"

"I'm in a bit of a hurry myself," says the man.

"If that train hadn't started moving, I don't know what I would have done." I shake my head. "You feel so . . . impotent!"

"I know exactly what you mean," says the man intensely. "They don't realize that some of us . . ." He gestures toward me. "We aren't just idly traveling. It *matters* whether we arrive or not."

"Absolutely!" I say. "Where are you off to?"

"My wife's in labor," he says. "Our fourth."

"Oh," I say, taken aback. "Well . . . Gosh. Congratulations. I hope you—"

"She took an hour and a half last time," says the man, rubbing his damp forehead. "And I've been on this tube for forty minutes already. Still. At least we're moving now."

He gives a little shrug, then smiles at me.

"How about you? What's your urgent business?"

Oh God.

"I . . . ahm . . . I'm going to . . ."

I stop feebly and clear my throat, feeling rather sheepish. I *can't* tell this man that my urgent business consists of picking up a scarf from Denny and George.

I mean, a scarf. It's not even a suit or a coat, or something worthy like that.

"It's not that important," I mumble.

"I don't believe that," he says nicely.

Oh, now I feel awful. I glance up—and thank goodness, it's my stop.

"Good luck," I say, hastily getting up. "I really hope you get there in time."

As I walk along the pavement I'm feeling a bit shamefaced. I should have got out my 120 quid and given it to that man for his baby, instead of buying a pointless scarf. I mean, when you think about it, what's more important? Clothes—or the miracle of new life?

As I ponder this issue, I feel quite deep and philosophical. In fact, I'm so engrossed, I almost walk past my turning. But I look up just in time and turn the corner—and feel a jolt. There's a girl coming toward me and she's carrying a Denny and George carrier bag. And suddenly everything is swept from my mind.

Oh my God.

What if she's got my scarf?

What if she asked for it specially and that assistant sold it to her, thinking I wasn't going to come back?

My heart starts to beat in panic and I begin to stride along the street toward the shop. As I arrive at the door and push it open, I can barely breathe for fear. What if it's gone? What will I do?

But the blond girl smiles as I enter.

"Hi!" she says. "It's waiting for you."

"Oh, thanks," I say in relief and subside weakly against the counter.

I honestly feel as though I've run an obstacle course to get here. In fact, I think, they should list shopping as a cardiovascular activity. My heart never beats as fast as it does when I see a "reduced by 50 percent" sign.

I count out the money in tens and twenties and wait, almost shivering as she ducks behind the counter and produces the green box. She slides it into a thick glossy bag with dark green cord handles and hands it to me, and I almost want to cry out loud, the moment is so wonderful.

That moment. That instant when your fingers curl round the handles of a shiny, uncreased bag—and all the gorgeous new things inside it become yours. What's it like? It's like going hungry for days, then cramming your mouth full of warm buttered toast. It's like waking up and realizing it's the weekend. It's like the better moments of sex. Everything else is blocked out of your mind. It's pure, selfish pleasure.

I walk slowly out of the shop, still in a haze of delight. I've got a Denny and George scarf. I've got a Denny and George scarf! I've got . . .

"Rebecca." A man's voice interrupts my thoughts. I look up and my stomach gives a lurch of horror. It's Luke Brandon.

Luke Brandon is standing on the street, right in front of me, and he's staring down at my carrier bag. I feel myself growing flustered. What's he doing here on the pavement anyway? Don't people like that have chauffeurs? Shouldn't he be whisking off to some vital financial reception or something?

"Did you get it all right?" he says, frowning slightly.

"What?"

"Your aunt's present."

"Oh yes," I say, and swallow. "Yes, I . . . I got it."

"Is that it?" He gestures to the bag and I feel a guilty blush spread over my cheeks.

"Yes," I say eventually. "I thought a . . . a scarf would be nice."

"Very generous of you. Denny and George." He raises his eyebrows. "Your aunt must be a stylish lady."

"She is," I say, and clear my throat. "She's terribly creative and original."

"I'm sure she is," says Luke, and pauses. "What's her name?"

Oh God. I should have run as soon as I saw him, while I had a chance. Now I'm paralyzed. I can't think of a single female name.

"Erm . . . Ermintrude," I hear myself saying.

"Aunt Ermintrude," says Luke thoughtfully. "Well, give her my best wishes."

He nods at me, and walks off, and I stand, clutching my bag, trying to work out if he guessed or not.

Ms. Rebecca Bloomwood
Flat 2
4 Burney Rd.
London SW6 8FD

17 November 1999

Dear Ms. Bloomwood:

I am sorry to hear that you have glandular fever.

When you have recovered, perhaps you would be kind
enough to ring my assistant, Erica Parnell, and arrange a
meeting to discuss your situation.

Yours sincerely,

Derek Smeath
Manager

Three

I WALK THROUGH THE DOOR of our flat to see Suze, my flatmate, sitting in one of her strange yoga positions, with her eyes closed. Her fair hair is scrunched up in a knot, and she's wearing black leggings together with the ancient T-shirt she always wears for yoga. It's the one her dad was wearing when he rowed Oxford to victory, and she says it gives her good vibes.

For a moment I'm silent. I don't want to disturb her in case yoga is like sleepwalking and you're not meant to wake people when they're doing it. But then Suze opens her eyes and looks up—and the first thing she says is "Denny and George! Becky, you're not serious."

"Yes," I say, grinning from ear to ear. "I bought myself a scarf."

"Show me!" says Suze, unwinding herself from the floor. "Show-me-show-me-show-me!" She comes over and starts tugging at the strings of the carrier, like a kid. "I want to see your new scarf! Show me!"

This is why I love sharing a flat with Suze. Julia, my old flatmate, would have wrinkled her brow and said, "Denny and who?" or, "That's a lot of money for a scarf." But Suze completely and utterly understands. If anything, she's worse than me.

But then, she can afford to be. Although she's twenty-five, like me, her parents still give her pocket money. It's called an "allowance" and apparently comes from some family trust—but as far as I can see, it's pocket money. Her parents also bought her a flat in Fulham as a twenty-first birthday present and she's been living in it ever since, half working and half dossing about.

She was in PR for a (very) short while, and that's when I met her, on a press trip to an offshore bank on Guernsey. As a matter of fact, she was working for Brandon Communications. Without being rude—she admits it herself—she was the worst PR girl I've ever come across. She completely forgot which bank she was supposed to be promoting, and started talking enthusiastically about one of their competitors. The man from the bank looked crosser and crosser, while all the journalists pissed themselves laughing. Suze got in big trouble over that. In fact, that's when she decided PR wasn't the career for her. (The other way of putting it is that Luke Brandon gave her the sack as soon as they got back to London. Another reason not to like him.)

But the two of us had a whale of a time sloshing back wine until the early hours. Actually, Suze had a secret little weep at about two A.M. and said she was hopeless at every job she'd tried and what was she going to do? I said I thought she was *far* too interesting and creative to be one of those snooty Brandon C girls. Which I wasn't just saying to be nice, it's completely true. I gave her a big hug and she cried some more, then we both cheered up and ordered another bottle of wine, and tried on all each other's clothes. I lent Suze my belt with the square silver buckle, which, come to think of it, she's never given back. And we kept in touch ever since.

Then, when Julia suddenly upped and ran off with the professor supervising her Ph.D. (she was a dark horse, that one), Suze suggested I move in with her. I'm sure the rent she charges is too low, but I've never insisted I pay the full market rate, because I couldn't afford it. As market rates go, I'm nearer Elephant and Castle than Fulham on my salary. How can normal people afford to live in such hideously expensive places?

"Bex, open it up!" Suze is begging. "Let me see!" She's grabbing inside the bag with eager long fingers, and I pull it away quickly before she rips it. This bag is going on the back of my door along with my other prestige carrier bags, to be used in a casual manner when I need to impress. (Thank God they didn't print special "Sale" bags. I *hate* shops that do that. What's the point of having a posh bag with "Sale" splashed all over it?)

Very slowly, I take the dark green box out of the bag, remove the lid, and unfold the tissue paper. Then, almost reverentially, I lift up the scarf. It's beautiful. It's even more beautiful here than it was in the shop. I drape it around my neck and grin stupidly at Suze.

"Oh, Bex," she murmurs. "It's gorgeous!"

For a moment we are both silent. It's as though we're communing with a higher being. The god of shopping.

Then Suze has to go and ruin it all.

"You can wear it to see James this weekend," she says.

"I can't," I say almost crossly, taking it off again. "I'm not seeing him."

"How come?"

"I'm not seeing him anymore." I try to give a nonchalant shrug.

"Really?" Suze's eyes widen. "Why not? You didn't tell me!"

"I know." I look away from her eager gaze. "It's a bit . . . awkward."

"Did you chuck him? You hadn't even shagged him!" Suze's voice is rising in excitement. She's desperate to know. But am I desperate to tell? For a moment I consider being discreet. Then I think, oh, what the hell?

"I know," I say. "That was the problem."

"What do you mean?" Suze leans forward. "Bex, what are you talking about?"

I take a deep breath and turn to face her.

"He didn't want to."

"Didn't fancy you?"

"No. He—" I close my eyes, barely able to believe this myself. "He doesn't believe in sex before marriage."

"You're joking." I open my eyes to see Suze looking at me in horror—as if she's just heard the worst profanity known to mankind. "You are joking, Becky." She's actually pleading with me.

"I'm not." I manage a weak smile. "It was a bit embarrassing, actually. I kind of . . . pounced on him, and he had to fight me off."

The cringingly awful memory which I had successfully suppressed starts to resurface. I'd met James at a party a few weeks back, and this was the crucial third date. We'd been out for a really nice meal, which he'd insisted on paying for, and had gone back to his place, and had ended up kissing on the sofa.

Well, what was I *supposed* to think? There he was, there I was—and make no mistake, if his mind was saying no, his body was certainly saying yes, yes, yes. So, being a modern girl, I reached for his trouser zip and began to pull it down. When he reached down and brushed me aside I thought he was playing games, and carried on, even more enthusiastically.

Thinking back, perhaps it took me longer than it should have to guess that he wasn't playing ball, so to speak. In fact, he actually had to punch me in the face to get me off him—although he was very apologetic about it afterward.

Suze is gazing at me incredulously. Then she breaks into gurgles of laughter.

"He had to fight you off? Bex, you man-eater!"

"Don't!" I protest, half laughing, half embarrassed. "He was really sweet about it. He asked, was I prepared to wait for him?"

"And you said, not bloody likely!"

"Sort of." I look away.

In fact, carried away with the moment, I seem to remember issuing him a bit of a challenge. "Resist me now if you can, James," I recall saying in a husky voice, gazing at him with what I thought were limpid, sexual eyes. "But you'll be knocking at my door within the week."

Well, it's been over a week now, and I haven't heard a peep. Which, if you think about it, is pretty unflattering.

"But that's hideous!" Suze is saying. "What about sexual compatibility?"

"Dunno." I shrug. "I guess he's willing to take that gamble."

Suze gives a sudden giggle. "Did you get a look at his . . ."

"No! He wouldn't let me near it!"

"But could you feel it? Was it tiny?" Suze's eyes gleam wickedly. "I bet it's teeny. He's hoping to kid some poor girl into marrying him and being stuck with a teeny todger all her life. Narrow escape, Bex!" She reaches for her packet of Silk Cut and lights up.

"Stay away!" I say. "I don't want my scarf smelling of smoke!"

"So what *are* you doing this weekend?" she asks, taking a drag. "Will you be OK? Do you want to come down to the country?"

This is how Suze always refers to her family's second home in Hampshire. *The Country*. As though her parents own some small, independent nation that nobody else knows about.

"No, 's'OK," I say, morosely picking up the TV guide. "I'm going to Surrey. Visit my parents."

"Oh well," says Suze. "Give your mum my love."

"I will," I say. "And you give my love to Pepper."

Pepper is Suze's horse. She rides him about three times a year, if that, but whenever her parents suggest selling him she gets all hysterical. Apparently he costs £15,000 a year to run. Fifteen thousand pounds. And what does he do for his money? Just stands in a stable and eats apples. I wouldn't mind being a horse.

"Oh yeah, that reminds me," says Suze. "The council tax bill came in. It's three hundred each."

"Three hundred pounds?" I look at her in dismay. "What, straight away?"

"Yeah. Actually, it's late. Just write me a check or something."

"Fine," I say airily. "Three hundred quid coming up."

I reach for my bag and write a check out straight away. Suze is so generous about the rent, I always pay my share of the bills, and sometimes add a bit extra. But still, I'm feeling cold as I hand it over. Three hundred pounds gone, just like that. And I've still got that bloody VISA bill to think of. Not a great month.

"Oh, and someone called," adds Suze, and squints at a piece of paper. "Erica Parsnip. Is that right?"

"Erica *Parsnip*?" Sometimes I think Suze's mind has been expanded just a little too often.

"Parnell. Erica Parnell from Endwich Bank. Can you call her."

I stare at Suze, frozen in horror.

"She called here? She called this number?"

"Yes. This afternoon."

"Oh shit." My heart starts to thump. "What did you say? Did you say I've got glandular fever?"

"What?" It's Suze's turn to stare. "Of course I didn't say you've got bloody glandular fever!"

"Did she ask about my leg? Anything about my health at all?"

"No! She just said where were you? And I said you were at work—"

"Suze!" I wail in dismay.

"Well, what was I *supposed* to say?"

"You were supposed to say I was in bed with glandular fever and a broken leg!"

"Well, thanks for the warning!" Suze gazes at me, eyes narrowed, and crosses her legs back into the lotus position. Suze has got the longest, thinnest, wiriest legs I've ever known. When she's wearing black leggings she looks just like a spider. "What's the big deal, anyway?" she says. "Are you overdrawn?"

Am I overdrawn?

I smile back as reassuringly as I can. If Suze had any idea of my real situation, she'd need more than yoga to calm her down.

"Just a tad." I give a careless shrug. "But I'm sure it'll work itself out. No need to worry!"

There's silence, and I look up to see Suze tearing up my check. For a moment I'm completely silenced, then I stutter, "Suze! Don't be stupid!"

"Pay me back when you're in the black," she says firmly.

"Thanks, Suze," I say in a suddenly thickened voice— and as I give her a big hug I can feel tears jumping into my eyes. Suze has got to be the best friend I've ever had.

But there's a tense feeling in my stomach, which stays with me all evening and is still there when I wake up the next morning. A feeling I can't even shift by thinking about my Denny and George scarf. I lie in bed staring up at the ceiling and, for the first time in months, calculate how much I owe to everybody. The bank, VISA, my Harvey Nichols card, my Debenhams card, my Fenwicks card . . . And now Suze, too.

It's about . . . let's think . . . it's about £6,000.

A cold feeling creeps over me as I contemplate this figure. How on earth am I going to find £6,000? I could save £6 a week for a thousand weeks. Or £12 a week for five hundred weeks. Or . . . or £60 a week for a hundred weeks. That's more like it. But how the hell am I going to find £60 a week?

Or I could bone up on lots of general knowledge and go on a game show. Or invent something really clever. Or I could . . . win the lottery. At the thought, a lovely warm glow creeps over me, and I close my eyes and snuggle back down into bed. The lottery is by far the best solution.

I wouldn't aim to win the jackpot of course— that's *completely* unlikely. But one of those minor prizes. There seem to be heaps of those going around. Say, £100,000. That would do. I could pay off all my debts, buy a car, buy a flat . . .

Actually, better make it £200,000. Or a quarter of a million.

Or, even better, one of those shared jackpots. "The five winners will each receive £1.3 million." (I love the way they say that: "One point three." As if that extra £300,000 is a tiny, insignificant amount. As if you wouldn't notice whether it was there or not.)

One point three million should see me straight. And

it's not being greedy, is it, to want to share your jackpot? Please, God, I think, let me win the lottery and I promise to share nicely.

And so, on the way down to my parents' house I stop off at a petrol station to buy a couple of lottery tickets. Choosing the numbers takes about half an hour. I know 44 always does well, and 42. But what about the rest? I write out a few series of numbers on a piece of paper and squint at them, trying to imagine them on the telly.

1   6   9   16   23   44

No! Terrible! What am I thinking of? One never comes up, for a start. And 6 and 9 look wrong, too.

3   14   21   25   36   44

That's a bit better. I fill in the numbers on the ticket.

5   11   18   27   28   42

I'm quite impressed by this one. It *looks* like a winner. I can just imagine Moira Stewart reading it out on the news. "One ticket-holder, believed to live in southwest London, has won an estimated jackpot of £10 million."

For a moment, I feel faint. What'll I do with £10 million? Where will I start?

Well, a huge party to begin with. Somewhere smart but cool, with loads of champagne and dancing and a taxi service so no one has to drive. And going-home presents, like really nice bubble bath or something. (Does Calvin Klein do bubble bath?)

Then I'll buy houses for all my family and friends, of course. I lean against the lottery stand and close my eyes to concentrate. Suppose I buy twenty houses at £250,000 each. That'll leave me . . . 5 million. Plus about £50,000 on the party.

So that's £4,950,000. Oh, and I need £6,000 to pay off all my credit cards and overdraft. Plus £300 for Suze. Call it £7,000. So that leaves . . . £4,943,000.

Obviously, I'll do loads for charity. In fact, I'll probably set up a charitable foundation. I'll support all those unfashionable charities that get ignored, like skin diseases and home helps for the elderly. And I'll send a great big check to my old English teacher, Mrs. James, so she can restock the school library. Perhaps they'll even rename it after me. The Bloomwood Library.

Oh, and £300 for that swirly coat in Whistles, which I *must* buy before they're all snapped up. So how much does that leave? Four million, nine hundred and forty-three thousand, minus—

"Excuse me." A voice interrupts me and I look up dazedly. The woman behind is trying to get at the pen.

"Sorry," I say, and politely make way. But the interruption has made me lose track of my calculations. Was it 4 million or 5 million?

Then, as I see the woman looking at my bit of paper covered in scribbled numbers, an awful thought strikes me. What if one of my rejected sets of numbers actually comes up? What if **1 6 9 16 23 44** comes up tonight and I haven't entered it? All my life, I'd never forgive myself.

I quickly fill in tickets for all the combinations of numbers written on my bit of paper. That's nine tickets in all. Nine quid—quite a lot of money, really. I almost feel bad about spending it. But then, that's nine times as many chances of winning, isn't it?

And I now have a very good feeling about **1 6 9 16 23 44**. Why has that particular set of numbers leapt into my mind and stayed there? Maybe someone, some-where, is trying to tell me something.

Four

WHEN I ARRIVE at my parents' house, they are in the middle of an argument. Dad is halfway up a stepladder in the garden, poking at the gutter on the side of the house, and Mum is sitting at the wrought-iron garden table, leafing through a Past Times catalogue. Neither of them even looks up when I walk through the patio doors.

"All I'm saying is that they should set a good example!" Mum is exclaiming. She's looking good, I think as I sit down. New hair color—pale brown with just a hint of gray—and a very nice red polo-neck jumper. Perhaps I'll borrow that tomorrow.

"And you think exposing themselves to danger is a good example, is it?" replies Dad, looking down from the ladder. He's got quite a few more gray hairs, I notice with a slight shock. Mind you, gray hair looks quite distinguished on him. "You think that would solve the problem?"

"Danger!" says Mum derisively. "Don't be so melodramatic, Graham. Is that the opinion you really have of British society?"

"Hi, Mum," I say. "Hi, Dad."

"Becky agrees with me. Don't you, darling?" says Mum, and points to a page of Past Times, full of 1930s reproduction jewelry and trinket boxes. "Lovely cardigan," she adds *sotto voce*. "Look at that embroidery!" I follow her gaze and see a long, purple coatlike garment covered in colorful Art Deco swirls. I'd save the page and get it for her birthday—if I didn't know she'll probably have bought it herself by next week.

"Of course Becky doesn't agree with you!" retorts my dad. "It's the most ridiculous idea I've ever heard."

"No it's not!" says Mum indignantly. "Becky, you think it would be a good idea for the royal family to travel by public transport, don't you, darling?"

"Well . . ." I say cautiously. "I hadn't really . . ."

"You think the queen should travel to official engagements on the ninety-three bus?" scoffs Dad.

"And why not? Maybe then the ninety-three bus would become more efficient!"

"So," I say, sitting down next to Mum. "How are things?"

"You realize this country is on the verge of gridlock?" says Mum, as if she hasn't heard me. "If more people don't start using public transport, our roads are going to seize up."

My dad shakes his head.

"And you think the queen traveling on the ninety-three bus would solve the problem. Never mind the security problems, never mind the fact that she'd be able to do far fewer engagements . . ."

"I didn't mean the queen, necessarily," retorts Mum. "But some of those others. Princess Michael of Kent, for example. She could travel by tube, every so often, couldn't she? These people need to learn about real life."

The last time my mum traveled on the tube was about 1983.

"Shall I make some coffee?" I say brightly.

"If you ask me, this gridlock business is utter nonsense," says my dad. He jumps down from the stepladder and brushes the dirt off his hands. "It's all propaganda."

"Propaganda?" exclaims my mum in outrage.

"Right," I say hurriedly. "Well, I'll go and put the kettle on."

I walk back into the house, flick the kettle on in the kitchen, and sit down at the table in a nice patch of sunshine. I've already forgotten what my mum and dad are arguing about. They'll just go round and round in circles and agree it's all the fault of Tony Blair. Anyway, I've got more important things to think about. I'm trying to figure out exactly how much I should give to Philip, my boss, after I win the lottery. I can't leave him out, of course—but is cash a bit tacky? Would a present be better? Really nice cufflinks, perhaps. Or one of those picnic hampers with all the plates inside. (Clare Edwards, obviously, will get nothing.)

Sitting alone in the sunny kitchen, I feel as though I have a little glowing secret inside me. I'm going to win the lottery. Tonight, my life is going to change. God, I can't wait. Ten million pounds. Just think, tomorrow I'll be able to buy anything I want. Anything!

The newspaper's open in front of me at the property section and I carelessly pick it up to peruse expensive houses. Where shall I live? Chelsea? Notting Hill? Mayfair? *Belgravia*, I read. *Magnificent seven-bedroom detached house with staff annex and mature garden*. Well, that sounds all right. I could cope with seven bedrooms in Belgravia. My eye flicks complacently down to the price and stops still with shock. Six point five million pounds. That's how much they're asking. Six and a half million.

I feel stunned and slightly angry. Are they serious? I haven't got anything like £6.5 million. I've only got about . . . 4 million left. Or was it 5? I stare at the page, feeling cheated. Lottery winners are supposed to be able to buy anything they want—but already I'm feeling poor and inadequate.

I shove the paper aside and reach for a freebie brochure full of gorgeous white duvet covers at £100 each. That's more like it. When I've won the lottery I'll only ever have crisp white duvet covers, I decide. And I'll have a white cast-iron bed and painted wooden shutters and a fluffy white dressing gown . . .

"So, how's the world of finance?" Mum's voice interrupts me and I look up. She's bustling into the kitchen, still holding her Past Times catalogue. "Have you made the coffee? Chop chop, darling!"

"I was going to," I say, and make a half move from my chair. But, as always, Mum's there before me. She reaches for a ceramic storage jar I've never seen before and spoons coffee into a new gold cafétière.

Mum's terrible. She's always buying new stuff for the kitchen—and she just gives the old stuff to charity shops. New kettles, new toasters . . . We've already had three new rubbish bins this year—dark green, then chrome, and now yellow translucent plastic. I mean, what a waste of money.

"That's a nice skirt!" she says, looking at me as though for the first time. "Where's that from?"

"DKNY," I mumble back.

"Very pretty," she says. "Was it expensive?"

"Not really," I say. "About fifty quid."

This is not strictly true. It was nearer 150. But there's

no point telling Mum how much things really cost, because she'd have a coronary. Or, in fact, she'd tell my dad first—and then they'd both have coronaries, and I'd be an orphan.

So what I do is work in two systems simultaneously. Real prices and Mum prices. It's a bit like when everything in the shop is 20 percent off, and you walk around mentally reducing everything. After a while, you get quite practiced.

The only difference is, I operate a sliding-scale system, a bit like income tax. It starts off at 20 percent (if it really cost £20, I say it cost £16) and rises up to . . . well, to 90 percent if necessary. I once bought a pair of boots that cost £200, and I told Mum they were £20 in the sale. And she believed me.

"So, are you looking for a flat?" she says, glancing over my shoulder at the property pages.

"No," I say sulkily, and flick over a page of my brochure. My parents are always on at me to buy a flat. Do they know how much flats cost?

"Apparently, Thomas has bought a very nice little starter home in Reigate," she says, nodding toward our next-door neighbors. "He commutes." She says this with an air of satisfaction, as though she's telling me he's won the Nobel Peace Prize.

"Well, I can't afford a flat," I say. "*Or* a starter home."

Not yet, anyway, I think. Not until eight o'clock tonight. Hee hee hee.

"Money troubles?" says Dad, coming into the kitchen. "You know, there are two solutions to money troubles."

His eyes are twinkling, and I just know he's about to give me some clever little aphorism. Dad has a saying for every subject under the sun—as well as a wide selection of limericks and truly terrible jokes. Sometimes I like listening to them. Sometimes I don't.

"C.B.," says Dad, his eyes twinkling. "Or M.M.M."

He pauses for effect and I turn the page of my brochure, pretending I can't hear him.

"Cut Back," says my dad, "or Make More Money. One or the other. Which is it to be, Becky?"

"Oh, both, I expect," I say airily, and turn another page of my brochure. To be honest, I almost feel sorry for Dad. It'll be quite a shock for him when his only daughter becomes a multimillionaire overnight.

After lunch, Mum and I go along to a craft fair in the local primary school. I'm really just going to keep Mum company, and I'm certainly not planning to buy anything—but when we get there, I find a stall full of amazing handmade cards, only £1.50 each! So I buy ten. After all, you always need cards, don't you? There's also a gorgeous blue ceramic plant holder with little elephants going round it—and I've been saying for ages we should have more plants in the flat. So I buy that, too. Only fifteen quid. Craft fairs are such a bargain, aren't they? You go along thinking they'll be complete rubbish—but you can always find *something* you want.

Mum's really happy, too, as she's found a pair of candlesticks for her collection. She's got collections of candlesticks, toast racks, pottery jugs, glass animals, embroidered samplers, and thimbles. (Personally, I don't think the thimbles count as a proper collection, because she got the whole lot, including the cabinet, from an ad at the back of the *Mail on Sunday* magazine. But she never tells anybody that. In fact, I shouldn't have mentioned it.)

So anyway, we're both feeling rather pleased with ourselves, and decide to go for a cup of tea. Then, on the way out, we pass one of those really sad stalls which no one is going near; the kind people glance at once, then quickly walk past. The poor guy behind it looks really sorry for himself, so I pause to have a look. And no wonder no one's stopping. He's selling weird-shaped wooden bowls, and matching wooden cutlery. What on earth is the point of wooden cutlery?

"That's nice!" I say brightly, and pick one of the bowls up.

"Hand-crafted applewood," he says. "Took a week to make."

Well, it was a waste of a week, if you ask me. It's shapeless and the wood's a nasty shade of brown. But as I go to put it back down again, he looks so doleful I feel sorry for him and turn it over to look at the price, thinking if it's a fiver I'll buy it. But it's eighty quid! I show the price to Mum, and she pulls a little face.

"That particular piece was featured in *Elle Decoration* last month," says the man mournfully, and produces a cutout page. And at his words, I freeze. *Elle Decoration*? Is he joking?

He's not joking. There on the page, in full color, is a picture of a room, completely empty except for a suede beanbag, a low table, and a wooden bowl. I stare at it incredulously.

"Was it this exact one?" I ask, trying not to sound too excited. "This exact bowl?" As he nods, my grasp tightens round the bowl. I can't believe it. I'm holding a piece of *Elle Decoration*. How cool is that? Now I feel incredibly stylish and trendy—and wish I were wearing white linen trousers and had my hair slicked back like Yasmin Le Bon to match.

It just shows I've got good taste. Didn't I pick out this bowl—sorry, this *piece*—all by myself? Didn't I spot its quality? Already I can see our sitting room redesigned entirely around it, all pale and minimalist. Eighty quid. That's nothing for a timeless piece of style like this.

"I'll have it," I say determinedly, and reach inside my bag for my checkbook. The thing is, I remind myself, buying cheap is actually a false economy. It's much better to spend a little more and make a serious purchase that'll last for a lifetime. And this bowl is quite clearly a classic. Suze is going to be *so* impressed.

When we get back home, Mum goes straight inside, but I stay in the driveway, carefully transferring my purchases from her car to mine.

"Becky! What a surprise!"

Oh God. It's Martin Webster from next door, leaning over the fence with a rake in his hand and a huge friendly smile on his face. Martin has this way of always making me feel guilty, I don't know why.

Actually I do know why. It's because I know he was always hoping I would grow up and marry Tom, his son. And I haven't. The history of my relationship with Tom is: he asked me out once when we were both about sixteen and I said no, I was going out with Adam Moore. That was the end of it and thank God for that. To be perfectly honest, I would rather marry Martin himself than marry Tom.

"Hi!" I say overenthusiastically. "How are you?"

"Oh, we're all doing well," says Martin. "You heard Tom's bought a house?"

"Yes," I say. "In Reigate. Fantastic!"

"It's got two bedrooms, shower room, reception room, and open-plan kitchen," he recites. "Limed oak units in the kitchen."

"Gosh," I say. "How fab."

"Tom's thrilled with it," says Martin. "Janice!" he adds in a yell. "Come and see who's here!"

A moment later, Janice appears on the front doorstep, wearing her floral apron.

"Becky!" she says. "What a stranger you've become! How long is it?"

Now I feel guilty for not visiting my parents more often.

"Well," I say, trying to give a nonchalant smile. "You know. I'm quite busy with my job and everything."

"Oh yes," says Janice, giving an awe-stricken nod. "Your *job*."

Somewhere along the line, Janice and Martin have got it into their heads that I'm this high-powered financial whiz kid. I've tried telling them that really, I'm not—but the more I deny it, the more high powered they think I am. It's a catch-22. They now think I'm high powered *and* modest.

Still, who cares? It's actually quite fun, playing a financial genius.

"Yes, actually we've been quite busy lately," I say coolly. "What with the merger of SBG and Rutland."

"Of course," breathes Janice.

"You know, that reminds me," says Martin suddenly. "Becky, wait there. Back in two ticks." He disappears before I can say anything, and I'm left awkwardly with Janice.

"So," I say inanely. "I hear Tom's got limed oak units in his kitchen!"

This is literally the only thing I can think of to say. I smile at Janice, and wait for her to reply. But instead, she's beaming at me delightedly. Her face is all lit up— and suddenly I realize I've made a huge mistake. I shouldn't have mentioned Tom's bloody starter home. I shouldn't have mentioned the limed oak units. She'll think I suddenly fancy Tom, now he's got a starter home to his name.

"It's limed oak and Mediterranean tiles," she says proudly. "It was a choice of Mediterranean or Farmhouse Quarry, and Tom chose Mediterranean."

For an instant I consider saying I would have chosen Farmhouse Quarry. But that seems a bit mean.

"Lovely," I say. "And two bedrooms!"

Why can't I get off the subject of this bloody starter home?

"He wanted two bedrooms," says Janice. "After all, you never know, do you?" She smiles coyly at me, and ridiculously, I feel myself start to blush. Why am I blushing? This is so stupid. Now she thinks I fancy Tom. She's picturing us together in the starter home, making supper together in the limed oak kitchen.

I should say something. I should say, "Janice, I don't fancy Tom. He's too tall and his breath smells." But how on earth can I say that?

"Well, do give him my love," I hear myself saying instead.

"I certainly will," she says, and pauses. "Does he have your London number?"

Aarrgh!

"I think so," I lie, smiling brightly. "And he can always get me here if he wants." Now everything I say sounds like some saucy double entendre. I can just imagine how this conversation will be reported back to Tom. "She was asking *all* about your starter home. And she asked you to call her!"

Life would be a lot easier if conversations were rewindable and erasable, like videos. Or if you could instruct people to disregard what you just said, like in a courtroom. *Please strike from the record all references to starter homes and limed oak kitchens.*

Luckily, at that moment, Martin reappears, clutching a piece of paper.

"Thought you might cast your eye over this," he says. "We've had this with-profits fund with Flagstaff Life for fifteen years. Now we're thinking of transferring to their new unit-linked growth fund. What do you think?"

I don't know. What's he talking about, anyway? Some kind of savings plan? Please don't ask me, I want to say. Please ask someone who knows what they're talking about. But there's no way they'll believe that I'm not a financial genius—so I'll just have to do the best I can.

I run my eye over the piece of paper in what I hope looks like a knowledgeable fashion and nod several times. It's a letter making some kind of special offer if investors switch to this new fund. Sounds reasonable enough.

"The company wrote to us, saying we might want a higher return in our retirement years," says Martin. "There's a guaranteed sum, too."

"And they'll send us a carriage clock," chimes in Janice. "Swiss-made."

"Mmm," I say, studying the letterhead intently. "Well, I should think that's quite a good idea."

Flagstaff Life, I'm thinking. I'm sure I've heard something about them recently. Which ones are Flagstaff Life? Oh yes! They're the ones who threw a champagne party at Soho Soho. That's right. And Elly got incredibly pissed and told David Salisbury from *The Times* that she loved him. It was a bloody good party, come to think of it. One of the best.

Hmm. But wasn't there something else? Something I've heard recently? I wrinkle my nose, trying to remember . . . but it's gone. I've probably got it wrong, anyway.

"D'you rate them as a company?" says Martin.

"Oh yes," I say, looking up. "They're very well regarded among the profession."

"Well then," says Martin, looking pleased. "If Becky thinks it's a good idea . . ."

"Yes, but, I really wouldn't just listen to me!" I say quickly. "I mean, a financial adviser or someone would know far more . . ."

"Listen to her!" says Martin with a little chuckle. "The financial expert herself."

"You know, Tom sometimes buys your magazine," puts in Janice. "Not that he's got much money now, what with the mortgage and everything . . . But he says your articles are very good! Tom says—"

"How nice!" I cut in. "Well, look, I really must go. Lovely to see you. And love to Tom!"

And I turn into the house so quickly, I bump my knee on the door frame. Then I feel a bit bad, and wish I'd said good-bye nicely. But honestly! If I hear one more word about bloody Tom and his bloody kitchen, I'll go mad.

By the time I sit down in front of the National Lottery, however, I've forgotten all about them. We've had a nice supper—chicken Provençale from Marks and Spencer, and a nice bottle of Pinot Grigio, which I brought. I know the chicken Provençale comes from Marks and Spencer because I've bought it myself, quite a few times. I recognized the sun-dried tomatoes and the olives, and everything. Mum, of course, still acted like she'd made it from scratch, from her own recipe.

I don't know why she bothers. It isn't like anyone would care—especially when it's just me and Dad. And I mean, it's pretty obvious that there are never any raw ingredients in our kitchen. There are lots of empty cardboard boxes and lots of fully prepared meals—and nothing in between. But still Mum never ever admits she's bought a ready-made meal, not even when it's a pie in a foil container. My dad will eat one of those pies, full of plastic mushrooms and gloopy sauce, and then say, with a perfectly straight face, "Delicious, my love." And my mum will smile back, looking all pleased with herself.

But tonight it's not foil pie, it's chicken Provençale. (To be fair, I suppose it almost does look homemade—except no one would ever cut a red pepper up that small for themselves, would they? People have more important things to do.) So anyway, we've eaten it and we've drunk a fair amount of the Pinot Grigio, and there's an apple crumble in the oven—and I've suggested, casually, that we all go and watch telly. Because I know from looking at the clock that the National Lottery program has already started. In a matter of minutes, it's all going to happen. I cannot wait.

Luckily, my parents aren't the sort who want to make conversation about politics or talk about books. We've already caught up with all the family news, and I've told them how my work's going, and they've told me about their holiday in Corsica—so by now, we're grinding to a bit of a halt. We need the telly on, if only as a conversational sounding board.

So we all troop into the sitting room, and my dad lights the gas flame-effect fire and turns on the telly. And there it is! The National Lottery, in glorious Technicolor. The lights are shining, and Dale Winton is joshing with Tiffany from *EastEnders,* and every so often the audience gives an excited whoop. My stomach's getting tighter and tighter, and my heart's going thump-thump-

thump. Because in a few minutes those balls are going to fall. In a few minutes I'm going to be a millionaire. I just *know* I am.

I lean calmly back on the sofa and think what I'll do when I win. At the very instant that I win, I mean. Do I scream? Do I keep quiet? Maybe I shouldn't tell anyone for twenty-four hours. Maybe I shouldn't tell anyone *at all.*

This new thought transfixes me. I could be a secret winner! I could have all the money and none of the pressure. If people asked me how I could afford so many designer clothes I'd just tell them I was doing lots of freelance work. Yes! And I could transform all my friends' lives anonymously, like a good angel.

I'm just working out how big a house I could manage to buy without everyone twigging, when a voice on the screen alerts me.

"Question to number three."

What?

"My favorite animal is the flamingo because it's pink, fluffy, and has long legs." The girl sitting on the stool excitedly unwinds a pair of long glossy legs, and the audience goes wild. I stare at her dazedly. What's going on? Why are we watching *Blind Date*?

"Now, this show used to be fun," says Mum. "But it's gone downhill."

"You call this rubbish fun?" retorts my dad incredulously.

"Listen, Dad, actually, could we turn back to—"

"I didn't say it was fun *now*. I said—"

"Dad!" I say, trying not to sound too panicky. "Could we just go back to BBC1 for a moment?"

Blind Date disappears and I sigh with relief. The next moment, an earnest man in a suit fills the screen.

"What the police failed to appreciate," he says in a nasal voice, "is that the witnesses were not sufficiently—"

"Dad!"

"Where's the television guide?" he says impatiently. "There's got to be something better than this."

"There's the lottery!" I almost scream. "I want to watch the lottery!"

I know strictly speaking that whether I watch it or not won't affect my chances of winning—but I don't want to miss the great moment, do I? You might think I'm a bit mad, but I feel that if I watch it, I can kind of communicate with the balls through the screen. I'll stare hard at them as they get tossed around and silently urge on my winning numbers. It's a bit like supporting a team. *Team 1 6 9 16 23 44.*

Except the numbers never come out in order, do they?

Team 44 1 23 6 9 16. Possibly. Or *Team 23 6 1 . . .*

Suddenly there's a round of applause and Martine McCutcheon's finished her song. Oh my God. It's about to happen. My life is about to change.

"The lottery's become terribly commercialized, hasn't it?" says my mum, as Dale Winton leads Martine over to the red button. "It's a shame, really."

"What do you mean, it's *become* commercialized?" retorts my dad.

"People used to play the lottery because they wanted to support the charities."

"No they didn't! Don't be ridiculous! No one gives a fig about the charities. This is all about self, self, self." Dad gestures toward Dale Winton with the remote control and the screen goes dead.

"Dad!" I wail.

"So you think no one cares about the charities?" says my mum into the silence.

"That's not what I said."

"Dad! Put it back on!" I screech. "Put-it-back-on!" I'm about to wrestle him for the remote control when he flicks it back on again.

I stare at the screen in utter disbelief. The first ball has already dropped. And it's 44. My number 44.

". . . last appeared three weeks ago. And here comes the second ball . . . And it's number 1."

I can't move. It's taking place, before my very eyes. I'm actually winning the lottery. I'm winning the bloody lottery!

Now that it's happening, I feel surprisingly calm about it. It's as if I've known, all my life, that this would happen. Sitting here silently on the sofa, I feel as though I'm in a fly-on-the-wall documentary about myself. "Becky Bloomwood always secretly knew she would win the lottery one day. But on the day it happened, even she couldn't have predicted . . ."

"And another low one. Number 3."

What? My mind snaps to and I stare perplexedly at the screen. That can't be right. They mean 23.

"And number 2, last week's bonus ball."

I feel cold all over. What the hell is going on? What *are* these numbers?

"And another low one! Number 4. A popular number—it's had twelve appearances so far this year. And finally . . . number 5! Well, I never! This is a bit of a first! Now, lining them up in order . . ."

No. This can't be serious. This has to be a mistake. The winning lottery numbers cannot possibly be 1, 2, 3, 4, 5, 44. That's not a lottery combination, it's a . . . it's an act of torture.

And I was winning. I was *winning*.

"Look at that!" my mum's saying. "Absolutely incredible! One–two–three–four–five–forty-four."

"And why should that be incredible?" replies Dad. "It's as likely as any other combination."

"It can't be!"

"Jane, do you know *anything* about the laws of probability?"

Quietly I get up and leave the room, as the National Lottery theme tune blares out of the telly. I walk into the kitchen, sit down at the table, and bury my head in my hands. I feel slightly shaky, to tell you the truth. How could I lose? I was living in a big house and going on holiday to Barbados with all my friends, and walking into Agnès b and buying anything I wanted. It felt so real.

And now, instead, I'm sitting in my parents' kitchen, and I can't afford to go on holiday and I've just spent eighty quid on a wooden bowl I don't even like.

Miserably, I turn on the kettle, pick up a copy of *Woman's Journal* lying on the counter, and flick through it—but even that doesn't cheer me up. Everything seems to remind me of money. Maybe my dad's right, I find myself thinking dolefully. Maybe Cut Back is the answer. Suppose . . . suppose I cut back enough to save sixty quid a week. I'd have £6,000 in a hundred weeks.

And suddenly my brain is alert. Six thousand quid. That's not bad, is it? And if you think about it, it can't be *that* hard to save sixty quid a week. It's only the same as a couple of meals out. I mean, you'd hardly notice it.

God, yes. That's what I'll do. Sixty quid a week, every week. Maybe I'll even pay it into a special account. That new Lloyds high-yield sixty-day access account with the tiered interest rates. It'll be fantastic! I'll be completely on top of my finances—and when I've paid off my bills I'll just keep saving. It'll become a habit to be frugal. And at the end of every year I'll splash out on one classic investment like an Armani suit. Or maybe Christian Dior. Something really classy, anyway.

I'll start on Monday, I think excitedly, spooning chocolate Ovaltine into a cup. What I'll do is, I just won't spend *anything*. All my spare money will mount up, and I'll be rich. This is going to be so great.

OCTAGON ▶ *flair...style...vision*

Ms. Rebecca Bloomwood   *Charge Card Number 7854 4567*
Flat 2
4 Burney Rd.
London SW6 8FD

2 March 2000

Dear Ms. Bloomwood:

Our records suggest that we have not received payment for your latest Octagon Silver Card bill. If you have paid within the last few days, please ignore this letter.

Your outstanding bill is currently £235.76. The minimum payment is £43.00. You may pay by cash, check, or on the enclosed bank giro credit slip. We look forward to receiving your payment.

Yours sincerely,

John Hunter
Customer Accounts Manager

OCTAGON ▶ *flair...style...vision*

FINANCIAL SERVICES DEPARTMENT
8TH FLOOR   TOWER HOUSE
LONDON ROAD   WINCHESTER SO 44   3DR

Ms. Rebecca Bloomwood   *Charge Card Number 7854 4567*
Flat 2
4 Burney Rd.
London SW6 8FD

2 March 2000

Dear Ms. Bloomwood:

There's never been a better time to spend!

For a limited time, we are offering EXTRA POINTS on
all purchases over £50 made with your Octagon Silver
Card*—so take the opportunity now to add more points
to your total and take advantage of some of our
Pointholders' Gifts.

Some of the fantastic gifts we are offering include:

An Italian leather bag	**1,000 points**
A case of pink champagne	**2,000 points**
Two flights to Paris**	**5,000 points**

    (Your current level is: 35 points)

And remember, during this special offer period, you will
gain two points for every £5 spent! We look forward to
welcoming you soon to take advantage of this unique offer.

Yours sincerely,

Adrian Smith
Customer Services Manager

*excluding purchases at restaurants, pharmacy, newsstand, and hairdresser
**certain restrictions apply—see enclosed leaflet

Five

FRUGALITY. SIMPLICITY. These are my new watch-words. A new, uncluttered, Zen-like life, in which I spend nothing. Spend *nothing*. I mean, when you think about it, how much money do we all waste every day? No wonder I'm in a little bit of debt. And really, it's not my fault. I've merely been succumbing to the Western drag of materialism—which you have to have the strength of elephants to resist. At least, that's what it says in my new book.

You see, yesterday, when Mum and I went into Waterstone's to buy her paperback for the week, I sidled off to the self-help section and bought the most won-derful book I've ever read. Quite honestly, it's going to change my life. I've got it now, in my bag. It's called *Controlling Your Cash* by David E. Barton, and it's fantas-tic. What it says is that we can all fritter away money without realizing it, and that most of us could easily cut our cash consumption by half in just one week.

In one week!

You just have to do things like make your own sand-wiches instead of eating in restaurants and ride a bike to work instead of taking the tube. When you start think-ing about it, you can save money everywhere. And as

David E. Barton says, there are lots of free pleasures which we forget because we're so busy spending money, like parks and museums and the simple joy of a country walk.

Come to think of it, why don't we put information like this in *Successful Saving*? It's so much more useful than knowing about some fancy new unit trust which might make a profit or might not. I mean, with this scheme you start making money straight away!

It's all so easy and straightforward. And the best thing is, you have to start out by going shopping! The book says you should begin by itemizing every single purchase in a single normal spending day and plot it on a graph. It stresses that you should be honest and not suddenly curtail or alter your spending pattern—which is lucky, because it's Suze's birthday on Friday and I've got to get her a present.

So on Monday morning, I stop off at Lucio's on the way into work and buy an extralarge cappuccino and a chocolate muffin, just like I usually do. I have to admit I feel a bit sorrowful as I hand over my money, because this is my last-ever cappuccino and my last-ever chocolate muffin. My new frugality starts tomorrow—and cappuccinos aren't allowed. David E. Barton says if you have a coffee habit you should make it at home and take it into the office in a flask, and if you like eating snacks you should buy cheap cakes from the supermarket. "The coffee merchants are fleecing you for what is little more than hot water and polystyrene," he points out— and I suppose he's right. But I will miss my morning cappuccino. Still, I've promised myself I'll follow the rules of the book—and I will.

As I come out of the coffee shop, clutching my last-ever cup, I realize I don't actually have a flask for coffee. But that's OK, I'll buy one. There are some lovely sleek chrome ones in Habitat. Flasks are actually quite trendy these days. I think Alessi might even do one. Wouldn't that be cool? Drinking coffee out of an Alessi flask. Much cooler than a take-away cappuccino.

So I'm feeling quite happy as I walk along the street. When I get to Smiths I pop in and stock up on a few magazines to keep me going—and I also buy a sweet little silver notebook and pen to write down everything I spend. I'm going to be really rigorous about this, because David E. Barton says the very act of noting down purchases should have a curtailing effect. So when I get into work, I start my list.

Cappuccino	£1.50
Muffin	£1.00
Notebook	£3.99
Pen	£1.20
Magazines	£6.40

Which makes a grand total so far of . . . £14.09.

Gosh. I suppose that's quite a lot, bearing in mind it's only nine-forty in the morning.

But the notebook and pen don't count, do they? They're like course requirements. I mean, how on earth are you supposed to note down all your purchases without a notebook and pen? So I subtract both of those, and now my total comes to . . . £8.90. Which is much better.

Anyway, I'm at work now. I probably won't spend anything else all day.

But somehow, spending nothing is absolutely impossible. First of all, Guy from Accounts comes round with yet another leaving present to give to. Then I have to go out and get some lunch. I'm very restrained with my sandwich—I choose egg and cress, which is the cheapest one at Boots, and I don't even like egg and cress.

David E. Barton says that when you make a real effort, particularly in the early stages, you should reward yourself—so I pick up some coconut bath oil from the Natural range as a little treat. Then I notice there are double advantage points on the moisturizer I use.

I *love* advantage points. Aren't they a wonderful invention? If you spend enough, you can get really good prizes, like a beauty day at a hotel. Last Christmas I was really canny—I let my points build up until I'd accumulated enough to buy my granny's Christmas present. What happened in fact was, I'd already built up 1,653 points—and I needed 1,800 to buy her a heated roller set. So I bought myself a great big bottle of Samsara perfume, and that gave me 150 extra points on my card—and then I got the heated roller set absolutely free! The only thing is, I don't much like Samsara perfume—but I didn't realize that until I got home. Still, never mind.

The clever way to use advantage points—as with all special offers—is to spot the opportunity and use it, because it may not come your way again. So I grab three pots of moisturizer and buy them. Double advantage points! I mean, it's just free money, isn't it?

Then I have to get Suze's birthday present. I've actually already bought her a set of aromatherapy oils—but the other day I saw this gorgeous pink angora cardigan in Benetton, and I know she'd love it. I can always take the aromatherapy oils back or give them to someone for Christmas.

So I go into Benetton and pick up the pink cardigan. I'm about to pay . . . when I notice they've got it in gray as well. The most perfect, soft, dove-gray angora cardigan, with little pearly buttons.

Oh *God*. You see, the thing is, I've been looking for a

nice gray cardigan for ages. Honestly, I have. You can ask Suze, my mum, anybody. And the other thing is, I'm not actually *on* my new frugal regime yet, am I? I'm just monitoring myself.

David E. Barton says I should act as naturally as possible. So really, I *ought* to act on my natural impulses and buy it. It would be false not to. It would ruin the whole point.

It only costs forty-five quid. And I can put it on VISA.

Look at it another way—what's forty-five quid in the grand scheme of things? I mean, it's nothing, is it?

So I buy it. The most perfect little cardigan in the world. People will call me the Girl in the Gray Cardigan. I'll be able to *live* in it. Really, it's an investment.

After lunch, I have to go and visit Image Store to choose a front-cover picture for the next issue. This is my absolute favorite job—I can't understand why Philip always offloads it onto someone else. It basically means you get to go and sit drinking coffee all afternoon, looking at rows and rows of transparencies.

Because, of course, we don't have the editorial budget to create our own front covers. God, no. When I first started out in journalism, I thought I'd be able to go to shoots, and meet models, and have a really glamorous time. But we don't even have a cameraman. All our sorts of magazines use picture libraries like Image Store, and the same images tend to go round and round. There's a picture of a roaring tiger that's been on at least three personal finance covers in the last year. Still, the readers don't mind, do they? They're not exactly buying the magazines to look at Kate Moss.

The good thing is that Elly's editor doesn't like

choosing front covers either—and they use Image Store, too. So we always try to work it that we'll go together and have a good natter over the pics. Even better, Image Store is all the way over in Notting Hill Gate, so you can legitimately take ages getting there and back. Usually I don't bother going back to the office. Really, it's the perfect way to spend a weekday afternoon.

I get there before Elly and mutter, "Becky Bloomwood from *Successful Saving*," to the girl at reception, wishing I could say "Becky Bloomwood from *Vogue*" or "Becky Bloomwood from *Wall Street Journal*." Then I sit on a squashy black leather chair, flicking through a catalogue of pictures of glossy happy families, until one of the trendy young men who works there comes and leads me to my own illuminated table.

"I'm Paul," he says, "and I'll be looking after you today. Do you know what you're looking for?"

"Well . . ." I say, and pull out my notebook. We had a meeting about the cover yesterday and eventually decided on "Portfolio Management: Getting the Right Balance." And before your head falls off with boredom, let me just point out that last month, the cover line was "Deposit Accounts: Put to the Test."

Why can't we just *once* put self-tanning creams to the test instead? Oh well.

"I'm looking for pictures of scales," I say, reading off my list. "Or tightropes, unicycles . . ."

"Balancing images," says Paul. "No problem. Would you like a coffee?"

"Yes, please," I beam, and relax back in my chair. You see what I mean? It's so nice here. And I'm being *paid* to sit in this chair, doing nothing at all.

A few moments later, Elly appears with Paul, and I look at her in surprise. She's looking really smart, in an aubergine-colored suit and high heels.

"So it's swimmers, boats, and European images," says Paul to her.

"That's it," says Elly, and sinks into the chair beside me.

"Let me guess," I say. "Something about floating currencies."

"Very good," says Elly. "Actually, it's 'Europe: Sink or Swim'?" She says it in an incredibly dramatic voice, and Paul and I both start giggling. When he's walked away, I look her up and down.

"So how come you're so smart?"

"I always look smart," she parries. "You know that." Paul's already wheeling trolley-loads of transparencies toward us and she looks over at them. "Are these yours or mine?"

She's avoiding the subject. What's going on?

"Have you got an interview?" I say, in a sudden flash of genius. She looks at me, flushes, then pulls a sheet of transparencies out of the trolley.

"Circus acts," she says. "People juggling. Is that what you wanted?"

"Elly! Have you got an interview? Tell me!"

There's silence for a while. Elly stares down at the sheet, then looks up.

"Yes," she says, and bites her lip. "But—"

"That's fantastic!" I exclaim, and a couple of smooth-looking girls in the corner look up. "Who for?" I say more quietly. "It's not *Cosmo,* is it?"

We're interrupted by Paul, who comes over with a coffee and puts it in front of Elly.

"Swimmers coming up," he says, then grins and walks off.

"Who's it for?" I repeat. Elly applies for so many jobs, I lose track.

"It's Wetherby's," she says, and a pink flush creeps over her face.

"Wetherby's Investments?" She gives a very slight nod, and I frown in bemusement. Why is she applying to Wetherby's Investments? "Have they got an in-house magazine or something?"

"I'm not applying to be a journalist," she says in a low voice. "I'm applying to be a fund manager."

"*What?*" I say, appalled.

I know friends should be supportive of each other's life decisions and all that. But I'm sorry, a *fund manager*?

"I probably won't even get it," she says, and looks away. "It's no big deal."

"But . . ."

I'm speechless. How can Elly even be thinking of becoming a fund manager? Fund managers aren't real people. They're the characters we laugh at on press trips.

"It's just an idea," she says defensively. "Maybe I want to show Carol I can do something else. You know?"

"So it's like . . . a bargaining tool?" I hazard.

"Yes," she says, and gives a little shrug. "That's it. A bargaining tool."

But she doesn't sound exactly convinced—and she's not nearly as chatty as usual during the rest of the afternoon. What's happened to her? I'm still puzzling over it as I make my way home from Image Store. I walk down to High Street Kensington, cross over the road, and hesitate in front of Marks and Spencer.

The tube is to my right. The shops are to my left.

I must *ignore* the shops. I must practice frugality, go straight home, and plot my expenditure graph. If I need entertainment, I can watch some nice free television and perhaps make some inexpensive, nutritious soup.

But there's nothing good on tonight, at least not until *EastEnders*. And I don't want soup. I really feel as if I need something to cheer me up. And besides—my mind's working fast—I'll be giving it all up tomorrow, won't I? It's like the beginning of Lent. This is my Shopping Pancake Day. I need to cram it all in before the fast begins.

With a surge of excitement I hurry toward the Barkers Centre. I won't go mad, I promise myself. Just one little treat to see me through. I've already got my cardigan— so not clothes . . . and I bought some new kitten heels the other day—so not that . . . although there are some nice Prada-type shoes in Hobbs . . . Hmm. I'm not sure.

I arrive at the cosmetics department of Barkers and suddenly I know. Makeup! That's what I need. A new mascara, and maybe a new lipstick. Happily I start to wander around the bright, heady room, dodging sprays of perfume and painting lipsticks onto the back of my hand. I want a really pale lipstick, I decide. Sort of nudey beige/pink, and a lip liner to go with it . . .

At the Clarins counter, my attention is grabbed by a big promotional sign.

BUY TWO SKIN-CARE PRODUCTS, AND RECEIVE FREE
BEAUTY BAG, CONTAINING TRIAL-SIZE CLEANSER,
TONER, AND MOISTURIZER, AUTUMN BLAZE LIPSTICK,
EXTRA STRENGTH MASCARA AND SAMPLE-SIZE EAU
DYNAMISANTE. STOCKS LIMITED SO HURRY.

But this is fantastic! Do you know how much Clarins lipstick usually costs? And here they are, giving it away! Excitedly I start rooting through all the skin-care products, trying to decide which two to buy. How about some neck cream? I've never used that before. And some of this Revitalizing Moisturizer. And then I'll get a free lipstick! It's a complete bargain.

"Hi," I say to the woman in the white uniform. "I'd

like the Neck Cream and the Revitalizing Moisturizer. And the beauty bag," I add, suddenly petrified that I might be too late; that the limited stocks might have run out.

But they haven't! Thank God. As my VISA card's processing, the woman hands me my shiny red beauty bag (which I have to admit is a bit smaller than I was expecting) and I excitedly open it up. And there, sure enough, is my free lipstick!

It's a kind of browny-red color. A bit weird, actually. But if I mix it up a bit with some of my others and add a bit of lip gloss, it'll look really good.

By the time I get home, I'm exhausted. I open the door to the flat and Suze comes rushing up, like a puppy.

"What did you get?" she cries.

"Don't look!" I cry back. "You're not allowed to look! It's your present."

"My present!" Suze gets overexcited about birthdays. Well, to be honest, so do I.

I hurry into my bedroom and hide the Benetton bag in the wardrobe. Then I unpack all the rest of my shopping and get out my little silver notebook to itemize my purchases. David E. Barton says this should be done *straight away,* before items can be forgotten.

"D'you want a drink?" comes Suze's voice through the door.

"Yes, please!" I shout back, writing in my book, and a moment later she comes in with a glass of wine.

"*EastEnders* in a minute," she says.

"Thanks," I say absently, and keep on writing. I'm following the rules of the book exactly, taking out all my receipts and writing them all down, and I'm feeling really pleased with myself. It just shows, as David E. Barton says, that with a bit of application, anyone can gain control of their finances.

Come to think of it, I've bought quite a lot of moisturizer today, haven't I? To be honest, when I was at the Clarins counter, buying my Revitalizing Moisturizer, I forgot about all those pots I'd bought at Boots. Still, never mind. You always need moisturizer. It's a staple, like bread and milk, and David E. Barton says you should never scrimp on staples. And apart from that, I don't think I've done too badly. Of course I haven't added it all up yet, but . . .

OK. So here is my final and complete list:

Cappuccino	£1.50
Muffin	£1.00
~~Notebook~~	~~£3.99~~
~~Pen~~	~~£1.20~~
Magazines	£6.40
Leaving present	£4.00
Egg and cress sandwich	99p
Coconut bath oil	£2.55
Boots Moisturizers	£20.97
Two cardigans	£90.00
Evening Standard	35p
Clarins Neck Cream	£14.50
Clarins Moisturizer	£32.50
Beauty Bag	Free!
Banana smoothie	£2.00
Carrot cake	£1.20

And that comes to a grand total of . . . £177.96

I stare at this figure in utter shock.

No, I'm sorry, that just can't be right. It *can't* be right. I can't have spent over £170 in one day.

I mean, it isn't even the weekend. I've been at work. I wouldn't have had *time* to spend that much. There has to be something wrong somewhere. Maybe I haven't added it up right. Or maybe I've entered something twice.

My eye runs more carefully down the list and suddenly stops in triumph. "Two cardigans." I knew it! I only bought . . .

Oh yes. I did buy two, didn't I? Blast. Oh, this is too depressing. I'm going to go and watch *EastEnders*.

OCTAGON ▶ *flair...style...vision*

FINANCIAL SERVICES DEPARTMENT
8TH FLOOR   TOWER HOUSE
LONDON ROAD WINCHESTER SO 44 3DR

Ms. Rebecca Bloomwood   *Charge Card Number 7854 4567*
Flat 2
4 Burney Rd.
London SW6 8FD

5 March 2000

Dear Ms. Bloomwood:

Thank you for your check for £43.00, received today.

Unfortunately, the check is unsigned. No doubt just an oversight on your part. I am therefore returning it to you and request that you sign it and return to us.

As you are no doubt aware, this payment is already late by eight days.

I look forward to receiving your signed check.

Yours sincerely,

John Hunter
Customer Accounts Manager

Ms. Rebecca Bloomwood
Flat 2
4 Burney Rd.
London SW6 8FD

5 March 2000

Dear Ms. Bloomwood:

Thank you for your answer-machine message of Sunday
4 March.

I am sorry to hear that your dog has died.

Nevertheless, I must insist that you make contact with
myself or my assistant, Erica Parnell, within the next few
days, in order to discuss your situation.

Yours sincerely,

Derek Smeath
Manager

Six

Oκ, I THINK FIRMLY the next day. The thing is not to get freaked out by how much I happened to spend yesterday. It's water under the bridge. The point is, today is the beginning of my new frugal life. From now on, I'm just going to spend absolutely nothing. David E. Barton says you should aim to cut your expenditure by half in the first week, but I reckon I can do much better than that. I mean, not wanting to be rude, but these self-help books are always for people with absolutely zero self-control, aren't they? And I gave up smoking easily enough. (Except socially, but that doesn't count.)

I feel quite exhilarated as I make myself a cheese sandwich and wrap it up in tinfoil. I've already saved a couple of quid, just by doing that! I haven't got a flask (must buy one at the weekend), so I can't take in coffee, but there's a bottle of Peach Herbal Blast in the fridge so I decide I'll take that instead. It'll be healthier, too.

In fact, it makes you wonder why people buy shop-made sandwiches at all. Look how cheap and easy it is to make your own. And it's the same with curries. David E. Barton says instead of forking out for expensive take-away meals you should learn how to make your own curries and stir-fries, for a fraction of the cost. So that's what I'm going to do this weekend, after I've been to a museum or maybe just walked along the river, enjoying the scenery.

As I walk along to the tube I feel pure and refreshed. Stern, almost. Look at all these people on the street, scurrying around, thinking about nothing but money. Money, money, money. It's an obsession. But once you relinquish money altogether, it ceases to have any relevance. Already I feel I'm in a completely different mindset. Less materialistic, more philosophical. More *spiritual*. As David E. Barton says, we all fail to appreciate each day just how much we already possess. Light, air, freedom, the companionship of friends . . . I mean, these are the things that matter, aren't they?

It's almost frightening, the transformation that's already occurred within me. For example, I walk past the magazine kiosk at the tube station and idly glance over, but I don't feel the slightest desire to buy any of the magazines. Magazines are irrelevant in my new life. (Plus I've already read most of them.)

So I get on the tube feeling serene and impervious, like a Buddhist monk. When I get off the tube at the other end, I walk straight past the discount shoe shop without even looking, and straight past Lucio's, too. No cappuccino today. No muffin. No spending at all—just straight to the office.

It's quite an easy time of the month for *Successful Saving*. We've only just put the latest issue of the magazine to bed, which basically means we can laze around for a few days doing nothing, before getting our acts together for the next issue. Of course, we're meant to be starting on research for next month's article. In fact, I'm supposed to be making phone calls to a list of stockbrokers today, asking for their investment tips for the next six months. But I already know what they're all going to say. Jon Burrins will go on about the problems with e-commerce stocks, George Steadman will enthuse about some tiny biotechnology company, and Steve Fox will tell me how he wants to get out of the stockbroking game and start an organic farm.

Somehow the whole morning goes by and I haven't done anything, just changed the screen saver on my computer to three yellow fish and an octopus, and written out an expense claim form. To be honest, I can't really concentrate on proper work. I suppose I'm too exhilarated by my new pure self. I keep trying to work out how much I'll have saved by the end of the month and what I'll be able to afford in Jigsaw.

At lunchtime I take out my sandwich wrapped in foil—and for the first time that day, I feel a bit depressed. The bread's gone all soggy, and some pickle's leaked out onto the foil, and it really doesn't look very appetizing at all. What I crave at that moment is Pret à Manger walnut bread and a chocolate brownie.

Don't think about it, I instruct myself firmly. Think how much money you're saving. So somehow I force myself to eat my soggy effort, and swig down some Peach Herbal Blast. When I've finished, I throw away my foil, screw the top back on the Peach Herbal Blast bottle, and put it in our tiny office fridge. And that's about . . . five minutes of my lunch break gone.

So what am I supposed to do next? Where am I supposed to go?

I slump miserably at my desk. God, this frugality is hard going. I leaf dispiritedly through a few folders . . . then raise my head and stare out of the window, at all the busy Oxford Street shoppers clutching carrier bags. I want to get out there so desperately, I'm actually leaning forward in my chair, like a plant toward the light.

I'm craving the bright lights and warm air, the racks of merchandise, even the bleep of the cash registers. But I can't go. This morning I told myself that I wouldn't go near the shops all day. I *promised* myself—and I can't break my own promise.

Then a brilliant thought occurs to me. I need to get a curry recipe for my homemade takeaway, don't I? David E. Barton says recipe books are a waste of money. He says you should use the recipes printed on the sides of food packets, or take books out of the library. But I've got an even better idea. I'll go into Smith's and *copy out* a curry recipe to make on Saturday night. That way, I can go into a shop, but I don't need to spend any money. Already I'm scrambling to my feet, reaching for my coat. Shops, here I come!

As I walk into Smith's I feel my whole body expand in relief. There's a thrill about walking into a shop—any shop—which you can't beat. It's partly the anticipation, partly the buzzy, welcoming atmosphere, partly just the lovely *newness* of everything. Shiny new magazines, shiny new pencils, shiny new protractors. Not that I've needed a protractor since I was eleven—but don't they look nice, all clean and unscratched in their packets? There's a new range of leopard-print stationery that I haven't seen before, and for a moment I'm almost tempted to linger. But instead I force myself to stride on past, down to the back of the shop where the books are stacked.

There's a whole array of Indian recipe books, and I pick up one at random, flicking over the pages and wondering what sort of recipe I should go for. I hadn't realized quite how complicated this Indian cookery is. Perhaps I should write down a couple, to be on the safe side.

I look around cautiously and take out my notebook and pen. I'm a bit wary, because I know Smith's doesn't like you copying down stuff out of their books. The reason I know this is because Suze once got asked to leave the Smith's in Victoria. She was copying out a page of the street atlas, because she'd forgotten hers—and they told her she had to either buy it or leave. (Which doesn't make any sense, because they let you read the magazines for free, don't they?)

So anyway, when I'm sure no one's looking, I start copying out the recipe for "Tiger Prawn Biriani." I'm halfway through the list of spices when a girl in WHSmith uniform comes round the corner, so I quickly close the book and walk off a little, pretending I'm browsing. When I think I'm safe, I open it again—but before I can write anything down, an old woman in a blue coat says loudly, "Is that any good, dear?"

"What?" I say.

"The book!" She gestures to the recipe book with her umbrella. "I need a present for my daughter-in-law, and she comes from India. So I thought I'd get a nice Indian recipe book. Is that a good one, would you say?"

"I'm afraid I don't know," I say. "I haven't read it yet."

"Oh," she says, and starts to wander off. And I ought to keep my mouth shut and mind my own business—but I just can't leave it there, I have to clear my throat and say, "Excuse me—but doesn't she have lots of Indian recipes already?"

"Who, dear?" says the woman, turning round.

"Your daughter-in-law!" Already I'm regretting this. "If she's Indian, doesn't she already know how to cook Indian food?"

"Oh," says the old woman. She seems completely flummoxed. "Well, what should I get, then?"

Oh God.

"I don't know," I say. "Maybe a book on . . . on something else?"

"That's a good idea!" she says brightly, and comes toward me. "You show me, dear."

"Well," I say, looking helplessly around the racks of books. "What's she interested in? Does she . . . have any particular hobby?"

"She likes the fresh air," says the woman thoughtfully. "Walking in the countryside."

"Perfect!" I say in relief. "Why not try the travel section for a walking book?"

I point the woman in the right direction, then hurry off to do my copying. I reach the CD and video section, which is always quite empty, and hide behind a rack of Teletubbies videos. I glance around and check no one's about, then open the book again. Okay, turn to page 214, "Tiger Prawn Biriani" . . . I start copying again, and I've just got to the end of the list of spices, when a stern voice says in my ear, "Excuse me?"

I'm so startled, my pen jerks off my notebook and, to my horror, makes a blue line, straight across a photograph of perfectly cooked basmati rice. Quickly I shift my hand, almost covering up the mark, and turn round innocently. A man in a white shirt and a name badge is looking at me disapprovingly.

"This isn't a public library, you know," he says.

"I'm just browsing," I say hurriedly, and make to close the book. But the man's finger comes out of nowhere and lands on the page before I can get it shut. Slowly he opens the book out again and we both stare at my blue Biro line.

"Browsing is one thing," says the man sternly. "Defacing shop stock is another."

"It was an accident!" I say. "You startled me!"

"Hmm," says the man, and gives me a hard stare.

"Were you actually intending to buy this book? Or any book?"

There's a pause—then, rather shamefacedly, I say, "No."

"I see," says the man, tightening his lips. "Well, I'm afraid this matter will have to go to the manager. Obviously, we can't sell this book now, so it's our loss. If you could come with me and explain to her exactly what you were doing when the defacement occurred . . ."

Is he serious? Isn't he just going to tell me kindly that it doesn't matter and would I like a loyalty card? My heart starts to thud in panic. What am I going to do? Obviously, I can't buy the book, under my new frugal regime. But I don't want to go and see the manager, either.

"Lynn?" the man's calling to an assistant at the pen counter. "Could you page Glenys for me, please?"

He really is serious. He's looking all pleased with himself, as though he's caught a shoplifter. Can they prosecute you for making Biro marks in books? Maybe it counts as vandalism. I'll have a criminal record. I won't ever be able to go to America.

"Look, I'll buy it, okay?" I say breathlessly. "I'll buy the bloody book." I wrench it from the man's grasp and hurry off to the checkout before he can say anything else.

Standing at the next checkout is the old woman in the blue coat, and she calls triumphantly, "I took your advice! I've got her one of those traveling books. I think she'll really like it!"

"Oh good," I reply, handing my recipe book over to be scanned.

"It's called *The Rough Guide to India,*" says the old woman, showing me the fat blue paperback. "Have you heard of it?"

"Oh," I say. "Well, yes, but—"

"That's £24.99, please," says the girl at my till.

What? I look at the girl in dismay. Twenty-five quid, just for recipes? Why couldn't I have picked up some cheap paperback? Damn. *Damn*. Very reluctantly, I take out my credit card and hand it over. Shopping is one thing, being forced into purchases against your will is something else. I mean, I could have bought some nice underwear with that twenty-five quid.

On the other hand, I think as I walk away, that's quite a lot of new points on my Club Card. The equivalent to . . . fifty pence! And now I'll be able to make loads of delicious, exotic curries and save all that wasted take-away money. Really, I've got to think of this book as an investment.

I don't want to boast, but apart from that one purchase, I do incredibly well over the next couple of days. The only things I buy are a really nice chrome flask to take coffee into the office. (And some coffee beans and an electric grinder.) And some flowers and champagne for Suze's birthday.

But I'm allowed to get those, because, as David E. Barton says, you must treasure your friends. He says the simple act of breaking bread with friends is one of the oldest, most essential parts of human life. "Do not stop giving your friends gifts," he says. "They need not be extravagant—use your creativity and try making them yourself."

So I've bought Suze a half bottle of champagne instead of a whole one—and instead of buying expensive croissants from the patisserie, I'm going to make them out of that special dough you get in tubes.

In the evening we're going out to Terrazza for supper

with Suze's cousins Fenella and Tarquin—and, to be honest, it might be quite an expensive evening. But that's OK, because it counts as breaking bread with friends. (Except the bread at Terrazza is sun-dried tomato focaccia and costs £4.50 a basket.)

Fenella and Tarquin arrive at six o'clock, and as soon as she sees them, Suze starts squealing with excitement. I stay in my bedroom and finish my makeup, putting off the moment of having to go out and say hello. I'm not that keen on Fenella and Tarquin. In fact, to be honest with you, I think they're a bit weird. For a start, they look weird. They're both very skinny, but in a pale, bony way, and have the same slightly protruding teeth. Fenella does make a bit of an effort with clothes and makeup, and doesn't look *too* bad. But Tarquin, frankly, looks just like a stoat. Or a weasel. Some bony little creature, anyway. They do strange things, too. They ride around on a tandem and wear matching jumpers knit-ted by their old nanny and have this family language which no one else can understand. Like they call sand-wiches "witchies." And a drink is a "titchy" (except if it's water, which is "Ho"). Take it from me, it gets irritating after a while.

But Suze loves them. She spent all her childhood summers with them in Scotland and she just can't see that they're a bit strange. The worst thing is, *she* starts talking about witchies and titchies when she's with them.

Still, there's nothing I can do about it—they're here now. I finish brushing on my mascara and stand up, looking at my reflection. I'm pretty pleased with what I see. I'm wearing a really simple black top and black trousers—and, tied loosely round my neck, my gorgeous, *gorgeous* Denny and George scarf. God, that was a good buy. It looks fantastic.

I linger a bit, then resignedly open my bedroom door.

"Hi, Bex!" says Suze, looking up with bright eyes. She's sitting cross-legged on the floor of the corridor, ripping open a present, while Fenella and Tarquin stand nearby, looking on. They're not wearing matching jumpers today, thank God, but Fenella's wearing a very odd red skirt made out of hairy tweed, and Tarquin's double-breasted suit looks as if it were tailored during the First World War.

"Hi!" I say, and kiss each of them politely.

"Oh, wow!" cries Suze, as she pulls out a picture in an old gilt frame. "I don't believe it! I don't *believe* it!" She's looking from Tarquin to Fenella with shining eyes, and I look at the picture interestedly over her shoulder. But to be honest, I can't say I'm impressed. For a start it's really dingy—all sludgy greens and browns—and for another start, it just shows a horse standing still in a field. I mean, couldn't it have been jumping over a fence or rearing up or something? Or maybe trotting along in Hyde Park, ridden by a girl in one of those lovely *Pride and Prejudice* dresses.

"Happy Bad Day!" Tarquin and Fenella chime in unison. (That's another thing. They call birthdays bad days, ever since . . . Oh God. It really is too boring to explain.)

"It's absolutely gorgeous!" I say enthusiastically. "Absolutely beautiful!"

"It is, isn't it?" says Tarquin earnestly. "Just look at those colors."

"Mmm, lovely," I say, nodding.

"And the brushwork. It's exquisite. We were thrilled when we came across it."

"It's a really wonderful picture," I say. "Makes you want to just . . . gallop off over the downs!"

What is this drivel I'm coming out with? Why can't I just be honest and say I don't like it?

"Do you ride?" says Tarquin, looking up at me in slight surprise.

I've ridden once. On my cousin's horse. And I fell off and vowed never to do it again. But I'm not going to admit that to Mr. Horse of the Year.

"I used to," I say, and give a modest little smile. "Not very well."

"I'm sure you'd get back into it," says Tarquin, gazing at me. "Have you ever hunted?"

Hunted? Little furry foxes? Is he joking?

"Hey," says Suze, fondly propping the picture against the wall. "Shall we have a titchy before we go?"

"Absolutely!" I say, turning quickly away from Tarquin. "Good idea."

"Oooh, yes," says Fenella. "Have you got any champagne?"

"Should have," says Suze, and goes into the kitchen. At that moment the phone rings and I go to answer it.

"Hello?"

"Hello, may I speak to Rebecca Bloomwood?" says a strange woman's voice.

"Yes," I say idly. I'm listening to Suze opening and shutting cupboard doors in the kitchen and wondering if we have actually got any champagne, apart from the dregs of the half bottle we drank for breakfast . . . "Speaking."

"Ms. Bloomwood, this is Erica Parnell from Endwich Bank," says the voice, and I freeze.

Shit. It's the bank. Oh God, they sent me that letter, didn't they, and I never did anything about it.

What am I going to say? Quick, what am I going to say? "Ms. Bloomwood?" says Erica Parnell.

OK, what I'll say is, I'm fully aware that my overdraft is slightly larger than it should be, and I'm planning to take remedial action within the next few days. Yes, that sounds good. "Remedial action" sounds very good. OK—go.

Firmly I tell myself not to panic—these people are human—and take a big breath. And then, in one seamless, unplanned movement, my hand puts down the receiver.

I stare at the silent phone for a few seconds, not quite able to believe what I've just done. *What* did I do that for? Erica Parnell knew it was me, didn't she? Any minute, she'll ring back. She's probably pressing redial now, and she'll be really angry . . .

Quickly I take the phone off the hook and hide it under a cushion. Now she can't get me. I'm safe.

"Who was that?" says Suze, coming into the room.

"No one," I say, and force a bright smile. I don't want to spoil Suze's birthday with my stupid problems. "Just a wrong . . . Listen, let's not have drinks here. Let's go out!"

"Oh," says Suze. "OK!"

"Much more fun," I gabble, trying to head her away from the phone. "We can go to some really nice bar and have cocktails, and then go on to Terrazza."

What I'll do in future, I'm thinking, is screen all my calls. Or answer in a foreign accent. Or, even better, change the number. Go ex-directory.

"What's going on?" says Fenella, appearing at the door.

"Nothing!" I hear myself say. "We're going out for a titchy and then on to sups."

Oh, I don't believe it. I'm turning into one of them.

As we arrive at Terrazza, I'm feeling a lot calmer. Of course, Erica Parnell will have thought we were cut off by a fault on the line or something. She'll never have thought I put the phone down on her. I mean, we're two civilized adults, aren't we? Adults just don't *do* things like that.

And if I ever meet her, which I hope to God I never do, I'll just keep very cool and say, "It was odd what happened, that time you phoned me, wasn't it?" Or even better, I'll accuse *her* of putting the phone down on *me*. (In a jokey way, of course.)

Terrazza is full, buzzing with people and cigarette smoke and chatter, and as we sit down with our huge silver menus I feel myself relax even more. I love eating out. And I reckon I deserve a real treat, after being so frugal over the last few days. It hasn't been easy, keeping to such a tight regime, but somehow I've managed it. I'm keeping to it so well! On Saturday I'm going to monitor my spending pattern again, and I'm sure it'll have gone down by at least 70 percent.

"What shall we have to drink?" says Suze. "Tarquin, you choose."

"Oh, look!" shrieks Fenella. "There's Eddie Lazenby! I must just say hello." She leaps to her feet and makes for a balding guy in a blazer, ten tables away. How she spotted him in this throng, I've no idea.

"Suze!" cries another voice, and we all look up. A blond girl in a tiny pastel-pink suit is heading toward our table, arms stretched out for a hug. "And Tarkie!"

"Hello, Tory," says Tarquin, getting to his feet. "How's Mungo?"

"He's over there!" says Tory. "You must come and say hello!"

How is it that Fenella and Tarquin spend most of their time in the middle of Perthshire, but the minute they set foot in London, they're besieged by long-lost friends?

"Eddie says hi," announces Fenella, returning to the table. "Tory! How are you? How's Mungo?"

"Oh, he's fine," says Tory. "But listen, have you heard? Caspar's back in town!"

"No!" everyone exclaims, and I'm almost tempted to join in. No one has bothered to introduce me to Tory, but that's the way it goes. You join the gang by osmosis. One minute you're a complete stranger, the next you're shrieking away with the rest of them, going "Did you *hear* about Venetia and Sebastian?"

"Look, we *must* order," says Suze. "We'll come and say hello in a minute, Tory."

"Okay, ciao," says Tory, and she sashays off.

"Suze!" cries another voice, and a girl in a little black dress comes rushing up. "And Fenny!"

"Milla!" they both cry. "How are you? How's Benjy?"

Oh God, it just doesn't stop. Here I am, staring at the menu, pretending to be really interested in the starters but really feeling like some utter loser that no one wants to talk to. It's not fair. *I* want to table-hop, too. *I* want to bump into old friends I've known since babyhood. (Although to be honest, the only person I've known that long is Tom from next door, and he'll be in his limed oak kitchen in Reigate.)

But just in case, I lower my menu and gaze hopefully around the restaurant. Please, God, just once, let there be someone I recognize. It doesn't have to be anyone I like, or even know that well—just someone I can rush up to and go mwah mwah and shriek, "We must do lunch!" *Anyone*'ll do. Anyone at all . . .

And then, with a disbelieving thrill, I spot a familiar face, a few tables away! It's Luke Brandon, sitting at a table with a smartly dressed older man and woman.

Well, he's not exactly an old friend—but I know him, don't I? And I *so* want to table-hop like the others.

"Oh look, there's Luke!" I shriek (quietly, so he doesn't hear). "I simply *must* go and say hello!"

As the others look at me in surprise, I toss my hair back, leap to my feet, and hurry off, full of a sudden exhilaration. I can do it, too! I'm table-hopping at Terrazza. I'm an It-girl!

It's only when I get within a few feet of his table that I slow down and wonder what I'm actually going to say to him.

Well . . . I'll just be polite. Say hello and—ah, genius! I can thank him again for his kind loan of twenty quid.

Shit, I did pay him back, didn't I?

Yes. Yes, I sent him that nice recycled card with poppies on it and a check. That's right. Now don't panic, just be cool and It.

"Hi!" I say as soon as I get within earshot of his table, but the hubbub around us is so loud, he doesn't hear me. No wonder all Fenella's friends have got such screechy voices. You need about sixty-five decibels, just to be heard. "Hi!" I try again, louder, but still no response. Luke is talking earnestly to the older man, and the woman's listening intently. None of them even glances up.

This is getting a bit embarrassing. I'm standing, marooned, being utterly ignored by the person I want to table-hop with. Nobody else ever seems to have this problem. Why isn't he leaping up, shrieking "Have you *heard* about Foreland Investments?" It's not fair. What shall I do? Shall I just creep away? Shall I pretend I was heading toward the Ladies'?

A waiter barges past me with a tray, and I'm pushed helplessly forward, toward Luke's table—and at that moment, he looks up. He stares at me blankly as though he doesn't even know who I am, and I feel my stomach give a little flip of dismay. But I've got to go through with it now.

"Hi, Luke!" I say brightly. "I just thought I'd say . . . hello!"

"Well, hello," Luke says eventually. "Mum, Dad, this is Rebecca Bloomwood. Rebecca—my parents."

Oh God. What have I done? I've table-hopped an intimate family gathering. Leave, quick.

"Hello," I say, and give a feeble smile. "Well, I won't keep you from . . ."

"So how do you know Luke?" inquires Mrs. Brandon.

"Rebecca is a leading financial journalist," says Luke, taking a sip of wine. (Is that really what he thinks? Gosh, I must drop that into a conversation with Clare Edwards. And Philip, come to that.)

I grin confidently at Mr. Brandon, feeling like a mover and a shaker. I'm a leading financial journalist hobnobbing with a leading entrepreneur at a leading London restaurant. How cool is that?

"Financial journalist, eh?" grunts Mr. Brandon, and lowers his reading glasses to have a better look at me. "So what do *you* think of the chancellor's announcement?"

I'm never going to table-hop again. Never.

"Well," I begin confidently, wondering if I could suddenly pretend to spot an old friend across the room.

"Dad, I'm sure Rebecca doesn't want to talk shop," says Luke, his lips twitching slightly.

"Quite right!" says Mrs. Brandon, and smiles at me. "That's a lovely scarf, Rebecca. Is it Denny and George?"

"Yes, it is!" I say brightly, full of relief. "I was so pleased, I got it last week in the sale!"

Out of the corner of my eye, I can see that Luke Brandon is staring at me with an odd expression. Why? Why is he looking so . . .

Oh fuck. How can I be so *stupid*?

"In the sale . . . for my aunt," I continue, trying to think as quickly as I can. "I bought it for my aunt, as a present. But she . . . died."

There's a shocked silence and I look down. I can't quite believe what I've just said.

"Oh dear," says Mr. Brandon gruffly.

"Aunt Ermintrude died?" says Luke in a strange voice.

"Yes," I reply, forcing myself to look up. "It was terribly sad."

"How awful!" says Mrs. Brandon sympathetically.

"She was in hospital, wasn't she?" says Luke, pouring himself a glass of water. "What was wrong with her?"

For an instant I'm silenced.

"It was . . . her leg," I hear myself say.

"Her leg?" Mrs. Brandon's staring at me anxiously. "What was wrong with her leg?"

"It . . . swelled up and got septic," I say after a pause. "And they had to amputate it and then she died."

"Christ," says Mr. Brandon, shaking his head. "Bloody doctors." He gives me a suddenly fierce look. "Did she go private?"

"Umm . . . I'm not sure," I say, starting to back away. Why didn't I just say she *gave* me the bloody scarf? "Anyway, lovely to see you, Luke. Must dash, my friends will be missing me!"

I give a nonchalant kind of wave without quite

looking Luke in the eye and then quickly turn round and walk back to Suze, my legs trembling and my fingers twisted tightly by my sides. God, what a fiasco.

I've managed to recompose myself by the time our food arrives. The food! I've ordered grilled scallops and as I take my first bite, I nearly swoon. After so many torturous days of cheap, functional food, this is like going to heaven. I feel almost tearful—like a prisoner returning to the real world, or children after the war, when rationing stopped. After my scallops I have steak béarnaise and chips—and when all the others say no thanks to the pudding menu, I order chocolate mousse. Because who knows when I'm next going to be in a restaurant like this? There could be months ahead of cheese sandwiches and homemade coffee in a flask, with nothing to relieve the monotony.

While I'm waiting for my chocolate mousse, Suze and Fenella decide they simply must go and talk to Benjy, on the other side of the room. So they leap up, both lighting cigarettes as they do so, and Tarquin stays behind to keep me company. He doesn't seem quite as into table-hopping as the others. In fact, he's been pretty quiet all evening. I've also noticed that he's drunk more than any of us. Any moment I'm expecting his head to land on the table.

For a while there's silence between us. To be honest, Tarquin is so weird, I don't know how to talk to him. Then, suddenly, he says, "Do you like Wagner?"

"Oh yes," I say at once. I'm not sure I've ever heard any Wagner, but I don't want to sound uncultured. And I have been to the opera before, though I think that was Mozart.

" 'The Liebestod' from *Tristan*," he says, and shakes his head. " 'The Liebestod.' "

"Mmm," I say, and nod in what I hope is an intelligent manner. I pour myself some wine, fill his glass up, too, and look around to see where Suze has got to. Typical of her just to disappear off and leave me with her drunken cousin.

"Dah-dah-*dah*-dah, daaaah dah dah . . ."

Oh my God, now he's singing. Not loudly, but really intensely. And he's staring into my eyes as though he expects me to join in.

"Dah-dah-*dah*-dah . . ."

Now he's closed his eyes and is swaying. This is getting embarrassing.

"Da diddle-idy da-a-da-a daaaah dah . . ."

"Lovely," I say brightly. "You can't beat Wagner, can you?"

"*Tristan*," he says. "*Und Isolde*." He opens his eyes. "You'd make a beautiful Isolde."

I'd make a *what*? While I'm still staring at him, he lifts my hand to his lips and starts kissing it. For a few seconds I'm too shocked to move.

"Tarquin," I say as firmly as I can, trying to pull my hand away. "Tarquin, please—" I look up and desperately scan the room for Suze—and, as I do so, meet the eye of Luke Brandon, making his way out of the restaurant. He frowns slightly, lifts his hand in farewell, then disappears out of the door.

"Your skin smells like roses," murmurs Tarquin against my skin.

"Oh, shut up!" I say crossly, and yank my hand out of his grasp so hard I get a row of teeth marks on my skin. "Just leave me alone!"

I would slap him, but he'd probably take it as a come-on.

Just then, Suze and Fenella arrive back at the table, full of news about Binky and Minky—and Tarquin reverts into silence. And for the rest of the evening, even when we say good-bye, he barely looks at me. Thank God. He must have got the message.

Seven

It DOESN'T SEEM he has, though, because on Saturday, I receive a card of a pre-Raphaelite girl looking coyly over her shoulder. Inside, Tarquin has written:

> Many apologies for my uncouth behavior. I hope to make it up to you. Tickets to Bayreuth—or, failing that, dinner?
>
> Tarquin.

Dinner with Tarquin. Can you imagine? And what's he going on about, anyway? I've never heard of Bayreuth. Is it a new show or something? Or does he mean Beirut? Why would we want to go to Beirut, for God's sake?

Anyway, I've got more important things to think about today. This is my sixth day of Cutting Back—and, crucially, my first weekend. David E. Barton says this is often when one's frugal regime cracks, as the office routine is no longer there as a distraction and the day stretches empty, waiting to be filled with the familiar comfort of shopping.

But I'm too strong-willed to crack. I've got my day

completely sussed—and I'm not going *near* any shops. This morning I'm going to visit a museum and then tonight, instead of wasting lots of money on an expensive takeaway, I'm cooking a homemade curry for me and Suze. I'm actually quite excited about it.

My entire budget for today is as follows:

Travel to museum:	*free (I already have a travelcard)*
Museum:	*free*
Curry:	*£2.50 (David E. Barton says you can make a wonderful curry for four people for less than £5.00—and there are only two of us.)*
Total daily expenditure:	*£2.50*

That's more like it. Plus I get to experience culture instead of mindless materialism. I have chosen the Victoria & Albert Museum because I have never been to it before. In fact, I'm not even sure what they have in it. Statues of Queen Victoria and Prince Albert, or something?

Anyway, whatever they have, it will be very interesting and stimulating, I'm sure. And above all, free!

As I come out of South Kensington tube, the sun's shining brightly and I stride along, feeling pleased with myself. Normally I waste my Saturday mornings watching *Live and Kicking* and getting ready to go to the shops. But look at this! I suddenly feel very grown-up and metropolitan, like someone in a Woody Allen film. I just need a long woolly scarf and some sunglasses and I'll look like Diane Keaton.

And on Monday, when people ask me how my weekend was, I'll be able to say, "Actually, I went to the V&A." No, what I'll say is "I caught an exhibition." That sounds much cooler. (Why *do* people say they "caught" an exhibition, by the way? It's not as though all the paintings were thundering past like bulls at Pamplona.) Then they'll say, "Really? I didn't know you were into art, Rebecca." And I'll say, "Oh yes. I spend most of my free time at museums." And they'll give me an impressed look and say . . .

Come to think of it, I've walked straight past the entrance. Silly me. Too busy thinking about the conversation between me and . . . actually, the person I realize I've pictured in this little scene is Luke Brandon. How weird. Why should that be? Because I table-hopped with him, I suppose. Anyway. Concentrate. Museum.

Quickly I retrace my steps and walk nonchalantly into the entrance hall, trying to look as though I come here all the time. Not like that bunch of Japanese tourists clustering round their guide. Ha! I think proudly, I'm no tourist. This is my heritage. *My* culture. I pick up a map carelessly as though I don't really need it, and look at a list of talks on things like *Ceramics of the Yuan and Early Ming Dynasties*. Then, casually, I begin to walk through to the first gallery.

"Excuse me?" A woman at a desk is calling to me. "Have you paid?"

Have I *what*? You don't have to pay to get into museums! Oh, of course—she's just joking with me. I give a friendly little laugh, and carry on.

"Excuse me!" she says, in a sharper voice, and a bloke in security uniform appears out of nowhere. "Have you paid for admission?"

"It's free!" I say in surprise.

"I'm afraid not," she says, and points to a sign behind

me. I turn to read it, and nearly keel over in astonishment.

Admission £5.00.

I feel quite faint with shock. What's happened to the world? They're *charging* for admission to a museum. This is outrageous. Everyone knows museums are supposed to be free. If you start charging for museums, no one will ever go! Our cultural heritage will be lost to a whole generation, excluded by a punitive financial barrier. The nation will be dumbed down still further, and civilized society will face the very brink of collapse. Is that what you want, Tony Blair?

Plus, I don't have £5. I deliberately came out with no cash except £2.50 for my curry ingredients. Oh God, this is annoying. I mean, here I am, all ready for some culture. I *want* to go in and look at . . . well, whatever's in there—and I can't!

Now all the Japanese tourists are staring at me, as if I'm some sort of criminal. Go away! I think crossly. Go and look at some art.

"We take credit cards," says the woman. "VISA, Switch, American Express."

"Oh," I say. "Well . . . OK."

"The season ticket is £15," she says, as I reach for my purse, "but it gives you unlimited access for a year."

Unlimited access for a year! Now wait just a minute. David E. Barton says what you're supposed to do, when you make any purchase, is estimate the "cost per use," which you get by dividing the price by the number of times you use it. Let's suppose that from now on I come to the V&A once a month. (I should think that's quite realistic.) If I buy a season ticket, that's only . . . £1.25 a visit.

Well, that's a bargain, isn't it? It's actually a very good investment, when you come to think of it.

"OK, I'll have the season ticket," I say, and hand over my VISA card. Hah! Culture here I come.

I start off really well. I look at my little map, and peer at each exhibit, and carefully read all the little cards.

Chalice made from silver, Dutch, 16th century
Plaque depicting Holy Trinity, Italian mid–15th century
Blue and white earthenware bowl, early 17th century

That bowl's really nice, I find myself thinking in sudden interest, and wonder how much it is. It looks quite expensive . . . I'm just peering to see if there's a price tag when I remember where I am. Of course. There aren't any prices here.

Which is a bit of a mistake, I think. Because it kind of takes the fun out of it, doesn't it? You wander round, just looking at things, and it all gets a bit boring after a while. Whereas if they put price tags on, you'd be far more interested. In fact, I think all museums should put prices on their exhibits. You'd look at a silver chalice or a marble statue or the *Mona Lisa* or whatever, and admire it for its beauty and historical importance and everything—and then you'd reach for the price tag and gasp, "Hey, look how much this one is!" It would really liven things up.

I might write to the Victoria & Albert and suggest this to them. I am a season-ticket holder, after all. They should listen to my opinion.

In the meantime, let's move on to the next glass case.

Carved goblet, English, mid–15th century

God, I could die for a cup of coffee. How long have I been here? It must be . . .

Oh. Only fifteen minutes.

When I get to the gallery showing a history of fashion, I become quite rigorous and scholarly. In fact, I spend longer there than anywhere else. But then the dresses and shoes come to an end and it's back to more statues and little fiddly things in cases. I keep looking at my watch, and my feet hurt . . . and in the end I sink down onto a sofa.

Don't get me wrong, I like museums. I do. And I'm really interested in Korean art. It's just that the floors are really hard, and I'm wearing quite tight boots, and it's hot so I've taken off my jacket but now it keeps slithering around in my arms. And it's weird, but I keep thinking I can hear the sound of a cash till. It must be in my imagination.

I'm sitting blankly, wondering if I can summon the energy to stand up again, when the group of Japanese tourists comes into the gallery, and I feel compelled to get to my feet and pretend I'm looking at something. I peer vaguely at a piece of tapestry, then stride off down a corridor lined with exhibits of old Indian tiles. I'm just thinking that maybe we should get the Fired Earth catalogue and retile the bathroom, when I glimpse something through a metal grille and stop dead with shock.

Am I dreaming? Is it a mirage? I can see a cash register, and a queue of people, and a display cabinet with price tags . . .

Oh my God, I was right! It's a shop! There's a *shop*, right there in front of me!

Suddenly my steps have more spring in them; my energy has miraculously returned. Following the bleeping sound of the cash register, I hurry round the corner to the shop entrance and pause on the threshold, telling myself not to raise my hopes, not to be disappointed if it's just bookmarks and tea towels.

But it's not. It's bloody fantastic! Why isn't this place better known? There's a whole range of gorgeous jewelry, and loads of really interesting books on art, and there's all this amazing pottery, and greeting cards, and . . .

Oh. But I'm not supposed to be buying anything today, am I? Damn.

This is awful. What's the point of discovering a new shop and then not being able to buy anything in it? It's not fair. Everyone else is buying stuff, everyone else is having fun. For a while I hover disconsolately beside a display of mugs, watching as an Australian woman buys a pile of books on sculpture. She's chatting away to the sales assistant, and suddenly I hear her say something about Christmas. And then I have a flash of pure genius.

Christmas shopping! I can do all my Christmas shopping here! I know March is a bit early, but why not be organized? And then when Christmas arrives I won't have to go near the horrible Christmas crowds. I can't believe I haven't thought of doing this before. And it's not breaking the rules, because I'd have to buy Christmas presents *sometime,* wouldn't I? All I'm doing is shifting the buying process forward a bit. It makes perfect sense.

And so, about an hour later, I emerge happily with two carrier bags. I've bought a photograph album covered in William Morris print, an old-fashioned wooden jigsaw puzzle, a book of fashion photographs, and a fantastic ceramic teapot. God, I *love* Christmas shopping. I'm not sure what I'll give to who—but the point is, these are all timeless and unique items that would enhance any home. (Or at least the ceramic teapot is, because that's what it said on the little leaflet.) So I reckon I've done really well.

In fact, this morning has been a great success. As I emerge from the museum, I feel incredibly content and uplifted. It just shows the effect that a morning of pure culture has on the soul. From now on, I decide, I'm going to spend every Saturday morning at a museum.

When I get back home, the second post is on the doormat and there's a square envelope addressed to me in writing I don't recognize. I rip it open as I lug my carrier bags to my room—and then stop in surprise. It's a card from Luke Brandon. How did he get my home address?

> *Dear Rebecca*, it says, *It was good to bump into you the other night, and I do hope you had an enjoyable evening. I now realize that I never thanked you for the prompt repayment of my loan. Much appreciated.*
>
> *With all best wishes—and, of course, deepest sympathy on the loss of your Aunt Ermintrude. (If it's any consolation, I can't imagine that scarf could suit anyone better than you.)*
>
> *Luke.*

For a while I stare at it silently. I'm quite taken aback. Gosh, I think cautiously. It's nice of him to write, isn't it? A nice handwritten card like this, just to thank me for *my* card. I mean, he's not just being polite, is he? You don't have to send a thank-you card to someone just because they repaid your twenty quid.

Or do you? Maybe, these days, you do. Everyone seems to send cards for everything. I haven't got a clue what's done and what's not anymore. (I *knew* I should have read that etiquette book I got in my stocking.) Is this card just a polite thank-you? Or is it something else? And if so . . . what?

Is he taking the piss?

Oh God, that's it. He knows Aunt Ermintrude doesn't exist. He's just pulling my leg to embarrass me.

But then . . . would he go to all the trouble of buying a card, writing in it, and sending it, just to pull my leg?

Oh, I don't know. Who cares? I don't even like him, anyway.

Having been so cultured all morning, I deserve a bit of a treat in the afternoon, so I buy myself *Vogue* and a bag of Minstrels, and lie on the sofa for a bit. God, I've missed little treats like this. I haven't read a magazine for . . . well, it must be a week, except Suze's copy of *Cosmo* yesterday. And I can't *remember* the last time I tasted chocolate.

I can't spend too long enjoying myself, though, because I've got to go out and buy the stuff for our home-made curry. So after I've read my horoscope, I close *Vogue* and get out my new Indian recipe book. I'm quite excited, actually. I've never made curry before.

I've gone off the tiger prawn recipe because it turns out tiger prawns are very expensive. So what I'm going to make instead is chicken and mushroom Balti. It all looks very cheap and easy, and I just need to write out my shopping list.

When I've finished I'm a bit taken aback. The list is quite a lot longer than I'd thought it would be. I hadn't realized you needed so many spices just to make one curry. I've just looked in the kitchen, and we don't have a Balti pan, or a grinder for grinding spices, or a blender for making the aromatic paste. Or a wooden spoon or any scales that work.

Still, never mind. What I'll do is quickly go to Peter Jones and buy all the equipment we need for the kitchen, and then I'll get the food and come back and start cooking. The thing to remember is, we only have to buy all this stuff once—and then we're fully equipped to make delicious curries every night. I'll just have to think of it as an investment.

By the time Suze arrives back from Camden Market that evening, I am dressed in my new stripy apron, grinding up roasted spices in our new grinder.

"Phew!" she says, coming into the kitchen. "What a stink!"

"It's aromatic spices," I say a bit crossly, and take a swig of wine. To be honest, this is all a bit more difficult than I'd thought. I'm trying to make something called Balti masala mix, which we will be able to keep in a jar and use for months, but all the spices seem to be disappearing into the grinder and refusing to come back out. Where are they going?

"I'm absolutely starving," says Suze, pouring herself a glass of wine. "Will it be ready soon?"

"I don't know," I say, peering into the grinder. "If I can just get these bloody spices out . . ."

"Oh well," says Suze. "I might just make some toast." She pops a couple of pieces of bread in the toaster and then starts picking up all my little bags and pots of spices and looking at them.

"What's allspice?" she says, holding up a pot curiously. "Is it all the spices, mixed together?"

"I don't know," I say, banging the grinder on the

counter. A tiny dusting of powder falls out and I stare at it angrily. What happened to a whole jarful that I could keep for months? Now I'll have to roast some more of the bloody things.

"Because if it is, couldn't you just use that and forget all the others?"

"No!" I say. "I'm making a fresh and distinct Balti blend."

"OK," says Suze, shrugging. "You're the expert."

Right, I think, taking another swig of wine. Start again. Coriander seeds, fennel seeds, cumin seeds, peppercorns . . . By this time, I've given up measuring, I'm just throwing everything in. They say cooking should be instinctive, anyway.

"What's this?" says Suze, looking at Luke Brandon's card on the kitchen table. "Luke Brandon? How come he sent you a card?"

"Oh, you know," I say, shrugging casually. "He was just being polite."

"Polite?" Suze wrinkles her brow, turning the card over in her hands. "No way. You don't have to send a card to someone just because they returned your twenty quid."

"Really?" My voice is slightly higher than usual, but that must be because of the roasting aromatic spices. "I thought maybe that's what people did these days."

"Oh no," says Suze assuredly. "What happens is, the money's lent, it's returned with a thank-you letter, and that's the end of the matter. This card"—she waves it at me—"this is something extra."

This is why I love sharing a flat with Suze. She knows stuff like this, because she mixes in the right social circles. You know she once had dinner with the duchess of Kent? Not that I'm boasting, or anything.

"So what do you think it means?" I say, trying not to sound too tense.

"I reckon he's being friendly," she says, and puts the card back on the table.

Friendly. Of course, that's it. He's being friendly. Which is a good thing, of course. So why do I feel ever so slightly disappointed? I stare at the card, which has a face by Picasso on the front. What does that mean?

"Are those spices supposed to be going black, by the way?" says Suze, spreading peanut butter on her toast.

"Oh God!" I whip the Balti pan off the stove and look at the blackened coriander seeds. This is driving me crazy. Okay, tip them away and start again. Coriander seeds, fennel seeds, cumin seeds, peppercorns, bay leaves. That's the last of the bay leaves. This one had better not go wrong.

Somehow, miraculously, it doesn't. Forty minutes later, I actually have a curry bubbling away in my Balti pan! This is fantastic! It smells wonderful, and it looks just like it does in the book—and I didn't even follow the recipe very carefully. It just shows, I have a natural affinity with Indian cookery. And the more I practice, the more accomplished I'll become. Like David E. Barton says, I'll be able to knock up a quick, delicious curry in the time it takes to call the delivery firm. And look how much money I've saved!

Triumphantly I drain my basmati rice, take my ready-made nans out of the oven, and serve everything out onto plates. Then I sprinkle chopped fresh coriander over everything—and honestly, it looks like something out of *Marie-Claire*. I carry the plates through and put one in front of Suze.

"Wow!" she says. "This looks fantastic!"

"I know," I say proudly, sitting down opposite her. "Isn't it great?"

I watch as she takes her first forkful—then put a forkful into my mouth.

"Mmm! Delicious!" says Suze, chewing with relish. "Quite hot," she adds after a while.

"It's got chili powder in," I say. "And fresh chilies. But it's nice, though, isn't it?"

"It's wonderful!" says Suze. "Bex, you're so clever! I could never make this in a million years!"

But as she's chewing, a slightly strange expression is coming over her face. To be honest, I'm feeling a bit breathless, too. This curry is quite hot. In fact, it's bloody hot.

Suze has put down her plate and is taking a large slug of wine. She looks up, and I see her cheeks are red.

"OK?" I say, forcing myself to smile through the pain in my mouth.

"Yeah, great!" she says, and takes a huge bite of nan. I look down at my plate and resolutely take another forkful of curry. Immediately, my nose starts to run. Suze is sniffing, too, I notice, but as I meet her eye she smiles brightly.

Oh God, this is hot. My mouth can't stand it. My cheeks are burning, and my eyes are starting to water. How much chili powder did I put in this bloody thing? Only about one teaspoonful . . . or maybe it was two. I just kind of trusted my instincts and chucked in what looked about right. Well, so much for my instincts.

Tears start running down my face, and I give an enormous sniff.

"Are you OK?" says Suze in alarm.

"I'm fine!" I say, putting down my fork. "Just . . . you know. A bit hot."

But actually, I'm not OK. And it's not just the heat that's making tears run down my face. Suddenly I feel like a complete failure. I can't even get a quick and easy curry right. And look how much money I spent on it, with the Balti pan and the apron and all the spices . . . Oh, it's all gone wrong, hasn't it? I haven't Cut Back at all. This week's been a complete disaster.

I give a huge sob and put my plate on the floor.

"It's horrible!" I say miserably, and tears begin to stream down my face. "Don't eat it, Suze. It'll poison you."

"Bex! Don't be silly!" says Suze. "It's fantastic!" She looks at me, then puts her own plate on the floor. "Oh, Bex." She shuffles across the floor, reaches up, and gives me a hug. "Don't worry. It's just a bit hot. But otherwise, it's brilliant! And the nan is delicious! Honestly. Don't get upset."

I open my mouth to reply, and instead hear myself giving another huge sob.

"Bex, don't!" wails Suze, practically crying herself. "It's delicious! It's the most delicious curry I've ever tasted."

"It's not just the curry!" I sob, wiping my eyes. "The point was, I was supposed to be Cutting Back. This curry was only supposed to cost £2.50."

"But . . . why?" asks Suze perplexedly. "Was it a bet, or something!"

"No!" I wail. "It was because I'm in debt! And my dad said I should Cut Back or Make More Money. So I've been trying to Cut Back. But it hasn't worked . . ." I break off, shuddering with sobs. "I'm just a complete failure."

"Of course you're not a failure!" says Suze at once. "Bex, you're the opposite of a failure. It's just . . ." She hesitates. "It's just that maybe . . ."

"What?"

There's silence, then Suze says seriously, "I think you might have chosen the wrong option, Becky. I don't think you're a Cut Back kind of person."

"Really?" I sniff, and wipe my eyes. "Do you think?"

"I think you should go for Make More Money instead." Suze pauses thoughtfully. "In fact, to be honest, I don't know why anyone would choose Cut Back. I think Make More Money is a *much* better option. If I ever had to choose, that's definitely the one I'd go for."

"Yes," I say slowly. "Yes, maybe you're right. Maybe that's what I should do." I reach down with a shaky hand and take a bite of warm nan—and Suze is right. Without the curry, it's delicious. "But how shall I do it?" I say eventually. "How shall I make more money?"

There's silence for a while, with both of us thoughtfully chewing on nan. Then Suze brightens.

"I know. Look at this!" She reaches for a magazine and flips to the classified ads at the back. "Look what it says here. 'Need extra money? Join the Fine Frames family. Make thousands, working from home in your spare time. Full kit supplied.' You see? It's easy."

Wow. I'm quite impressed. Thousands. That's not bad.

"Yes," I say shakily, "maybe I'll do that."

"Or you could invent something," says Suze.

"Like what?"

"Oh, anything," she says confidently. "You're really clever. Remember when the coffee filter broke, and you made a new one out of a knee-high?"

"Yes," I say, and a tiny glow of pride spreads over me. "Yes, I did, didn't I?"

"You could easily be an inventor. Or . . . I know! Set up an Internet company. They're worth millions!"

You know, she's right. There's loads of things I could

do to Make More Money. Loads of things! It's just a question of lateral thinking. Suddenly I feel a lot better. Suze is *such* a good friend. I reach forward and give her a hug.

"Thanks, Suze," I say. "You're a star."

"No problem," she says, and hugs me back. "So, you cut out this ad and start making your thousands . . ." She pauses. "And I'll go and phone up for a takeaway curry, shall I?"

"Yes please," I say in a small voice. "A takeaway would be lovely."

REBECCA BLOOMWOOD'S CUT-BACK PROJECT

HOMEMADE CURRY, SATURDAY 24TH MARCH

Proposed Budget: £2.50

Actual Expenditure:

Balti pan	£15.00
Electric grinder	£14.99
Blender	£18.99
Wooden spoon	35p
Apron	£9.99
Two chicken breasts	£1.98
300g mushrooms	79p
Onion	29p
Coriander seeds	£1.29
Fennel seeds	£1.29
Allspice	£1.29
Cumin seeds	£1.29
Cloves	£1.39
Ground ginger	£1.95
Bay leaves	£1.40
Chili powder	

OH GOD, FORGET IT

PGNI FIRST BANK VISA

7 CAMEL SQUARE
LIVERPOOL LI 5NP

Ms. Rebecca Bloomwood
Flat 2
4 Burney Rd.
London SW6 8FD

6 March 2000

Dear Ms. Bloomwood:

PGNI First Bank VISA Card No. 1475839204847586

Thank you for your letter of 2 March.

I can assure you that our computers are regularly checked,
and that the possibility of a "glitch," as you put it, is
remote. Nor have we been affected by the millennium
bug. All accounts are entirely accurate.

You may write to Anne Robinson at *Watchdog* if you wish,
but I am sure she will agree that you have no grounds for
complaint.

Our records inform us that payment on your VISA account
is now overdue. As you will see from your most recent
VISA card statement, the minimum payment required is
£105.40. I look forward to receiving your payment, as
soon as possible.

Yours sincerely,

Peter Johnson
Customer Accounts Executive

Eight

OK, SO PERHAPS the Cutting Back didn't go that well. But it doesn't matter, because that's all in the past. That was negative thinking—now I'm seriously into positive thinking. Onward and upward. Growth and prosperity. M.M.M. It's the obvious solution, when you think about it. And you know what? Suze is absolutely right. Making More Money suits my personality far better than Cutting Back did. I'm already feeling much happier. Just the fact that I don't have to make any more grotty cheese sandwiches, or go to any more museums, has lifted a huge weight off my soul. And I'm allowed to buy all the cappuccinos I like, and start looking in shop windows again. Oh, the relief! I've even chucked *Controlling Your Cash* in the bin. I never did think it was any good.

The only small thing—tiny niggle—is I'm not quite sure how I'm going to do it. Make More Money, I mean. But now I've decided to go ahead with it, something will turn up. I'm sure of it.

When I get into work on Monday, Clare Edwards is already at her desk—surprise—and on the phone.

"Yes," she's saying softly. "Well, it's certainly been a wonderful first year."

When she sees me, to my surprise, she blushes a faint pink and turns away slightly. "Yes, I understand," she whispers, scribbling in her notepad. "But what about the future?"

God knows why she's being so secretive. As if I'm interested in her tedious life. I sit down at my desk, briskly flip on my computer, and open my diary. Oh goody, I've got a press conference in the City. Even if it is some boring old pensions launch, at least it means a trip out of the office and, with any luck, a nice glass of champagne. Work can be quite fun, sometimes. And Philip isn't in yet, which means we can sit and gossip for a while.

"So, Clare," I say, as she puts the phone down, "how was your weekend?"

I look over, expecting to hear the usual thrilling account of what shelf she put up where with her boyfriend—but Clare doesn't even seem to have heard what I said.

"Clare?" I say puzzledly. She's staring at me with pink cheeks, as though I've caught her stealing pens from the stationery cupboard.

"Listen," she says in a rush. "That conversation you heard me having just now . . . could you not mention it to Philip?"

I stare at her in bemusement. What's she talking about? Oh wow—is she having an affair? But then, why should Philip care? He's her editor, not her—

Oh my God. She's not having an affair with *Philip,* is she?

"Clare, what's going on!" I say excitedly.

There's a long pause, as Clare blushes deep red. I can't believe this. A piece of office scandal at last! And involving Clare Edwards, of all people!

"Oh, come on, Clare," I whisper. "You can tell me. I

won't tell anyone." I lean forward sympathetically. "I might even be able to help."

"Yes," says Clare, rubbing her face. "Yes, that's true. I could do with a bit of advice. The pressure's starting to get to me."

"Start from the beginning," I say calmly, just like Dear Abby. "When did it all begin?"

"OK, I'll tell you," whispers Clare, and looks nervously about. "It was about . . . six months ago."

"And what happened?"

"It all began on that Scottish press trip," she says slowly. "I was away from home . . . I said yes without even thinking. I suppose I was flattered, more than anything else."

"It's the old story," I say wisely. God, I'm enjoying this.

"If Philip knew what I was doing, he'd go crazy," she says despairingly. "But it's just so easy. I use a different name—and no one knows!"

"You use a different name?" I say, impressed in spite of myself.

"Several," she says, and gives a bitter little laugh. "You've probably seen some of them around." She exhales sharply. "I know I'm taking a risk—but I can't stop. To be honest, you get used to the money."

Money? Is she a *prostitute*?

"Clare, what exactly are you—"

"At first it was just a little piece on mortgages in *The Mail*," she says, as though she hasn't heard me. "I thought I could handle it. But then I was asked to do a full-length feature on life insurance in *The Sunday Times*. Then *Pension* and *Portfolio* got in on the act. And now it's about three articles every week. I have to do it all in secret, try to act normally . . ." She breaks off and shakes her head. "Sometimes it gets me down. But I just can't say no anymore. I'm hooked."

I do not believe it. She's talking about work. Work! There I was, thinking she was having a steamy affair, ready to hear all the exciting details—and all the time it was just boring old . . .

Then something she's just said tweaks at my mind.

"Did you say the money was good?" I say casually.

"Oh yes," she says. "About three hundred quid a piece. That's how we could afford our flat."

Three hundred quid!

Nine hundred quid a week! Bloody hell!

This is the answer. It's easy. I'll become a high-flying freelance journalist, just like Clare, and earn nine hundred quid a week. What I have to do is start networking and making contacts at events instead of always sitting at the back with Elly. I must shake hands firmly with all the finance editors of the nationals and wear my name badge prominently instead of putting it straight in my bag, and then phone them up with ideas when I get back to the office. And then I'll have £900 a week. Hah!

So when I arrive at the press conference, I pin my name badge on firmly, take a cup of coffee (no champagne— blast), and head toward Moira Channing of the *Daily Herald*.

"Hello," I say, nodding in what I hope is a serious manner. "Becky Bloomwood, *Successful Saving*."

"Hello," she says without interest, and turns back to the other woman in the group. "So we had the second lot of builders back, and *really* read them the riot act."

"Oh, Moira, you poor thing," says the other woman. I squint at her badge and see that she's Lavinia Bellimore, freelance. Well, there's no point impressing her—she's the competition.

Anyway, she doesn't give me a second glance. The two chat away about extensions and school fees, completely ignoring me—and after a bit I mutter, "Good to meet you," and creep away. God, I'd forgotten how unfriendly they are. Still, never mind. I'll just have to find someone else.

So after a bit I sidle up to a very tall guy on his own, and smile at him.

"Becky Bloomwood, *Successful Saving,*" I say.

"Geoffrey Norris, freelance," he says, and flashes his badge at me. Oh for God's sake. The place is crawling with freelancers!

"Who do you write for?" I ask politely, thinking at least I might pick up some tips.

"It depends," he says shiftily. His eyes keep darting backward and forward, and he's refusing to meet my eye. "I used to be on *Monetary Matters.* But they sacked me."

"Oh dear," I say.

"They're bastards over there," he says, and drains his coffee. "Bastards! Don't go near them. That's my advice."

"OK, I'll remember that!" I say brightly, edging away. "Actually, I just have to . . ." And I turn, and walk quickly away. Why do I always find myself talking to weirdos?

Just then, a buzzer goes off, and people start to find their seats. Deliberately, I head for the second row, pick up the glossy brochure that's waiting for me on my seat, and take out my notebook. I wish I wore glasses, then I'd look even more serious. I'm just writing down Sacrum Asset Management Pension Fund Launch in capitals at the top of the page, when a middle-aged man I've never seen before plonks himself down next to me. He's got disheveled brown hair and smells of cigarettes, and is wearing an old-looking jacket over a dark red shirt with no tie. Plus, I suddenly notice, sneakers on his feet. *Sneakers* to a press conference? He sits down, leans back comfortably, and looks around with twinkling brown eyes.

"It's a joke, isn't it?" he murmurs, then meets my eye. "All this gloss. All this show." He gestures around. "You don't fall for it, do you?"

Oh God. *Another* weirdo.

"Absolutely not," I say politely, and look for his name badge, but I can't see one.

"Glad to hear it," says the man, and shakes his head. "Bloody fat cats." He gestures to the front, where three men in expensive suits are sitting down behind the table. "You won't find *them* surviving on fifty quid a week, will you?"

"Well . . . no," I say. "More like fifty quid a minute." The man gives an appreciative laugh.

"That's a good line. I might use that." He extends his hand. "Eric Foreman, *Daily World.*"

"*Daily World?*" I say, impressed in spite of myself. Gosh, *The Daily World.* I have to confess a little secret here—I really like *The Daily World.* I know it's only a tabloid, but it's so easy to read, especially if you're on a train. (My arms must be very weak or something, because holding *The Times* makes them ache after a while. And then all the pages get messed up. It's a nightmare.) And some of the articles in the "Female World" section are actually rather interesting.

But hang on—surely I've met *The Daily World*'s personal finance editor. Surely it's that drippy woman called Marjorie? So who's this guy?

"I haven't seen you around before," I say casually. "Are you new?"

Eric Foreman gives a chuckle. "I've been on the paper for ten years. But this finance stuff isn't usually my scene." He lowers his voice. "I'm here to stir up a bit of trouble, as it goes. The editor's brought me on board for a new campaign we're running, 'Can We Trust the Money Men?' "

He even *talks* in a tabloid voice.

"That sounds great," I say.

"Could be, could be. As long as I can get past all this technical stuff." He pulls a face. "Never been good at figures."

"I wouldn't worry," I say kindly. "You don't actually need to know very much. You'll soon pick up what's important. Basically, these guys are launching a new pension plan . . ." I glance at the brochure ". . . and the gimmick is, there's a discount for investors under the age of twenty-five. Which makes sense, of course, because the sooner you start retirement planning, the better."

"Oh absolutely," echoes Eric Foreman, a tiny smile at his mouth. "May I ask, do you have a pension?"

"Well . . . no," I admit. "I don't at the moment . . . but I'm absolutely intending to, as soon as I decide which one."

Which is true. As *soon* as I clear all my debts, I'm going to start a pension plan, and also invest in a long-term equity-based investment fund. I may even put some spare money into emerging markets. I mean, it makes sense, doesn't it?

"Glad to hear it," says Eric Foreman, grinning. "Very wise of you." He peers at my name badge. "And you are . . ."

"Rebecca Bloomwood, *Successful Saving*," I say, in my best networking manner.

"Glad to meet you, Rebecca," he says, and fishes in his pocket for a business card.

"Oh, thanks," I say, hastily reaching into my bag for my own business cards. Yes! I think triumphantly as I hand it over. I'm networking with the national newspapers! I'm swapping business cards!

Just then the microphones all come on with a screech of feedback, and a dark-haired girl at the podium clears her throat. Behind her is a lit-up screen, with the words *Sacrum Asset Management* against a sunset.

I remember this girl now. She was really snotty to me at a press briefing last year. But Philip likes her, because she sends him a bottle of champagne every Christmas, so I'll have to give this new pension plan a nice write-up.

"Ladies and gentlemen," she says. "My name is Maria Freeman, and I'm delighted to welcome you all to the launch of the Sacrum Asset Management Pension Series. This is an innovative range of products designed to combine flexibility and security with the powerful performance associated with Sacrum."

A graph appears on the screen before us, with a wiggly red line rising and falling above a thinner black one.

"As Graph 1 shows," says Maria Freeman confidently, pointing to the wiggly red line, "our UK Enterprise Fund has consistently outperformed the rest of its particular sector."

"Hmm," murmurs Eric Foreman to me, frowning at his brochure. "So, what's going on here, then? I heard a rumor that Sacrum Asset Management wasn't doing too well." He jabs at the graph. "But look at this. Outperforming the sector."

"Yeah, right," I murmur back. "And what sector would that be? The Crap Investments Sector? The Lose All Your Money Sector?"

Eric Foreman looks at me and his mouth twists slightly.

"You think they've fiddled their figures?" he whispers.

"It's not exactly fiddling," I explain. "They just compare themselves to whoever's worse than themselves, and then call themselves the winners." I point to the graph in the brochure. "Look. They haven't actually specified what this so-called sector is."

"Well, blow me," says Eric Foreman, and looks up at the Sacrum team sitting on the platform. "They're canny bastards, aren't they?"

Really, this guy has no idea. I feel almost sorry for him.

Maria Freeman is droning on again, and I stifle a yawn. The trouble with sitting near the front is you have to pretend to look interested and be writing notes. "Pensions," I write, and draw a swirly line underneath. Then I make the line into the stem of a vine and start drawing little bunches of grapes and leaves all the way along.

"In a moment I'll be introducing Mike Dillon, who heads up the investment team, and he'll be telling you a little about their methods. In the meantime, if there are any questions . . ."

"Yes," says Eric Foreman. "I've got a question." I look up from my grapevine, slightly surprised.

"Oh yes?" Maria Freeman smiles sweetly at him. "And you are . . ."

"Eric Foreman, *Daily World*. I'd like to know, how much do you all get paid?" He gestures with his hand along the table.

"What?" Maria Freeman turns pink, then regains her composure. "Oh, you mean charges. Well, we'll be dealing with those . . ."

"I don't mean charges," says Eric Foreman. "I mean, how-much-do-you-get-paid? You, Mike Dillon." He jabs at him with his finger. "What are you on? Six figures, is it? And bearing in mind what a *disaster* the performance of Sacrum Asset Management was last year—shouldn't you be out on the streets?"

I'm absolutely stunned. I've never seen anything like this at a press conference. Never!

There's a kerfuffle at the table, and then Mike Dillon leans forward toward his microphone.

"If we could get on with the presentation," he says, "and . . . and leave other questions for later." He's looking decidedly uncomfortable.

"Just one more thing," says Eric Foreman. "What would you say to one of our readers who invested in your Safe Prospects plan and lost ten grand?" He glances briefly at me and winks. "Show them a nice reassuring graph like that one, would you? Tell them you were 'top of the sector'?"

Oh, this is fantastic! All the Sacrum people look like they want to die.

"A press release on the subject of Safe Prospects was issued at the time," says Maria and smiles icily at Eric. "However, this press conference is restricted to the subject of the new Pension Series. If you could just wait until the presentation is over . . ."

"Don't worry," says Eric Foreman comfortably. "I won't be staying to hear the bullshit. I reckon I've got everything I need already." He stands up and grins at me. "Good to meet you, Rebecca," he says quietly. "And thanks for your expertise." He extends his hand and I shake it, without quite knowing what I'm doing. And then, as everyone is turning in their seats and whispering, he makes his way along the row and out of the room.

"Ladies and gentlemen," says Maria Freeman, two bright spots burning on her cheeks. "Due to this . . . disturbance, we will have a short break before we resume. Please help yourself to tea and coffee. Thank you." She turns off the microphone, climbs down from the podium, and hurries over to the huddle of Sacrum Asset Management personnel.

"You should *never* have let him in!" I hear one of them saying.

"I didn't know who he was!" replies Maria defensively. "He said he was a stringer for *The Wall Street Journal*!"

Well, this is more like it! I haven't seen so much excitement since Alan Derring from the *Daily Investor* stood up at a Provident Assurance press conference and told everyone he was becoming a woman and wanted us all to call him Andrea.

I head toward the back to get another cup of coffee, and find Elly standing by the coffee table. Excellent. I haven't seen Elly for ages.

"Hi," she grins. "I like your new friend. Very entertaining."

"I know!" I say delightedly. "Isn't he cool?" I reach for a posh chocolate biscuit wrapped in gold foil, and give my cup to the waitress to be refilled. Then I take another couple of biscuits and pop them in my bag. (No point wasting them.)

Around us there is an excited buzz of conversation; the Sacrum people are still clustered at the front. This is great. We'll be able to natter for hours.

"So listen," I say to Elly. "Have you applied for any jobs recently?" I take a sip of coffee. "Because I saw one for *New Woman* the other day in the *Media Guardian,* and I meant to ring you. It said it was essential to have experience on a consumer title, but I thought you could say—"

"Becky," interrupts Elly in an odd voice, "you know which job I've been going for."

"What?" I stare at her. "Not that fund manager job. But that wasn't serious. That was just a bargaining tool."

"I took it," she says, and I gaze at her in shock.

Suddenly a voice comes from the podium, and we both look up.

"Ladies and gentlemen," Maria is saying. "If you would like to resume your seats . . ."

I'm sorry, but I can't go and sit back down there. I *have* to hear about this.

"Come on," I say quickly to Elly. "We don't need to stay. We've got our press packs. Let's go and have lunch."

There's a pause—and for an awful moment I think she's going to say no, she *wants* to stay and hear about personal pensions. But then she grins and takes my arm—and to the obvious dismay of the girl at the door, we waltz out of the room.

There's a Café Rouge around the corner, and we go straight in and order a bottle of white wine. I'm still in slight shock, to tell you the truth. Elly Granger is going to become a Wetherby's fund manager. She's deserting me. I won't have anyone to play with anymore.

And how *can* she? She wanted to be beauty editor on *Marie-Claire,* for God's sake!

"So, what decided you?" I say cautiously as our wine arrives.

"Oh, I don't know," she says, and sighs. "I just kept thinking, where am I going? You know, I keep applying

for all these glam jobs in journalism and never even getting an interview . . ."

"You would have got one eventually," I say robustly.
"I know you would."

"Maybe," she says. "Or maybe not. And in the meantime, I'm writing about all this boring financial stuff—
and I suddenly thought, why not just sod it and *do*
boring financial stuff? At least I'll have a proper career."

"You were in a proper career!"

"No I wasn't, I was hopeless! I was paddling around
with no aim, no game plan, no prospects . . ." Elly
breaks off as she sees my face. "I mean, I was quite
different from you," she adds hurriedly. "You're much
more sorted out than I was."

Sorted out? Is she joking?

"So when do you start?" I say, to change the subject—
because to be honest, I feel a bit thrown by all this. I
don't have a game plan, I don't have prospects. Maybe
I'm hopeless, too. Maybe I should rethink my career.
Oh God, this is depressing.

"Next week," says Elly, and takes a swig of wine. "I'm
going to be based at the Silk Street office."

"Oh right," I say miserably.

"And I've had to buy loads of new clothes," she
adds, and pulls a little face. "They're all really smart at
Wetherby's."

New clothes? *New clothes?* Right, now I really am
jealous.

"I went into Karen Millen and practically bought it
out," she says, eating a marinated olive. "Spent about a
thousand quid."

"Blimey," I say, feeling slightly awe-stricken. "A thousand quid, all at once?"

"Well, I had to," she says apologetically. "And anyway, I'll be earning more now."

"Really?"

"Oh yes," she says, and gives a little laugh. "Lots more."

"Like . . . how much?" I ask, feeling tweaks of curiosity.

"I'm starting off on forty grand," she says, and gives a careless shrug. "After that, who knows? What they said is . . ."

And she starts talking about career structures and ladders and bonuses. But I can't hear a word, I'm too shell-shocked.

Forty grand?

Forty grand? But I only earn—

Actually, should I be telling you how much I earn? Isn't it one of those things like religion, you're not supposed to mention in polite company? Or maybe we're all allowed to talk about money these days. Suze would know.

Oh well, sod it. You know everything else, don't you? The truth is, I earn £21,000. And I thought that was a lot! I remember really well, when I moved jobs, I jumped from £18,000 to £21,000, and I thought I'd made the big time. I was so excited about it, I used to write endless lists of what I would buy with all that extra money.

But now it sounds like nothing. I should be earning forty grand, like Elly, and buying all my clothes at Karen Millen. Oh, it's not fair. My life's a complete disaster.

As I'm walking back to the office, I feel pretty morose. Maybe I should give up journalism and become a fund manager, too. Or a merchant banker. They earn a pretty good whack, don't they? Maybe I could join Goldman Sachs or somewhere. They earn about a million a year, don't they? God, that would be good. I wonder how you get a job like that.

But on the other hand . . . do I really want to be a banker? I wouldn't mind the clothes-from-Karen-Millen part of it. In fact, I think I'd do that really well. But I'm not so sure about the rest. The getting-up-early-and-working-hideously-hard part. Not that I'm lazy or anything—but I quite like the fact that I can go and spend the afternoon at Image Store, or flick through the papers pretending to be doing research, and no one gives me a hard time. It doesn't sound as if Elly will be doing much of that in her new job. In fact, there doesn't seem to be anything remotely fun or creative about it. And aren't bankers rather humorless? Their press conferences certainly are—so imagine *working* with them. It all sounds quite scary.

Hmm. If only there were some way that I could get all the nice clothes—but not have to do the dreary work. One but not the other. If only there were a way . . . My eyes are automatically flicking into all the shop windows as I pass, checking out the displays—and suddenly I stop in my tracks.

This is a sign from God. It has to be.

I'm standing outside Ally Smith—which has some gorgeous full-length coats in the window—and there's a handwritten sign in the glass pane of the door. "Wanted. Saturday sales assistants. Inquire within."

I almost feel faint as I stare at the sign. It's as though lightning has struck, or something. Why on *earth* haven't I thought of this before? It's pure genius. I'll get a Saturday job! I'll work in a clothes shop! That way, I'll make loads of extra money *and* I'll get a discount on all the clothes! And let's face it, working in a shop has got to be more fun than becoming a fund manager, hasn't it? I can choose all my own clothes as I help the customers. I'll actually be getting *paid* to go shopping!

This is bloody fantastic, I think, striding into the

shop with a friendly smile on my face. I *knew* something good was going to happen today. I just had a feeling about it.

Half an hour later, I come out with an even bigger smile on my face. I've got a job! I've got a Saturday job! I'm going to work from eight-thirty to five-thirty every Saturday, and get £4.80 an hour, and 10 percent off all the clothes! And after three months, it goes up to 20 percent! All my money troubles are over.

Thank God it was a quiet afternoon. They let me fill in the application form on the spot, and Danielle, the manager, gave me an interview straight away. At first, she looked a bit dubious—especially when I said I had a full-time job as a financial journalist and was doing this to get extra money and clothes. "It'll be hard work," she kept saying. "You do realize that? It'll be very hard work." But I think what changed her mind was when we started talking about the stock. I love Ally Smith— so of course I knew the price of every single item in the shop and whether they have anything similar in Jigsaw or French Connection. Eventually Danielle gave me a funny look and said, "Well, you obviously like clothes." And then she gave me the job! I can't wait. I start this Saturday. Isn't it great?

As I arrive back at the office I feel exhilarated with my success. I look around—and suddenly this mundane office life seems far too boring and limited for a creative spirit like mine. I don't belong here, among fusty piles of press releases and grimly tapping computers. I belong out there, among the bright spotlights and cashmere cardigans of Ally Smith. Maybe I'll go into retail full time, I think, as I sit back down at my desk. Maybe I'll start my own chain of designer stores! I'll be one of those people featured in articles about incredibly successful entrepreneurs. "Becky Bloomwood was working as a financial journalist when she devised the innovative concept of Bloomwood Stores. Now a successful chain around the country, the idea came to her one day as she . . ."

The phone rings and I pick it up.

"Yes?" I say absently. "Rebecca Bloomwood here." I nearly add, "of Bloomwood Stores," but maybe that's a tad premature.

"Ms. Bloomwood, this is Derek Smeath from Endwich Bank."

What? I'm so shocked, I drop the phone onto my desk with a clatter and have to scrabble around to pick it up. All the while, my heart's thumping like a rabbit. How does Derek Smeath know where I work? How did he get my number?

"Are you OK?" says Clare Edwards curiously.

"Yes," I gulp. "Yes, fine."

And now she's looking at me. Now I can't just put the phone down and pretend it was a wrong number. I've got to talk to him. OK, what I'll do is be really brisk and cheerful and try and get rid of him as quickly as possible.

"Hi!" I say into the phone. "Sorry about that! The thing is, I was just a bit busy with something else. You know how it is!"

"Ms. Bloomwood, I've written you several letters," says Derek Smeath. "And to none of them have I had a satisfactory response."

Oh, he sounds really cross. This is horrible. Why did he have to come along and spoil my day?

"I've been very busy, I'm afraid," I say. "My . . . my aunt was very ill. I had to go and be with her."

"I see," he says. "Nevertheless—"

"And then she died," I add.

"I'm sorry to hear that," says Derek Smeath. He doesn't *sound* sorry. "But that doesn't alter the fact that your current account stands at a balance of—"

Has this man got no heart? As he starts talking about balances and overdrafts and agreements, I deliberately tune out so I don't hear anything that will upset me. I'm staring at the fake wood-grain on my desk, wondering if I could pretend to drop the receiver accidentally back down onto the phone. This is awful. What am I going to do? *What am I going to do?*

"And if the situation is not resolved," he's saying sternly, "I'm afraid I will be forced to—"

"It's OK," I hear myself interrupting. "It's OK, because . . . I'm coming into some money soon." Even as I say the words, I feel my cheeks flame guiltily. But I mean, what else am I supposed to do?

"Oh yes?"

"Yes," I say, and swallow. "The thing is, my . . . my aunt left me some money in her will."

Which is kind of almost true. I mean, obviously Aunt Ermintrude would have left me some money. After all, I was her favorite niece, wasn't I? Did anyone else buy her Denny and George scarves? "I'll get it in a couple of weeks," I add for good measure. "A thousand pounds."

Then I realize I should have made it ten thousand— that would have really impressed him. Oh well, too late now.

"You're saying that in two weeks' time you'll be paying a check for a thousand pounds into your account," says Derek Smeath.

"Erm . . . yes," I say after a pause. "I suppose I am."

"I'm glad to hear it," he says. "I've made a note of our

conversation, Ms. Bloomwood, and I'll be expecting the arrival of a thousand pounds into your account on Monday 26 March."

"Good," I say boldly. "Is that it?"

"For the moment. Good-bye, Ms. Bloomwood."

"Good-bye," I say, and put the phone down.

Got rid of him. Thank God.

OCTAGON ▶ *flair...style...vision*

FINANCIAL SERVICES DEPARTMENT
8TH FLOOR   TOWER HOUSE
LONDON ROAD   WINCHESTER S0 44 3DR

Ms. Rebecca Bloomwood   Charge Card Number 7854 4567
Flat 2
4 Burney Rd.
London SW6 8FD

9 March 2000

Dear Ms. Bloomwood:

Thank you for your prompt return of a signed check for
£43.

Unfortunately, although this check is signed, it appears to
be dated 14 February 2200. No doubt just an oversight on
your part.

Octagon Shops cannot accept postdated checks as
payment, and I am therefore returning it to you with the
request that you return to us a signed check, dated with
the date of signature.

Alternatively you can pay by cash or on the enclosed bank
giro credit slip. A leaflet is enclosed for your information.

I look forward to receiving your payment.

Yours sincerely,

John Hunter
Customer Accounts Manager

Nine

WHEN I GET HOME that night, there's a pile of post in the hall for me—but I ignore it because my package from Fine Frames has arrived! It cost me £100 to buy, which is quite expensive, but apparently it will give you a return of £300 in only a few hours. Inside the package there's a leaflet full of photographs of people who make fortunes from doing Fine Frames—some of them make a hundred thousand a year! It makes me wonder what I'm doing, being a journalist.

So after supper, I sit down in front of *Changing Rooms* and open the kit. Suze is out tonight, so it's nice and easy to concentrate.

"Welcome to the best-kept secret in Britain . . ." says the leaflet. "The Fine Frames home-working family! Join other members and earn £££ in the comfort of your own home. Our easy-to-follow instructions will aid you as you embark on the biggest money-making enterprise of your life. Perhaps you will use your earnings to buy a car, or a boat—or to treat someone special. And remember—the amount you earn is completely up to you!"

I'm utterly gripped. Why on earth haven't I done this

before? This is a *fantastic* scheme! I'll work incredibly hard for two weeks, then pay off all my debts, go on holiday, and buy loads of new clothes.

I start ripping at the packaging, and suddenly a pile of fabric strips falls onto the floor. Some are plain, and some are a flowered pattern. It's a pretty hideous pattern actually—but then, who cares? My job is just to make the frames and collect the money. I reach for the instructions and find them under a load of cardboard pieces. And sure enough, they're incredibly simple. What you have to do is glue wadding onto the cardboard frame, put the fabric over the top for that luxury uphol-stered effect, then glue braid along the back to hide the join. And that's it! It's completely simple and you get £2 a frame. There are 150 in the package—so if I do thirty a night for a week I'll have made three hundred quid just like that in my spare time!

OK, let's get started. Frame, wadding, glue, fabric, braid.

Oh God. Oh *God*. Who designed these bloody things? There just isn't enough fabric to fit over the frame and the wadding. Or at least you have to stretch it really hard—and it's such flimsy fabric, it rips. I've got glue on the carpet, and I've bent two of the cardboard frames from pulling them, and the only frame I've actually completed looks really wonky. And I've been doing it for . . .

I yawn, look at the time, and feel a jolt of shock. It's eleven-thirty, which means I've been working for three hours. In that time I've made one dodgy-looking frame which I'm not sure they'll accept, and ruined two. And I was supposed to be making thirty!

At that moment the door opens and Suze is back.

"Hi!" she says, coming into the sitting room. "Nice evening?"

"Not really," I begin disgruntledly. "I've been making these things . . ."

"Well, never mind," she says dramatically. "Because guess what? You've got a secret admirer."

"What?" I say, startled.

"Someone really likes you," she says, taking off her coat. "I heard it tonight. You'll never guess who!"

Luke Brandon pops into my mind before I can stop it. How ridiculous. And how would Suze have found that out, anyway? Stupid idea. Very stupid. Impossible.

She could have bumped into him at the cinema, whispers my brain. She does know him, after all, doesn't she? And he could have said . . .

"It's my cousin!" she says triumphantly. "Tarquin. He *really* likes you."

Oh for God's sake.

"He's got this secret little crush on you," she continues happily. "In fact, he's had one ever since he met you!"

"Really?" I say. "Well, I had sort of . . . guessed." Suze's eyes light up.

"So you already know about it?"

"Well," I say, and shrug awkwardly. What can I say? I can't tell her that her beloved cousin gives me the creeps. So instead I start to pick at the fabric on the photo frame in front of me, and a delighted smile spreads over Suze's face.

"He's really keen on you!" she says. "I said he should just ring you and ask you out. You wouldn't mind, would you?"

"Of course not," I say feebly.

"Wouldn't that be great?" said Suze. "If you two got married. I could be bridesmaid!"

"Yes," I say, and force myself to smile brightly. "Lovely."

What I'll do, I think, is agree to a date just to be polite—and then cancel at the last moment. And hopefully Tarquin'll have to go back to Scotland or something, and we can forget all about it.

But to be honest, I could really do without it. Now I've got two reasons to dread the phone ringing.

However, to my relief, Saturday arrives and I haven't heard a word from Tarquin. *Or* Derek Smeath. Everyone's finally leaving me alone to get on with my life!

On the slightly more negative side, I was planning to make 150 frames this week—but so far I've only made three, and none of them looks like the one in the picture. One doesn't have enough wadding in it, one doesn't quite meet at the corner, and the third has got a smear of glue on the front, which hasn't come off. I just can't understand why I'm finding it so difficult. Some people make hundreds of these things every week, without any effort. Mrs. S. of Ruislip even takes her family on a cruise every year on her earnings. How come they can do it and I can't? It's really depressing. I mean, I'm supposed to be bright, aren't I? I've got a degree, for God's sake.

Still, never mind, I tell myself. It's my new job at Ally Smith today—so at least I'll be earning some extra money there.

And I'm quite excited about it. Here starts a whole new career in fashion! I spend a long time choosing a cool outfit to wear on my first day—and eventually settle on black trousers from Jigsaw, a little cashmere (well, half cashmere) T-shirt, and a pink wraparound top, which actually came from Ally Smith.

I'm quite pleased with the way I look, and am expecting Danielle to make some appreciative comment when I arrive at the shop—but she doesn't even seem to notice. She just says, "Hi. The trousers and T-shirts are in the stock room. Pick out your size and change in the cubicle."

Oh, right. Now I come to think of it, all the assistants at Ally Smith do wear the same outfits. Almost like a . . . well, a uniform, I suppose. Reluctantly I get changed and look at myself—and, to tell you the truth, I'm disappointed. These gray trousers don't really flatter me—and the T-shirt's just plain boring. I'm almost tempted to ask Danielle if I can pick out another outfit to wear—but she seems a bit busy, so I don't. Maybe next week I'll have a little word.

But even though I don't like the outfit, I still feel a frisson of excitement as I come out onto the shop floor. The spotlights are shining brightly; the floor's all shiny and polished; music's playing and there's a sense of anticipation in the air. It's almost like being a performer. I glance at myself in a mirror and murmur, "How can I help you?" Or maybe it should be "*Can* I help you?" I'm going to be the most charming shop assistant ever, I decide. People will come here just to be assisted by me, and I'll have a fantastic rapport with all the customers. And then I'll appear in the *Evening Standard* in some quirky column about favorite shops.

No one's told me what to do yet, so—using my initiative, very good—I walk up to a woman with blond hair, who's tapping away at the till, and say, "Shall I have a quick go?"

"What?" she says, not looking up.

"I'd better learn how to work the till, hadn't I? Before all the customers arrive?"

Then the woman does look up and, to my surprise, bursts into laughter.

"On the till? You think you're going to go straight onto the till?"

"Oh," I say, blushing a little. "Well, I thought . . ."

"You're a beginner, darling," she says. "You're not going near the till. Go with Kelly. She'll show you what you'll be doing today."

Folding jumpers. Folding bloody jumpers. That's what I'm here to do. Rush round after customers who have picked up cardigans and left them all crumpled—and fold them back up again. By eleven o'clock I'm absolutely exhausted—and, to be honest, not enjoying myself very much at all. Do you know how depressing it is to fold a cardigan in exactly the right Ally Smith way and put it back on the shelf, all neatly lined up—just to see someone casually pull it down again, look at it, pull a face, and discard it? You want to scream at them, LEAVE IT ALONE IF YOU'RE NOT GOING TO BUY IT! I watched one girl even pick up a cardigan *identical* to the one she already had on!

And I'm not getting to chat to the customers, either. It's as if they see through you when you're a shop assistant. No one's asked me a single interesting question, like "Does this shirt go with these shoes?" or, "Where can I find a really nice black skirt under £60?" I'd *love* to answer stuff like that. I could really help people! But the only questions I've been asked are "Is there a loo?" and, "Where's the nearest Midland cashpoint?" I haven't built up a single rapport with anyone.

Oh, it's depressing. The only thing that keeps me going is an end-of-stock reduced rack at the back of the shop. I keep sidling toward it and looking at a pair of zebra-print jeans, reduced from £180 to £90. I remember those jeans. I've even tried them on. And here they are, out of the blue—reduced. I just can't keep my eyes off them. They're even in my size.

I mean, I know I'm not really supposed to be spending money—but this is a complete one-off. They're the coolest jeans you've ever seen. And £90 is *nothing* for a pair of really good jeans. If you were in Gucci, you'd be paying at least £500. Oh God, I want them. I *want* them.

I'm just loitering at the back, eyeing them up for the hundredth time, when Danielle comes striding up and I jump guiltily. But all she says is "Can you go onto fitting room duty now? Sarah'll show you the ropes."

No more folding jumpers! Thank God!

To my relief, this fitting room lark is a lot more fun. Ally Smith has really nice fitting rooms, with lots of space and individual cubicles, and my job is to stand at the entrance and check how many items people are taking in with them. It's really interesting to see what people are trying on. One girl's buying *loads* of stuff, and keeps saying how her boyfriend told her to go mad for her birthday, and he would pay.

Huh. Well, it's all right for some. Still, never mind, at least I'm earning money. It's eleven-thirty, which means I've earned . . . £14.40 so far. Well, that's not bad, is it? I could get some nice makeup for that.

Except that I'm not going to waste this money on makeup. Of course not—I mean, that's not why I'm here, is it? I'm going to be really sensible. What I'm going to do is buy the zebra-print jeans—just because they're a one-off and it would be a crime not to—and then put all the rest toward my bank balance. I just can't *wait* to put them on. I get a break at two-thirty, so what

I'll do is nip to the reduced rack and take them to the staff room, just to make sure they fit, and . . .

Suddenly my face freezes. Hang on.

Hang on a moment. What's that girl holding over her arm? She's holding my zebra-print jeans! She's coming toward the fitting rooms. Oh my God. She wants to try them on. But they're mine! I saw them first!

I'm almost giddy with panic. I mean, a normal pair of jeans, I wouldn't bother about. But these are unique. They're *meant* for me. I've mentally reorganized my entire wardrobe around them, and have already planned to wear them at least three times next week. I can't lose them. Not now.

"Hi!" she says brightly as she approaches.

"Hi," I gulp, trying to stay calm. "Ahm . . . how many items have you got?"

"Four," she says, showing me the hangers. Behind me are tokens hanging on the wall, marked One, Two, Three, and Four. The girl's waiting for me to give her a token marked Four and let her in. But I can't.

I physically cannot let her go in there with my jeans.

"Actually," I hear myself saying, "you're only allowed three items."

"Really?" she says in surprise. "But . . ." She gestures to the tokens.

"I know," I say. "But they've just changed the rules. Sorry about that." And I flash her a quick smile.

"Oh, OK," says the girl. "Well, I'll leave out—"

"These," I say, and grab the zebra-print jeans.

"No," she says. "Actually, I think I'll—"

"We have to take the top item," I explain hurriedly. "Sorry about that."

Thank *God* for bossy shop assistants and stupid pointless rules. People are so used to them that this girl doesn't even question me. She just rolls her eyes, grabs the Three token, and pushes her way past into the fitting room, leaving me holding the precious jeans.

OK, now what? From inside the girl's cubicle, I can hear zips being undone and hangers being clattered. She won't take long to try on those three things. And then she'll be out, wanting the zebra-print jeans. Oh God. What can I do? For a few moments I'm frozen with indecision. Then the sound of a cubicle curtain being rattled back jolts me into action. It's not her—but it could have been. Quickly I stuff the zebra-print jeans out of sight behind the curtain and stand up again, a bright smile on my face.

Please let the girl find something else she likes, I pray feverishly. Please let her forget all about the jeans. Maybe she's not even that keen on them. Maybe she picked them up on impulse. She didn't really look like a jeans person to me.

A moment later, Danielle comes striding up, a clipboard in her hands.

"All right?" she says. "Coping, are you?"

"I'm doing fine," I say. "Really enjoying it."

"I'm just rostering in breaks," she says. "If you could manage to last until three, you can have an hour then."

"Fine," I say in my positive, employee-of-the-month voice, even though I'm thinking *Three? I'll be starving!*

"Good," she says, and moves off into the corner to write on her piece of paper, just as a voice says,

"Hi. Can I have those jeans now?"

It's the girl, back again. How can she have tried on all those other things so quickly? Is she Houdini?

"Hi!" I say, ignoring the last bit of what she said. "Any good? That black skirt's really nice. I think it would really suit you. The way the splits go at the—"

"Not really," she says, interrupting me, and shoves

the lot back at me, all mussed up and off their hangers. "It was really the jeans I wanted. Can I have them?"

I stare at her desperately. I *can't* relinquish my trea-sured jeans. I just know this girl wouldn't love them like I would. She'd probably wear them once and chuck them out—or never wear them at all! And I *saw them first.*

"What jeans were they?" I say, wrinkling my brow sympathetically. "Blue ones? You can get them over there, next to the—"

"No!" says the girl impatiently. "The zebra-print jeans I had a minute ago."

"Oh," I say vaguely. "Oh yes. I'm not sure where they went. Maybe someone else took them."

"Oh for God's sake!" she says, looking at me as if I'm an imbecile. "This is ridiculous! I gave them to you about thirty seconds ago! How can you have lost them?"

Shit. She's really angry. Her voice is getting quite loud, and people are starting to look. Oh, *why* couldn't she have liked the black skirt instead?

"Is there a problem?" chimes in a syrupy voice, and I look up in horror. Danielle's coming over toward us, a sweet-but-menacing look on her face. OK, keep calm, I tell myself firmly. No one can prove anything either way.

"I gave this assistant a pair of jeans to look after be-cause I had four items, which is apparently too many," the girl begins explaining.

"Four items?" says Danielle. "But you're allowed four items in the fitting room." And she turns to look at me with an expression which isn't very friendly.

"*Are* you?" I say innocently. "Oh God, I'm sorry. I thought it was three. I'm new," I add apologetically.

"I *thought* it was four!" says the girl. "I mean, you've got tokens with bloody 'Four' written on them!" She gives an impatient sigh. "So anyway, I gave her the jeans, and tried on the other things—and then I came out for the jeans, and they've gone."

"Gone?" says Danielle sharply. "Gone where?"

"I'm not sure," I say, trying to look as baffled as the next person. "Maybe another customer took them."

"But you were holding them!" says the girl. "So what— did someone just come up to you and whip them out of your fingers?"

I flinch at the tone of her voice. I would never speak to a shop assistant like that, even if I was cross. Anyway, how can she be so obsessed with a pair of *jeans*?

"Maybe you could get another pair from the rack," I say, trying to sound helpful. "Or some capri pants? I bet you'd look really nice in—"

"There *isn't* another pair," she says icily. "They were from the reduced rack. And I don't like capri pants."

"Rebecca, think!" says Danielle. "Did you put the jeans down somewhere?"

"I must have done," I say, twisting my fingers into a knot. "It's been so busy in here, I must have put them on the rail, and . . . and I suppose another customer must have walked off with them." I give an apologetic little shrug as though to say "Customers, eh?"

"Wait a minute!" says the girl sharply. "What's that?"

I follow her gaze and freeze. The zebra-print jeans have rolled out from under the curtain. For a moment we all stare at them.

"Gosh!" I manage at last. "There they are!"

"And what exactly are they doing down there?" asks Danielle.

"I don't know!" I say. "Maybe they . . ." I swallow, trying to think as quickly as I can. "Maybe . . ."

"You *took* them!" says the girl incredulously. "You bloody took them! You wouldn't let me try them on, and then you hid them!"

"That's ridiculous!" I say, trying to sound convincing—but I can feel my cheeks flushing a guilty red.

"You little . . ." The girl breaks off and turns to Danielle. "I want to make an official complaint."

"Rebecca," says Danielle. "Into my office, please."

I jump in fright at her voice and follow her slowly to her office. Around the shop, I can see all the other staff looking at me and nudging each other. How utterly mortifying. Still, it'll be OK. I'll just say I'm really sorry and promise not to do it again, and maybe offer to work overtime. Just as long as I don't get . . .

I don't believe it. She's fired me. I haven't even worked there for a day, and I've been kicked out. I was so shocked when she told me, I almost became tearful. I mean, apart from the incident with the zebra-print jeans, I thought I was doing really well. But apparently hiding stuff from customers is one of those automatic-firing things. (Which is really unfair, because she never told me that at the interview.)

As I get changed out of my gray trousers and T-shirt, there's a heavy feeling in my heart. My retail career is over before it's even begun. I was only given twenty quid for the hours I've done today—and Danielle said that was being generous. And when I asked if I could quickly buy some clothes using my staff discount, she looked at me as if she wanted to hit me.

It's all gone wrong. No job, no money, no discount, just twenty bloody quid. Miserably I start to walk along the street, shoving my hands in my pockets. Twenty bloody quid. What am I supposed to do with—

"Rebecca!" My head jerks up and I find myself looking dazedly at a face which I know I recognize. But who is it? It's . . . it's . . . it's . . .

"Tom!" I exclaim in the nick of time. "Hi there! What a surprise!"

Well, blow me down. Tom Webster, up in London. He's just as tall and gangly as ever—but somehow looking slightly cooler with it than usual. He's wearing a thin blue sweater over a T-shirt and . . . are those really Armani jeans? This doesn't make sense. What's he doing here anyway? Shouldn't he be in Reigate, grouting his Mediterranean tiles or something?

"This is Lucy," he says proudly, and pulls forward a slim girl with big blue eyes, holding about sixty-five carrier bags. And I don't believe it. It's the girl who was buying all that stuff in Ally Smith. The girl whose boyfriend was paying. *Surely* she didn't mean . . .

"You're going out together?" I say stupidly. "You and her?"

"Yes," says Tom, and grins at me. "Have been for some time now."

But this doesn't make any sense. Why haven't Janice and Martin mentioned Tom's girlfriend? They've mentioned every other bloody thing in his life.

And fancy Tom having a girlfriend!

"Hi," says Lucy.

"Hi there," I say. "I'm Rebecca. Next-door neighbor. Childhood friend. All that."

"Oh, *you're* Rebecca," she says, and gives a swift glance at Tom.

What does that mean? Have they been talking about me? God, does Tom still fancy me? How embarrassing.

"That's me!" I say brightly, and give a little laugh.

"You know, I'm sure I've seen you somewhere before," says Lucy thoughtfully—and then her eyes crinkle in recognition. "You work at Ally Smith, don't you?"

"No!" I say, a little too sharply.

"Oh," she says. "I thought I saw you—"

God, I can't have it going back to my parents that I work in a shop. They'll think I've been lying about my entire life in London and that secretly I'm broke and living in squalor.

"Research," I say quickly. "I'm a journalist, actually."

"Rebecca's a financial journalist," says Tom. "Really knows her stuff."

"Oh, right," says Lucy, and I give her a supercilious smile.

"Mum and Dad always listen to Rebecca," says Tom. "Dad was talking about it just the other day. Said you'd been very helpful on some financial matter. Switching funds or something."

I nod vaguely, and give him a special, old-friends smile. Not that I'm jealous, or anything—but I do feel a little twinge seeing Tom smiling down at this Lucy character who, frankly, has very boring hair, even if her clothes are quite nice. Come to think of it, Tom's wearing quite nice clothes himself. Oh, what's going on? This is all wrong. Tom belongs in his starter home in Reigate, not prancing around expensive shops looking halfway decent.

"Anyway," he says. "We must get going."

"Train to catch?" I say patronizingly. "It must be hard, living so far out."

"It's not so bad," says Lucy. "I commute to Wetherby's every morning and it only takes forty minutes."

"You work for Wetherby's?" I say, aghast. Why am I *surrounded* by City high-flyers?

"Yes," she says. "I'm one of their political advisers."

What? What does that mean? Is she really brainy, or something? Oh God, this gets worse and worse.

"And we're not catching our train just yet," says Tom, smiling down at Lucy. "We're off to Tiffany first. Choose a little something for Lucy's birthday next week." He lifts a hand and starts twisting a lock of her hair round his finger.

I can't cope with this anymore. It's not fair. Why haven't *I* got a boyfriend to buy me stuff in Tiffany's?

"Well, lovely to see you," I gabble. "Give my love to your mum and dad. Funny they didn't mention Lucy," I can't resist adding. "I saw them the other day, and they didn't mention her once."

I shoot an innocent glance at Lucy. But she and Tom are exchanging looks again.

"They probably didn't want to—" begins Tom, and stops abruptly.

"What?" I say.

There's a long, awkward silence. Then Lucy says, "Tom, I'll just look in this shop window for a second," and walks off, leaving the two of us alone.

God, what drama! I'm obviously the third person in their relationship.

"Tom, what's going on?" I say, and give a little laugh.

But it's obvious, isn't it? He's still hankering after me. And Lucy knows it.

"Oh God," says Tom, and rubs his face. "Look, Rebecca, this isn't easy for me. But the thing is, Mum and Dad are aware of your . . . feelings for me. They didn't want to mention Lucy to you, because they thought you'd be . . ." He exhales sharply. "Disappointed."

What? Is this some kind of *joke*? I have never been more dumbfounded in all my life. For a few seconds I can't even move for astonishment.

"My feelings for *you*?" I stutter at last. "Are you joking?"

"Look, it's pretty obvious," he says, shrugging. "Mum and Dad told me how the other day, you kept on asking how I was, and all about my new house . . ." There's a slightly pitying look in his eye. Oh my God, I can't stand this. How can he think . . . "I really like you, Becky," he adds. "I just don't . . ."

"I was being *polite*!" I roar. "I don't *fancy* you!"

"Look," he says. "Let's just leave it, shall we?"

"But I *don't*!" I cry furiously. "I never did fancy you! That's why I didn't go out with you when you asked me! When we were both sixteen, remember?"

I break off and look at him triumphantly—to see that his face hasn't moved a bit. He isn't listening. Or if he is, he's thinking that the fact I've dragged in our teenage past means I'm obsessed by him. And the more I try to argue the point, the more obsessed he'll think I am. Oh God, this is horrendous.

"OK," I say, trying to gather together the remaining shreds of my dignity. "OK, we're obviously not communicating here, so I'll just leave you to it." I glance over at Lucy, who's looking in a shop window and obviously pretending not to be listening. "Honestly, I'm not after your boyfriend," I call. "And I never was. Bye."

And I stride off down the street, a nonchalant smile plastered stiffly across my face.

As I round the corner, however, the smile gradually slips, and I sit heavily down on a bench. I feel humiliated. Of course, the whole thing's laughable. That Tom Webster should think I'm in love with *him*. Just serves me right for being too polite to his parents and feigning interest in his bloody limed oak units. Next time I'll yawn loudly, or walk away. Or produce a boyfriend of my own.

I know all this. I know I shouldn't care two hoots what Tom Webster or his girlfriend think. But even so . . . I have to admit, I feel a bit low. Why haven't I got a boyfriend? There isn't even anyone I fancy at the moment. The last serious boyfriend I had was Robert Hayman, who sells advertising for *Portfolio News,* and we split up three months ago. And I didn't even much like him. He used to call me "Love" and jokingly put his hands over my eyes during the rude bits in films. Even when I told him not to, he still kept doing it. It used to drive me *mad.* Just remembering it now makes me feel all tense and scratchy.

But still, he was a boyfriend, wasn't he? He was someone to phone up during work, and go to parties with and use as ammunition against creeps. Maybe I shouldn't have chucked him. Maybe he was all right.

I give a gusty sigh, stand up, and start walking along the street again. All in all, it hasn't been a great day. I've lost a job and been patronized by Tom Webster. And now I haven't got anything to do tonight. I thought I'd be too knackered after working all day, so I didn't bother to organize anything.

Still, at least I've got twenty quid.

Twenty quid. I'll buy myself a nice cappuccino and a chocolate brownie. And a couple of magazines.

And maybe something from Accessorize. Or some boots. In fact I really *need* some new boots—and I've seen some really nice ones in Hobbs with square toes and quite a low heel. I'll go there after my coffee, and look at the dresses, too. God, I deserve a treat, after to-day. And I need some new tights for work, and a nail file. And maybe a book to read on the tube . . .

By the time I join the queue at Starbucks, I feel happier already.

Ms. Rebecca Bloomwood
Flat 2
4 Burney Rd.
London SW6 8FD

10 March 2000

Dear Ms. Bloomwood:

PGNI First Bank VISA Card No. 1475839204847586

Thank you for your letter of 6 March.

Your offer of a free subscription to *Successful Saving* magazine is most kind, as is your invitation to dinner at The Ivy. Unfortunately, employees of PGNI First Bank are prohibited from accepting such gifts.

I look forward to receiving your outstanding payment of £105.40, as soon as possible.

Yours sincerely,

Peter Johnson
Customer Accounts Executive

Ten

On Monday morning I wake early, feeling rather hollow inside. My gaze flits to the pile of unopened carrier bags in the corner of my room and then quickly flits away again. I know I spent too much money on Saturday. I know I shouldn't have bought two pairs of boots. I know I shouldn't have bought that purple dress. In all, I spent . . . Actually, I don't want to think about how much I spent. Think about something else, quick, I instruct myself. Something else. Anything'll do.

I'm well aware that at the back of my mind, thumping quietly like a drumbeat, are the twin horrors of Guilt and Panic.

Guilt Guilt Guilt Guilt.

Panic Panic Panic Panic.

If I let them, they'd swoop in and take over. I'd feel completely paralyzed with misery and fear. So the trick I've learned is simply not to listen. My mind is very well trained like that.

My other trick is to distract myself with different thoughts and activities. So I get up, switch the radio on, take a shower, and get dressed. The thumping's still there at the back of my head, but gradually, gradually, it's fading away. As I go into the kitchen and make a cup of coffee, I can barely hear it anymore. A cautious relief floods over me, like that feeling you get when a painkiller finally gets rid of your headache. I can relax. I'm going to be all right.

On the way out I pause in the hall to check my appearance in the mirror (Top: River Island, Skirt: French Connection, Tights: Pretty Polly Velvets, Shoes: Ravel) and reach for my coat (Coat: House of Fraser sale). Just then the post plops through the door, and I go to pick it up. There's a handwritten letter for Suze and a postcard from the Maldives. And for me, there are two ominous-looking window envelopes. One from VISA, one from Endwich Bank.

For a moment, my heart stands still. Why another letter from the bank? And VISA. What do they want? Can't they just leave me alone?

Carefully I place Suze's post on the ledge in the hall and shove my own two letters in my pocket, telling myself I'll read them on the way to work. Once I get on the tube, I'll open them both and I'll read them, however unpleasant they may be.

Honestly. As I'm walking along the pavement, I promise my intention is to read the letters.

But then I turn into the next street—and there's a skip outside someone's house. A huge great yellow skip, already half full of stuff. Builders are coming in and out of the house, tossing old bits of wood and upholstery into the skip. Loads of rubbish, all jumbled up together.

And a little thought creeps into my mind.

My steps slow down as I approach the skip and I pause, staring intently at it as though I'm interested in the words printed on the side. I stand there, trying to appear casual, until the builders have gone back into the house and no one's looking. Then, in one motion, I reach for the two letters, pull them out of my pocket, and drop them over the side, into the skip.

Gone.

As I'm standing there, a builder pushes past me with two sacks of broken plaster, and heaves them into the skip. And now they really are gone. Buried beneath a layer of plaster, unread. No one will ever find them.

Gone for good.

Quickly I turn away from the skip and begin to walk on again. Already my step's lighter and I'm feeling buoyant.

Before long, I'm feeling completely purged of guilt. I mean, it's not my fault if I never read the letters, is it? It's not my fault if I never got them, is it? As I bound along toward the tube station I honestly feel as though neither of those letters ever existed.

When I arrive at work, I switch on my computer, click efficiently to a new document, and start typing my piece on pensions. Perhaps if I work really hard, it's occurred to me, Philip will give me a raise. I'll stay late every night and impress him with my dedication to the job, and he'll realize that I'm considerably undervalued. Perhaps he'll even make me associate editor, or something.

"These days," I type briskly, "none of us can rely on the government to take care of us in our old age. Therefore pension planning should be done as early as possible, ideally as soon as you are earning an income."

"Morning, Clare," says Philip, coming into the office in his overcoat. "Morning, Rebecca."

Hah! Now is the time to impress him.

"Morning, Philip," I say, in a friendly-yet-professional manner. Then, instead of leaning back in my chair and asking him how his weekend was, I turn back to my computer and start typing again. In fact, I'm typing so fast that the screen is filled with lots of splodgy typos. It has to be said, I'm not the best typist in the world. But who cares? I look very businesslike, that's the point.

"The bwst ootion is oftwn yoor compaamy occupatinoa Ischeme, bt if tehis is not posibsle, a wide vareiety of peronanlas penion lans is on ther markte, ranign from . . ." I break off, reach for a pension brochure, and flip quickly through it, as though scanning for some crucial piece of information.

"Good weekend, Rebecca?" says Philip.

"Fine, thanks," I say, glancing up from the brochure as though surprised to be interrupted while I'm at work.

"I was round your neck of the woods on Saturday," he says. "The Fulham Road. Trendy Fulham."

"Right," I say absently.

"It's the place to be, these days, isn't it? My wife was reading an article about it. Full of It-girls, all living on trust funds."

"I suppose so," I say vaguely.

"That's what we'll have to call you," he says, and gives a little guffaw. "The office It-girl."

"Right," I say, and smile at him. After all, he's the boss. He can call me whatever he—

Hang on a minute. Philip hasn't got the idea that I'm rich, has he? He doesn't think I've got a trust fund or something ridiculous, does he?

"Rebecca," says Clare, looking up from her telephone. "I've got a call for you. Someone called Tarquin."

Philip gives a little grin, as though to say "What

else?" and ambles off to his desk. I stare after him in frustration. This is all wrong. If Philip thinks I've got some kind of private income, he'll never give me a raise.

But what on earth could have given him that idea?

"Becky," says Clare meaningfully, gesturing to my ringing phone.

"Oh," I say. "Yes, OK." I pick up the receiver, and say, "Hi. Rebecca Bloomwood here."

"Becky" comes Tarquin's unmistakable, reedy voice. He sounds rather nervous, as if he's been gearing up to this phone call for ages. Perhaps he has. "It's so nice to hear your voice. You know, I've been thinking about you a lot."

"Really?" I say, trying not to sound too encouraging. I mean, he is Suze's cousin and I don't want to hurt the poor bloke.

"I'd . . . I'd very much like to spend some more time in your company," he says. "May I take you out to dinner?"

Oh God. What am I supposed to say to that? It's such an innocuous request. I mean, it's not as if he's said, Can I sleep with you? or even Can I kiss you? If I say no to dinner, it's like saying "You're so unbearable, I can't even stand sharing a table with you for two hours."

And Suze has been so sweet to me recently, and if I turn her darling Tarkie down flat, she'll be really upset.

"I suppose so," I say, aware that I don't sound too thrilled—and also aware that maybe I should just come clean and say "I don't fancy you." But somehow I can't face it. To be honest, it would be a lot easier just to go out to dinner with him. I mean, how bad can it be?

And anyway, I don't have to actually *go*. I'll call at the last moment and cancel. Easy.

"I'm in London until Sunday," says Tarquin.

"Let's make it Saturday night, then!" I say brightly. "Just before you leave."

"Seven o'clock?"

"How about eight?" I suggest.

"OK," he says. "Eight o'clock." And he rings off, without mentioning a venue. But since I'm not actually going to meet him, this doesn't really matter. I put the phone down, give an impatient sigh, and start typing again.

"Although solid investment performance is important, flexibility is equally vital when choosing a pension plan, particularly for the younger investor. New on the market this year is the . . ." I break off and reach for a brochure. "Sun Assurance 'Later Years' Retirement Plan, which . . ."

"So, was that guy asking you out?" says Clare Edwards.

"Yes, he was, actually," I say, looking up carelessly. And in spite of myself, I feel a little flip of pleasure. Because Clare doesn't know what Tarquin's like, does she? For all she knows, he's incredibly good-looking and witty. "We're going out on Saturday night." I give her a nonchalant smile and start typing again.

"Oh right," she says, and snaps an elastic band round a pile of letters. "You know, Luke Brandon was asking me if you had a boyfriend the other day."

For an instant I can't move. Luke Brandon wants to know if I've got a boyfriend?

"Really?" I say, trying to sound normal. "When . . . when was this?"

"Oh, just the other day," she says. "I was at a briefing at Brandon Communications, and he asked me. Just casually. You know."

"And what did you say?"

"I said no," said Clare, and gives me a little grin. "You don't fancy him, do you?"

"Of course not," I say, and roll my eyes.

But I have to admit, I feel quite cheerful as I turn back

to my computer and start typing again. Luke Brandon. I mean, not that I like him or anything—but still. "This plan," I type, "offers full death benefits and an optional lump sum on retirement. For example, assuming 7 percent growth, a typical woman aged 30 who invested £100 a month would receive . . ."

You know what? I suddenly think, stopping mid-sentence. This is boring. I'm better than this.

I'm better than sitting here in this crappy office, typing out the details from a brochure, trying to turn them into some kind of credible journalism. I deserve to do something more interesting than this. Or more well paid. Or both.

I stop typing and rest my chin on my hands. It's time for a new start. Why don't I do what Elly's doing? I'm not afraid of a bit of hard work, am I? Why don't I get my life in order, go to a City head-hunter, and land myself a new job? I'll have a huge income and a company car and wear Karen Millen suits every day. And I'll never have to worry about money again.

I feel exhilarated. This is it! This is the answer to everything. I'll be a . . .

"Clare?" I say casually. "Who earns the most in the City?"

"I don't know," says Clare, frowning thoughtfully. "Maybe futures brokers?"

That's it, then. I'll be a futures broker. Easy.

And it is easy. So easy that ten o'clock the next morning sees me walking nervously up to the front doors of William Green, top City head-hunters. As I push the door open I glimpse my own reflection and feel a little thrill go through my stomach. Am I *really* doing this?

You bet I am. I'm wearing my smartest black suit,

and tights and high heels, with an *FT* under my arm, obviously. And I'm carrying the briefcase with the combination lock, which my mum gave me one Christmas and which I've never used. This is partly because it's really heavy and bumpy—and partly because I've forgotten the combination, so I can't actually open it. But it looks the part. And that's what counts.

Jill Foxton, the woman I'm meeting, was really nice on the phone when I told her about wanting to change careers, and sounded pretty impressed by all my experience. I quickly typed up a curriculum vitae and e-mailed it to her—and, OK, I padded it a bit, but that's what they expect, isn't it? It's all about selling yourself. And it worked, because she phoned back only about ten minutes after receiving it, and asked if I'd come in and see her, as she thought she had some interesting opportunities for me.

I was so excited, I could barely keep still. I went straight into Philip and told him I wanted to take tomorrow off to take my nephew to the zoo—and he didn't suspect a thing. He's going to be gobsmacked when he finds out I've turned overnight into a high-flying futures broker.

"Hi," I say confidently to the woman at reception. "I'm here to see Jill Foxton. It's Rebecca Bloomwood."

"Of . . ."

I can't say *Successful Saving*. It might get back to Philip that I've been looking for a new job.

"Of . . . just of nowhere, really," I say and give a relaxed little laugh. "Just Rebecca Bloomwood. I have a ten o'clock appointment."

"Fine," she says, and smiles. "Take a seat."

I pick up my briefcase and walk over to the black leather chairs, trying not to give away how nervous I feel. I sit down, run my eye hopefully over the magazines on the coffee table (but there's nothing interesting, just things like *The Economist*), then lean back and look around. This foyer is pretty impressive, I have to admit. There's a fountain in the middle, and glass stairs rising in a curve—and, what seems like several miles away, I can see lots of state-of-the-art lifts. Not just one lift, or two—but about ten. Blimey. This place must be huge.

"Rebecca?" A blond girl in a pale trouser suit is suddenly in front of me. Nice suit, I think. Very nice suit.

"Hi!" I say. "Jill!"

"No, I'm Amy," she smiles. "Jill's assistant."

Wow. That's pretty cool. Sending your assistant to pick up your visitors, as if you're too grand and busy to do it yourself. Maybe that's what I'll get my assistant to do when I'm an important futures broker and Elly comes over for lunch. Or maybe I'll have a *male* assistant—and we'll fall in love! God, it would be just like a movie. The high-flying woman and the cute but sensitive . . .

"Rebecca?" I come to and see Amy staring at me curiously. "Are you ready?"

"Of course!" I say gaily, and pick up my briefcase. As we stride off over the glossy floor, I surreptitiously run my gaze over Amy's trouser suit again—and find my eye landing on an Emporio Armani label. I can't quite believe it. The *assistants* wear Emporio Armani! So what's Jill herself going to be in? Couture Dior? God, I love this place already.

We go up to the sixth floor and begin to walk along endless carpeted corridors.

"So you want to be a futures broker," says Amy after a while.

"Yes," I say. "That's the idea."

"And you already know a bit about it."

"Well, you know." I give a modest smile. "I've written

extensively on most areas of finance, so I do feel quite well equipped."

"That's good," says Amy, and gives me a smile. "Some people turn up with no idea. Then Jill asks them a few standard questions, and . . ." She makes a gesture with her hand. I don't know what it means, but it doesn't look good.

"Right!" I say, forcing myself to speak in an easy tone. "So—what sort of questions?"

"Oh, nothing to worry about!" says Amy. "She'll probably ask you . . . oh, I don't know. Something like 'How do you trade a butterfly?' or, 'What's the difference between open outlay and OR?' Or, 'How would you calculate the expiry date of a futures instrument?' Really basic stuff."

"Right," I say, and swallow. "Great."

Something in me is telling me to turn and run—but we've already arrived at a pale blond-wood door.

"Here we are," says Amy, and smiles at me. "Would you like tea or coffee?"

"Coffee, please," I say, wishing I could say "A stiff gin, please." Amy knocks on the door, opens it and ushers me in, and says, "Rebecca Bloomwood."

"Rebecca!" says a dark-haired woman behind the desk, and gets up to shake my hand.

To my slight surprise, Jill is not nearly as well dressed as Amy. She's wearing a blue, rather mumsy-looking suit, and boring court shoes. But still, never mind, she's the boss. And her office is pretty amazing.

"It's very good to meet you," she says, gesturing to a chair in front of her desk. "And let me say straight away, I was extremely impressed by your CV."

"Really?" I say, feeling relief creep over me. That can't be bad, can it? *Extremely impressed.* Maybe it won't matter I don't know the answers to those questions.

"Particularly by your languages," adds Jill. "*Very* good. You do seem to be one of those rare breeds, an all-rounder."

"Well, my French is really only conversational," I say modestly. "*Voici la plume de ma tante,* and all that!"

Jill gives an appreciative laugh, and I beam back at her.

"But Finnish!" she says, reaching for the cup of coffee on her desk. "That's quite unusual."

I keep smiling and hope we move off the subject of languages. To be honest, "fluent in Finnish" went in because I thought "conversational French" looked a bit bare on its own. And after all, who speaks Finnish, for God's sake? No one.

"And your financial knowledge," she says, pulling my CV toward her. "You seemed to have covered a lot of different areas during your years in financial journalism." She looks up. "What attracts you to derivatives in particular?"

What? What's she talking about? Oh yes. Derivatives. They're futures, aren't they? And they have something to do with the price of a security. Or a commodity. Something like that.

"Well," I begin confidently—and am interrupted as Amy comes in with a cup of coffee.

"Thanks," I say, and look up, hoping we've moved onto something else. But she's still waiting for an answer. "I think the excitement of futures is the . . . um, their speculative nature, combined with the ability to control risk with hedge positions," I hear myself saying.

Wow. How on earth did I come out with that?

"They're an extremely challenging area," I add quickly, "and I think . . ." What do I think? Should I throw in a quick reference to butterflies or expiry dates or something? Or Barings Bank? Probably better not. "I think I'd be well suited to that particular field," I finish at last.

"I see," says Jill Foxton, and leans back in her chair. "The reason I ask is, there's a position we have in banking, which I think might also suit you. I don't know what you would feel about that."

A position in banking? Has she actually found me a job? I don't believe it!

"Well, that would be fine by me," I say, trying not to sound too joyful. "I mean, I'd miss the futures—but then, banking's good, too, isn't it?"

Jill laughs. I think she thinks I'm joking or something.

"The client is a triple-A-rated foreign bank, looking for a new recruit in the London arm of their debt financing division."

"Right," I say intelligently.

"I don't know whether you're familiar with the principles of European back-to-back arbitrage?"

"Absolutely," I say confidently. "I wrote an article on that very subject last year."

Which isn't *quite* true, but I can always read a book about it, can't I?

"Obviously I'm not trying to rush you into any decision," she says, "but if you do want a change of career, I'd say this would be perfect for you. There'd be an interview, but I can't see any problems there." She smiles at me. "And we'll be able to negotiate you a very attractive package."

"Really?" Suddenly, I can't quite breathe. She's going to negotiate an attractive package. For me!

"Oh yes," says Jill. "Well, you must realize you're a bit of a one-off." She gives me a confidential smile. "You know, when your CV came through yesterday, I actually whooped! I mean, the *coincidence*!"

"Absolutely," I say, beaming at her. God, this is fantastic. This is a bloody dream come true. I'm going to be a banker! And not just any old banker—a triple-A-rated banker!

"So," says Jill casually. "Shall we go and meet your new employer?"

"What?" I say in astonishment, and a little smile spreads over her face.

"I didn't want to tell you until I'd met you—but the recruitment director of Bank of Helsinki is over here for a meeting with our managing director. I just *know* he's going to love you. We can have the whole thing wrapped up by this afternoon!"

"Excellent!" I say, and get to my feet. Ha-ha-ha! I'm going to be a banker!

It's only as we're halfway down the corridor that her words begin to impinge on my mind. Bank of Helsinki.

Bank of Helsinki. That doesn't mean . . . Surely she doesn't think . . .

"I can't wait to hear the two of you talking away in Finnish," says Jill pleasantly, as we begin to climb a flight of stairs. "It's not a language I know at all."

Oh my God. *Oh my God. No.*

"But then, my languages have always been hopeless," she adds comfortably. "I'm not talented in that department, not like you!"

I flash her a little smile and keep walking, without missing a step. But I can hardly breathe. Shit. What am I going to do? *What the fuck am I going to do?*

We turn a corner and begin to walk calmly down another corridor. And I'm doing pretty well. As long as we just keep walking, I'm OK.

"Was Finnish a hard language to learn?" asks Jill.

"Not that hard," I hear myself saying in a scratchy voice. "My . . . my father's half Finnish."

"Yes, I thought it must be something like that," says Jill. "I mean, it's not the sort of thing you learn at school, is it?" And she gives a jolly little laugh.

It's all right for her, I think desperately. She's not the one being led to her death. Oh God, this is terrible. People keep passing us and glancing at me and smiling, as if to say "So that's the Finnish-speaker!"

Why did I put I was fluent in Finnish? *Why?*

"All right?" says Jill. "Not nervous?"

"Oh no!" I say at once, and force a grin onto my face. "Of course I'm not nervous!"

Maybe I'll be able to busk it, I think suddenly. I mean, the guy won't conduct the whole bloody interview in Finnish, will he? He'll just say "Haållø," or whatever it is, and I'll say "Haållø" back, and then before he can say anything else, I'll quickly say, "You know, my technical Finnish is a bit rusty these days. Would you mind if we spoke in English?" And he'll say . . .

"Nearly there," says Jill, and smiles at me.

"Good," I say brightly, and clasp my sweaty hand more tightly round my briefcase handle. Oh God. Please save me from this. Please . . .

"Here we are!" she says, and stops at a door marked "Conference Room." She knocks twice, then pushes it open. There's a roomful of people sitting round a table, and they all turn to look at me.

"Jan Virtanen," she says. "I'd like you to meet Rebecca Bloomwood."

A bearded man rises from his chair, give me a huge smile, and extends his hand.

"Neiti Bloomwood," he says cheerfully. "Nautin erittain paljon tapaamisestamme. Onko oiken, etta teilla on jonkinlainen yhteys Suomeen?"

I stare speechlessly at him. My face is glowing, as

though I'm consumed with happiness. Everyone in the room is waiting for me to answer, I've got to say something.

"I . . . erm . . . erm . . . Haållø!" I lift my hand in a friendly little wave and smile around the room.

But nobody smiles back.

"Erm . . . I've just got to . . ." I start backing away. "Just got to . . ."

I turn. And I run.

Eleven

I ARRIVE BACK DOWN in the foyer, panting slightly. Which is not surprising, since I've just run about a half marathon along endless corridors, trying to get out of this place. I descend the final flight of stairs (couldn't risk waiting for the elevators in case the Finnish brigade suddenly turned up), then pause to catch my breath. I straighten my skirt, transfer my briefcase from one sweaty hand to the other, and begin to walk calmly across the foyer toward the door, as though I've come out of an utterly ordinary, utterly unspectacular meeting. I don't look right and I don't look left. I don't think about the fact that I've just completely shredded any chances I had of becoming a top City banker. All I can think about is getting to that glass door and getting outside before anyone can . . .

"Rebecca!" comes a voice behind my voice, and I freeze. Shit. They've got me.

"Haållø!" I gulp, turning round. "Haåll . . . Oh. Hell . . . Hello."

It's Luke Brandon.

It's Luke Brandon, standing right in front of me, looking down at me with that amused smile he always seems to have.

"This isn't the sort of place I would have expected to find you," he says. "You're not after a City job, are you?"

And why shouldn't I be? Doesn't he think I'm clever enough?

"Actually," I say haughtily, "I'm thinking of a change of career. Maybe into foreign banking. Or futures broking."

"Really?" he says. "That's a shame."

A shame? What does that mean? Why is it a shame? As I look up at him, his dark eyes meet mine, and I feel a little flicker, deep inside me. Out of nowhere, Clare's words pop into my head. *Luke Brandon was asking me if you had a boyfriend.*

"What . . ." I clear my throat. "What are *you* doing here, anyway?"

"Oh, I recruit from here quite often," he says. "They're very efficient. Soulless, but efficient." He shrugs, then looks at my shiny briefcase. "Have they fixed you up with anything yet?"

"I've . . . I've got a number of options open to me," I say. "I'm just considering my next move."

Which, to be honest, is straight out the door.

"I see," he says, and pauses. "Did you take the day off to come here?"

"Yes," I say. "Of course I did."

What does he think? That I just sloped off for a couple of hours and said I was at a press conference?

Actually, that's not a bad idea. I might try that next time.

"So—what are you up to now?" he asks.

Don't say "nothing." *Never* say "nothing."

"Well, I've got some bits and pieces to do," I say. "Calls to make, people to see. That kind of thing."

"Ah," he says, nodding. "Yes. Well. Don't let me keep

you." He looks around the foyer. "And I hope it all works out for you, job-wise."

"Thanks," I say, giving him a businesslike smile.

And then he's gone, walking off toward the doors, and I'm left holding my clunky briefcase, feeling just a bit disappointed. I wait until he's disappeared, then wander slowly over to the doors myself and go out onto the street. And then I stop. To tell you the truth, I'm not quite sure what to do next. I'd kind of planned to spend the day ringing everyone up and telling them about my fab new job as a futures broker. Instead of which . . . Well, anyway. Let's not think about that.

But I can't stand still on the pavement outside William Green all day. People will start thinking I'm a piece of installation art or something. So eventually I begin walking along the street, figuring I'll arrive at a tube soon enough and then I can decide what to do. I come to a corner and I'm just waiting for the traffic to stop, when a taxi pulls up beside me.

"I know you're a very busy woman, with a lot to do," comes Luke Brandon's voice, and my head jerks up in shock. There he is, leaning out of the taxi window, his dark eyes crinkled up in a little smile. "But if you had the odd half-hour to spare—you wouldn't be interested in doing a little shopping, would you?"

This day is unreal. Completely and utterly unreal.

I get into the taxi, put my clunky briefcase on the floor, and shoot a nervous look at Luke as I sit down. I'm already slightly regretting this. What if he asks me a question about interest rates? What if he wants to talk about the Bundesbank or American growth prospects? But all he says is "Harrods, please," to the driver.

As we zoom off, I can't stop a smile coming to my face. I thought I was going to have to go home and be all miserable on my own—and instead, I'm on my way to Harrods, and someone else is paying. I mean, you can't get more perfect than that.

As we drive along, I look out of the window at the crowded streets. Although it's March, there are still a few SALE signs in the shop windows left over from January, and I find myself peering at the displays, wondering if there are any bargains I might have missed. We pause outside a branch of Lloyds Bank. I look idly at the window, and at the queue of people inside, and hear myself saying "You know what? Banks should run January sales. Everyone else does."

There's silence and I look up, to see a look of amusement on Luke Brandon's face.

"Banks?" he says.

"Why not?" I say defensively. "They could reduce their charges for a month or something. And so could building societies. Big posters in the windows, 'Prices Slashed' . . ." I think for a moment. "Or maybe they should have April sales, after the end of the tax year. Investment houses could do it, too. 'Fifty percent off a selected range of funds.' "

"A unit trust sale," says Luke Brandon slowly. "Reductions on all upfront charges."

"Exactly," I say. "Everyone's a sucker for a sale. Even rich people."

The taxi moves on again, and I gaze out at a woman in a gorgeous white coat, wondering where she got it. Maybe at Harrods. Maybe I should buy a white coat, too. I'll wear nothing but white all winter. A snowy white coat and a white fur hat. People will start calling me the Girl in the White Coat.

When I look back again, Luke's writing something down in a little notebook. He looks up and meets my eye for a moment, then says, "Rebecca, are you serious about leaving journalism?"

"Oh," I say vaguely. To be honest, I'd forgotten all about leaving journalism. "I don't know. Maybe."

"And you really think banking would suit you better?"

"Who knows?" I say, feeling a bit rattled at his tone. It's all right for him. He doesn't have to worry about his career—he's got his own multimillion-pound company. I've only got my own multimillion-pound overdraft. "Elly Granger is leaving *Investor's Weekly News*," I add. "She's joining Wetherby's as a fund manager."

"I heard," he says. "Doesn't surprise me. But you're nothing like Elly Granger."

Really? This comment intrigues me. If I'm not like Elly, who am I like, then? Someone really cool like Kristin Scott Thomas, maybe.

"You have imagination," adds Luke. "She doesn't."

Wow! Now I really am gobsmacked. Luke Brandon thinks I have imagination? Gosh. That's good, isn't it. That's quite flattering, really. *You have imagination.* Mmm, yes, I like that. Unless . . .

Hang on. It's not some polite way of saying he thinks I'm stupid, is it? Or a liar? Like "creative accounting." Perhaps he's trying to say that none of my articles is accurate.

Oh God, now I don't know whether to look pleased or not.

To cover up my embarrassment, I look out of the window. We've stopped at a traffic light, and a very large lady in a pink velour jogging suit is trying to cross the road. She's holding several bags of shopping and a pug dog, and she keeps losing grasp of one or other of them

and having to put something down. I almost want to
leap out and help her. Then, suddenly, she loses her
grasp of one of the bags, and drops it on the ground. It
falls open—and three huge tubs of ice cream come out
of it and start rolling down the road.

Don't laugh, I instruct myself. Be mature. Don't
laugh. I clamp my lips together, but I can't stop a little
giggle escaping.

I glance at Luke, and his lips are clamped together,
too.

Then the woman starts chasing her ice cream down
the road, pug dog in tow, and that's it. I can't stop myself
giggling. And when the pug dog reaches the ice cream
before the lady, and starts trying to get the lid off with its
teeth, I think I'm going to die laughing. I look over at
Luke, and I can't believe it. He's laughing helplessly, too,
wiping the tears from his eyes. I didn't think Luke
Brandon *ever* laughed.

"Oh God," I manage at last. "I know you shouldn't
laugh at people. But I mean . . ."

"That dog!" Luke starts laughing again. "That bloody
dog!"

"That outfit!" I give a little shudder as we start to
move off again, past the pink woman. She's bending
over the ice cream, her huge pink bottom thrust up in
the air . . . "I'm sorry, but pink velour jogging suits
should be banned from this planet."

"I couldn't agree more," says Luke, nodding seriously. "Pink velour jogging suits are hereby banned.
Along with cravats."

"And men's briefs," I say without thinking—then
blush pink. How could I mention men's briefs in front
of Luke Brandon? "And toffee-flavored popcorn," I
quickly add.

"Right," says Luke. "So we're banning pink velour

jogging suits, cravats, men's briefs, toffee-flavored pop-corn . . ."

"And punters with no change," comes the taxi driver's voice from the front.

"Fair enough," says Luke, giving a little shrug. "Punt-ers with no change."

"And punters who vomit. They're the worst."

"OK . . ."

"And punters who don't know where the fuck they're going."

Luke and I exchange glances and I begin to giggle again.

"And punters who don't speak the bloody language. Drive you crazy."

"Right," says Luke. "So . . . most punters, in fact."

"Don't get me wrong," says the taxi driver. "I've got nothing against foreigners . . ." He pulls up outside Harrods. "Here we are. Going shopping, are you?"

"That's right," says Luke, getting out his wallet.

"So—what're you after?"

I look at Luke expectantly. He hasn't told me what we're here to buy. Clothes? A new aftershave? Will I have to keep smelling his cheek? (I wouldn't mind that, actually.) Furniture? Something dull like a new desk?

"Luggage," he says, and hands a tenner to the driver. "Keep the change."

Luggage! Suitcases and holdalls and stuff like that. As I wander round the department, looking at Louis Vuitton suitcases and calfskin bags, I'm quite thrown. Quite shocked by myself. Luggage. Why on earth have I never considered luggage before?

I should explain—for years now, I've kind of oper-ated under an informal shopping cycle. A bit like a farmer's crop rotation system. Except, instead of wheat-maize-barley-fallow, mine pretty much goes clothes-makeup-shoes-clothes. (I don't usually bother with fallow.) Shopping is actually very similar to farming a field. You can't keep buying the same thing—you have to have a bit of variety.

But look what I've been missing out on all this time. Look what I've been denying myself. I feel quite shaky as I realize the opportunities I've just been throwing away over the years. Suitcases, weekend bags, mono-grammed hatboxes . . . With weak legs I wander into a corner and sit down on a carpeted pedestal next to a red leather vanity case.

How can I have overlooked luggage for so long? How can I have just blithely led my life *ignoring an entire retail sector*?

"So—what do you think?" says Luke, coming up to me. "Anything worth buying?"

And now, of course, I feel like a fraud. Why couldn't he have wanted to buy a really good white shirt, or a cashmere scarf? Or even hand cream? I would have been able to advise him authoritatively and even quote prices. But luggage. I'm a beginner at luggage.

"Well," I say, playing for time. "It depends. They all look great."

"They do, don't they?" He follows my gaze around the department. "But which one would you choose? If you had to buy one of these suitcases, which one would it be?"

It's no good. I can't bluff.

"To be honest," I say, "this isn't really my field."

"What isn't?" he says, sounding incredulous. "Shop-ping?"

"Luggage," I explain. "It's not an area I've put a lot of time into. I should have done, I know, but . . ."

"Well . . . never mind," says Luke, his mouth twisting into a smile. "As a nonexpert, which one would you choose?"

Well, that's different.

"Hmm," I say, and get to my feet in a businesslike manner. "Well, let's have a closer look."

God, we have fun. We line up eight suitcases in a row, and give them marks for looks, heaviness, quality of lining, number of interior pockets, and efficiency of wheels. (I test this by striding the length of the department, pulling the case behind me. By this time, the assistant has just given up and left us to it.) Then we look to see if they have a matching holdall and give that marks, too.

The prices don't seem to matter to Luke. Which is a bloody good thing, because they're astronomical—and at first sight, so scary, they make me want to run away. But it's amazing how quickly £1,000 can start to seem like a very reasonable sum for a suitcase—especially since the Louis Vuitton monogrammed trunk costs about ten times as much. In fact, after a while I find myself thinking quite seriously that I too should really invest in a quality suitcase, instead of my battered old canvas bag.

But today is Luke's shopping trip, not mine. And, strangely enough, it's almost more fun choosing for someone else than for yourself. In the end, we narrow it down to a dark green leather case, which has wonderful trundly wheels, or the palest beige calfskin case, which is a bit heavier, but has a stunning silk lining and is so soft, I can't stop running my fingers over it. And it has a matching holdall and vanity case—and they're just as beautiful. God, if it were me, I'd . . .

But then, it's not up to me, is it? It's Luke who's buying the case. He's the one who's got to choose. We sit down on the floor, side by side, and look at them.

"The green one would be more practical," says Luke eventually.

"Mmm," I say noncommittally. "I suppose it would."

"It's lighter—and the wheels are better."

"Mmm."

"And that pale calfskin would probably scuff in a matter of minutes. Green's a more sensible color."

"Mmm," I say, trying to sound as though I agree with him.

He gives me a quizzical look and says, "Right, well, I think we've made our choice, don't you?" And, still sitting on the floor, he calls over the assistant.

"Yes, sir?" says the assistant, and Luke nods at him.

"I'd like to buy one of these pale beige suitcases, please."

"Oh!" I say, and I can't stop a smile of delight spreading over my face. "You're getting the one I liked best!"

"Rule of life," says Luke, getting to his feet and brushing down his trousers. "If you bother to ask someone's advice, then bother to listen to it."

"But I didn't say which one . . ."

"You didn't have to," says Luke, reaching out a hand to pull me to my feet. "Your mmms gave it all away."

His hand is surprisingly strong round mine, and as he pulls me up, I feel a slight swooping in my stomach. He smells nice, too. Some expensive aftershave, which I don't recognize. For a moment, neither of us says anything.

"Right," says Luke at last. "Well, I'd better pay for it, I suppose."

"Yes," I say, suddenly feeling ridiculously nervous. "Yes, I suppose you had."

He walks off to the checkout and starts talking to the assistant, and I perch next to a display of leather suit-carriers, suddenly feeling a bit awkward. I mean, what happens next?

Well, we'll just say good-bye politely, won't we? Luke'll probably have to get back to the office. He can't hang around shopping all day. And if he asks me what I'm doing next, I tell myself, I really will say I'm busy. I'll pretend I've got some important meeting arranged or something.

"All sorted out," he says, coming back. "Rebecca, I'm incredibly grateful to you for your help."

"Great!" I say brightly. "Well, I must be on my—"

"So I was wondering," says Luke, before I can continue. "Would you like some lunch?"

This is turning into my perfect day. Shopping at Harrods, and lunch at Harvey Nichols. I mean, what could be better than that? We go straight up to the Fifth Floor restaurant, and Luke orders a bottle of chilled white wine and raises his glass in a toast.

"To luggage," he says, and smiles.

"Luggage," I reply happily, and take a sip. It's just about the most delicious wine I've ever tasted. Luke picks up his menu and starts to read it, and I pick mine up, too—but to be honest, I'm not reading a word. I'm just sitting in a happy glow. I'm looking around with relish at all the smart women coming in to have lunch here, and making notes of their outfits and wondering where that girl over there got her pink boots from. And now, for some reason, I'm thinking about that nice card Luke sent me. And I'm wondering whether it was just being friendly—or . . . or whether it was something else.

At this thought, my stomach flips so hard I almost feel sick, and very quickly I take another sip of wine. Well, a gulp, really. Then I put down my glass, count to five, and say casually, "Thanks for your card, by the way."

"What?" he says, looking up. "Oh, you're welcome." He reaches for his glass and takes a sip of wine. "It was nice to bump into you that night."

"It's a great place," I say. "Great for table-hopping."

As soon as I've said this, I feel myself blush. But Luke just smiles and says, "Indeed." Then he puts down his glass and says, "Do you know what you want?"

"Ahm . . ." I say, glancing hurriedly at the menu. "I think I'll just have . . . erm . . . fish cakes. And rocket salad."

Damn, I've just spotted squid. I should have had that. Oh well, too late now.

"Good choice," says Luke, smiling at me. "And thanks again for coming along today. It's always good to have a second opinion."

"No problem," I say lightly, and take a sip of wine. "Hope you enjoy the case."

"Oh, it's not for me," he says after a pause. "It's for Sacha."

"Oh, right," I say pleasantly. "Who's Sacha? Your sister?"

"My girlfriend," says Luke, and turns away to beckon to a waiter.

And I stare at him, unable to move.

His girlfriend. I've been helping him choose a suitcase for his girlfriend.

Suddenly I don't feel hungry anymore. I don't want

fish cakes and rocket salad. I don't even want to be here. My happy glow is fading away, and underneath I feel chilly and rather stupid. Luke Brandon's got a girlfriend. Of course he has. Some beautiful smart girl called Sacha, who has manicured nails and travels everywhere with expensive cases. I'm a fool, aren't I? I should have known there'd be a Sacha somewhere on the scene. I mean, it's obvious.

Except . . . Except it's not that obvious. In fact, it's not obvious at all. Luke hasn't mentioned his girlfriend all morning. Why hasn't he? Why didn't he just *say* the suitcase was for her in the first place? Why did he let me sit on the floor beside him in Harrods and laugh as I marched up and down, testing the wheels? I wouldn't have behaved anything like that if I'd known we were buying a case for his girlfriend. And he must have known that. He must have known.

A cold feeling begins to creep over me. This is all wrong.

"All right?" says Luke, turning back to me.

"No," I hear myself saying. "No, it's not. You didn't tell me that case was for your girlfriend. You didn't even tell me you *had* a girlfriend."

Oh God. I've done it now. I've been completely un-cool. But somehow I don't care.

"I see," says Luke after a pause. He picks up a piece of bread and begins to break it up with his fingers, then looks up. "Sacha and I have been together awhile now," he says kindly. "I'm sorry if I gave . . . any other impression."

He's patronizing me. I can't bear it.

"That's not the point," I say, feeling my cheeks flushing beet red. "It's just . . . it's all wrong."

"Wrong?" he says, looking amused.

"You should have told me we were choosing a case for your girlfriend," I say doggedly, staring down at the table. "It would have made things . . . different."

There's silence and I raise my eyes, to see Luke looking at me as though I'm crazy.

"Rebecca," he says, "you're getting this all out of proportion. I wanted your opinion on suitcases. End of story."

"And are you going to tell your girlfriend you asked my advice?"

"Of course I am!" says Luke, and gives a little laugh. "I expect she'll be rather amused."

I stare at him in silence, feeling mortification creep over me. My throat's tight, and there's a pain growing in my chest. *Amused.* Sacha will be amused when she hears about me.

Well, of course she will. Who wouldn't be amused by hearing about the girl who spent her entire morning testing out suitcases for another woman? The girl who got completely the wrong end of the stick. The girl who was so stupid, she thought Luke Brandon might actually like her.

I swallow hard, feeling sick with humiliation. For the first time, I'm realizing how Luke Brandon sees me. How they all see me. I'm just the comedy turn, aren't I? I'm the scatty girl who gets things wrong and makes people laugh. The girl who didn't know SBG and Rutland Bank had merged. The girl no one would ever think of taking seriously. Luke didn't bother telling me we were choosing a suitcase for his girlfriend because I don't matter. He's only buying me lunch because he hasn't got anything else to do—and probably because he thinks I might do something entertaining like drop my fork, which he can laugh about when he gets back to the office.

"I'm sorry," I say in a wobbly voice, and stand up. "I haven't got time for lunch after all."

"Rebecca, don't be silly!" says Luke. "Look, I'm sorry you didn't know about my girlfriend." He raises his eyebrows quizzically, and I almost want to hit him. "But we can still be friends, can't we?"

"No," I say stiffly, aware that my voice is thick and my eyes smarting. "No, we can't. Friends treat each other with respect. But you don't respect me, do you, Luke? You just think I'm a joke. A nothing. Well . . ." I swallow hard. "Well, I'm not."

And before he can say anything else I turn and quickly make my way out of the restaurant, half blinded by disappointed tears.

PGNI FIRST BANK VISA

7 CAMEL SQUARE
LIVERPOOL LI 5NP

Ms. Rebecca Bloomwood
Flat 2
4 Burney Rd.
London SW6 8FD

15 March 2000

Dear Ms. Bloomwood:

PGNI First Bank VISA Card No. 1475839204847586

Thank you for your payment of £10.00, received on 13 March.

As I have pointed out several times, the minimum payment required was in fact £105.40.

The balance currently overdue is therefore £95.40. I look forward to receiving your payment as soon as possible.

If satisfactory payment is not received within seven days, further action will have to be taken.

Yours sincerely,

Peter Johnson
Customer Accounts Executive

Ms. Rebecca Boomwood
Flat 2
4 Burney Rd.
London SW6 8FD

18 March 2000

Dear Ms. Boomwood:

Just think ...

What kind of difference would a personal loan make to your life?

A new car, perhaps. Improvements to the home. A boat for those weekend breaks. Or maybe just the peace of mind, knowing that all those bills can easily be taken care of.

Bank of London will offer loans for almost any purpose—so don't wait any longer! Turn your life into the lifestyle you deserve.

With a Bank of London Easifone Loan, you don't even have to fill in any forms. Simply call one of our friendly 24-hour operators on **0100 45 46 47 48** and let us do the rest.

Just think ...

We look forward to hearing from you.

Yours sincerely,

Sue Skepper
Marketing Executive

P.S. Why delay? Pick up the phone now and dial 0100 45 46 47 48. It couldn't be easier!

Twelve

I ARRIVE HOME that afternoon, feeling weary and miserable. Suddenly, triple-A-rated jobs in banking and Harrods with Luke Brandon seem miles away. Real life isn't swanning round Knightsbridge in a taxi, choosing £1,000 suitcases, is it? This is real life. Home to a tiny flat which still smells of curry, and a pile of nasty letters from the bank, and no idea what to do about them.

I put my key in the lock, and as I open the door, I hear Suze cry, "Bex? Is that you?"

"Yes!" I say, trying to sound cheerful. "Where are you?"

"Here," she says, appearing at the door of my bedroom. Her face is all pink, and there's a shine in her eyes. "Guess what! I've got a surprise for you!"

"What is it?" I say, putting down my briefcase. To be honest, I'm not in the mood for one of Suze's surprises. She'll just have moved my bed to a different place, or something. And all I want is to sit down and have a cup of tea and something to eat. I never did get any lunch.

"Come and see. No, no, shut your eyes, first. I'll lead you."

"OK," I say reluctantly. I close my eyes and allow her

to take my hand. We start to walk along the corridor—
and of course, as we near my bedroom door, I start feeling a little tingle of anticipation in spite of myself. I
always fall for things like this.

"Da-daaa! You can look now!"

I open my eyes and look dazedly around my room,
wondering what mad thing Suze has done. At least she
hasn't painted the walls or touched the curtains, and my
computer's safely switched off. So what on earth can she
have . . .

And then I see them. On my bed. Piles and piles
of upholstered frames. All made up perfectly, with no
wonky corners, and the braid glued neatly in place. I
can't quite believe my eyes. There must be at least . . .

"I've done a hundred," says Suze behind me. "And
I'm going to do the rest tomorrow! Aren't they fab?"

I turn and stare incredulously at her. "You . . . you
did all these?"

"Yes!" she says proudly. "It was easy, once I got into a
rhythm. I did it in front of *Morning Coffee*. Oh, I wish
you'd seen it. They had *such* a good phone-in, about
men who dress up in women's clothes! Emma was being
all sympathetic, but Rory looked like he wanted to—"

"Wait," I say, trying to get my head round this. "Wait.
Suze, I don't understand. This must have taken you
ages." My eye runs disbelievingly over the pile of frames
again. "Why . . . why on earth did you—"

"Well, you weren't getting very far with them, were
you?" says Suze. "I just thought I'd give you a helping
hand."

"A helping hand?" I echo weakly.

"I'll do the rest tomorrow, and then I'll ring up the
delivery people," says Suze. "You know, it's a very good
system. You don't have to post them, or anything. They

just come and pick them up! And then they'll send you a check. It should come to about £284. Pretty good, huh?"

"Hang on." I turn round. "What do you mean, they'll send me a check?" Suze looks at me as though I'm stupid.

"Well, Bex, they are *your* frames."

"But you made them! Suze, you should get the money!"

"But I did them for you!" says Suze, and stares at me. "I did them so you could make your three hundred quid!"

I stare at her silently, feeling a sudden thickness in my throat. Suze made all these frames for me. Slowly I sit down on the bed, pick up one of the frames, and run my finger along the fabric. It's absolutely perfect. You could sell it in Liberty's.

"Suze, it's your money. Not mine," I say eventually. "It's your project now."

"Well, that's where you're wrong," says Suze, and a triumphant look spreads over her face. "I've got my own project."

She comes over to the bed, reaches behind the pile of made-up frames, and pulls something out. It's a photo frame, but it's nothing like a Fine Frame. It's upholstered in silver furry fabric, and the word ANGEL is appliquéd in pink across the top, and there are little silver pom-poms at the corners. It's the coolest, kitschest frame I've ever seen.

"Do you like it?" she says, a bit nervously.

"I love it!" I say, grabbing it from her hands and looking more closely at it. "Where did you get it?"

"I didn't get it anywhere," she says. "I made it."

"What?" I stare at her. "You . . . made this?"

"Yes. During *Neighbours*. It was awful, actually. Beth found out about Joey and Skye."

I'm completely astounded. How come Suze suddenly turns out to be so talented?

"So what do you reckon?" she says, taking the frame back and turning it over in her fingers. "Could I sell these?"

Could she sell these?

"Suze," I say quite seriously. "You're going to be a millionaire."

And we spend the rest of the evening getting very pissed and eating ice cream, as we always do when something good or bad happens to either one of us. We map out Suze's career as a high-flying businesswoman, and get quite hysterical trying to decide if she should wear Chanel or Prada when she goes to meet the queen. Somehow the discussion ends with us trying on each other's smartest outfits (Suze looks really good in my new Hobbs dress, much better than me), and by the time I get into bed, I've forgotten all about Luke Brandon, and Bank of Helsinki, and the rest of my disastrous day.

The next morning, it all comes rushing back to me like a horror movie. I wake up feeling pale and shaky, and desperately wishing I could take a sickie. I don't want to go to work. I want to stay at home under the duvet, watching daytime telly and being a millionairess entrepreneur with Suze.

But it's the busiest week of the month, and Philip'll never believe I'm ill.

So, somehow, I haul myself out of bed and into some clothes and onto the tube. At Lucio's I buy myself an extralarge cappuccino, and a muffin, *and* a chocolate brownie. I don't care if I get fat. I just need sugar and caffeine and chocolate, and as much as possible.

Luckily it's so busy, no one's talking very much, so I

don't have to bother telling everyone at the office what I did on my day off. Clare's tapping away at something and there's a pile of pages on my desk, ready for me to proofread. So after checking my e-mails—none—I scrunch miserably up in my chair, pick up the first one, and start to scan it.

"Market efficiencies dictate that greater risks must accompany greater reward. Fund managers understand the balance sheets and market momentum driving volatile stocks."

Oh God, this is boring.

"These experts therefore minimize risk in a way that the average investor cannot. For the small-time investor . . ."

"Rebecca?" I look up, to see Philip approaching my desk, holding a piece of paper. He doesn't look very happy, and for one terrible moment, I think he's spoken to Jill Foxton at William Green, has discovered everything, and is about to fire me. But as he gets nearer, I see it's only some dull-looking press release.

"I want you to go to this instead of me," he says. "It's on Friday. I'd go myself, but I'm going to be tied up here with Marketing."

"Oh," I say without enthusiasm, and take the piece of paper. "OK. What is it?"

"Personal Finance Fair at Olympia," he says. "We always cover it."

Yawn. Yawn yawn yawn . . .

"Barclays are giving a champagne lunchtime reception," he adds.

"Oh right!" I say, with more interest. "Well, OK. It sounds quite good. What exactly is it—"

I glance down at the paper, and my heart stops as I see the Brandon Communications logo at the top of the page.

"It's basically just a big fair," says Philip. "All sectors

of personal finance. Talks, stands, events. Just cover whatever sounds interesting. I leave it up to you."

"OK," I say after a pause. "Fine."

I mean, what do I care if Luke Brandon might be there? I'll just ignore him. I'll show him about as much respect as he showed me. And if he tries to talk to me, I'll just lift my chin firmly in the air, and turn on my heel, and . . .

"How are the pages going?" says Philip.

"Oh, great," I say, and pick the top one up again. "Should be finished soon." He gives a little nod and walks away, and I begin to read again.

". . . for the small-time investor, the risks attached to such stocks may outweigh the potential for reward."

Oh God, this is boring. I can't even bring myself to focus on what the words mean.

"More and more investors are therefore demanding the combination of stock-market performance with a high level of security. One option is to invest in a Tracker fund, which automatically 'tracks' the top one hundred companies at any time . . ."

Hmm. Actually, that gives me a thought. I reach for my Filofax, flip it open, and dial Elly's new direct number at Wetherby's.

"Eleanor Granger," comes her voice, sounding a bit far-off and echoey. Must be a dodgy line.

"Hi, Elly, it's Becky," I say. "Listen, whatever happened to Tracker bars? They're really yummy, aren't they? And I haven't eaten one for . . ."

There's a scuffly sort of sound on the line, and I gape at the receiver in surprise. In the distance, I can hear Elly, saying "I'm sorry. I'll just be a . . ."

"Becky!" she hisses down the phone. "I was on speakerphone! Our head of department was in my office."

"Oh God!" I say, aghast. "Sorry! Is he still there?"

"No," says Elly, and sighs. "God knows what he thinks of me now."

"Oh well," I say reassuringly. "He's got a sense of humor, hasn't he?"

Elly doesn't reply.

"Oh well," I say again, less certainly. "Anyway, are you free for a drink at lunchtime?"

"Not really," she says. "Sorry, Becky, I've really got to go." And she puts the phone down.

No one likes me anymore. Suddenly I feel a bit small and sad, and I scrunch up even more in my chair. Oh God, I hate today. I hate everything. I want to go hooome.

By the time Friday arrives, I have to say I feel a lot more cheerful. This is primarily because:

1. It's Friday.
2. I'm spending all day out of the office.
3. Elly phoned yesterday and said sorry she was so abrupt, but someone else came into the office just as we were talking. And she's going to be at the Personal Finance Fair.

Plus:

4. I have completely put the Luke Brandon incident from my mind. Who cares about him, anyway?

So as I get ready to go, I feel quite bouncy and positive. I put on my new gray cardigan over a short black shirt, and my new Hobbs boots—dark gray suede—and I have to say, I look bloody good in them. God, I love new clothes. If everyone could just wear new clothes every day, I reckon depression wouldn't exist anymore.

As I'm about to leave, a pile of letters comes through the letterbox for me. Several of them look like bills, and one is yet another letter from Endwich Bank. But I have a clever new solution to all these nasty letters: I just put them in my dressing table drawer and close it. It's the only way to stop getting stressed out about it. And it really does work. As I thrust the drawer shut and head out of the front door, I've already forgotten all about them.

The conference is buzzing by the time I get there. I give my name to the press officer at reception and I'm given a big, shiny courtesy carrier bag with the logo of HSBC on the side. Inside this, I find an enormous press pack complete with a photo of all the conference organizers lifting glasses of champagne to each other, a voucher for two drinks at the Sun Alliance Pimm's Stand, a raffle ticket to win £1,000 (invested in the unit trust of my choice), a big lollipop advertising Eastgate Insurance, and my name badge with PRESS stamped across the top. There's also a white envelope with the ticket to the Barclays Champagne Reception inside, and I put that carefully in my bag. Then I fasten my name badge prominently on my lapel and start to walk around the arena.

Normally, of course, the rule is to throw away your name badge. But the great thing about being PRESS at one of these events is that people fall over themselves to ply you with free stuff. A lot of it's just boring old leaflets about savings plans, but some of them are giving out free gifts and snacks, too. So after an hour, I've accumulated two pens, a paper knife, a mini box of

Ferrero Rocher chocolates, a helium balloon with Save & Prosper on the side, and a T-shirt with a cartoon on the front, sponsored by some mobile phone company. I've had two free cappuccinos, a *pain au chocolat,* some apple cider (from Somerset Savings), a mini pack of Smarties, and my Pimm's from Sun Alliance. (I haven't written a single note in my notebook, or asked a single question—but never mind.)

I've seen that some people are carrying quite neat little silver desk clocks, and I wouldn't mind one of those, so I'm just wandering along, trying to work out what direction they're coming from, when a voice says, "Becky!"

I look up—and it's Elly! She's standing at the Wetherby's display with a couple of guys in suits, waving at me to come over.

"Hi!" I say delightedly. "How *are* you?"

"Fine!" she says, beaming. "Really getting along well." And she does look the part, I have to say. She's wearing a bright red suit (Karen Millen, no doubt), and some really nice square-toed shoes, and her hair's tied back. The only thing I don't go for is the earrings. Why is she suddenly wearing pearl earrings? Maybe it's just to blend in with the others.

"God, I can't believe you're actually one of them!" I say, lowering my voice slightly. "I'll be interviewing you next!" I tilt my head earnestly, like Martin Bashir on *Panorama.* " 'Ms. Granger, could you tell me the aims and principles of Wetherby's Investments?' "

Elly gives a little laugh, then reaches into a box beside her.

"I'll give you this," she says, and hands me a brochure.

"Oh thanks," I say ironically, and stuff it into my bag.

I suppose she has to look good in front of her colleagues.

"It's actually quite an exciting time at Wetherby's," continues Elly. "You know we're launching a whole new range of funds next month? There are five altogether. UK Growth, UK Prospects, European Growth, European Prospects, and . . ."

Why is she telling me this, exactly?

"Elly . . ."

"And US Growth!" she finishes triumphantly. There isn't a flicker of humor in her eyes. Suddenly I find myself remembering Luke saying he wasn't surprised by Elly joining Wetherby's.

"Right," I say after a pause. "Well, that sounds . . . fab!"

"I could arrange for our PR people to give you a call, if you like," she says. "Fill you in a bit more."

What?

"No," I say hurriedly. "No, it's OK. So, erm . . . what are you doing afterward? Do you want to go for a drink?"

"No can do," she says apologetically. "I'm going to look at a flat."

"Are you moving?" I say in surprise. Elly lives in the coolest flat in Camden, with two guys who are in a band and get her into loads of free gigs and stuff. I can't think why she'd want to move.

"Actually, I'm buying," she says. "I'm looking around Streatham, Tooting . . . I just want to get on the first rung of that property ladder."

"Right," I say feebly. "Good idea."

"You should do it yourself, you know, Becky," she says. "You can't hang around in a student flat forever. Real life has to begin sometime!" She glances at one of her men in suits, and he gives a little laugh.

It's not a student flat, I think indignantly. And anyway, who defines "real life"? Who says "real life" is property ladders and hideous pearl earrings? "Shit-boring tedious life," more like.

"Are you going to the Barclays Champagne Reception?" I say as a last gasp, thinking maybe we can go and have some fun together. But she pulls a little face and shakes her head.

"I might pop in," she says, "but I'll be quite tied up here."

"OK," I say. "Well, I'll . . . I'll see you later."

I move away from the stand and slowly start walking toward the corner where the Champagne Reception's being held, feeling slightly dispirited. In spite of myself, a part of me starts wondering if maybe Elly's right and I'm wrong. Maybe I should be talking about property ladders and growth funds, too. Oh God, I'm missing the gene which makes you grow up and buy a flat in Streatham and start visiting Homebase every weekend. Everyone's moving on without me, into a world I don't understand.

But as I get near the entrance to the Champagne Reception, I feel my spirits rising. Whose spirits *don't* rise at the thought of free champagne? It's all being held in a huge tent, and there's a huge banner, and a band playing music, and a girl in a sash at the entrance, handing out Barclays key rings. When she sees my badge, she gives me a wide smile, hands me a white glossy press pack, and says, "Bear with me a moment." Then she walks off to a little group of people, murmurs in the ear of a man in a suit, and comes back. "Someone will be with you soon," she says. "In the meantime, let me get you a glass of champagne."

You see what I mean about being PRESS? Everywhere you go, you get special treatment. I accept a glass of champagne, stuff the press pack into my carrier bag, and take a sip. Oh, it's delicious. Icy cold and sharp and bubbly. Maybe I'll stay here for a couple of hours, I think, just drinking champagne until there's none left. They won't dare chuck me out, I'm PRESS. In fact, maybe I'll . . .

"Rebecca. Glad you could make it."

I look up and feel myself freeze. The man in the suit was Luke Brandon. Luke Brandon's standing in front of me, with an expression I can't quite read. And suddenly I feel sick. All that stuff I planned about playing it cool and icy isn't going to work—because just seeing his face, I feel hot with humiliation, all over again.

"Hi," I mutter, looking down. Why am I even saying hi to him?

"I was hoping you'd come," he says in a low, serious voice. "I very much wanted to—"

"Yes," I interrupt. "Well, I . . . I can't talk, I've got to mingle. I'm here to work, you know."

I'm trying to sound dignified, but there's a wobble in my voice, and I can feel my cheeks flush as he keeps gazing at me. So I turn away before he can say anything else, and march off toward the other side of the tent. I don't quite know where I'm heading, but I've just got to keep walking until I find someone to talk to.

The trouble is, I can't see anyone I recognize. It's all just groups of bank-type people laughing loudly together and talking about golf. They all seem really tall and broad-shouldered, and I can't even catch anyone's eye. God, this is embarrassing. I feel like a six-year-old at a grown-up's party. In the corner I spot Moira Channing from the *Daily Herald,* and she gives me a half flicker of recognition—but I'm certainly not going to talk to her. OK, just keep walking, I tell myself. Pretend you're on your way somewhere. Don't panic.

Then I see Luke Brandon on the other side of the

tent. His head jerks up as he sees me, and and he starts heading toward me. Oh God, quick. Quick. I've *got* to find somebody to talk to.

Right, how about this couple standing together? The guy's middle-aged, the woman's quite a lot younger, and they don't look as if they know too many people, either. Thank God. Whoever they are, I'll just ask them how they're enjoying the Personal Finance Fair and whether they're finding it useful, and pretend I'm making notes for my article. And when Luke Brandon arrives, I'll be too engrossed in conversation even to notice him. OK, go.

I take a gulp of champagne, approach the man, and smile brightly.

"Hi there," I say. "Rebecca Bloomwood, *Successful Saving*."

"Hello," he says, turning toward me and extending his hand. "Derek Smeath from Endwich Bank. And this is my assistant, Erica."

Oh my God.

I can't speak. I can't shake his hand. I can't run. My whole body's paralyzed.

"Hi!" says Erica, giving me a friendly smile. "I'm Erica Parnell."

"Yes," I say, after a huge pause. "Yes, hi."

Please don't recognize my name. Please don't recognize my voice.

"Are you a journalist, then?" she says, looking at my name badge and frowning. "Your name seems quite familiar."

"Yes," I manage. "Yes, you . . . you might have read some of my articles."

"I expect I have," she says, and takes an unconcerned sip of champagne. "We get all the financial mags in the office. Quite good, some of them."

Slowly the circulation is returning to my body. It's going to be OK, I tell myself. They don't have a clue.

"You journalists have to be expert on everything, I suppose," says Derek, who has given up trying to shake my hand and is swigging his champagne instead.

"Yes, we do really," I reply, and risk a smile. "We get to know all areas of personal finance—from banking to unit trusts to life insurance."

"And how do you acquire all this knowledge?"

"Oh, we just pick it up along the way," I say smoothly.

You know what? This is quite fun, actually, now that I've relaxed. And Derek Smeath isn't at all scary in the flesh. In fact, he's rather cozy and friendly, like some nice sitcom uncle.

"I've often thought," says Erica Parnell, "that they should do a fly-on-the-wall documentary about a bank." She gives me an expectant look and I nod vigorously.

"Good idea!" I say. "I think that would be fascinating."

"You should *see* some of the characters we get in! People who have absolutely no idea about their finances. Don't we, Derek?"

"You'd be amazed," says Derek. "Utterly amazed. The lengths people go to, just to avoid paying off their overdrafts! Or even talking to us!"

"Really?" I say, as though astonished.

"You wouldn't believe it!" says Erica. "I sometimes wonder—"

"Rebecca!" A voice booms behind me and I turn round in shock to see Philip, clutching a glass of champagne and grinning at me. What's *he* doing here?

"Hi," he says. "Marketing canceled the meeting, so I thought I'd pop along after all. How's it all going?"

"Oh, great!" I say, and take a gulp of champagne.

"This is Derek, and Erica . . . this is my editor, Philip Page."

"Endwich Bank, eh?" says Philip, looking at Derek Smeath's name badge. "You must know Martin Gollinger, then."

"We're not head office, I'm afraid," says Derek, giving a little laugh. "I'm the manager of our Fulham branch."

"Fulham!" says Philip. "Trendy Fulham."

And suddenly a warning bell goes off in my head. Dong-dong-dong! I've got to do something. I've got to say something; change the subject. But it's too late. I'm the spectator on the mountain, watching the trains collide in the valley below.

"Rebecca lives in Fulham," Philip's saying. "Who do you bank with, Rebecca? You're probably one of Derek's customers!" He laughs loudly at his own joke, and Derek laughs politely, too.

But I can't laugh. I'm frozen to the spot, watching Erica Parnell's face as it changes. As realization slowly dawns. She meets my eye, and I feel something icy drip down my spine.

"Rebecca Bloomwood," she says, in quite a different voice. "I *thought* I knew that name. Do you live in Burney Road, Rebecca?"

"That's clever!" says Philip. "How did you know that?" And he takes another swig of champagne.

Shut up, Philip, I think frantically. Shut *up*.

"So you do?" Her voice is sweet but sharp. Oh God, now Philip's looking at me, waiting for me to answer.

"Yes," I say in a strangled voice. I'm gripping my champagne glass so hard, I think I might break it.

"Derek, have you realized who this is?" says Erica pleasantly. "This is Rebecca Bloomwood, one of our customers. I think you spoke to her the other day.

Remember?" Her voice hardens. "The one with the dead dog?"

There's silence. I don't dare look at Derek Smeath's face. I don't dare look at anything except the floor.

"Well, there's a coincidence!" says Philip. "More champagne, anyone?"

"Rebecca Bloomwood," says Derek Smeath. He sounds quite faint. "I don't believe it."

"Yes!" I say, desperately slugging back the last of my champagne. "Ha-ha-ha! It's a small world. Well, I must be off and interview some more . . ."

"Wait!" says Erica, her voice like a dagger. "We were hoping to have a little meeting with you, Rebecca. Weren't we, Derek?"

"Indeed we were," says Derek Smeath. I feel a sudden trickle of fear. This man isn't like a cozy sitcom uncle anymore. He's like a scary exam monitor, who's just caught you cheating. "That is," he adds pointedly, "assuming your legs are both intact and you aren't suffering from any dreaded lurgey?"

"What's this?" says Philip cheerfully.

"How *is* the leg, by the way?" says Erica sweetly.

"Fine," I mumble. "Fine, thanks."

"Good," says Derek Smeath. "So we'll say Monday at nine-thirty, shall we?" He looks at Philip. "You don't mind if Rebecca joins us for a quick meeting on Monday morning, do you?"

"Of course not!" says Philip.

"And if she doesn't turn up," says Derek Smeath, "we'll know where to find her, won't we?" He gives me a sharp look, and I feel my stomach contract in fright.

"Rebecca'll turn up!" says Philip. He gives me a jokey grin, lifts his glass, and wanders off. Oh God, I think in panic. Don't leave me alone with them.

"Well, I'll look forward to seeing you," says Derek Smeath. He pauses, and gives me a beady look. "And if I remember rightly from our telephone conversation the other day, you'll be coming into some funds by then."

Oh shit. I thought he'd have forgotten about that.

"That's right," I say after a pause. "Absolutely. My aunt's money. Well remembered! My aunt left me some money recently," I explain to Erica Parnell.

Erica Parnell doesn't look impressed.

"Good," says Derek Smeath. "Then I'll expect you on Monday."

"Fine," I say, and smile even more confidently at him. "Looking forward to it already!"

OCTAGON ▸ *flair...style...vision*

FINANCIAL SERVICES DEPARTMENT
8TH FLOOR   TOWER HOUSE
LONDON ROAD WINCHESTER SO 44 3DR

Ms. Rebecca Bloomwood   Charge Card Number 7854 4567
Flat 2
4 Burney Rd.
London SW6 8FD

15 March 2000

Dear Ms. Bloomwood:

FINAL REMINDER

Further to my letter of 9 March, there is still an outstanding balance of £235.76 on your Octagon Silver Card. Should payment not arrive within the next seven days, your account will be frozen and further action will be taken.

I was glad to hear that you have found the Lord and accepted Jesus Christ as your savior; unfortunately this has no bearing on the matter.

I look forward to receiving your payment shortly.

Yours sincerely,

Grant Ellesmore
Customer Finance Manager

Thirteen

THIS IS BAD. I mean, I'm not just being paranoid, am I? This is really bad.

As I sit on the tube on my way home, I stare at my reflection—outwardly calm and relaxed. But inside, my mind's scurrying around like a spider, trying to find a way out. Round and round and round, legs flailing, no escape . . . OK, stop. Stop! Calm down and let's go through the options one more time.

Option One: Go to meeting and tell the truth.

I just can't. I *can't* go along on Monday morning and admit that there isn't £1,000 from my aunt and there never will be. What will they do to me? They'll get all serious, won't they? They'll sit me down and start going through all my expenditures and . . . Oh God, I feel sick at the thought of it. I can't do it. I can't go. End of story.

Option Two: Go to meeting and lie.

So, what, tell them the £1,000 is absolutely on its way, and that further funds will be coming through soon. Hmm. Possible. The trouble is, I don't think they'll believe me. So they'll still get all serious, sit me down, give me a lecture. No way.

Option Three: Don't go to meeting.

But if I don't, Derek Smeath will phone Philip and they'll start talking. Maybe the whole story will come out, and he'll find out I didn't actually break my leg. Or have glandular fever. And after that I won't ever be able to go back into the office. I'll be unemployed. My life will be over at the age of twenty-five.

Option Four: Go to meeting with check for £1,000. Perfect. Waltz in, hand over the check, say "Will there be anything else?" and waltz out again.

But how do I get £1,000 before Monday morning? *How?*

Option Five: Run away.

Which would be very childish and immature. Not worth considering.

I wonder where I could go? Maybe abroad somewhere. Las Vegas. Yes, and I could win a fortune at the casinos. A million pounds or something. Even more, perhaps. And then, yes, then I'd fax Derek Smeath, saying I'm closing my bank account due to his lack of faith in me.

God yes! Wouldn't that be great? "Dear Mr. Smeath, I was a little surprised at your recent implication that I have insufficient funds to cover my overdraft. As this check for £1.2 million shows, I have ample funds at my disposal, which I will shortly be moving to one of your competitors. Perhaps they will treat me with more respect. P.S., I am copying this letter to your superiors."

I love this idea so much, I lean back and wallow in it for a while, amending the letter over and over in my head. "Dear Mr. Smeath, as I tried to inform you discreetly at our last encounter, I am in fact a millionairess. If only you had trusted me, things might have been different."

God, he'll be sorry, won't he? He'll probably phone

up and apologize. Try and keep my business and say he hadn't meant to offend me. But it'll be too late. Hah! Ha-ha-ha-ha . . .

Oh blast. Missed my stop.

When I get home, Suze is sitting on the floor, surrounded by magazines.

"Hi!" she says brightly. "Guess what? I'm going to be in *Vogue*!"

"What?" I say disbelievingly. "Were you spotted on the streets or something?" Suze has got an excellent figure. She could easily be a model. But still . . . *Vogue*!

"Not me, silly!" she says. "My frames."

"Your *frames* are going to be in *Vogue*?" Now I really am disbelieving.

"In the June issue! I'm going to be in a piece called 'Just Relax: Designers Who Are Bringing the Fun Back into Interiors.' It's cool, isn't it? The only thing is, I've only made two frames so far, so I need to make a few more in case people want to buy them."

"Right," I say, trying to grasp all this. "So—how come *Vogue* is doing a piece about you? Did they . . . hear about you?" I mean, she only started making frames four days ago!

"No, silly!" she says, and laughs. "I phoned up Lally. Have you met Lally?" I shake my head. "Well, she's fashion editor of *Vogue* now, and she spoke to Perdy, who's the interiors editor, and Perdy phoned me back—and when I told her what my frames were like, she just went wild."

"Gosh," I say. "Well done."

"She told me what to say in my interview, too," Suze adds, and clears her throat importantly. "I want to create spaces for people to enjoy, not admire. There's a bit of the child in all of us. Life's too short for mini-malism."

"Oh right," I say. "Great!"

"No, wait, there was something else, too." Suze frowns thoughtfully. "Oh yes, my designs are inspired by the imaginative spirit of Gaudi. I'm going to phone up Charlie now," she adds happily. "I'm *sure* he's something at *Tatler*."

"Great," I say again.

And it is great.

I'm really glad for Suze. Of course I am. If Suze gets in *Vogue*, I'll be the proudest person in the world.

But at the same time there's a part of me that's think-ing, How come everything happens so easily for her? I bet Suze has never had to face a nasty bank manager in her life. And I bet she never will have to, either.

Immediately I feel a huge spasm of guilt. Why can't I just be glad for Suze and nothing else? Dispiritedly I sink down onto the floor and begin to flip through a magazine.

"By the way," says Suze, looking up from the phone. "Tarquin rang about an hour ago, to arrange your date." She grins wickedly. "Are you looking forward to it?"

"Oh," I say dully. "Of course I am."

I'd forgotten all about it, to be honest. But it's OK—I'll just wait until tomorrow afternoon and say I've got period pain. Easy. No one ever questions that, especially men.

"Oh yes," says Suze, gesturing to a *Harper's and Queen* open on the floor. "And look who I came across just now in the Hundred Richest Bachelors list! Oh hi, Charlie," she says into the phone. "It's Suze! Listen—"

I look down at the open *Harper's and Queen* and freeze. Luke Brandon is staring out of the page at me, an easy smile on his face.

Number 31, reads the caption. *Age 32. Estimated wealth: £10 million. Scarily intelligent entrepreneur. Lives in Chelsea; currently dating Sacha de Bonneville, daughter of the French billionaire.*

I don't want to know this. Why would I be interested in who Luke Brandon is dating? Not remotely interested.

Sacha. Sacha, with her million-pound suitcase and perfect figure and whole wardrobe full of Prada. She'll have immaculate nails, won't she? Of course she will. And hair that never goes wrong. And some really sexy French accent, and incredibly long legs . . .

Anyway, I'm not interested. Savagely I flip the page backward and start reading about Number 17, who sounds much nicer.

Dave Kington. Age 28. Estimated wealth: £20 million. Former striker for Manchester United, now management guru and sportswear entrepreneur. Lives in Hertfordshire, recently split from girlfriend, model Cherisse.

And anyway, Luke Brandon's boring. Everyone says so. All he does is work. Obsessed with money, probably.

Number 16, Ernest Flight. Age 52. Estimated wealth: £22 million. Chairman and major shareholder of the Flight Foods Corporation. Lives in Nottinghamshire, recently divorced from third wife Susan.

I don't even think he's that good-looking. Too tall. And he probably doesn't go to the gym or anything. Too busy. He's probably hideous underneath his clothes.

Number 15, Tarquin Cleath-Stuart. Age 26. Estimated wealth: £25 million. Landowner since inheriting family estate at age 19. V. publicity-shy. Lives in Perthshire and London with old nanny; currently single.

Anyway, what kind of man buys luggage as a present? I mean, a *suitcase*, for God's sake, when he had the whole of Harrods to choose from. He could have bought his girlfriend a necklace, or some clothes. Or he could have . . . He could have . . .

Hang on a moment, what was that?

What was that?

No. That can't be—Surely that's not—

And suddenly, I can't breathe. I can't move. My entire frame is concentrated on the blurry picture in front of me. Tarquin Cleath-Stuart? Tarquin Suze's-Cousin? *Tarquin?*

Tarquin . . . has . . . twenty-five . . . million . . . pounds?

I think I'm going to pass out, if I can ever ungrip my hand from this page. I'm staring at the fifteenth richest bachelor in Britain—and I know him.

Not only do I know him, I'm having dinner with him tomorrow night.

OH. MY. GOD.

I'm going to be a millionairess. A multimillionairess. I knew it. Didn't I know it? I *knew* it. Tarquin's going to fall in love with me and ask me to marry him and we'll get married in a gorgeous Scottish castle just like in *Four Weddings* (except with nobody dying on us).

Of course, I'll love him, too. By then.

I know I haven't exactly been attracted to him in the past . . . but it's all a matter of willpower, isn't it? I bet that's what most long-term successful couples would say counts in a relationship. Willpower and a desire to make it work. Both of which I absolutely have. You know what? I actually fancy him more already. Well, not exactly *fancy* . . . but just the thought of him makes me feel all excited, which must mean something, mustn't it?

It's going to happen. I'm going to be Mrs. Tarquin Cleath-Stuart and have £25 million.

And what will Derek Smeath say *then*? Hah!
Hah!

"D'you want a cup of tea?" says Suze, putting down
the phone. "Charlie's such a poppet. He's going to feature me in Britain's Up-and-Coming-Talent."

"Excellent," I say vaguely, and clear my throat.
"Just . . . just looking at Tarquin here."

I have to check. I have to check there isn't some other
Tarquin Cleath-Stuart. Please God, *please* let me be going out with the rich one.

"Oh yes," says Suze casually. "He's always in those
things." She runs her eyes down the text and shakes her
head. "God, they always exaggerate everything. Twenty-
five million pounds!"

My heart stops.

"Hasn't he got £25 million, then?" I says carelessly.

"Oh, no!" She laughs as though the idea's ridiculous.
"The estate's worth about . . . Oh, I don't know, £18
million."

Eighteen million pounds. Well, that'll do. That'll do
nicely.

"These magazines!" I say, and roll my eyes sympathetically.

"Earl Grey?" says Suze, getting up. "Or normal?"

"Earl Grey," I say, even though I actually prefer
Typhoo. Because I'd better start acting posh, hadn't I, if
I'm going to be the girlfriend of someone called Tarquin
Cleath-Stuart.

Rebecca Cleath-Stuart.

Becky Cleath-Stuart.

*Hi, it's Rebecca Cleath-Stuart here. Yes, Tarquin's wife.
We met at . . . Yes, I was wearing Chanel. How clever of
you!*

"By the way," I add, "did Tarquin say where I should
meet him?"

"Oh, he's going to come and pick you up," says Suze.

But of course he is. The fifteenth richest bachelor in Britain doesn't just meet you at a tube station, does he? He doesn't just say "See you under the big clock at Waterloo." He comes and picks you up.

Oh, this is it. This is it! Forget Luke Brandon, forget suitcases. My new life has finally begun.

I have never spent so long on getting ready for a date in my life. Never. The process starts at eight on Saturday morning when I look at my open wardrobe and realize that I don't have a *single* thing to wear—and only ends at seven-thirty that evening when I give my lashes another layer of mascara, spray myself in Coco Chanel, and walk into the sitting room for Suze's verdict.

"Wow!" she says, looking up from a frame she is upholstering in distressed denim. "You look . . . bloody amazing!"

And I have to say, I agree. I'm wearing all black—but expensive black. The kind of deep, soft black you fall into. A simple sleeveless dress from Whistles, the highest of Jimmy Choos, a pair of stunning uncut amethyst earrings. And please don't ask how much it all cost, because that's irrelevant. This is investment shopping. The biggest investment of my life.

I haven't eaten anything all day so I'm nice and thin, and for once my hair has fallen perfectly into shape. I look . . . well, I've never looked better in my life.

But of course, looks are only part of the package, aren't they? Which is why I cannily stopped off at Waterstones on the way home and bought a book on Wagner. I've been reading it all afternoon, while I waited for my nails to dry, and have even memorized a few little passages to throw into the conversation.

I'm not sure what else Tarquin is into, apart from Wagner. Still, that should be enough to keep us going. And anyway, I expect he's planning to take me somewhere really glamorous with a jazz band, so we'll be too busy dancing cheek to cheek to make conversation.

The doorbell rings and I give a little start. I have to admit, my heart is pounding with nerves. But at the same time I feel strangely cool. This is it. Here begins my new multimillion-pound existence. Luke Brandon, eat your heart out.

"I'll get it," says Suze, grinning at me, and disappears out into the hall. A moment later I hear her saying "Tarkie!"

"Suze!"

I glance at myself in the mirror, take a deep breath, and turn to face the door, just as Tarquin appears. His head is as bony as ever, and he's wearing another of his odd-looking suits. But somehow none of that seems to matter anymore. In fact, I'm not really taking in the way he looks. I'm just staring at him. Staring and staring at him, unable to speak; unable to frame any thought at all except: twenty-five million pounds.

Twenty-five million pounds.

The sort of thought that makes you feel dizzy and elated, like a fairground ride. I suddenly want to run around the room, yelling "Twenty-five million! Twenty-five million!" throwing bank notes up in the air as if I were in some Hollywood comedy caper.

But I don't. Of course I don't. I say, "Hi, Tarquin," and give him a dazzling smile.

"Hi, Becky," he says. "You look wonderful."

"Thanks," I say, and look bashfully down at my dress.

"D'you want to stay for a titchy?" says Suze, who is looking on fondly, as if she's my mother and this is senior prom night and I'm dating the most popular boy in school.

"Ermm . . . no, I think we'll just get going," says Tarquin, meeting my eye. "What do you think, Becky?"

"Absolutely," I say. "Let's go."

Fourteen

A TAXI IS CHUGGING OUTSIDE in the road, and Tarquin ushers me inside. To be honest, I'm a bit disappointed it isn't a chauffeur-driven limousine—but still. This is pretty good, too. Being whisked off in a taxi by one of Britain's most eligible bachelors to . . . who knows where? The Savoy? Claridges? Dancing at Annabel's? Tarquin hasn't told me yet where we're going.

Oh God, maybe it'll be one of those mad places where everything is served under a silver dome and there's a million knives and forks and snooty waiters looking on, just waiting to catch you out.

"I thought we'd just have a nice quiet supper," says Tarquin, looking over at me.

"Lovely," I say. "Nice quiet supper. Perfect."

Thank God. That probably means we're not heading for silver domes. We're going to some tiny tucked-away place that hardly anyone knows about. Some little private club where you have to knock on an anonymous-looking door in a back street, and you get inside and it's packed with celebrities sitting on sofas, behaving like normal people. Yes! And maybe Tarquin knows them all!

But of course he knows them all. He's a multimillion-aire, isn't he?

I look out of the window and see that we're driving past Harrods. And for just a moment, my stomach tightens painfully as I remember the last time I was here. Bloody suitcases. Bloody Luke Brandon. Huh. In fact, I wish he was walking along the road right now, so I could give him a careless, I'm-with-the-fifteenth-richest-single-man-in-Britain wave.

"OK," says Tarquin suddenly to the taxi driver. "You can drop us here." He grins at me. "Practically on the doorstep."

"Great," I say, and reach for the door.

Practically on the doorstep of where? As I get out I look around, wondering where on earth we're going. We're at Hyde Park Corner. What's at Hyde Park Corner? I turn round slowly, and glimpse a sign—and suddenly I realize what's going on. We're going to the Lanesborough!

Wow. How classy is that? Dinner at the Lanesborough. But naturally. Where else would one go on a first date?

"So," says Tarquin, appearing at my side. "I just thought we could get a bite to eat and then . . . see."

"Sounds good," I say, as we start walking.

Excellent! Dinner at the Lanesborough and then on to some glam nightclub. This is all shaping up wonderfully.

We walk straight past the entrance to the Lanesborough, but I'm not fazed by that. Everyone knows VIPs always go in through the back to avoid the paparazzi. Not that I can actually see any paparazzi, but it probably becomes a habit. We'll duck into some back alley, and walk through the kitchens while the chefs pretend they can't see us, and then emerge in the foyer. This is so cool.

"I'm sure you've been here before," says Tarquin apologetically. "Not the most original choice."

"Don't be silly!" I say, as we stop and head toward a pair of glass doors. "I simply adore . . ."

Hang on, where are we? This isn't the back entrance to anywhere. This is . . .

Pizza on the Park.

Tarquin's taking me to Pizza Express. I don't believe it. The fifteenth richest man in the country is taking me to bloody Pizza Express.

". . . pizza," I finish weakly. "Love the stuff."

"Oh good!" says Tarquin. "I thought we probably didn't want anywhere too flashy."

"Oh no." I pull what I think is a very convincing face. "I hate flashy places. Much better to have a nice quiet pizza together."

"That's what I thought," says Tarquin, turning to look at me. "But now I feel rather bad. You've dressed up so nicely . . ." He pauses doubtfully, gazing at my outfit. (As well he might. I didn't go and spend a fortune in Whistles for Pizza Express.) "I mean, if you wanted to, we could go somewhere a bit smarter. The Lanesborough's just around the corner . . ."

He raises his eyes questioningly, and I'm about to say "Oh, yes, please!" when suddenly, in a blinding flash, I realize what's going on. This is a test, isn't it? It's like choosing out of three caskets in a fairy tale. Everyone knows the rules. You *never* choose the gold shiny one. Or even the quite impressive silver one. What you're supposed to do is choose the dull little lead one, and then there's a flash of light and it turns into a mountain of jewels. So this is it. Tarquin's testing me, to see whether I like him for himself.

Which, frankly, I find rather insulting. I mean, who does he think I am?

"No, let's stay here," I say, and touch his arm briefly. "Much more relaxed. Much more . . . fun."

Which is actually quite true. And I do like pizza. And that yummy garlic bread. Mmm. You know, now I come to think about it, this is quite a good choice.

As the waiter hands us our menus, I give a cursory flash down the list, but I already know what I want. It's what I always have when I go to Pizza Express—Fiorentina. The one with spinach and an egg. I know, it sounds weird, but honestly, it's delicious.

"Would you like an aperitif?" says the waiter, and I'm about to say what I usually do, which is Oh, let's just have a bottle of wine, when I think, Sod it, I'm having dinner with a multimillionaire here. I'm bloody well going to have a gin and tonic.

"A gin and tonic," I say firmly, and look at Tarquin, daring him to look taken aback. But he grins at me and says, "Unless you wanted champagne?"

"Oh," I say, completely thrown.

"I always think champagne and pizza is a good combination," he says, and looks at the waiter. "A bottle of Moet, please."

Well, this is more like it. This is a lot more like it. Champagne and pizza. And Tarquin is actually being quite normal.

The champagne arrives and we toast each other and take a few sips. I'm really starting to enjoy myself. Then I spot Tarquin's bony hand edging slowly toward mine on the table. And in a reflex action—completely without meaning to—I whip my fingers away, pretending I have to scratch my ear. A flicker of disappointment passes over his face and I find myself giving a really fake, embarrassed cough and looking intently at a picture on the wall to my left.

I can do this, I tell myself firmly. I *can* be attracted to him. It's just a matter of self-control and possibly also getting very drunk. So I lift my glass and take several huge gulps. I can feel the bubbles surging into my head, singing happily "I'm going to be a millionaire's wife! I'm going to be a millionaire's wife!" And when I look back at Tarquin, he already seems a bit more attractive (in a stoaty kind of way). Alcohol is obviously going to be the key to our marital happiness.

My head is filled with a happy vision of our wedding day. Me in some wonderful designer dress; my mum and dad looking on proudly. No more money troubles ever. *Ever.* The fifteenth richest man in the country. A house in Belgravia. Mrs. Tarquin Cleath-Stuart. Just imagining it, I feel almost faint with longing.

I smile as warmly as I can at Tarquin, who hesitates—then smiles back. Phew. I haven't wrecked things. It's all still on. Now we just need to discover that we're utter soul mates with loads of things in common.

"I love the—" I say.

"Do you—"

We both speak at once.

"Sorry," I say. "Do carry on."

"No, *you* carry on," says Tarquin.

"Oh," I say. "Well . . . I was just going to say again how much I love the picture you gave Suze." No harm in complimenting his taste again. "I *love* horses," I add for good measure.

"Then we should go riding together," says Tarquin. "I know a very good livery near Hyde Park. Not quite the same as in the country, of course . . ."

"What a wonderful idea!" I say. "That would be such fun!"

There's no way anyone's getting me on a horse. Not even in Hyde Park. But that's OK, I'll just go along with the plan and then, on the day, say I've twisted my ankle or something.

"Do you like dogs?" asks Tarquin.

"I love dogs," I say confidently.

Which is sort of true. I wouldn't actually like to *have* a dog—too much hard work and hairs everywhere. But I like seeing Labradors running across the park. And cute little puppies. That kind of thing.

We lapse into silence, and I take a few sips of champagne.

"Do you like *EastEnders*?" I ask eventually. "Or are you a . . . a *Coronation Street* person?"

"I've never watched either, I'm afraid," says Tarquin apologetically. "I'm sure they're very good."

"Well . . . they're OK," I say. "Sometimes they're really good, and other times . . ." I tail off a bit feebly, and smile at him. "You know."

"Absolutely," exclaims Tarquin, as though I've said something really interesting.

There's another awkward silence. This is getting a bit sticky.

"Are there good shops, where you live in Scotland?" I say at last. Tarquin pulls a little face.

"I wouldn't know. Never go near shops if I can help it."

"Oh right," I say, and take a deep gulp of champagne. "No, I . . . I hate shops, too. Can't *stand* shopping."

"Really?" says Tarquin in surprise. "I thought all girls loved shopping."

"Not me!" I say. "I'd far rather be . . . out on the

moors, riding along. With a couple of dogs running behind."

"Sounds perfect," says Tarquin, smiling at me. "We'll have to do it sometime."

This is more like it! Common interests. Shared pursuits.

And OK, maybe I haven't been completely honest, maybe they aren't exactly my interests at the moment. But they could be. They *can* be. I can easily get to like dogs and horses, if I have to.

"Or . . . or listening to Wagner, of course," I say casually.

"Do you really like Wagner?" says Tarquin. "Not everyone does."

"I *adore* Wagner," I insist. "He's my favorite composer." OK, quick—what did that book say? "I love the . . . er . . . sonorous melodic strands which interweave in the Prelude."

"The Prelude to what?" says Tarquin interestedly.

Oh shit. Is there more than one Prelude? I take a gulp of champagne, playing for time, desperately trying to recall something else from the book. But the only other bit I can remember is "Richard Wagner was born in Leipzig."

"All the Preludes," I say at last. "I think they're all . . . fab."

"Right," says Tarquin, looking a bit surprised.

Oh God. That wasn't the right thing to say, was it? Change the subject. Change the subject.

Luckily, at that moment, a waiter arrives with our garlic bread, and we can get off the subject of Wagner. And Tarquin orders some more champagne. Somehow, I think we're going to need it.

Which means that by the time I'm halfway through my Fiorentina, I've drunk almost an entire bottle of champagne and I'm . . . Well, frankly, I'm completely pissed. My face is tingling and my eyes are sparkling, and my arm gestures are a lot more erratic than usual. But this doesn't matter. In fact, being pissed is a *good* thing—because it means I'm also delightfully witty and lively and am more-or-less carrying the conversation single-handedly. Tarquin is also pissed, but not as much as me. He's got quieter and quieter, and kind of thoughtful. And he keeps gazing at me.

As I finish my last scraps of pizza and lean back pleasurably, he stares at me silently for a moment, then reaches into his pocket and produces a little box.

"Here," he says. "This is for you."

I have to admit, for one heart-stopping moment I think, This is it! He's proposing!

But of course, he's not proposing, is he? He's just giving me a little present.

I knew that.

So I open it, and find a leather box, and inside is a little gold brooch in the shape of a horse. Lots of fine detail; beautifully crafted. A little green stone (emerald?) for the eye.

Really not my kind of thing.

"It's gorgeous," I breathe in awe. "Absolutely . . . stunning."

"It's rather jolly, isn't it?" says Tarquin. "Thought you'd like it."

"I *adore* it." I turn it over in my fingers then look up at him and blink a couple of times with misty eyes. God, I'm drunk. I think I'm actually *seeing* through champagne. "This is so thoughtful of you," I murmur.

Plus, I don't really wear brooches. I mean, where are you supposed to put them? Slap bang in the middle of a really nice top? I mean, come on. And they always leave great brooch-holes everywhere.

"It'll look lovely on you," says Tarquin after a pause—and suddenly I realize he's expecting me to put it on.

Aaargh! It'll ruin my lovely Whistles dress! And who wants a horse galloping across their tits, anyway!

"I *must* put it on," I say, and open the clasp. Gingerly, I thread it through the fabric of my dress and clasp it shut, already feeling it pull the dress out of shape.

"It looks wonderful," says Tarquin, meeting my gaze. "But then . . . you always look wonderful."

I feel a dart of apprehension as I see him leaning forward. He's going to try and hold my hand again, isn't he? And probably kiss me. I glance at Tarquin's lips— parted and slightly moist—and give an involuntary shudder. Oh God. I'm not quite ready for this. I mean, obviously I *do* want to kiss Tarquin, of course I do. In fact, I find him incredibly attractive. It's just . . . I think I need some more champagne first.

"That scarf you were wearing the other night," says Tarquin. "It was simply stunning. I looked at you in that, and I thought . . ."

Now I can see his hand edging toward mine.

"My Denny and George scarf!" I cut in brightly, before he can say anything else. "Yes, that's lovely, isn't it? It was my aunt's, but she died. It was really sad, actually."

Just keep talking, I think. Keep talking brightly and gesture a lot.

"But anyway, she left me her scarf," I continue hurriedly. "So I'll always remember her through that. Poor Aunt Ermintrude."

"I'm really sorry," says Tarquin, looking taken aback. "I had no idea."

"No. Well . . . her memory lives on through her good

works," I say, and give him a little smile. "She was a very charitable woman. Very . . . giving."

"Is there some sort of foundation in her name?" says Tarquin. "When my uncle died—"

"Yes!" I say gratefully. "Exactly that. The . . . the Ermintrude Bloomwood Foundation for . . . violinists," I improvise, catching sight of a poster for a musical evening. "Violinists in Mozambique. That was her cause."

"Violinists in Mozambique?" echoes Tarquin.

"Oh, absolutely!" I hear myself babbling. "There's a desperate shortage of classical musicians out there. And culture is so enriching, whatever one's material circumstances."

I can't *believe* I'm coming out with all this rubbish. I glance apprehensively up at Tarquin—and to my complete disbelief, he looks really interested.

"So, what exactly is the foundation aiming to do?" he asks.

What am I getting myself into here?

"To . . . to fund six violin teachers a year," I say after a pause. "Of course, they need specialist training, and special violins to take out there. But the results will be very worthwhile. They're going to teach people how to make violins, too, so they'll be self-sufficient and not dependent on the West."

"Really?" Tarquin's brow is furrowed. Have I said something that doesn't make sense?

"Anyway," I give a little laugh. "That's enough about me and my family. Have you seen any good films recently?"

This is good. We can talk about films, and then the bill will come, and then . . .

"Wait a moment," says Tarquin. "Tell me—how's the project going so far?"

"Oh," I say. "Ahm . . . quite well. Considering. I haven't

really kept up with its progress recently. You know, these things are always—"

"I'd really like to contribute something," he says, interrupting me.

What?

He'd like to *what*?

"Do you know who I should make the check payable to?" he says, reaching into his jacket pocket. "Is it the Bloomwood Foundation?"

And as I watch, paralyzed in astonishment, he brings out a Coutts checkbook.

A pale gray Coutts checkbook.

The fifteenth richest man in the country.

"I'm . . . I'm not sure," I hear myself say, as though from a great distance. "I'm not sure of the *exact* wording."

"Well, I'll make it payable to you, then, shall I?" he says. "And you can pass it on." Briskly he starts to write.

Pay Rebecca Bloomwood.
The sum of.
Five . . .

Five hundred pounds. It must be. He wouldn't just give five miserable . . .

Thousand pounds.
T. A. J. Cleath-Stuart.

I can't believe my eyes. Five thousand pounds, on a check, addressed to me.

Five thousand pounds, which belongs to Aunt Ermintrude and the violin teachers of Mozambique.

If they existed.

"Here you are," says Tarquin, and hands me the check—and as though in a dream, I find myself reaching out toward it.

Pay Rebecca Bloomwood the sum of five thousand pounds.

I read the words again slowly—and feel a wave of relief so strong, it makes me want to burst into tears. The sum of five thousand pounds. More than my overdraft and my VISA bill put together. This check would solve all my problems, wouldn't it? It would solve all my problems in one go. And, OK, I'm not exactly violinists in Mozambique—but Tarquin would never know the difference, would he?

And anyway, what's £5,000 to a multimillionaire like Tarquin? He probably wouldn't even notice whether I paid it in or not. A pathetic £5,000, when he's got £25 million! If you work it out as a fraction of his wealth it's . . . well, it's laughable, isn't it? It's the equivalent of about fifty pence to normal people. Why am I even hesitating?

"Rebecca?"

Tarquin is staring at me—and I realize my hand is still inches away from the check. *Come on, take it,* I instruct myself firmly. *It's yours. Take the check and put it in your bag.* With a heroic effort, I stretch out my hand further, willing myself to close my fingers around the check. I'm getting closer . . . closer . . . almost there . . . my fingers are trembling with the effort . . .

It's no good, I can't. I just can't do it. I can't take his money.

"I can't take it," I say in a rush. I pull my hand away and feel myself flushing. "I mean . . . I'm not actually sure the foundation is accepting money yet."

"Oh right," says Tarquin, looking slightly taken aback.

"I'll tell you who to make a check payable to when I've got more details," I say, and take a deep gulp of champagne. "You'd better tear that up."

He slowly rips the paper, but I can't look. I stare into

my champagne glass, feeling like crying. Five thousand pounds. It would have changed my life. It would have solved everything. I would have written out checks immediately to Suze, to VISA, to Octagon . . . to all of them. Then I would have taken this check and presented it to Derek Smeath on Monday morning. Perhaps I wouldn't have cleared every single penny of overdraft, but I would have made a start. A bloody good start.

Tarquin reaches for the box of matches on the table, sets the scraps of paper alight in the ashtray, and we both watch as they briefly flame. Then he puts down the matches, smiles at me, and says, "Do excuse me a minute."

He gets up from the table and heads off toward the back of the restaurant, and I take another gulp of champagne. Then I lean my head in my hands and give a little sigh. Oh well, I think, trying to be philosophical. Maybe I'll win £5,000 in a raffle or something. Maybe Derek Smeath's computer will go haywire and he'll be forced to cancel all my debts and start again. Maybe some utter stranger really *will* pay off my VISA bill for me by mistake.

Maybe Tarquin will come back from the loo and ask me to marry him.

I raise my eyes, and they fall with an idle curiosity on the Coutts checkbook, which Tarquin has left on the table. That's the checkbook of the fifteenth richest unmarried man in the country. Wow. I wonder what it's like inside? He probably writes enormous checks all the time, doesn't he? He probably spends more money in a day than I spend in a year.

On impulse, I pull the checkbook toward me and open it. I don't know quite what I'm looking for—really, I'm just hoping to find some excitingly huge amount. But the first stub is only for £30. Pathetic! I flip on a bit, and find £520. Payable to Arundel & Son, whoever they are. Then, a bit later on, there's one for £7,515 to American Express. Well, that's more like it. But I mean, really, it's not the most exciting read in the world. This could be anybody's checkbook. This could practically be mine.

I close it and push it back toward his place, and glance up. As I do so, my heart freezes. Tarquin is staring straight at me.

He's standing by the bar, being directed to the other side of the restaurant by a waiter. But he isn't looking at the waiter. He's looking at me. As our eyes meet, my stomach lurches. Oh, damn.

Damn. What exactly did he see?

Quickly I pull my hand back from his checkbook and take a sip of champagne. Then I look up and pretend to spot him for the first time. I give a bright little smile, and after a pause he smiles back. Then he disappears off again and I sink back into my chair, trying to look relaxed.

OK, don't panic, I instruct myself. Just behave naturally. He probably didn't see you. And even if he did— it's not the hugest crime in the world, is it, looking at his checkbook? If he asks me what I was doing, I'll say I was . . . checking he'd filled in his stub correctly. Yes. That's what I'll say I was doing if he mentions it.

But he doesn't. He comes back to the table, silently pockets his checkbook, and says politely, "Have you finished?"

"Yes," I say. "Yes, I have, thanks."

I'm trying to sound as natural as possible—but I'm aware my voice sounds guilty, and my cheeks are hot.

"Right," he says. "Well, I've paid the bill . . . so shall we go?"

And that's it. That's the end of the date. With impeccable courtesy, Tarquin ushers me to the door of Pizza

on the Park, hails a taxi, and pays the driver the fare
back to Fulham. I don't dare ask him if he'd like to
come back or go for a drink somewhere else. There's a
coldness about my spine which stops me uttering the
words. So we kiss each other on the cheek and he tells
me he had a delightful evening, and I thank him again
for a lovely time.

And I sit in the taxi all the way back to Fulham with
a jumpy stomach, wondering what exactly he saw.

I say good-night to the taxi driver and reach for my
keys. I'm thinking that I'll go and run a hot bath and sit
in it, and calmly try to work out exactly what happened
back there. Did Tarquin really see me looking through
his checkbook? Maybe he just saw me pushing it back
toward his place in a helpful manner. Maybe he saw
nothing at all.

But then why did he suddenly become all stiff and
polite? He must have seen something; suspected something. And then he'll have noticed the way I flushed and
couldn't meet his eye. Oh God, why do I always have to
look so guilty? I wasn't even *doing* anything. I was just
curious.

Perhaps I should have quickly said something—
made some joke about it. Turned it into a lighthearted,
amusing incident. But what kind of joke can you make
about leafing through someone's private checkbook?
Oh God, I'm so *stupid*. Why did I ever touch the bloody
thing? I should have just sat, quietly sipping my drink.

But in my defense . . . he left it on the table, didn't
he? He can't be that secretive about it. And I don't *know*
that he saw me looking through it, do I? Maybe I'm just
paranoid.

As I put my key into the lock, I'm actually feeling quite positive. OK, so Tarquin wasn't that friendly just now—but he might have been feeling ill or something. Or maybe he just didn't want to rush me. What I'll do is, tomorrow I'll send a nice chatty note to him, saying thanks again, and suggesting we go and see some Wagner together. Excellent idea. And I'll mug up a bit about the Preludes, so that if he asks me which one again, I'll know exactly what to say. Yes! This is all going to be fine. I need never have worried.

I swing the door open, taking off my coat—and then my heart gives a flip. Suze is waiting for me in the hall. She's sitting on the stairs, waiting for me—and there's a reproachful expression on her face.

"Oh, Bex," she says, and shakes her head. "I've just been speaking to Tarquin."

"Oh right," I say, trying to sound natural—but aware that my voice is a frightened squeak. I turn away, take my coat, and slowly unwind my scarf, playing for time. What exactly has he said to her?

"I don't suppose there's any point asking you *why*?" she says after a pause.

"Well," I falter, feeling sick. God, I could do with a cigarette.

"I'm not *blaming* you, or anything. I just think you should have . . ." She shakes her head and sighs. "Couldn't you have let him down more gently? He sounded quite upset. The poor thing was really keen on you, you know."

This isn't quite making sense. Let him down more gently?

"What exactly—" I lick my dry lips. "What exactly did he say?"

"Well, he was only really phoning to tell me you'd

left your umbrella behind," says Suze. "Apparently one of the waiters came rushing out with it. But of course I asked him how the date had gone . . ."

"And . . . and what did he say?"

"Well," says Suze, and gives a little shrug. "He said you'd had a really nice time—but you'd pretty much made it clear you didn't want to see him again."

"Oh."

I sink down onto the floor, feeling rather weak. So that's it. Tarquin did see me leafing through his checkbook. I've ruined my chances with him completely.

But he didn't tell Suze what I'd done. He protected me. Pretended it was my decision not to carry things on. He was a gentleman.

In fact—he was a gentleman all evening, wasn't he? He was kind to me, and charming, and polite. And all I did, all throughout the date, was tell him lies.

Suddenly I want to cry.

"I just think it's such a shame," says Suze. "I mean, I know it's up to you and everything—but he's such a sweet guy. And he's had a crush on you for ages! You two would go perfectly together." She gives me a wheedling look. "Isn't there *any* chance you might go out with him again?"

"I . . . I honestly don't think so," I say in a scratchy voice. "Suze . . . I'm a bit tired. I think I'll go to bed."

And without meeting her eye, I get up and slowly walk down the corridor to my room.

Ms. Rebecca Boomwood
Flat 2
4 Burney Rd.
London SW6 8FD

23 March 2000

Dear Ms. Boomwood:

Thank you very much for your application for a Bank of London Easifone Loan.

Unfortunately, "buying clothes and makeup" was not deemed a suitable purpose for such a substantial unsecured loan, and your application has been turned down by our credit team.

Thank you very much for considering Bank of London.

Yours sincerely,

Margaret Hopkins
Loans Adviser

Ms. Rebecca Bloomwood
Flat 2
4 Burney Rd.
London SW6 8FD

23 March 2000

Dear Ms. Bloomwood:

I am writing to confirm our meeting at 9:30 A.M. on
Monday 26 March, here at our Fulham office. Please ask
for me at reception.

I look forward to seeing you then.

Yours sincerely,

Derek Smeath
Manager

Fifteen

I HAVE NEVER IN MY LIFE felt as terrible as I do when I wake up the next morning. Never.

The first thing I feel is pain. Exploding sparks of pain as I try to move my head; as I try to open my eyes; as I try to work out a few basics like: Who am I? What day is it? Where should I be right now?

For a while I lie quite still, panting with the exertion of just being alive. In fact, my face is growing scarlet and I'm almost starting to hyperventilate, so I force myself to slow down and breathe regularly. *In . . . out, in . . . out*. And then surely everything will come back to me and I will feel better. *In . . . out, in . . . out*.

OK . . . Rebecca. That's right. I'm Rebecca Bloomwood, aren't I? *In . . . out, in . . . out*.

What else? Dinner. I had dinner somewhere last night. *In . . . out, in . . . out*.

Pizza. I had pizza. And who was I with, again? *In . . . out, in . . .*

Tarquin.

Out.

Oh God. Tarquin.

Leafing through checkbook. Everything ruined. All my own fault.

A familiar wave of despair floods over me and I close my eyes, trying to calm my throbbing head. At the same time, I remember that last night, when I went back to my room, I found the half bottle of malt whisky which Scottish Prudential once gave me, still sitting on my dressing table. I opened it up—even though I don't like whisky—and drank . . . well, certainly a few cupfuls. Which might possibly explain why I'm feeling so ill now.

Slowly I struggle to a sitting position and listen for sounds of Suze, but I can't hear anything. The flat's empty. It's just me.

Me and my thoughts.

Which, to be honest, I can't endure. My head's pounding and I feel pale and shaky—but I've got to get moving; distract myself. I'll go out, have a cup of coffee somewhere quiet and try to get myself together.

I manage to get out of bed, stagger to my chest of drawers, and stare at myself in the mirror. I don't like what I see. My skin's green, my mouth is dry, and my hair's sticking to my skin in clumps. But worst of all is the expression in my eyes: a blank, miserable self-loathing. Last night I was given a chance—a fantastic opportunity on a silver platter. I threw it in the bin—and hurt a really sweet, decent chap, to boot. God, I'm a disaster. I don't deserve to live.

I head to King's Road, to lose myself in the anonymous bustle. The air's crisp and fresh, and as I stride along it's almost possible to forget about last night. Almost, but not quite.

I go into Aroma, order a large cappuccino, and try to drink it normally. As if everything's fine and I'm just another girl out on a Sunday for some shopping. But I can't do it. I can't escape my thoughts. They're churning round in my head, like a record that won't stop, over and over and over.

If only I hadn't picked up his checkbook. If only I hadn't been so *stupid*. It was all going so well. He really liked me. We were holding hands. He was planning to ask me out again. If only I could go back; if only I could play the evening again . . .

Don't think about it. Don't think about what could have been. It's too unbearable. If I'd played it right, I'd probably be sitting here drinking coffee with Tarquin, wouldn't I? I'd probably be well on my way to becoming the fifteenth richest woman in the country.

Instead of which, I have unpaid bills stacked up in my dressing table drawer. I have a meeting with my bank manager on Monday morning. I have no idea what I'm going to do. No idea at all.

Miserably I take a sip of coffee and unwrap my little chocolate. I'm not in the mood for chocolate, but I stuff it into my mouth anyway.

The worst thing—the very worst thing of all—is that I was actually starting to quite like Tarquin. Maybe he isn't God's gift in the looks department, but he's very kind, and quite funny, in his own way. And that brooch—it's really quite sweet.

And the way he didn't tell Suze what he'd seen me doing. And the way he *believed* me when I told him I liked dogs and Wagner and bloody violinists in Mozambique. The way he was so completely, utterly unsuspicious.

Now I really am going to start crying.

Roughly I brush at my eyes, drain my cup, and stand up. Out on the street I hesitate, then begin walking briskly again. Maybe the breeze will blow these unbearable thoughts out of my head.

But I stride and stride, and I still feel no better. My

head's aching and my eyes are red and I could really do with a drink or something. Just a little something, to make me feel a bit better. A drink, or a cigarette, or . . .

I look up, and I'm in front of Octagon. My favorite shop in the whole world. Three floors of clothes, accessories, furnishings, gifts, coffee shops, juice bars, and a florist which makes you want to buy enough bouquets to fill your house.

I've got my purse with me.

Just something small, to cheer me up. A T-shirt or something. Or even some bubble bath. I *need* to buy myself something. I won't spend much. I'll just go in, and . . .

I'm already pushing my way through the doors. Oh God, the relief. The warmth, the light. This is where I belong. This is my natural habitat.

Except that even as I'm heading toward the T-shirts, I'm not quite as happy as I should be. I look through the racks, trying to summon the excitement I usually feel at buying myself a little treat—but somehow today I feel a bit empty. Still, I choose a cropped top with a silver star in the middle and put it over my arm, telling myself I feel better already. Then I spot a rack of dressing gowns. I could do with a new dressing gown, as a matter of fact.

As I finger a lovely white waffle robe, I can hear a little voice at the back of my head, like a radio turned down low. *Don't do it. You're in debt. Don't do it. You're in debt.*

But quite frankly, what does it matter now? It's too late to make any difference. I'm already in debt; I might as well be more in debt. Almost savagely, I pull the dressing gown down from the rack and put it over my arm. Then I reach for the matching waffle slippers. No point buying one without the other.

The checkout point is directly to my left, but I ignore it. I'm not done yet. I head for the escalators and go up to the home- furnishing floor. Time for a new duvet set. White, to match my new dressing gown. And a pair of bolster cushions.

Every time I add something to my pile, I feel a little whoosh of pleasure, like a firework going off. And for a moment, everything's all right. But then, gradually, the light and sparkles disappear, and I'm left with cold dark blackness again. So I look feverishly around for something else. A huge scented candle. A bottle of Jo Malone shower gel. A bag of handmade potpourri. As I add each one, I feel a whoosh—and then blackness. But the whooshes are getting shorter and shorter each time. Why won't the pleasure stay? Why don't I feel happier?

"Can I help you?" says a voice, interrupting my thoughts. A young assistant, dressed in the Octagon outfit of white shirt and linen trousers, has come up and is looking at my pile of stuff on the floor. "Would you like me to hold some of these while you continue shopping?"

"Oh," I say blankly, and look down at the stuff I've accumulated. It's actually quite a lot by now. "No, don't worry. I'll just . . . I'll just pay for this lot."

Somehow, between us, we manage to lug all my shopping across the beechwood floor to the stylish granite checkout point in the middle, and the assistant begins to scan everything through. The bolster cushions have been reduced, which I hadn't realized, and while she's checking the exact price, a queue begins to form behind me.

"That'll be £370.56," she says eventually, and smiles at me. "How would you like to pay?"

"Erm . . . debit card," I say, and reach for my purse. As she's swiping it, I eye up my carrier bags and wonder how I'm going to get all this stuff home.

But immediately my thoughts bounce away. I don't want to think about home. I don't want to think about Suze, or Tarquin, or last night. Or any of it.

"I'm sorry," says the girl apologetically, "but there's something wrong with your card. It won't authorize the purchase." She hands it back to me. "Do you have anything else?"

"Oh," I say, slightly flustered. "Well . . . here's my VISA card."

How embarrassing. And anyway, what's wrong with my card? It looks all right to me. I must call the bank about this.

The bank. Meeting tomorrow, with Derek Smeath. Oh God. Quick, think about something else. Look at the floor. Glance about the shop. There's quite a big line of people now, and I can hear coughing and clearing of throats. Everyone's waiting for me. As I meet the eye of the woman behind me, I smile awkwardly.

"No," says the girl. "This one's no good either."

"What?" I whip round in shock. How can my VISA card be no good? It's my *VISA* card, for God's sake. Accepted all over the world. What's going on? It doesn't make any sense. It doesn't make any . . .

My words stop midstream, and a nasty chill feeling begins to creep over me. All those letters. Those letters I've been putting in my dressing table drawer. Surely they can't have . . .

No. They can't have done.

My heart starts to thump in panic. I know I haven't been that great at paying my bills—but I need my VISA card. I *need* it. They can't just cancel it, just like that.

"There are other people waiting," says the girl, gesturing to the queue. "So if you aren't able to pay . . ."

"Of course I'm able to pay," I say stiffly. With trembling hands I scrabble in my purse and eventually produce my silver Octagon charge card. It was buried under all the others, so I can't have used it for a while. "Here," I say. "I'll put it all on this."

"Fine," says the girl curtly, and swipes the card.

It's only as we're waiting silently for the authorization that I begin to wonder whether I've actually paid off my Octagon account. They sent me a nasty letter a while ago, didn't they? Something about an outstanding balance. But I'm sure I paid it off, ages ago. Or at least some of it. Didn't I? I'm sure I . . .

"I'm just going to have to make a quick call," says the assistant, staring at her machine. She reaches for the phone next to the till.

"Hi," she says. "Yes, if I can give you an account number . . ."

Behind me, somebody sighs loudly. I can feel my face growing hotter and hotter. I don't dare look round. I don't dare move.

"I see," says the assistant eventually, and puts down the phone. She looks up—and at the sight of her face, my stomach gives a lurch. Her expression isn't apologetic or polite anymore. It's plain unfriendly.

"Our financial services department would like you to contact them urgently," she says curtly. "I'll give you the number."

"Right," I say, trying to sound relaxed. As though this is a fairly normal request. "OK. Well, I'll do that. Thanks." I hold my hand out for my charge card. I'm not interested in my shopping anymore. All I want to do is get out of here as quickly as possible.

"I'm sorry, I'm afraid your account's been frozen," says the assistant without lowering her voice. "I'm going to have to retain your card."

I stare at her in disbelief, feeling my face prickling with shock. Behind me there's an interested rustle as everybody hears this and starts nudging each other.

"So, unless you have another means of paying . . ." she adds, looking at my heap of stuff on the counter. My waffle robe. My new duvet set. My scented candle. A huge, conspicuous pile of stuff. Stuff I don't need. Stuff I can't pay for. Suddenly the sight of it all makes me feel sick.

Numbly I shake my head. I feel as if I've been caught stealing.

"Elsa," calls the assistant. "Will you deal with this, please? The customer isn't going to make the purchase after all." She gestures to the pile of stuff, and the other assistant moves it along the counter, out of the way, her face deliberately blank.

"Next, please."

The woman behind me steps forward, avoiding my eye in embarrassment, and slowly I turn away. I have never felt so humiliated in all my life. The whole floor seems to be looking at me—all the customers, all the sales assistants, all whispering and nudging. *Did you see? Did you see what happened?*

With wobbling legs I walk away, not looking right or left. This is a nightmare. I just have to get out, as quickly as possible. I have to get out of the shop and onto the street and go . . .

Go where? Home, I suppose.

But I can't go back and face Suze. She's been so kind to me and how have I behaved? She has no idea what a horrible person I am. If I go home, I'll have to hear her telling me again how sweet Tarquin is. Or even worse, risk bumping into him. Oh God. The very thought makes me feel sick.

What am I going to do? Where am I going to go?

Shakily I begin to walk along the pavement, looking away from the mocking window displays. What can I do? Where can I go? I feel empty, almost light-headed with panic.

I pause at a corner, waiting for a traffic light to change, and look blankly at a display of cashmere jumpers to my left. And suddenly, at the sight of a scarlet Pringle golfing jumper, I feel tears of relief springing to my eyes. There's one place I can go. One place I can always go.

Sixteen

WHEN I TURN UP at my parents' house that afternoon without warning, saying I want to stay for a few
days, I can't say they seem shocked.

In fact, so unsurprised do they seem that I begin to
wonder if they've been expecting this eventuality all
along, ever since I moved to London. Have they been
waiting every week for me to arrive on the doorsteps
with no luggage and red eyes? They're certainly behaving as calmly as a hospital casualty team operating an
emergency procedure.

Except that surely the casualty team wouldn't keep
arguing about the best way to resuscitate the patient?
After a few minutes, I feel like going outside, letting
them decide on their plan of action, and ringing the bell
again.

"You go upstairs and have a nice hot bath," says
Mum, as soon as I've put down my handbag. "I expect
you're exhausted!"

"She doesn't have to have a bath if she doesn't want
to!" retorts Dad. "She might want a drink! D'you want a
drink, darling?"

"Is that *wise*?" says Mum, shooting him a meaningful

what- if-she's-an-alkie? look, which presumably I'm not supposed to notice.

"I don't want a drink, thanks," I say. "But I'd love a cup of tea."

"Of course you would!" says Mum. "Graham, go and put the kettle on." And she gives him another meaningful look. As soon as he's disappeared into the kitchen, she comes close to me and says, in a lowered voice, "Are you feeling all right, darling? Is anything . . . wrong?"

Oh God, there's nothing like your mother's sympathetic voice to make you want to burst into tears.

"Well," I say, in a slightly uncertain voice. "Things have been better. I'm just . . . in a bit of a difficult situation at the moment. But it'll be all right in the end." I give a small shrug and look away.

"Because . . ." She lowers her voice even more. "Your father isn't as old-fashioned as he seems. And I know that if it were a case of us looking after a . . . a little one, while you pursued your career . . ."

What?

"Mum, don't worry!" I exclaim sharply. "I'm not pregnant!"

"I never said you were," she says, and flushes a little. "I just wanted to offer you our support."

My parents watch too many soap operas, that's their trouble. In fact, they were probably *hoping* I was pregnant. By my wicked married lover whom they could then murder and bury under the patio.

And what's this "offer you our support" business, anyway? My mum would never have said that before she started watching Ricki Lake.

"Well, come on," she says. "Let's sit you down with a nice cup of tea."

And so I follow her into the kitchen, and we all sit

down with a cup of tea. And I have to say, it is very nice. Hot strong tea and a chocolate bourbon biscuit. Perfect. I close my eyes and take a few sips, and then open them again, to see both my parents gazing at me with naked curiosity all over their faces. Immediately my mother changes her expression to a smile, and my father gives a little cough—but I can tell, they are *gagging* to know what's wrong.

"So," I say cautiously, and both their heads jerk up. "You're both well, are you?"

"Oh yes," says my mother. "Yes, *we're* fine."

There's another silence.

"Becky?" says my father gravely, and both Mum and I swivel to face him. "Are you in some kind of trouble we should know about? Only tell us if you want to," he adds hastily. "And I want you to know—we're there for you."

That's another bloody Ricki Lake–ism, too. My parents should really get out more.

"Are you all right, darling?" says Mum gently—and she sounds so kind and understanding that, in spite of myself, I find myself putting down my cup with a bit of a clatter and saying "To tell you the truth, I am in a spot of bother. I didn't want to worry you, so I haven't said anything before now . . ." I can feel tears gathering in my eyes.

"What is it?" says Mum in a panicky voice. "You're on drugs, aren't you?"

"No, I'm not on drugs!" I exclaim. "I'm just . . . It's just that I . . . I'm . . ." I take a deep gulp of tea. This is even harder than I thought it would be. Come on, Rebecca, just *say* it.

I close my eyes and clench my hand tightly around my mug.

"The truth is . . ." I say slowly.

"Yes?" says Mum.

"The truth is . . ." I open my eyes. "I'm being stalked. By a man called . . . called Derek Smeath."

There's silence apart from a long hiss as my father sucks in breath.

"I knew it!" says my mother in a sharp, brittle voice. "I knew it! I knew there was something wrong!"

"We all knew there was something wrong!" says my father, and rests his elbows heavily on the table. "How long has this been going on, Becky?"

"Oh, ahm . . . months now," I say, staring into my tea. "It's just . . . pestering, really. It's not serious or anything. But I just couldn't deal with it anymore."

"And who is this Derek Smeath?" says Dad. "Do we know him?"

"I don't think so. I came across him . . . I came across him through work."

"Of course you did!" says Mum. "A young, pretty girl like you, with a high-profile career . . . I knew this was going to happen!"

"Is he another journalist?" says Dad, and I shake my head.

"He works for Endwich Bank. He does things like . . . like phone up and pretend he's in charge of my bank account. He's really convincing."

There's silence while my parents digest this and I eat another chocolate bourbon.

"Well," says Mum at last. "I think we'll have to phone the police."

"No!" I exclaim, spluttering crumbs all over the table. "I don't want the police! He's never threatened me or anything. In fact, he's not really a stalker at all. He's just a pain. I thought if I disappeared for a while . . ."

"I see," says Dad, and glances at Mum. "Well, that makes sense."

"So what I suggest," I say, meshing my hands tightly in my lap, "is that if he rings, you say I've gone abroad and you don't have a number for me. And . . . if anyone else rings, say the same thing. Even Suze. I've left her a message saying I'm OK—but I don't want anyone to know where I am."

"Are you sure?" says Mum, wrinkling her brow. "Wouldn't it be better to go to the police?"

"No!" I say quickly. "That would only make him feel important. I just want to vanish for a bit."

"Fine," says Dad. "As far as we're concerned, you're not here."

He reaches across the table and clasps my hand. And as I see the worry on his face, I hate myself for what I'm doing.

But I simply can't tell my kind, loving parents that their so-called successful daughter with her so-called top job is in fact a disorganized, deceitful mess, up to her eyeballs in debt.

And so we have supper (Waitrose Cumberland Pie) and watch an Agatha Christie adaption together, and then I go upstairs to my old bedroom, put on an old nightie, and go to bed. And when I wake up the next morning, I feel more happy and rested than I have for weeks.

Above all, staring at my old bedroom ceiling, I feel safe. Cocooned from the world; wrapped up in cotton wool. No one can get me here. No one even *knows* I'm here. I won't get any nasty letters and I won't get any nasty phone calls and I won't get any nasty visitors. It's like a sanctuary. I feel as if I'm fifteen again, with nothing to worry about but my homework. (And I haven't even got any of that.)

It's at least nine o'clock before I rouse myself and get out of bed, and as I do so, it occurs to me that miles away in London, Derek Smeath is expecting me to arrive for a meeting in half an hour. A slight twinge passes through my stomach and for a moment I consider phoning up the bank and giving some excuse. But even as I'm considering it, I know I'm not going to do it. I don't even want to acknowledge the bank's existence. I want to forget all about it.

None of it exists anymore. Not the bank, not VISA, not Octagon. All eliminated from my life, just like that.

The only call I make is to the office, because I don't want them sacking me in my absence. I phone at nine-twenty—before Philip gets in—and get Mavis on reception.

"Hello, Mavis?" I croak. "It's Rebecca Bloomwood here. Can you tell Philip I'm ill?"

"You poor thing!" says Mavis. "Is it bronchitis?"

"I'm not sure," I croak. "I've got a doctor's appointment later. I must go. Bye."

And that's it. One phone call, and I'm free. No one suspects anything—why should they? I feel light with relief. It's so easy to escape. I should have done this long ago.

At the back of my mind, like a nasty little gremlin, is the knowledge that I won't be able to stay here forever. That sooner or later things will start to catch up with me. But the point is—not yet. And in the meantime, I'm not even going to think about it. I'm just going to have a nice cup of tea and watch *Morning Coffee* and blank my mind out completely.

As I go into the kitchen, Dad's sitting at the table, reading the paper. There's the smell of toast in the air, and Radio Four in the background. Just like when I was younger and lived at home. Life was simple then. No bills, no demands, no threatening letters. An enormous wave of nostalgia overcomes me, and I turn away to fill the kettle, blinking slightly.

"Interesting news," says Dad, jabbing at *The Daily Telegraph*.

"Oh yes?" I say, putting a tea bag in a mug. "What's that?"

"Scottish Prime has taken over Flagstaff Life."

"Oh right," I say vaguely. "Right. Yes, I think I'd heard that was going to happen."

"All the Flagstaff Life investors are going to receive huge windfall payments. The biggest ever, apparently."

"Gosh," I say, trying to sound interested. I reach for a copy of *Good Housekeeping,* flick it open, and begin to read my horoscope.

But something's niggling at my mind. Flagstaff Life. Why does that sound familiar? Who was I talking to about . . .

"Martin and Janice next door!" I exclaim suddenly. "They're with Flagstaff Life! Have been for fifteen years."

"Then they'll do very well," says Dad. "The longer you've been with them, the more you get, apparently."

He turns the page with a rustle, and I sit down at the table with my cup of tea and a *Good Housekeeping* article on making Easter cakes. It's not fair, I find myself thinking resentfully. Why can't I get a windfall payment? Why doesn't Endwich Bank get taken over? Then they could pay me a windfall big enough to wipe out my overdraft.

"Any plans for the day?" says Dad, looking up.

"Not really," I say, and take a sip of tea.

Any plans for the rest of my life? Not really.

In the end, I spend a pleasant, unchallenging morning helping Mum sort out a pile of clothes for a jumble sale, and at twelve-thirty we go into the kitchen to make a sandwich. As I look at the clock, the fact that I was supposed to be at Endwich Bank three hours ago flickers through my mind—but very far off, like a distant clock chiming. My whole London life seems remote and unreal now. *This* is where I belong. Away from the madding crowd; at home with Mum and Dad, having a nice relaxed uncomplicated time.

After lunch I wander out into the garden with one of Mum's mail-order catalogues, and go and sit on the bench by the apple tree. A moment later, I hear a voice from over the garden fence, and look up. It's Martin from next door. Hmm. I'm not feeling very well disposed toward Martin at the moment.

"Hello, Becky," he says softly. "Are you all right?"

"I'm fine, thanks," I say shortly. *And I don't fancy your son*, I feel like adding.

"Becky," says Janice, appearing beside Martin, holding a garden trowel. She gives me an awestricken look. "We heard about your . . . *stalker*," she whispers.

"It's criminal," says Martin fiercely. "These people should be locked up."

"If there's anything we can do," says Janice. "Anything at all. You just let us know."

"I'm fine, really," I say, softening. "I just want to stay here for a while. Get away from it all."

"Of course you do," says Martin. "Wise girl."

"I was saying to Martin this morning," says Janice, "you should hire a bodyguard."

"Can't be too careful," says Martin. "Not these days."

"The price of fame," says Janice, sorrowfully shaking her head. "The price of fame."

"Well, anyway," I say, trying to get off the subject of my stalker. "How are you?"

"Oh, we're both well," says Martin. "I suppose." To

my surprise there's a forced cheerfulness to his voice. He glances at Janice, who frowns and shakes her head slightly.

"Anyway, you must be pleased with the news," I say brightly. "About Flagstaff Life."

There's silence.

"Well," says Martin. "We would have been."

"No one could have known," says Janice, giving a little shrug. "It's just one of those things. Just the luck of the draw."

"What is?" I say, puzzled. "I thought you were getting some huge great windfall."

"It appears . . ." Martin rubs his face. "It appears not in our case."

"But . . . but why?"

"Martin phoned them up this morning," says Janice. "To see how much we would be getting. They were saying in the papers that long-term investors would be getting *thousands*. But—" She glances at Martin.

"But what?" I say, feeling a twinge of alarm.

"Apparently we're no longer eligible," says Martin awkwardly. "Since we switched our investment. Our old fund would have qualified, but . . ." He coughs. "I mean, we will get *something*—but it'll only be about £100."

I stare at him blankly.

"But you only switched—"

"Two weeks ago," he says. "That's the irony. If we'd just held on a little bit longer . . . Still, what's done is done. No point whining about it." He gives a resigned shrug and smiles at Janice, who smiles back.

And I look away and bite my lip.

A nasty cold feeling is creeping over me. They took the decision to switch their money based on my advice, didn't they? They asked me if they should switch funds, and I said go ahead. But now I come to think of it . . . hadn't I already heard a rumor about this take-over? Oh God. Could I have stopped this?

"We could never have known these windfalls would happen," says Janice, and puts her hand comfortingly on his arm. "They keep these things secret right up until the last minute, don't they, Becky?"

My throat's too tight to answer. I can remember exactly now. It was Alicia who first mentioned the take-over. The day before I came down here. And then Philip said something about it in the office. Something about with-profits holders doing well. Except . . . I wasn't really listening. I think I was doing my nails at the time.

"Twenty thousand pounds, they reckon we would have got if we'd stayed," says Martin gloomily. "Makes you sick to think about it. Still, Janice is right. We couldn't have known. Nobody knew."

Oh God. This is all my fault. It's all my fault. If I'd just used my brain and *thought* for once . . .

"Oh, Becky, don't look so upset!" says Janice. "This isn't your fault! You didn't know! Nobody knew! None of us could have—"

"I knew," I hear myself saying miserably.

There's a flabbergasted silence.

"What?" says Janice faintly.

"I didn't *know,* exactly," I say, staring at the ground. "But I heard a sort of rumor about it a while ago. I should have said something when you asked me. I should have warned you to wait. But I just . . . didn't think. I didn't re-member." I force myself to look up and meet Martin's as-tonished gaze. "I . . . I'm really sorry. It's all my fault."

There's silence, during which Janice and Martin glance at each other and I hunch my shoulders, loathing myself. Inside, I can hear the phone ringing, and footsteps as someone goes to answer it.

"I see," says Martin eventually. "Well . . . not to worry. These things happen."

"Don't blame yourself, Becky," says Janice kindly. "It was our decision to switch funds, not yours."

"And remember, you've been under a lot of pressure yourself recently," adds Martin, putting a sympathetic hand on my arm. "What with this dreadful stalking business."

Now I really feel like dirt. I don't deserve these people's kindness. I've just lost them £20,000, through being too bloody lazy to keep up with events I'm supposed to know about. I'm a financial journalist, for God's sake.

And suddenly, standing there in my parents' garden on a Monday afternoon, I'm plunged to the lowest ebb of my life. What have I got going for me? Nothing. Not one thing. I can't control my money, I can't do my job, and I haven't got a boyfriend. I've hurt my best friend, I've lied to my parents—and now I've ruined my neighbors.

"Becky?"

My father's voice interrupts us all, and I look up in surprise. He's striding across the lawn toward us, a perturbed look on his face.

"Becky, don't be alarmed," he says, "but I've just had that Derek Smeath chap on the phone."

"What?" I say, feeling my face drain in horror.

"The stalker?" exclaims Janice, and Dad gives a sober nod.

"Quite an unpleasant fellow, I would say. He was really quite aggressive toward me."

"But how does he know Becky's here?" says Janice.

"Obviously just taking potluck," says Dad. "I was very civil, simply told him you weren't here and that I had no idea where you were."

"And . . . and what did he say?" I say in a strangled voice.

"Came out with some nonsense about a meeting you'd set up with him." Dad shakes his head. "The chap's obviously deluded."

"You should change your number," advises Martin. "Go ex-directory."

"But where was he phoning from?" says Janice, her voice rising in alarm. "He could be anywhere!" She starts looking agitatedly around the garden as though expecting him to jump out from behind a bush.

"Exactly," says Dad. "So, Becky, I think maybe you should come inside now. You never know with these characters."

"OK," I say numbly. I can't quite believe this is happening. I look at Dad's kind, concerned face and suddenly I can barely meet his eye. Oh, *why* didn't I tell him and Mum the truth? Why did I let myself get into this situation?

"You look quite shaken up, dear," says Janice, and pats me on the shoulder. "You go and have a nice sit down."

"Yes," I say. "Yes, I think I will."

And Dad leads me off gently toward the house, as though I were some kind of invalid.

This is all getting out of hand. Now not only do I feel like an utter failure, I don't feel safe anymore, either. I feel exposed and edgy. I sit on the sofa next to Mum, drinking tea and watching *Countdown*, and every time there's a sound outside, I jump.

What if Derek Smeath's on his way here? How long would it take him to drive here from London? An hour and a half? Two, if the traffic's bad?

He wouldn't do that. He's a busy man.

But he *might*.

Or send the bailiffs round. Oh God. Threatening men in leather jackets. My stomach is squeezed tight with fear. In fact, I'm beginning to feel as though I genuinely am being stalked.

As the commercial break begins, Mum reaches for a catalogue full of gardening things. "Look at this lovely birdbath," she says. "I'm going to get one for the garden."

"Great," I mutter, unable to concentrate.

"They've got some super window boxes, too," she says. "You could do with some nice window boxes in your flat."

"Yes," I say. "Maybe."

"Shall I put you down for a couple? They're not expensive."

"No, it's OK."

"You can pay by check, or VISA . . ." she says, flipping over the page.

"No, really, Mum," I say, my voice sharpening slightly.

"You could just phone up with your VISA card, and have them delivered—"

"Mum, stop it!" I cry. "I don't want them, OK?"

Mum gives me a surprised, slightly reproving look and turns to the next page of her catalogue. And I gaze back at her, full of a choking panic. My VISA card doesn't work. My debit card doesn't work. Nothing works. And she has no idea.

Don't think about it. Don't think about it. I grab for an ancient copy of the *Radio Times* on the coffee table and begin to leaf through it blindly.

"It's a shame about poor Martin and Janice, isn't it?" says Mum, looking up. "Fancy switching funds two weeks before the takeover! Such bad luck!"

"I know," I mumble, staring down at a page of listings. I don't want to be reminded about Martin and Janice.

"It seems a terrible coincidence," says Mum, shaking her head. "That the company should launch this new fund just before the takeover. You know, there must be a lot of people who did exactly what Martin and Janice did, who have lost out. Dreadful, really." She looks at the television. "Oh look, it's starting again."

The cheery *Countdown* music begins to play, and a round of applause rattles noisily from the television. But I'm not listening to it, or even paying any attention to the vowels and consonants. I'm thinking about what Mum has just said. A terrible coincidence—but it wasn't exactly a coincidence, was it? The bank actually wrote to Janice and Martin, suggesting that they switch funds. They even offered an incentive, didn't they? A carriage clock.

Suddenly I feel alert. I want to see the letter from Flagstaff Life—and find out exactly how long before the takeover they sent it.

" 'ENDING,' " says Mum, staring at the screen. "That's six. Ooh, there's an S. Can you have 'ENDINGS'?"

"I'm just . . . popping next door," I say, getting to my feet. "I won't be a minute."

As Martin opens the front door, I see that he and Janice have also been sitting in front of the telly, watching *Countdown*.

"Hi," I say sheepishly. "I was just wondering—could I have a quick chat?"

"Of course!" says Martin. "Come on in! Would you like a sherry?"

"Oh," I say, a little taken aback. I mean, not that I'm

against drinking, obviously—but it isn't even five o'clock yet. "Well—OK then."

"Never too early for a sherry!" says Martin.

"I'll have another one, thanks, Martin," comes Janice's voice from the sitting room.

Blow me down. They're a pair of alcoholics!

Oh God, perhaps this is my fault too. Perhaps their financial mishap has driven them to seek solace in alcohol and daytime television.

"I was just wondering," I say nervously as Martin pours dark brown sherry into a schooner. "Just out of interest, could I have a look at that letter you got from Flagstaff Life, asking you to switch funds? I was wondering when they sent it."

"It arrived the very day we saw you," says Martin. "Why do you want to see it?" He raises his glass. "Your good health."

"Cheers," I say, and take a sip. "I'm just wondering—"

"Come into the living room," he interrupts, and ushers me through from the hall. "Here you are, my love," he adds, and gives Janice her sherry. "Bottoms up!"

"Sssh," she replies. "It's the numbers game! I need to concentrate."

"I thought I might do a little investigation into this," I whisper to Martin as the *Countdown* clock ticks round. "I feel so bad about it."

"Fifty times 4 is 200," says Janice suddenly. "Six minus 3 is 3, times 7 is 21 and add it on."

"Well done, love!" says Martin, and roots about in a carved oak sideboard. "Here's the letter," he says. "So—do you want to write an article or something?"

"Possibly," I say. "You wouldn't mind, would you?"

"Mind?" He gives a little shrug. "No, I wouldn't think so."

"Sssh!" says Janice. "It's the Countdown Conundrum."

"Right," I whisper. "Well, I'll just . . . I'll just take this, shall I?"

"Explicate!" yells Janice. "No, exploited!"

"And . . . thanks for the sherry." I take a huge gulp, shuddering slightly at its sticky sweetness, then put my glass down and tiptoe out of the room.

Half an hour later, sitting in my bedroom, I've read the letter from Flagstaff Life six times and I'm sure there's something fishy about it. How many investors must have switched funds after receiving this crappy carriage clock offer—and missed out on their windfall? More to the point, how much money must Flagstaff Life have saved? Suddenly I really want to know. There's a growing indignation in me; a growing determination to find out exactly what's been going on and, if it's what I suspect, to expose it. To print the truth and warn others. For the first time in my life, I'm actually *interested* in a financial story.

And I don't just want to write it up for *Successful Saving*, either. This deserves the widest audience possible. Eric Foreman's card is still in my purse, with his direct telephone number printed at the top, and I take it out. I go to the phone and quickly punch in the number before I can change my mind.

"Eric Foreman, *Daily World*," comes his voice, booming down the line.

Am I really doing this?

"Hi," I say nervously. "I don't know if you remember me. Rebecca Bloomwood from *Successful Saving*. We met at the Sacrum Asset Management press conference."

"That's right, so we did," he says cheerfully. "How are you, my love?"

"I'm fine," I say, and clench my hand tightly around the receiver. "Absolutely fine. Ahm . . . I was just wondering, are you still running your series on 'Can We Trust the Money Men?' "

"We are, as it goes," says Eric Foreman. "Why?"

"It's just . . ." I swallow. "I think I've got a story that might interest you."

Seventeen

I HAVE NEVER before worked so hard on an article. Never.

Mind you, I've never before been asked to write one so quickly. At *Successful Saving,* we get a whole month to write our articles—and we complain about that. When Eric Foreman said, "Can you do it by tomorrow?" I thought he was joking at first. I jauntily replied, "Of course!" and nearly added, "In fact, I'll have it with you in five minutes' time!" Then, *just* in time, I realized he was serious. Crikey.

So I'm round at Martin and Janice's first thing the next morning with a Dictaphone, writing down exactly all the information on their investment and trying to get in lots of heart-wrenching details as advised by Eric.

"We need human interest," he told me over the phone. "None of your dull financial reporting here. Make us feel sorry for them. Make us weep. A hardworking, ordinary couple, who thought they could rely on a few savings to see them through their old age. Ripped off by the fat cats. What kind of house do these people live in?"

"Ahmm . . . a four-bedroom detached house in Surrey."

"Well, for Christ's sake don't put that in!" he boomed. "I want honest, poor, and proud. Never demanded a penny off the state, saved to provide for themselves. Trusted a respectable financial institution. And all it did was kick them in the face." He paused, and it sounded as if he might be picking his teeth. "That kind of thing. Think you can manage it?"

"I . . . ahm . . . yes! Of course!" I stuttered.

Oh God, I thought as I put down the phone. What have I got myself into?

But it's too late to change my mind now. So the next thing is to persuade Janice and Martin that they don't mind appearing in *The Daily World*. The trouble is, it's not exactly *The Financial Times,* is it? Or even the normal *Times.* (Still, it could be a lot worse. It could be *The Sun*—and they'd end up sandwiched between a topless model and a blurred paparazzi shot of Posh Spice.)

Luckily, however, they're so bowled over that I'm making all this effort on their behalf, they don't seem to care which newspaper I'm writing for. And when they hear that a photographer's coming over at midday to take their picture, you'd think the queen was coming to visit.

"My hair!" says Janice in dismay, staring into the mirror. "Have I time to get Maureen in to give me a blow-dry?"

"Not really. And it looks lovely," I say reassuringly. "Anyway, they want you as natural as possible. Just . . . honest, ordinary people." I glance around the living room, trying to pick up poignant details to put into my article.

An anniversary card from their son stands proudly on the

well-polished mantelpiece. But there will be no celebration this year for Martin and Janice Webster.

"I must phone Phyllis!" says Janice. "She won't believe it!"

"You weren't ever a soldier, or anything?" I say thoughtfully to Martin. "Or a . . . a fireman? Anything like that. Before you became a travel agent."

"Not really, love," says Martin, wrinkling his brow. "Just the Cadets at school."

"Oh, right," I say, brightening. "That might do."

Martin Webster fingers the Cadet badge he was so proud to wear as a youth. His life has been one of hard work and service for others. Now, in his retirement years, he should be enjoying the rewards he deserves.

But the fat cats have conned him out of his nest egg. The Daily World asks . . .

"I've photocopied all the documents for you," says Martin. "All the paperwork. I don't know if it'll be any use . . ."

"Oh thanks," I say, taking the pile of pages from him. "I'll have a good read through these."

When honest Martin Webster received a letter from Flagstaff Life, inviting him to switch investment funds, he trusted the money men to know what was best for him.

Two weeks later he discovered they had tricked him out of a £20,000 windfall.

"My wife is ill as a result of all this," he said. "I'm so worried."

Hmm.

"Janice?" I say, looking up casually. "Do you feel all right? Not . . . unwell, or anything?"

"A bit nervous, to be honest, dear," she says, looking round from the mirror. "I'm never very good at having my picture taken."

"My nerves are shot to pieces," said Mrs. Webster in a ragged voice. "I've never felt so betrayed in all my life."

"Well, I think I've got enough now," I say, getting up and switching off my Dictaphone. "I might have to *slightly* digress from what's on the tape—just to make the story work. You don't mind, do you?"

"Of course not!" says Janice. "You write what you like, Becky! We trust you."

I look at her soft, friendly face and feel a sudden shot of determination. This time I'll get it right.

"So what happens now?" says Martin.

"I'll have to go and talk to Flagstaff Life," I say. "Get them to give their defense."

"What defense?" says Martin. "There is no defense for what they did to us!"

I grin at him. "Exactly."

I'm full of happy adrenaline. All I need to do is get a quote from Flagstaff Life, and I can start writing the piece. I haven't got long: it needs to be finished by two o'clock if it's going to make tomorrow's edition. Why has work never seemed so exciting before?

Briskly I reach for the phone and dial Flagstaff's number—only to be told by the switchboard operator that all press inquiries are dealt with out of house. She gives me a number, which seems rather familiar, and I frown at it for a moment, then punch it in.

"Hello," says a smooth voice. "Brandon Communications."

Of course. Suddenly I feel a bit shaky. The word *Brandon* has hit me right in the stomach like a punch. I'd forgotten all about Luke Brandon. To be honest, I'd forgotten all about the rest of my life. And frankly, I don't want to be reminded of it.

But it's OK—I don't have to speak to him personally, do I?

"Hi!" I say. "It's Rebecca Bloomwood here. Ermm . . . I just wanted to talk to somebody about Flagstaff Life."

"Let me check . . ." says the voice. "Yes, that's Luke Brandon's client. I'll just put you through to his assistant . . ." And the voice disappears before I can say anything.

Oh God.

I can't do this. I can't speak to Luke Brandon. My questions are jotted down on a piece of paper in front of me, but as I stare at them, I'm not reading them. I'm remembering the humiliation I felt that day in Harvey Nichols. That horrible plunge in my stomach, as I heard the patronizing note in his voice and suddenly realized what he thought of me. A nothing. A joke.

OK, I *can* do this, I tell myself firmly. I'll just be very stern and businesslike and ask my questions, and . . .

"Rebecca!" comes a voice in my ear. "How are you! It's Alicia here."

"Oh," I say in surprise. "I thought I was going to speak to Luke. It's about Flagstaff Life."

"Yes, well," says Alicia. "Luke Brandon is a very busy man. I'm sure I can answer any questions you have."

"Oh, right," I say, and pause. "But they're not your client, are they?"

"I'm sure that won't matter in this case," she says, and gives a little laugh. "What did you want to know?"

"Right," I say, and look at my list. "Was it a deliberate strategy for Flagstaff Life to invite their investors to move out of with- profits just before they announced windfalls? Some people lost out a lot, you know."

"Right . . ." she says. "Thanks, Camilla, I'll have smoked salmon and lettuce."

"What?" I say.

"Sorry, yes, I am with you," she says. "Just jotting it down . . . I'll have to get back to you on that, I'm afraid."

"Well, I need a response soon!" I say, giving her my number. "My deadline's in a few hours."

"Got that," says Alicia. Suddenly her voice goes muffled. "No, smoked salmon. OK then, Chinese chicken. Yes." The muffle disappears. "So, Rebecca, any other questions? Tell you what, shall I send you our latest press pack? That's bound to answer any other queries. Or you could fax in your questions."

"Fine," I say curtly. "Fine, I'll do that." And I put the phone down.

For a while I stare straight ahead in brooding silence. Stupid patronizing cow. Can't even be bothered to take my questions seriously.

Then gradually it comes to me that this is the way I always get treated when I ring up press offices. No one's ever in any hurry to answer my questions, are they? People are always putting me on hold, saying they'll ring me back and not bothering. I've never minded before—I've rather enjoyed hanging on to a phone, listening to "Greensleeves." I've never cared before whether people took me seriously or not.

But today I do care. Today what I'm doing *does* seem important, and I *do* want to be taken seriously. This article isn't just about a press release and a bunch of numbers. Martin and Janice aren't hypothetical examples dreamed up by some marketing department. They're real people with real lives. That money would have made a huge difference to them.

I'll show Alicia, I think fiercely. I'll show them all, Luke Brandon included. Show them that I, Rebecca Bloomwood, am not a joke.

With a sudden determination I reach for my dad's typewriter. I feed in some paper, switch on my Dicta-phone, take a deep breath, and begin to type.

Two hours later, I fax my 950-word article to Eric Foreman.

Eighteen

THE NEXT MORNING, I wake at six o'clock. It's pathetic, I know, but I'm as excited as a little kid on Christmas Day (or as me on Christmas Day, to be perfectly honest).

I lie in bed, telling myself to be grown-up and laidback and not think about it—but I just can't resist it. My mind swims with images of the piles of newspapers in newsstands all over the country. Of the copies of *The Daily World* being dropped on people's doormats this morning; all the people who are going to be opening their papers, yawning, wondering what's in the news.

And what are they going to see?

They're going to see my name! Rebecca Bloomwood in print in *The Daily World*! My first national byline: "By Rebecca Bloomwood." Doesn't that sound cool? "By Rebecca Bloomwood."

I know the piece has gone in, because Eric Foreman phoned me up yesterday afternoon and told me the editor was really pleased with it. And they've got it on a color page—so the picture of Janice and Martin will be in full color. Really high profile. I can't quite believe it. *The Daily World!*

Even as I'm lying here, it occurs to me, there's already

a whole pile of *Daily World*s at the newsstand in the parade of shops round the corner. A whole pile of pristine,
unopened copies. And the newsstand opens at . . . what
time? Six, I seem to remember. And now it's five past
six. So in *theory*, I could go and buy one right now if I
wanted to. I could just get up, slip on some clothes, go
down to the newsstand, and buy one.

Not that I would, of course. I'm not quite so sad and
desperate that I'm going to rush down as soon as the
shop's opened, just to see my name. I mean, what do
you take me for? No, what I'll do is just saunter down
casually later on—perhaps at eleven or midday—pick
up the paper and flip through it in mild interest and
then saunter home again. I probably won't even bother
to buy a copy. I mean—I've seen my name in print before. It's hardly a big deal. No need to make a song and
dance about it.

I'm going to turn over now and go back to sleep. I
can't think why I'm awake so early. Must be the birds or
something. Hmm . . . close my eyes, plump up my pil-
low, think about something else . . . I wonder what I'll
have for breakfast when I get up?

But I've never seen my name in *The Daily World,* says
a little voice in my head. I've never seen it in a national
newspaper.

This is killing me. I can't wait any longer, I've *got* to
see it.

Abruptly I get out of bed, throw on my clothes, and
tiptoe down the stairs. As I close the door, I feel just like
the girl in that Beatles song about leaving home. Outside the air has a sweet, new-day smell, and the road is
completely quiet. Gosh, it's nice being up early. Why on
earth don't I get up at six more often? I should do this
every day. A power walk before breakfast, like people
do in New York. Burn off loads of calories and then

return home to an energizing breakfast of oats and freshly squeezed orange juice. Perfect. This will be my new regime.

But as I reach the little parade of shops I feel a stab of nerves, and without quite meaning to, I slow my walk to a funereal pace. Maybe I'll just buy myself a Mars Bar and go home again. Or a Mint Aero, if they've got them.

Cautiously, I push at the door and wince at the ping! as it opens. I really don't want to draw attention to myself this morning. What if the guy behind the counter has read my article and thinks it's rubbish? This is nerve-racking. I should never have become a journalist. I should have become a beautician, like I always wanted to. Maybe it's not too late. I'll retrain, open my own boutique . . .

"Hello, Becky!"

I look up and feel my face jerk in surprise. Martin Webster's standing at the counter, holding a copy of *The Daily World.* "I just happened to be awake," he explains sheepishly. "Thought I'd just come down, have a little look . . ."

"Oh," I say. "Erm . . . me too." I give a nonchalant shrug. "Since I was awake anyway . . ."

My eye falls on the newspaper and I feel my stomach flip over. I'm going to expire with nerves. Please, just kill me quickly.

"So—what . . . what's it like?" I say in a strangled voice.

"Well," says Martin, gazing at the page as though perplexed. "It's certainly big." He turns the paper round to face me, and I nearly keel over. There, in full color, is a picture of Martin and Janice staring miserably up at the camera, below the headline COUPLE CHEATED BY FAT CATS AT FLAGSTAFF LIFE.

Shaking slightly, I take the paper from Martin. My eye skips across the page to the first column of text . . .

and there it is! "By Rebecca Bloomwood." That's my name! That's me!

There's a ping at the door of the shop, and we both look round. And there, to my utter astonishment, is Dad.

"Oh," he says, and gives an embarrassed little cough. "Your mother wanted me to buy a copy. And since I was awake anyway . . ."

"So was I," says Martin quickly.

"Me too," I say.

"Well," says Dad. "So—is it in?"

"Oh yes," I say, "it's in." I turn the paper round so he can see it.

"Gosh," he says. "It's big, isn't it?"

"The photo's good, don't you think?" says Martin enthusiastically. "Brings out the flowers in our curtains beautifully."

"Yes, the photo's great," I agree.

I'm not going to demean myself by asking what he thought of the article itself. If he wants to compliment my writing, he will. If he doesn't—then it really doesn't matter. The point is, *I'm* proud of it.

"And Janice looks very nice, I thought," says Martin, still gazing at the photograph.

"Very nice," agrees Dad. "If a little mournful."

"You see, these professionals, they know how to light a shot," says Martin. "The way the sunlight falls just here, on her—"

"What about my article?" I wail piteously. "Did you like that?"

"Oh, it's very good!" says Martin. "Sorry, Becky, I should have said! I haven't read it all yet, but it seems to capture the situation exactly. Makes me out to be quite a hero!" He frowns. "Although I never did fight in the Falklands, you know."

"Oh well," I say hurriedly. "That's neither here nor there, really."

"So you wrote all this yesterday?" says Dad. "On my typewriter?" He seems astounded.

"Yes," I say smugly. "It looks good, doesn't it? Have you seen my byline? 'By Rebecca Bloomwood.' "

"Janice'll be thrilled," says Martin. "I'm going to buy two copies."

"I'm going to buy three," says Dad. "Your granny will love to see this."

"And I'll buy one," I say. "Or two, perhaps." I carelessly reach for a handful and plonk them on the counter.

"Six copies?" says the cashier. "Are you sure?"

"I need them for my records," I say, and blush slightly.

When we get home, Mum and Janice are both waiting at our front door, desperate to see a copy.

"My hair!" wails Janice as soon as she sees the picture. "It looks terrible! What have they done to it?"

"No, it doesn't, love!" protests Martin. "You look very nice."

"Your curtains look lovely, Janice," says Mum, looking over her shoulder.

"They do, don't they?" says Martin eagerly. "That's just what I said."

I give up. What kind of family have I got, that are more interested in curtains than top financial journalism? Anyway, I don't care. I'm mesmerized by my byline. "By Rebecca Bloomwood." "By Rebecca Bloomwood."

After everyone's peered at the paper, Mum invites Janice and Martin round to our house for breakfast, and Dad goes and puts on some coffee. There's a rather

festive air to the proceedings, and everyone keeps laughing a lot. I don't think any of us can quite believe that
Janice and Martin are in *The Daily World.* (And me, of
course. "By Rebecca Bloomwood.")

At ten o'clock, I slope off and ring up Eric Foreman.
Just casually, you know. To let him know I've seen it.

"Looks good, doesn't it?" he says cheerfully. "The
editor's really going for this series, so if you come up
with any more stories like this just give me a shout. I
like your style. Just right for *The Daily World.*"

"Excellent," I say, feeling a glow of pleasure.

"Oh, and while I'm at it," he adds, "you'd better give
me your bank details."

My stomach gives a nasty lurch. Why does Eric
Foreman want my bank details? Shit, is he going to
check that my own finances are in order or something?
Is he going to run a credit check on me?

"Everything's done by transfer these days," he's saying. "Four hundred quid. That all right?"

What? What's he—

Oh my God, he's going to *pay* me. But of course he is.
Of course he is!

"That's fine," I hear myself say. "No problem. I'll just,
ahm . . . give you my account number, shall I?"

Four hundred quid! I think dazedly as I scrabble for
my checkbook. Just like that! I can't quite believe it.

"Excellent," says Eric Foreman, writing the details
down. "I'll sort that out for you with Accounts." Then
he pauses. "Tell me, would you be in the market for
writing general features? Human interest stories, that
kind of thing?"

Would I be in the market? Is he kidding?

"Sure," I say, trying not to sound too thrilled. "In
fact . . . I'd probably prefer it to finance."

"Oh right," he says. "Well, I'll keep an eye out for bits

that might suit you. As I say, I think you've got the right style for us."

"Great," I say. "Thanks."

As I put the phone down, there's a huge smile on my face. I've got the right style for *The Daily World*! Hah!

The phone rings again, and I pick it up, wondering if it's Eric Foreman offering me some more work already.

"Hello, Rebecca Bloomwood," I say in a businesslike voice.

"Rebecca," says Luke Brandon's curt voice—and my heart freezes. "Could you please tell me what the fuck is going on?"

Shit.

He sounds really angry. For an instant I'm paralyzed. My throat feels dry; my hand is sweaty round the receiver. Oh God. What am I going to say? What am I going to say to him?

But hang on a minute. *I* haven't done anything wrong.

"I don't know what you mean," I say, playing for time. Keep calm, I tell myself. Calm and cool.

"Your tawdry effort in *The Daily World*," he says scathingly. "Your one-sided, unbalanced, probably libelous little story."

For a second I'm so shocked I can't speak. Tawdry? Libelous?

"It's not tawdry!" I splutter at last. "It's a good piece. And it's certainly not libelous. I can prove everything I said."

"And I suppose getting the other side of the story would have been inconvenient," he snaps. "I suppose you were too busy writing your purple prose to approach Flagstaff Life and ask for their version of events. You'd rather have a good story than spoil it by trying to give a balanced picture."

"I *tried* to get the other side of the story!" I exclaim

furiously. "I phoned your PR company yesterday and told them I was writing the piece!"

There's silence.

"Who did you speak to?" says Luke.

"Alicia," I reply. "I asked her a very clear question about Flagstaff's policy on switching funds, and she told me she'd get back to me. I *told* her I had an urgent deadline."

Luke gives an impatient sigh. "What the fuck were you doing, speaking to Alicia? Flagstaff's my client, not hers."

"I know! I said that to her! But she said you were a very busy man and she could deal with me."

"Did you tell her you were writing for *The Daily World*?"

"No," I say, and feel myself flush slightly red. "I didn't specify who I was writing for. But I would have told her if she'd asked me. She just didn't bother. She just assumed I couldn't possibly be doing anything important." In spite of myself, my voice is rising in emotion. "Well, she was wrong, wasn't she? You were all wrong. And maybe now you'll start treating everybody with respect. Not just the people you *think* are important."

I break off, panting slightly, and there's a bemused silence.

"Rebecca," says Luke at last, "if this is about what happened between us that day—if this is some kind of petty revenge—"

I'm really going to explode now.

"Don't you bloody insult me!" I yell. "Don't you bloody try and make this personal! This is about two innocent people being hoodwinked by one of your bigshot clients, nothing else. I told the truth, and if you didn't have a chance to respond, it's your own company's incompetence that's to blame. I was completely professional, I gave you every opportunity to put out your side of the story. *Every* opportunity. And if you blew it, that's not my fault."

And without giving him the chance to reply, I slam the phone down.

I'm feeling quite shaken as I go back into the kitchen. To think I ever liked Luke Brandon. To think I table-hopped with him. To think I let him lend me twenty quid. He's just an arrogant, self-centered, chauvinistic—

"Telephone!" says Mum. "Shall I get it?"

It'll be him again, won't it? Ringing back to apologize. Well, he needn't think I'm that easily won round. I stand by every word I said. And I'll tell him so. In fact, I'll add that—

"It's for you, Becky," says Mum.

"Fine," I say coolly, and make my way to the telephone. I don't hurry; I don't panic. I feel completely in control.

"Hello?" I say.

"Rebecca? Eric Foreman here."

"Oh!" I say in surprise. "Hi!"

"Bit of news about your piece."

"Oh yes?" I say, trying to sound calm. But my stomach's churning. What if Luke Brandon's spoken to him? Oh shit, I did check all the facts, didn't I?

"I've just had *Morning Coffee* on the phone," he says. "You know, the TV program? Rory and Emma. They're interested in your story."

"What?" I say stupidly.

"There's a new series they're doing on finance, 'Managing Your Money.' They get some financial expert in every week, tell the viewers how to keep tabs on their dosh." Eric Foreman lowers his voice. "Frankly, they're

running out of stuff to talk about. They've done mortgages, store cards, pensions, all the usual cobblers . . ."

"Right," I say, trying to sound focused. But as his
words slowly sink in, I'm a bit dazed. Rory and Emma
read my article? Rory and Emma themselves? I have
a sudden vision of them holding the paper together,
jostling for a good view.

But of course, that's silly, isn't it? They'd have a copy
each.

"So, anyway, they want to have you on the show tomorrow morning," Eric Foreman's saying. "Talk about
this windfall story, warn their viewers to take care. You
interested in that kind of thing? If not, I can easily tell
them you're too busy."

"No!" I say quickly. "No. Tell them I'm . . ." I swallow.
"I'm interested."

As I put down the phone, I feel faint. I'm going to be
on television.

BANK OF HELSINKI

Helsinki House
124 Lombard St.
London EC2D 9YF

Rebecca Bloomwood
c/o William Green Recruitment
39 Farringdon Square
London EC4 7TD

27 March 2000

Dere Rebecca Bloomwood:

Finnish Finnish Finnish Finnish Finnish Finnish Finnish
Finnish Finnish Finnish Finnish Finnish *"Daily World"*
Finnish Finnish Finnish Finnish Finnish Finnish Finnish
Finnish Finnish Finnish Finnish Finnish Finnish Finnish
Finnish Finnish Finnish Finnish Finnish Finnish Finnish
Finnish Finnish Finnish

More Finnish More Finnish More Finnish More Finnish
More Finnish More Finnish More Finnish More Finnish
More Finnish More Finnish More Finnish More Finnish
More Finnish More Finnish More Finnish More Finnish
More Finnish More Finnish More Finnish More Finnish
More Finnish

Finnish good-bye,

Jan Virtanen

Nineteen

THE CAR TO TAKE ME to the television studios arrives promptly at seven-thirty the next morning. When the doorbell rings, Mum, Dad, and I all jump, even though we've been waiting in a tense silence for ten minutes.

"Well," says Dad gruffly, glancing at his watch. "They're here, anyway."

Ever since I told him about the arrangements, Dad's been predicting that the car won't turn up and that he'll have to drive me to the studios himself. He even worked out a route last night, and phoned up Uncle Malcolm as a standby. (To be honest, I think he was quite looking forward to it.)

"Oh, Becky," says Mum in a trembling voice. "Good luck, darling." She looks at me, then shakes her head. "Our little Becky, on television. I can't believe it."

I start to get up, but Dad puts out a restraining arm.

"Now, before you answer the door, Becky," he says. "You are sure, aren't you? About the risk you're taking." He glances at Mum, who bites her lip.

"I'll be fine!" I say, trying to sound as soothing as possible. "Honestly, Dad, we've been over it all."

Last night, it suddenly occurred to Dad that if I went

on the telly, my stalker would know where I was. At first he was adamant I'd have to call the whole thing off— and it took an awful lot of persuasion to convince him and Mum I'd be perfectly safe in the TV studios. They were even talking about hiring a bodyguard, can you believe it? I mean, what on earth would I look like, turning up with a bodyguard?

Actually, I'd look pretty cool and mysterious, wouldn't I? That might have been quite a good idea.

The doorbell rings again and I leap to my feet.

"Well," says Dad. "You just be careful."

"I will, don't worry!" I say, picking up my bag. I walk to the door calmly, trying not to give away how excited I feel. Inside I feel as light as a bubble.

I just can't believe how well everything's going. Not only am I going to be on the telly, but everyone's being so nice to me! Yesterday I had several phone conversations with an assistant producer of *Morning Coffee,* who's a really sweet girl called Zelda. We went over exactly what I was going to say on the program, then she arranged for a car to come and pick me up—and when I told her I was at my parents' house with none of my clothes handy, she thought for a bit—then said I could choose something to wear from the wardrobe. I mean, how cool is that? Choosing any outfit I like from the wardrobe! Maybe they'll let me keep it afterward, too.

As I open the front door, my stomach gives an excited leap. There, waiting in the drive, is a portly, middle-aged man in a blue blazer and cap, standing next to a shiny black car. My own private chauffeur! This just gets better and better.

"Miss Bloomwood?" says the driver.

"Yes," I say, unable to stop myself from grinning in delight. I'm about to reach for the door handle—but he gets there before me, opens the car door with a flourish, and stands to attention, waiting for me to get in. God, this is like being a film star or something!

I glance back toward the house and see Mum and Dad standing on the front step, both looking utterly gobsmacked.

"Well—bye then!" I say, trying to sound casual, as though I always ride around in a chauffeur-driven car. "See you later!"

"Becky, is that you?" comes a voice from next door, and Janice appears on the other side of the hedge in her dressing gown. Her eyes grow large as they take in the car and she glances at Mum, who raises her shoulders, as though to say "I know, isn't it unbelievable?"

"Morning, Janice," says Dad.

"Morning, Graham," says Janice dazedly. "Oh, Becky! I've never seen anything like it. In all the years . . . If Tom could only see you . . ." She breaks off and looks at Mum. "Have you taken any photographs?"

"We haven't!" says Mum in dismay. "It didn't even occur to us. Graham, quick—go and get the camera."

"No, wait, I'll get our camcorder!" says Janice. "It won't take me two ticks. We could have the car arriving in the drive, and Becky walking out of the front door . . . and maybe we could use *The Four Seasons* as the sound-track, and then cut straight to . . ."

"No!" I say hastily, seeing a flicker of amusement pass across the face of the driver. And I was doing so well at looking nonchalant and professional. "We haven't got time for any pictures. I have to get to the studios!"

"Yes," says Janice, suddenly looking anxious. "Yes, you don't want to be late." She glances fearfully at her watch, as though afraid the program might already have started. "It's on at eleven, isn't it?"

"Eleven o'clock the program starts," says Dad. "Set the video for five to, that's what I've been telling people."

"That's what we'll do," says Janice. "Just in case." She gives a little sigh. "I shan't dare to go to the loo all morning, just in case I miss it!"

There's an awed silence as I get into the car. The driver closes the door smartly, then walks around to the driver's door. I press the button to lower my window and grin out at Mum and Dad.

"Becky, darling, what will you do afterward?" says Mum. "Come back here or go back to the flat?"

Immediately I feel my smile falter, and look down, pretending to fiddle with the window controls. I don't want to think about afterward.

In fact, I can't even visualize afterward. I'm going to be on the telly . . . and that's as far as it goes. The rest of my life is shut securely away in a box at the back of my head and I don't even want to remember it's there.

"I . . . I'm not sure," I say. "I'll see what happens."

"They'll probably take you out to lunch afterward," says Dad knowledgeably. "These showbiz types are always having lunch with each other."

"Liquid lunches," puts in Janice, and gives a little laugh.

"At The Ivy," says Mum. "That's where all the actors meet up, isn't it?"

"The Ivy's old hat!" retorts Dad. "They'll take her to the Groucho Club."

"The Groucho Club!" says Janice, clasping her hands. "Isn't that where Kate Moss goes?"

This is getting ridiculous.

"We'd better go," I say, and the driver nods.

"Good luck, sweetheart," calls Dad. I close the window and lean back, and the car purrs out of the drive.

For a while, we drive in silence. I keep casually glancing out of the window to see if anyone's looking at me in my chauffeur-driven car and wondering who I am (that new girl on *EastEnders,* perhaps). Although we're whizzing along the highway so fast, I probably look like a blur.

"So," says the driver after a while. "You're appearing on *Morning Coffee,* are you?"

"Yes, I am," I say, and immediately feel a joyful smile plaster itself over my face. God, I must *stop* this. I bet Jeremy Paxman doesn't start grinning inanely every time someone asks him if he's appearing on *University Challenge.*

"So what're you on for?" says the driver, interrupting my thoughts.

I'm about to reply "To be famous and maybe get some free clothes," when I realize what he means.

"A financial story," I say coolly. "I wrote a piece in *The Daily World,* and the producers read it and wanted me on the show."

"Been on television before?"

"No," I admit reluctantly. "No, I haven't."

We pull up at some lights and the driver turns round in his seat to survey me.

"You'll be fine," he says. "Just don't let the nerves get to you."

"Nerves?" I say, and give a little laugh. "I'm not nervous! I'm just . . . looking forward to it."

"Glad to hear it," says the driver, turning back. "You'll be OK, then. Some people, they get onto that sofa, thinking they're fine, relaxed, happy as a clam . . . then they see that red light, and it hits them that 2.5 million people around the country are all watching them. Makes some people start to panic."

"Oh," I say after a slight pause. "Well . . . I'm nothing like them! I'll be fine!"

"Good," says the driver.

"Good," I echo, a little less certainly, and look out of the window.

I'll be fine. Of course I will. I've never been nervous in my life before, and I'm certainly not going to start . . .

Two point five million people.

Gosh. When you think about it—that is quite a lot, isn't it? Two point five million people, all sitting at home, staring at the screen. Staring at my face. Waiting for what I'm going to say next.

OK, don't think about it. The important thing is just to keep remembering how well prepared I am. I rehearsed for ages in front of the mirror last night and I know what I'm going to say practically by heart.

It all has to be very basic and simple, Zelda said— because apparently 76 percent of the *Morning Coffee* audience are housewives looking after toddlers, who have very short attention spans. She kept apologizing for what she called the "dumbing-down effect" and saying a financial expert like myself must feel really frustrated by it—and of course, I agreed with her.

But to be honest, I'm quite relieved. In fact, the more dumbed down the better, as far as I'm concerned. I mean, writing a *Daily World* article with all my notes to hand was one thing, but answering tricky questions on live TV is quite another.

So anyway, I'm going to start off by saying "If you were offered a choice between a carriage clock and £20,000, which would you choose?" Rory or Emma will reply, "Twenty thousand pounds, of course!" and I'll say, "Exactly. Twenty thousand pounds." I'll pause briefly, to let that figure sink into the audience's mind, and then I'll say, "Unfortunately, when Flagstaff Life offered their customers a carriage clock to transfer their savings, they didn't tell them that if they did so, they would *lose* a £20,000 windfall!"

That sounds quite good, don't you think? Rory and Emma will ask a few very easy questions like "What can people do to protect themselves?" and I'll give nice simple answers. And right at the end, just to keep it light, we're going to talk about all the different things you could buy with £20,000.

Actually, that's the bit I'm looking forward to most of all. I've already thought of loads of things. Did you know, with £20,000 you could buy forty Gucci watches, *and* have enough left over for a bag?

The *Morning Coffee* studios are in Maida Vale, and as we draw near to the gates, familiar from the opening credits of the show, I feel a dart of excitement. I'm actually going to be on television!

The doorman waves us through the barrier, we pull up outside a pair of huge double doors, and the driver opens the door for me. As I get out, my legs are shaking slightly, but I force myself to walk confidently up the steps, into the reception hall, and up to the desk.

"I'm here for *Morning Coffee*," I say, and give a little laugh as I realize what I've just said. "I mean . . ."

"I know what you mean," says the receptionist, kindly but wearily. She looks up my name on a list, jabs a number into her phone, and says, "Jane? Rebecca Bloomwood's here." Then she gestures to a row of squashy chairs and says, "Someone will be with you shortly."

I walk over to the seating area and sit down opposite a middle-aged woman with lots of wild dark hair and a big amber necklace round her neck. She's lighting up a cigarette, and even though I don't really smoke anymore, I suddenly feel as though I could do with one myself.

Not that I'm nervous or anything. I just fancy a cigarette.

"Excuse me," calls the receptionist. "This is a no-smoking area."

"Damn," says the woman in a raspy voice. She takes a long drag, then stubs the cigarette out on a saucer and smiles at me conspiratorially. "Are you a guest on the show?" she says.

"Yes," I say. "Are you?"

The woman nods. "Promoting my new novel, *Blood Red Sunset*." She lowers her voice to a thrilling throb. "A searing tale of love, greed, and murder, set in the ruthless world of South American money launderers."

"Gosh," I say. "That sounds really—"

"Let me give you a copy," interrupts the woman. She reaches into a Mulberry holdall by her side and pulls out a vividly colored hardback book. "Remind me of your name?"

Remind her?

"It's Rebecca," I say. "Rebecca Bloomwood."

"To Becca," the woman says aloud, as she scrawls inside the front page. "With love and great affection." She signs with a flourish and hands the book to me.

"Thanks very much . . ." Quickly I look at the cover. "Elisabeth."

Elisabeth Plover. To be honest, I've never heard of her.

"I expect you're wondering how I came to know such a lot about such a violent, dangerous world," says Elisabeth. She leans forward and gazes at me with huge green eyes. "The truth is, I lived with a money launderer for three long months. I loved him; I learned from him . . . and then I betrayed him." Her voice dies to a trembling whisper. "I still remember the look he gave me as the police dragged him away. He knew what I'd done. He knew I was his Judas Iscariot. And yet, in a strange kind of way, I think he loved me for it."

"Wow," I say, impressed in spite of myself. "Did all this happen in South America?"

"Brighton," she says after a slight pause. "But money launderers are the same the world over."

"Rebecca?" says a voice, before I can think of a reply to this, and we both look up to see a girl with smooth dark hair, in jeans and a black polo neck, walking swiftly toward us. "I'm Zelda. We spoke yesterday?"

"Zelda!" exclaims Elisabeth, getting to her feet. "How have you been, my darling?" She holds out her arms, and Zelda stares at her.

"I'm sorry," she says, "have we—" She stops as her gaze falls on my copy of *Blood Red Sunset*. "Oh yes, that's right. Elisabeth Plover. One of the researchers will be down for you in a minute. Meanwhile, do help yourself to coffee." She flashes her a smile, then turns to me. "Rebecca, are you ready?"

"Yes!" I say eagerly, leaping up from my chair. (I have to admit, I feel quite flattered that Zelda's come down to get me herself. I mean, she obviously doesn't come down for everyone.)

"Great to meet you," says Zelda, shaking my hand. "Great to have you on the show. Now, as usual, we're completely frantic—so if it's OK by you, I thought we'd just head straight off to hair and makeup and we can talk on the way."

"Absolutely," I say, trying not to sound too excited. "Good idea."

Hair and makeup! This is so cool!

"There's been a slight change of plan which I need to fill you in on," says Zelda. "Nothing to worry about . . . Any word from Bella yet?" she adds to the receptionist.

The receptionist shakes her head, and Zelda mutters something which sounds like "Stupid cow."

"OK, let's go," she says, heading off toward a pair of swing doors. "I'm afraid it's even more crazy than usual today. One of our regulars has let us down, so we're searching for a replacement, and there's been an accident in the kitchen . . ." She pushes through the swing doors and now we're striding along a green-carpeted corridor buzzing with people. "Plus, we've got Heaven Sent 7 in today," she adds over her shoulder. "Which means the switchboard gets jammed with fans calling in, and we have to find dressing room space for seven enormous egos."

"Right," I say nonchalantly. But underneath I'm jumping with excitement. Heaven Sent 7? But I mean . . . they're really famous! And I'm appearing on the same show as them! I mean—I'll get to meet them and everything, won't I? Maybe we'll all go out for a drink afterward and become really good friends. They're all a bit younger than me, but that won't matter. I'll be like their older sister.

Or maybe I'll *go out* with one of them! God, yes. That nice one with the dark hair. Nathan. (Or is it Ethan? Whatever he's called.) He'll catch my eye after the show and quietly ask me out to dinner without the others. We'll go to some tiny little restaurant, and at first it'll be all quiet and discreet, but then the press will find out and we'll become one of those really famous couples who go to premieres all the time. And I'll wear . . .

"OK, here we are," says Zelda, and I look up dazedly.

We're standing in the doorway of a room lined with mirrors and spotlights. Three people are sitting in chairs in front of the mirrors, wearing capes and having makeup applied by trendy-looking girls in jeans; another is having her hair blow-dried. Music is playing in the background, there's a friendly level of chatter, and in the air are the mingled scents of hair spray, face powder, and coffee.

It's basically my idea of heaven.

"So," says Zelda, leading me toward a girl with red hair. "Chloe will do your makeup, and then we'll pop you along to wardrobe. OK?"

"Fine," I say, my eyes widening as I take in Chloe's collection of makeup. There's about a zillion brushes, pots, and tubes littered over the counter in front of us, all really good brands like Chanel and MAC.

"Now, about your slot," continues Zelda as I sit down on a swivel chair. "As I say, we've gone for a rather different format from the one we talked about previously . . ."

"Zelda!" comes a man's voice from outside. "Bella's on the line for you!"

"Oh shit," says Zelda. "Look, Rebecca, I've got to go and take this call, but I'll come back as soon as I can. OK?"

"Fine!" I say happily, as Chloe drapes a cape round me and pulls my hair back into a wide towel band. In the background, the radio's playing my favorite song by Lenny Kravitz.

"I'll just cleanse and tone, and then give you a base," says Chloe. "If you could shut your eyes . . ."

I close my eyes and, after a few seconds, feel a cool, creamy liquid being massaged into my face. It's the most delicious sensation in the world. I could sit here all day.

"So," says Chloe after a while. "What are you on the show for?"

"Errm . . . finance," I say vaguely. "A piece on finance."

To be honest, I'm feeling so relaxed, I can hardly remember what I'm doing here.

"Oh, yeah," says Chloe, efficiently smoothing foundation over my face. "They were talking earlier about some financial thing." She reaches for a palette of eyeshadows, blends a couple of colors together, then picks up a brush. "So, are you a financial expert, then?"

"Well," I say, a little awkwardly. "You know."

"Wow," says Chloe, starting to apply eyeshadow to my eyelids. "I don't understand the first thing about money."

"Me neither!" chimes in a dark-haired girl from across the room. "My accountant's given up trying to explain it all to me. As soon he says the word 'tax-year,' my mind glazes over."

I'm about to reply sympathetically "Me too!" and launch into a nice girly chat—but then I stop myself. The memory of Janice and Martin is a bit too raw for me to be flippant.

"You probably know quite a lot more about your finances than you realize," I say instead. "If you *really* don't know . . . then you should take advice from someone who does."

"You mean a financial expert like you?" says the girl.

I smile back, trying to look confident—but all this talk of my being a "financial expert" is unnerving me. I feel as though any minute now, someone's going to walk in, ask me an impossible question about South African bond yields, and then denounce me as a fraud. Thank goodness I know exactly what I'm going to say on air.

"Sorry, Rebecca," says Chloe, "I'm going to have to interrupt. Now, I was thinking a raspberry red for the lips. Is that OK by you?"

What with all this chatting, I haven't really been paying attention to what she's been doing to my face. But as

I look at my reflection properly, I can't quite believe it. My eyes are huge; I've suddenly got amazing cheekbones . . . honestly, I look like a different person. Why on earth don't I wear makeup like this every day?

"Wow!" I breathe.

"It's easier because you're so calm," observes Chloe, reaching into a black vanity case. "We get some people in here, really trembling with nerves. Even celebrities. We can hardly do their makeup."

"Really?" I say, and lean forward, ready to hear some insider gossip. But Zelda's voice interrupts us.

"Sorry about that, Rebecca!" she exclaims. "Right, how are we doing? Makeup looks good. What about hair?"

"It's nicely cut," says Chloe, picking up a few strands of my hair and dropping them back down again, just like Nicky Clarke on a makeover. "I'll just give it a blow-dry for sheen."

"Fine," says Zelda. "And then we'll get her along to wardrobe." She glances at something on her clipboard, then sits down on a swivel chair next to me. "OK, so, Rebecca, we need to talk about your item."

"Excellent," I say, matching her businesslike tone. "Well, I've prepared it all just as you wanted. Really simple and straightforward."

"Yup," says Zelda. "Well, that's the thing. We had a talk at the meeting yesterday, and you'll be glad to hear, we don't need it too basic, after all." She smiles. "You'll be able to get as technical as you like!"

"Oh, right," I say, taken aback. "Well . . . good! That's great! Although I might still keep it fairly low—"

"We want to avoid talking down to the audience. I mean, they're not morons!" Zelda lowers her voice slightly. "Plus we had some new audience research in yesterday, and apparently 80 percent of our viewers feel patronized by some or all of the show's content. Basically, we need to redress that balance. So we've had a complete change of plan for your item!" She beams at me. "What we thought is, instead of a simple interview, we'd have more of a high-powered debate."

"A high-powered debate?" I echo, trying not to sound as alarmed as I feel.

"Absolutely!" says Zelda. "What we want is a really heated discussion! Opinions flying, voices raised. That kind of thing."

Opinions?

"So is that OK?" says Zelda, frowning at me. "You look a bit—"

"I'm fine!" I force myself to smile brightly. "Just . . . looking forward to it! A nice high-powered debate. Great!" I clear my throat. "And . . . and who will I be debating with?"

"A representative from Flagstaff Life," says Zelda triumphantly. "Head-to-head with the enemy. It'll make great television!"

"Zelda!" comes a voice from outside the room. "Bella again!"

"Oh, for Christ's sake!" says Zelda, leaping up. "Rebecca, I'll be back in a sec."

"Fine," I manage. "See you in a minute."

"OK," says Chloe cheerfully. "While she's gone, let me put on that lipstick."

She reaches for a long brush and begins to paint in my lips, and I stare at my reflection, trying to keep calm, trying not to panic. But my throat's so tight, I can't swallow. I've never felt so frightened in all my life.

I can't talk in a high-powered debate!

Why did I ever want to be on television?

"Rebecca, could you try to keep your lips still?" says Chloe with a puzzled frown. "They're really shaking."

"Sorry," I whisper, staring at my reflection like a

frozen rabbit. She's right, I'm trembling all over. Oh God, this is no good. I've got to calm down. Think happy thoughts. Think Zen.

In an effort to distract myself, I focus on the reflection in the mirror. In the background I can see Zelda standing in the corridor, talking into a phone with a furious expression on her face.

"Yup," I can hear her saying curtly. "Yup. But the point is, Bella, we pay you a retainer to *be* available. What the fuck am I supposed to do now?" She looks up, sees someone, and lifts a hand in greeting. "OK, Bella, I do see that . . ."

A blond woman and two men appear in the corridor, and Zelda nods to them apologetically. I can't see their faces, but they're all wearing smart overcoats and holding briefcases, and one of the men is holding a folder bulging with papers. The blond woman's coat is actually rather nice, I find myself thinking. And she's got a *gorgeous* Louis Vuitton bag. I wonder who she is.

"Yup," Zelda's saying. "Yup. Well, if *you* can suggest an alternative phone-in subject . . ."

She raises her eyebrows at the blond woman, who shrugs and turns away to look at a poster on the wall. And as she does so, my heart nearly stops dead.

Because I recognize her. It's Alicia. Alicia from Brandon Communications is standing five yards away from me.

I almost want to laugh at the incongruity of it. What's she doing here? What's Alicia Bitch Long-legs doing here, for God's sake?

One of the men turns round to say something to her—and as I see his face, I think I recognize him, too. He's another one of the Brandon C lot, isn't he? One of those young, eager, baby-faced types.

But what on earth are they all doing here? What's going on? Surely it can't be—

They can't all be here because of—

No. Oh no. Suddenly I feel rather cold.

"Luke!" comes Zelda's voice from the corridor, and I feel a swoop of dismay. "*So* glad you could make it. We always love having you on the show. You know, I had no idea you represented Flagstaff Life, until Sandy said . . ."

This isn't happening. Please tell me this isn't happening.

"The journalist who wrote the piece is already here," Zelda's saying, "and I've primed her on what's happening. I think it's going to make really great television, the two of you arguing away!"

She starts moving down the corridor, and in the mirror I see Alicia and the eager young man begin to follow her. Then the third overcoated man starts to come into view. And although my stomach's churning painfully, I can't stop myself. I slowly turn my head as he passes the door.

I meet Luke Brandon's grave, dark eyes and he meets mine, and for a few still seconds, we just stare at each other. Then abruptly he looks away and strides off down the corridor. And I'm left, gazing helplessly at my painted reflection, feeling sick with panic.

POINTS FOR TELEVISION INTERVIEW

SIMPLE AND BASIC FINANCIAL ADVICE

1. Prefer clock/twenty grand? Obvious.
2. Flagstaff Life ripped off innocent customers. Beware.

Ermm . . .

3. Always be very careful with your money.
4. Don't put it all in one investment but diversify.
5. Don't lose it by mistake
6. Don't

THINGS YOU CAN BUY WITH £20,000

1. Nice car; e.g., small BMW
2. Pearl and diamond necklace from Aspreys plus big diamond ring
3. 3 couture evening dresses; e.g., from John Galliano
4. Steinway grand piano
5. 5 gorgeous leather sofas from the Conran shop
6. 40 Gucci watches, plus bag
7. Flowers delivered every month for 42 years
8. 55 pedigree Labrador puppies
9. 80 cashmere jumpers
10. 666 Wonderbras
11. 454 pots Helena Rubinstein moisturizer
12. 800 bottles of champagne
13. 2,860 Fiorentina pizzas
14. 15,384 tubes of Pringles
15. 90,909 packets of Polo mints
16.

Twenty

By ELEVEN TWENTY-FIVE, I'm sitting on a brown upholstered chair in the green room. I'm dressed in a midnight-blue Jasper Conran suit, sheer tights, and a pair of suede high heels. What with my makeup and blown-dry hair, I've never looked smarter in my life. But I can't enjoy any of it. All I can think of is the fact that in fifteen minutes, I've got to sit on a sofa and discuss high-powered finance with Luke Brandon on live television.

The very thought of it makes me feel like whimpering. Or laughing wildly. I mean, it's like some kind of sick joke. Luke Brandon against me. Luke Brandon, with his genius IQ and bloody photographic memory—against me. He'll walk all over me. He'll *massacre* me.

"Darling, have a croissant," says Elisabeth Plover, who's sitting opposite me, munching a *pain au chocolat.* "They're simply sublime. Every bite like a ray of golden Provençal sun."

"No thanks," I say. "I . . . I'm not really hungry."

I don't understand how she can eat. I honestly feel as though I'm about to throw up at any moment. How on earth do people appear on television every day? How does Fiona Phillips do it? No wonder they're all so thin.

"Coming up!" comes Rory's voice from the television monitor in the corner of the room, and both our heads automatically swivel round to see the screen filled with a picture of the beach at sunset. "What is it like, to live with a gangster and then, risking everything, betray him? Our next guest has written an explosive novel based on her dark and dangerous background . . ."

". . . And we introduce a new series of in-depth discussions," chimes in Emma. The picture changes to one of pound coins raining onto the floor, and my stomach gives a nasty flip. "*Morning Coffee* turns the spotlight on the issue of financial scandal, with two leading industry experts coming head-to-head in debate."

Is that me? Oh God, I don't want to be a leading industry expert. I want to go home and watch reruns of *The Simpsons.*

"But first!" says Rory cheerily. "Scott Robertson's getting all fired up in the kitchen."

The picture switches abruptly to a man in a chef's hat grinning and brandishing a blowtorch. I stare at him for a few moments, then look down again, clenching my hands tightly in my lap. I can't quite believe that in fifteen minutes it'll be me up on that screen. Sitting on the sofa. Trying to think of something to say.

To distract myself, I unscrew my crappy piece of paper for the thousandth time and read through my paltry notes. Maybe it won't be so bad, I find myself thinking hopefully, as my eyes circle the same few sentences again and again. Maybe I'm worrying about nothing. We'll probably keep the whole thing at the level of a casual chat. Keep it simple and friendly. After all . . .

"Good morning, Rebecca," comes a voice from the door. Slowly I look up—and as I do so, my heart sinks. Luke Brandon is standing in the doorway. He's wearing an immaculate dark suit, his hair is shining, and his face is bronze with makeup. There isn't an ounce of friendliness in his face. His jaw is tight; his eyes are hard and businesslike. As they meet mine, they don't even flicker.

For a few moments we gaze at each other without speaking. I can hear my pulse beating loudly in my ears; my face feels hot beneath all the makeup. Then, summoning all my inner resources, I force myself to say calmly, "Hello, Luke."

There's an interested silence as he walks into the room. Even Elisabeth Plover seems intrigued by him.

"I know that face," she says, leaning forward. "I know it. You're an actor, aren't you? Shakespearean, of course. I believe I saw you in *Lear* three years ago."

"I don't think so," says Luke curtly.

"You're right!" says Elisabeth, slapping the table. "It was *Hamlet*. I remember it well. The desperate pain, the guilt, the final tragedy . . ." She shakes her head solemnly. "I'll never forget that voice of yours. Every word was like a stab wound."

"I'm sorry to hear it," says Luke, and looks at me. "Rebecca—"

"Luke, here are the final figures," interrupts Alicia, hurrying into the room and handing him a piece of paper. "Hello, Rebecca," she adds, giving me a snide look. "All prepared?"

"Yes, I am, actually," I say, crumpling my paper into a ball in my lap. "Very well prepared."

"Glad to hear it," says Alicia, raising her eyebrows. "It should be an interesting debate."

"Yes," I say defiantly. "Very."

God, she's a cow.

"I've just had John from Flagstaff on the phone," adds Alicia to Luke in a lowered voice. "He was very keen that you should mention the new Foresight Savings Series. Obviously, I told him—"

"This is a damage limitation exercise," says Luke curtly. "Not a bloody plug-fest. He'll be bloody lucky if he . . ." He glances at me and I look away as though I'm not remotely interested in what he's talking about. Casually I glance at my watch and feel a leap of fright as I see the time. Ten minutes. Ten minutes to go.

"OK," says Zelda, coming into the room. "Elisabeth, we're ready for you."

"Marvelous," says Elisabeth, taking a last mouthful of *pain au chocolat*. "Now, I do *look* all right, don't I?" She stands up and a shower of crumbs falls off her skirt.

"You've got a piece of croissant in your hair," says Zelda, reaching up and removing it. "Other than that— what can I say?" She catches my eye and I have a hysterical desire to giggle.

"Luke!" says the baby-faced guy, rushing in with a mobile phone. "John Bateson on the line for you. And a couple of packages have arrived . . ."

"Thanks, Tim," says Alicia, taking the packages and ripping them open. She pulls out a bunch of papers and begins scanning them quickly, marking things every so often in pencil. Meanwhile, Tim sits down, opens a laptop computer, and starts typing.

"Yes, John, I do see your bloody point," Luke's saying in a low, tight voice. "But if you had just kept me better informed—"

"Tim," says Alicia, looking up. "Can you quickly check the return on the Flagstaff Premium Pension over the last three, five, and ten?"

"Absolutely," says Tim, and starts tapping at his computer.

"Tim," says Luke, looking up from the phone. "Can you print out the Flagstaff Foresight press release draft for me ASAP? Thanks."

I can't quite believe what I'm seeing. They've practically

set up an office, here in the *Morning Coffee* green room. An entire office of Brandon Communications staff complete with computers and modems and phones . . . pitted against me and my crumpled piece of notebook paper.

As I watch Tim's laptop efficiently spewing out pages, and Alicia handing sheets of paper to Luke, a resigned feeling starts to creep over me. I mean, let's face it. I'll never beat this lot, will I? I haven't got a chance. I should just give up now. Tell them I'm ill or something. Run home and hide under my duvet.

"OK, everyone?" says Zelda, poking her head round the door. "On in seven minutes."

"Fine," says Luke.

"Fine," I echo in a wobbly voice.

"Oh, and Rebecca, there's a package for you," says Zelda. She comes into the room and hands me a large, square box. "I'll be back in a minute."

"Thanks, Zelda," I say in surprise, and, with a sudden lift of spirits, begin to rip the box open. I've no idea what it is or who it's from—but it's got to be something helpful, hasn't it? Special last-minute information from Eric Foreman, maybe. A graph, or a series of figures that I can produce at the crucial moment. Or some secret document that Luke doesn't know about.

Out of the corner of my eye I can see that all the Brandonites have stopped what they're doing and are watching, too. Well, that'll show them. They're not the only ones to get packages delivered to the green room. They're not the only ones to have resources. Finally I get the sticky tape undone and open the flaps of the box.

And as everyone watches, a big red helium balloon, with "GOOD LUCK" emblazoned across it, floats up to the ceiling. There's a card attached to the string, and, without looking anyone in the eye, I rip it open.

Immediately I wish I hadn't.

"Good luck to you, good luck to you, whatever you're about to do," sings a tinny electronic voice.

I slam the card shut and feel a surge of embarrassment. From the other side of the room I can hear little sniggers going on, and I look up to see Alicia smirking. She whispers something into Luke's ear, and an amused expression spreads across his face.

He's laughing at me. They're all laughing at Rebecca Bloomwood and her singing balloon. For a few moments I can't move for mortification. My chest is rising and falling swiftly; I've never felt less like a leading industry expert in my life.

Then, on the other side of the room, I hear Alicia murmur some malicious little comment and give a snort of laughter. Deep inside me, something snaps. Sod them, I think suddenly. Sod them all. They're probably only jealous, anyway. They wish they had balloons, too.

Defiantly I open the card again to read the message.

"No matter if it's rain or shine, we all know that you'll be fine," sings the card's tinny voice at once. *"Hold your head up, keep it high—all that matters is you try."*

To Becky, I read. *With love and thanks for all your wonderful help. We're so proud to know you. From your friends Janice and Martin.*

I stare down at the card, reading the words over and over, and feel my eyes grow hot with tears. Janice and Martin *have* been good friends over the years. They've always been kind to me, even when I gave them such disastrous advice. I owe this to them. And I'm bloody well not going to let them down.

I blink a few times, take a deep breath, and look up to see Luke Brandon gazing at me, his eyes dark and expressionless.

"Friends," I say coolly. "Sending me their good wishes."

Carefully I place the card on the coffee table, making sure it stays open so it'll keep singing, then pull my balloon down from the ceiling and tie it to the back of my chair.

"OK," comes Zelda's voice from the door. "Luke and Rebecca. Are you ready?"

"Couldn't be readier," I say calmly, and walk past Luke to the door.

Twenty-one

As we stride along the corridors to the set, neither Luke nor I says a word. I dart a glance at him as we turn a corner—and his face is even steelier than it was before.

Well, that's fine. I can do hard and businesslike, too. Firmly I lift my chin and begin to take longer strides, pretending to be Alexis Carrington in *Dynasty*.

"So, do you two already know each other?" says Zelda, who's walking along between us.

"We do, as it happens," says Luke shortly.

"In a business context," I say, equally shortly. "Luke's always trying to promote some financial product or other. And I'm always trying to avoid his calls."

Zelda gives an appreciative laugh and I see Luke's eyes flash angrily. But I really don't care. I don't care how angry he gets. In fact, the angrier he gets, the better I feel.

"So—Luke, you must have been quite pissed off at Rebecca's article in *The Daily World*," says Zelda.

"I wasn't pleased," says Luke. "By any of it," he adds in a lower voice.

What does that mean? I turn my head, and to my

astonishment, he's looking at me with a sober expression. Almost apologetic. Hmm. This must be an old PR trick. Soften up your opponent and then go in for the kill. But *I'm* not going to fall for it.

"He phoned me up to complain," I say airily to Zelda. "Can't cope with the truth, eh, Luke? Can't cope with seeing what's under the PR gloss?"

There's silence and I dart another look at him. Now he looks so furious, I think for a terrifying moment that he's going to hit me. Then his face changes and, in an icily calm voice, he says, "Let's just get on the fucking set and get this over with, shall we?"

Zelda raises her eyebrows at me and I grin back. This is more like it.

"OK," says Zelda as we approach a set of double swing doors. "Here we are. Keep your voices down when we go in."

She pushes open the doors and ushers us in, and for a moment my cool act falters. I feel all shaky and awed, like Laura Dern in *Jurassic Park* when she sees the dinosaurs for the first time. Because there it is, in real life. The real live *Morning Coffee* set. With the sofa and all the plants and everything, all lit up by the brightest, most dazzling lights I've ever seen in my life.

This is just unreal. How many zillion times have I sat at home, watching this on the telly? And now I'm actually going to be part of it.

"We've got a couple of minutes till the commercial break," says Zelda, leading us across the floor, across a load of trailing cables. "Rory and Emma are still with Elisabeth in the library set."

She gestures to us to sit down on opposite sides of the coffee table, and, gingerly, I do so. The sofa's harder than I was expecting, and kind of . . . different. Everything's different. The plants seem bigger than they do on the screen, and the coffee table is smaller. God, this is weird. The lights are so bright on my face, I can hardly see anything, and I'm not quite sure how to sit. A girl comes and threads a microphone cable under my shirt and clips it to my lapel. Awkwardly, I lift my hand to push my hair back, and immediately Zelda comes hurrying over.

"Try not to move too much, OK, Rebecca?" she says. "We don't want to hear a load of rustling."

"Right," I say. "Sorry."

Suddenly my voice doesn't seem to be working properly. I feel as though a wad of cotton's been stuffed into my throat. I glance up at a nearby camera and, to my horror, see it zooming toward me.

"OK, Rebecca," says Zelda, hurrying over again, "one more golden rule—don't look at the camera, all right? Just behave naturally!"

"Fine," I say huskily.

Behave naturally. Easy-peasy.

"Thirty seconds till the news bulletin," she says, looking at her watch. "Everything OK, Luke?"

"Fine," says Luke calmly. He's sitting on his sofa as though he's been there all his life. Typical.

I shift on my seat, tug nervously at my skirt, and smooth my jacket down. They always say that television puts ten pounds on you, which means my legs will look really fat. Maybe I should cross them the other way. Or not cross them at all? But then maybe they'll look even fatter.

"Hello!" comes a high-pitched voice from across the set before I can make up my mind. My head jerks up, and I feel an excited twinge in my stomach. It's Emma March in the flesh! She's wearing a pink suit and hurrying toward the sofa, closely followed by Rory, who looks even more square-jawed than usual. God, it's weird seeing celebrities up close. They don't look quite real, somehow.

"Hello!" Emma says cheerfully, and sits down on the sofa. "So you're the finance people, are you? Gosh, I'm dying for a wee." She frowns into the lights. "How long is this slot, Zelda?"

"Hi there!" says Rory, and shakes my hand. "Roberta."

"It's Rebecca!" says Emma, and rolls her eyes at me sympathetically. "Honestly, he's hopeless." She wriggles on the sofa. "Gosh, I really need to go."

"Too late now," says Rory.

"But isn't it really unhealthy not to go when you need to?" Emma wrinkles her brow anxiously. "Didn't we have a phone-in on it once? That weird girl phoned up who only went once a day. And Dr. James said . . . what did he say?"

"Search me," says Rory cheerfully. "These phone-ins always go over my head. Now I'm warning you, Rebecca," he adds, turning to me, "I can never follow any of this finance stuff. Far too brainy for me." He gives me a wide grin and I smile weakly back.

"Ten seconds," calls Zelda from the side of the set, and my stomach gives a tweak of fear. Over the loudspeakers I can hear the *Morning Coffee* theme music, signaling the end of a commercial break.

"Who starts?" says Emma, squinting at the Tele-PrompTer. "Oh, me."

So this is it. I feel almost light-headed with fear. I don't know where I'm supposed to be looking; I don't know when I'm supposed to speak. My legs are trembling and my hands are clenched tightly in my lap. The lights are dazzling my eyes; a camera's zooming in on my left, but I've got to try to ignore it.

"Welcome back!" says Emma suddenly to the

camera. "Now, which would you rather have? A carriage clock or £20,000?"

What? I think in shock. But that's *my* line. That's what I was going to say.

"The answer's obvious, isn't it?" continues Emma blithely. "We'd all prefer the £20,000."

"Absolutely!" interjects Rory with a cheerful smile.

"But when some Flagstaff Life investors received a letter inviting them to move their savings recently," says Emma, suddenly putting on a sober face, "they didn't realize that if they did so, they would lose out on a £20,000 windfall. Rebecca Bloomwood is the journalist who uncovered this story—Rebecca, do you think this kind of deception is commonplace?"

And suddenly everyone's looking at me, waiting for me to reply. The camera's trained on my face; the studio's silent.

Two point five million people, all watching at home.

I can't breathe.

"Do you think investors need to be cautious?" prompts Emma.

"Yes," I manage in a strange, woolly voice. "Yes, I think they should."

"Luke Brandon, you represent Flagstaff Life," says Emma, turning away. "Do you think—"

Shit, I think miserably. That was pathetic. Pathetic! What's happened to my voice, for God's sake? What's happened to all my prepared answers?

And now I'm not even listening to Luke's reply. Come on, Rebecca. Concentrate.

"What you must remember," Luke's saying smoothly, "is that nobody's *entitled* to a windfall. This isn't a case of deception!" He smiles at Emma. "This is simply a case of a few investors being a little too greedy for their own good. They believe they've missed out—so they're deliberately stirring up bad publicity for the company. Meanwhile, there are thousands of people who *have* benefited from Flagstaff Life."

What? What's he saying?

"I see," says Emma, nodding her head. "So, Luke, would you agree that—"

"Wait a minute!" I hear myself interrupting. "Just . . . just wait a minute. Mr. Brandon, did you just call the *investors* greedy?"

"Not all," says Luke. "But some, yes."

I stare at him in disbelief, my skin prickling with outrage. An image of Janice and Martin comes into my mind—the sweetest, least greedy people in the world—and for a few moments I'm so angry, I can't speak.

"The truth is, the majority of investors with Flagstaff Life have seen record returns over the last five years," Luke's continuing to Emma, who's nodding intelligently. "And that's what they should be concerned with. Good-quality investment. Not flash-in-the-pan windfalls. After all, Flagstaff Life was originally set up to provide—"

"Correct me if I'm wrong, Luke," I cut in, forcing myself to speak calmly. "Correct me if I'm wrong—but I believe Flagstaff Life was originally set up as a mutual company? For the *mutual benefit* of all its members. Not to benefit some at the expense of others."

"Absolutely," replies Luke without flickering. "But that doesn't entitle every investor to a £20,000 windfall, does it?"

"Maybe not," I say, my voice rising slightly. "But surely it entitles them to believe they won't be misled by a company they've put their money with for fifteen years? Janice and Martin Webster trusted Flagstaff Life. They trusted the advice they were given. And look where that trust got them!"

"Investment is a game of luck," says Luke blandly. "Sometimes you win—"

"It wasn't luck!" I hear myself crying furiously. "Of course it wasn't luck! Are you telling me it was compete coincidence that they were advised to switch their funds two weeks before the windfall announcements?"

"My clients were simply making available an offer that they believed would add value to their customers' portfolios," says Luke, giving me a tight smile. "They have assured me that they were simply wishing to benefit their customers. They have assured me that—"

"So you're saying your clients are incompetent, then?" I retort. "You're saying they had all the best intentions—but cocked it up?"

Luke's eyes flash in anger and I feel a thrill of exhilaration.

"I fail to see—"

"Well, we could go on debating all day!" says Emma, shifting slightly on her seat. "But moving onto a slightly more—"

"Come on, Luke," I say, cutting her off. "Come *on*. You can't have it both ways." I lean forward, ticking points off on my hand. "Either Flagstaff Life were incompetent, or they were deliberately trying to save money. Whichever it is, they're in the wrong. The Websters were loyal customers and they should have gotten that money. In my opinion, Flagstaff Life deliberately encouraged them out of the with-profits fund to stop them receiving the windfall. I mean, it's obvious, isn't it?"

I look around for support and see Rory gazing blankly at me.

"It all sounds a bit technical for me," he says with a little laugh. "Bit complicated."

"OK, let's put it another way," I say quickly. "Let's . . ." I close my eyes, searching for inspiration. "Let's . . . suppose I'm in a clothes shop!" I open my eyes again. "I'm in a clothes shop, and I've chosen a wonderful cashmere Nicole Farhi coat. OK?"

"OK," says Rory cautiously.

"I love Nicole Farhi!" says Emma, perking up. "Beautiful knitwear."

"Exactly," I say. "OK, so imagine I'm standing in the checkout queue, minding my own business, when a sales assistant comes up to me and says, 'Why not buy this other coat instead? It's better quality—and I'll throw in a free bottle of perfume.' I've got no reason to distrust the sales assistant, so I think, Wonderful, and I buy the other coat."

"Right," says Rory, nodding. "With you so far."

"But when I get outside," I say carefully, "I discover that this other coat isn't Nicole Farhi and isn't real cashmere. I go back in—and the shop won't give me a refund."

"You were ripped off!" exclaims Rory, as though he's just discovered gravity.

"Exactly," I say. "I was ripped off. And the point is, so were thousands of Flagstaff Life customers. They were persuaded out of their original choice of investment, into a fund which left them £20,000 worse off." I pause, marshaling my thoughts. "Perhaps Flagstaff Life didn't break the law. Perhaps they didn't contravene any regulations. But there's a natural justice in this world, and they didn't just break that, they shattered it. Those customers deserved that windfall. They were loyal, long-standing customers, and they deserved it. And if you're honest, Luke Brandon, you *know* they deserved it."

I finish my speech breathlessly and look at Luke. He's staring at me with an unreadable expression on his face—and in spite of myself, I feel my stomach clench with nerves. I swallow, and try to shift my vision away from his—but somehow I can't move my head. It's as though our eyes are glued together.

"Luke?" says Emma. "Do you have a response to Rebecca's point?"

Luke doesn't respond. He's staring at me, and I'm staring back, feeling my heart thump like a rabbit.

"Luke?" repeats Emma slightly impatiently. "Do you have—"

"Yes," says Luke. "Yes I do. Rebecca—" He shakes his head, almost smiling to himself, then looks up again at me. "Rebecca, you're right."

There's a sudden still silence around the studio.

I open my mouth, but I can't make a sound.

Out of the corner of my eye, I see Rory and Emma glancing at each other puzzledly.

"Sorry, Luke," says Emma. "Do you mean—"

"She's right," says Luke, and gives a shrug. "Rebecca's absolutely right." He reaches for his glass of water, leans back on his sofa, and takes a sip. "If you want my honest opinion, those customers deserved that windfall. I very much wish they *had* received it."

He looks up at me, and he's wearing that same apologetic expression he had in the corridor. This can't be happening. Luke's agreeing with me. How can he be agreeing with me?

"I see," says Emma, sounding a bit affronted. "So, you've changed your position, then?"

There's a pause, while Luke stares thoughtfully into his glass of water. Then he looks up and says, "My company is employed by Flagstaff Life to maintain their public profile. But that doesn't mean that personally I agree with everything they do—or even that I know about it." He pauses. "To tell you the truth, I had no idea any of this was going on until I read about it in Rebecca's article in *The Daily World*. Which, by the way, was a fine piece of investigative journalism," he adds, nodding to me. "Congratulations."

I stare back helplessly, unable even to mutter "Thank you." I've never felt so wrong-footed in all my life. I want to stop and bury my head in my hands and think all of this through slowly and carefully—but I can't, I'm on live television. I'm being watched by 2.5 million people, all around the country.

I hope my legs look OK.

"If I were a Flagstaff customer and this had happened to me, I'd be very angry," Luke continues. "There is such a thing as customer loyalty; there is such a thing as playing straight. And I would hope that any client of mine, whom I represent in public, would abide by both of those principles."

"I see," says Emma, and turns to the camera. "Well, this is quite a turnaround! Luke Brandon, here to represent Flagstaff Life, now says that what they did was wrong. Any further comment, Luke?"

"To be honest," says Luke, with a wry smile, "I'm not sure I'll be representing Flagstaff Life any more after this."

"Ah," says Rory, leaning forward intelligently. "And can you tell us why that is?"

"Oh, honestly, Rory!" says Emma impatiently. She rolls her eyes and Luke gives a little snort of laughter.

And suddenly everyone's laughing, and I join in too, slightly hysterically. I catch Luke's eye and feel something flash in my chest, then quickly look away again.

"Right, well, anyway," says Emma abruptly, pulling herself together and smiling at the camera. "That's it from the finance experts—but, coming up after the break, the return of hot pants to the catwalk . . ."

". . . and cellulite creams—do they really work?" adds Rory.

"Plus our special guests—Heaven Sent 7—singing live in the studio."

The theme music blares out of the loudspeakers and both Emma and Rory leap to their feet.

"Wonderful debate," says Emma, hurrying off. "Sorry, I'm *dying* for a wee."

"Excellent stuff," adds Rory earnestly. "Didn't understand a word—but great television." He slaps Luke on the back, raises his hand to me, and then hurries off the set.

And all at once it's over. It's just me and Luke, sitting opposite each other on the sofas, with bright lights still shining in our eyes and microphones still clipped to our lapels. I feel slightly shell-shocked.

Did all that really just happen?

"So," I say eventually, and clear my throat.

"So," echoes Luke with a tiny smile. "Well done."

"Thanks," I say, and bite my lip awkwardly in the silence.

I'm wondering if he's in big trouble now. If attacking one of your clients on live TV is the PR equivalent of hiding clothes from the customers.

If he really changed his mind because of my article. Because of me.

But I can't ask that. Can I?

The silence is growing louder and louder and at last I take a deep breath.

"Did you—"

"I was—"

We both speak at once.

"No," I say, flushing red. "You go. Mine wasn't . . . You go."

"OK," says Luke, and gives a little shrug. "I was just going to ask if you'd like to have dinner tonight."

What does he mean, have dinner? Does he mean—

"To discuss a bit of business," he continues. "I very much liked your idea for a unit trust promotion along the lines of the January sales."

My what?

What idea? What's he . . .

Oh God, *that*. Is he serious? That was just one of my stupid, speak-aloud, brain-not-engaged moments.

"I think it could be a good promotion for a particular client of ours," he's saying, "and I was wondering whether you'd like to consult on the project. On a freelance basis, of course."

Consult. Freelance. Project.

He's serious.

"Oh," I say, and swallow, inexplicably disappointed. "Oh, I see. Well, I . . . I suppose I might be free tonight."

"Good," says Luke. "Shall we say the Ritz?"

"If you like," I say offhandedly, as though I go there all the time.

"Good," says Luke again, and his eyes crinkle into a smile. "I look forward to it."

And then—oh God. To my utter horror, before I can stop myself, I hear myself saying bitchily, "What about Sacha? Doesn't she have plans for you tonight?"

Even as the words hit the air, I feel myself redden. Oh shit. Shit! What did I say that for?

There's a long silence during which I want to slink off somewhere and die.

"Sacha left two weeks ago," says Luke finally, and my head pops up.

"Oh," I say feebly. "Oh dear."

"No warning—she packed up her calfskin suitcase and went." Luke looks up. "Still, it could be worse." He gives a deadpan shrug. "At least I didn't buy the holdall as well."

Oh God, now I'm going to giggle. I mustn't giggle. I *mustn't*.

"I'm really sorry," I manage at last.

"I'm not," says Luke, gazing at me seriously, and the laughter inside me dies away. I stare back at him nervously and feel a tingle spread across my face.

"Rebecca! Luke!"

Our heads jerk round to see Zelda approaching the set, clipboard in hand.

"Fantastic!" she exclaims. "Just what we wanted. Luke, you were great. And Rebecca . . ." She comes and sits next to me on the sofa and pats my shoulder. "You were so wonderful, we were thinking—how would you like to stand in as our phone-in expert later in the show?"

"What?" I stare at her. "But . . . but I can't! I'm not an expert on anything."

"Ha-ha-ha, very good!" Zelda gives an appreciative laugh. "The great thing about you, Rebecca, is you've got the common touch. We see you as finance guru meets girl next door. Informative but approachable. Knowledgeable but down-to-earth. The financial expert people really want to talk to. What do you think, Luke?"

"I think Rebecca will do the job perfectly," says Luke. "I can't think of anyone better qualified. I also think I'd better get out of your way." He stands up and smiles at me. "See you later, Rebecca. Bye, Zelda."

I watch in a daze as he picks his way across the cable-strewn floor toward the exit, half wishing he would look back.

"Right," says Zelda, and squeezes my hand. "Let's get you sorted."

Twenty-two

I WAS MADE TO GO ON TELEVISION. That's the truth. I was absolutely *made* to go on television.

We're sitting on the sofas again, Rory and Emma and me, and Anne from Leeds is admitting over the line that she's never given retirement planning a thought.

I glance at Emma and smile, and she twinkles back. I've never felt so warm and happy in all my life.

What's really strange is that when it was me being interviewed, I felt all tongue-tied and nervous—but on the other side of the sofa, I've been in my element right from the start. God, I could do this all day. I don't even mind the bright lights anymore. They feel normal. And I've practiced the most flattering way to sit in front of the mirror (knees together, feet crossed at the ankle), and I'm sticking to it.

"My mum used to tell me to take out a pension," says Anne, "and I used to laugh at her. But now I've started to panic I've left it too late."

"Rebecca?" says Emma. "Should Anne be concerned?"

Pensions, I think quickly. Come on, what do I know about pensions?

"Well," I say. "Of course, the earlier you start saving,

the more you'll accumulate. But that's no reason to panic, Anne. The good thing is, you're thinking about it *now*."

"How old are you exactly, Anne?" says Emma.

"I'm thirty," says Anne. "Thirty last month."

Yes! Thank you, God!

"Ah, well," I say knowledgeably. "A typical woman of thirty, who invested £100 a month, would receive an income of £9,000 on retirement at sixty. That's assuming 7 percent growth."

Bingo. Rory and Emma look *so* impressed. OK, quick, what else?

"But you should also look for flexibility, Anne," I continue. "Choose a scheme which allows you to take a 'holiday' from payments, because you never know when you might need it."

"That's true," says Anne thoughtfully. "I'd like to take a year off sometime and travel a bit."

"Well, there you are!" I say triumphantly. "If you do that, you'll want to be able to pause your pension payments. In fact, what I would do is—"

"Thanks, Rebecca," chimes in Emma. "Wise advice there! Now we're going to go briefly to Davina for news and weather . . ."

I'm rather disappointed at being interrupted. There were so many more things I could have said to Anne. All the points I made in my pensions article are popping up in my head—and now that there's a real person involved, they all suddenly seem a lot more interesting. In fact, the whole subject seems more interesting today. It's as though all this stuff has suddenly got a point.

Believe it or not, I'm really enjoying the questions on this phone-in. I know about mortgages and I know about life insurance and I know about unit trusts. I know so much more than I ever realized! A few minutes ago, Kenneth from St. Austell asked what the annual contribution limit for an ISA is—and the figure £5,000 just jumped right into my head. It's as if some bit of my mind has been storing every single bit of information I've ever written—and now, when I need it, it's all there.

"And after the break," Emma's saying, "since so many of you are ringing in, we'll be coming back to this phone-in: 'Managing Your Money.' "

"Lots of people with money problems out there," chimes in Rory.

"Absolutely," says Emma. "And we want to help. So whatever your query, however big or small, please call in for Rebecca Bloomwood's advice, on 0333 4567." She freezes for a moment, smiling at the camera, then relaxes back in her chair as the light goes off. "Well, this is going very well!" she says brightly, as a makeup girl hurries up and touches up her face with powder. "Isn't it, Zelda?"

"Fantastic!" says Zelda, appearing out of nowhere. "The lines haven't been this busy since we did 'I'd Like to Meet a Spice Girl.' " She looks curiously at me. "Have you ever done a course in television presenting, Rebecca?"

"No," I say honestly. "I haven't. But . . . I've watched a lot of telly."

Zelda roars with laughter. "Good answer! OK, folks, we're back in thirty."

Emma smiles at me and consults a piece of paper in front of her, and Rory leans back and examines his nails.

I've never felt so completely and utterly happy. Never. Not even that time I found a Vivienne Westwood bustier for £60 in the Harvey Nichols sale. (I wonder where that is, actually. I must get round to wearing it sometime.) This beats everything. Life is perfect.

I lean back, full of contentment, and am idly looking

around the studio when an oddly familiar figure catches my eye. I peer harder, and my skin starts to prickle in horror. There's a man standing in the gloom of the studio—and honestly, I must be hallucinating or something, because he looks exactly like—

"And . . . welcome back," says Rory, and my attention snaps back to the set. "This morning's phone-in is on financial problems, big and small. Our guest expert is Rebecca Bloomwood and our next caller is Fran from Shrewsbury. Fran?"

"Yes," says Fran. "Hi. Hi, Rebecca."

"Hi there, Fran," I say, smiling warmly. "And what seems to be the trouble?"

"I'm in a mess," says Fran. "I . . . I don't know what to do."

"Are you in debt, Fran?" says Emma gently.

"Yes," says Fran, and gives a shaky sigh. "I'm overdrawn, I owe money on all my credit cards, I've borrowed money off my sister . . . and I just can't stop spending. I just . . . love buying things."

"What sort of things?" says Rory interestedly.

"I don't know, really," says Fran after a pause. "Clothes for me, clothes for the kids, things for the house, just rubbish, really. Then the bills arrive . . . and I throw them away."

Emma gives me a significant look, and I raise my eyebrows back. But my cool act is starting to falter a little at Fran's story.

"It's like a vicious circle," Fran's saying. "The more in debt I am, the worse I feel, so I go out and spend more."

Outstanding bills. Credit card debts. Overdrafts. All the things I've been desperate not to think about are being thrust back into my mind. Desperately I thrust them back out again.

"Rebecca?" she says. "Fran's obviously in a bit of a spot. What should she be doing?"

For an instant I feel like crying *Why ask me?* But I can't crumble, I have to do this. I have to be Rebecca Bloomwood, top financial expert. Summoning all my strength, I force myself to smile sympathetically at the camera.

"Well, Fran," I say. "The first thing you've got to do is . . . is be brave and confront the issue. Contact the bank and tell them you're having trouble managing." I swallow hard, trying to keep my voice steady. "I know myself how hard it can be to tackle this kind of problem—but I can honestly tell you, running away doesn't solve anything. The longer you leave it, the worse it'll get."

"Rebecca," says Emma earnestly. "Would you say this is a common problem?"

"I'm afraid it is," I reply. "It's all too easy to forget those unpaid bills, to put them in a dressing table drawer, or . . . or throw them in a skip . . ."

"A skip?" says Rory, looking puzzled.

"Whatever," I say hurriedly. "Everybody's different."

"I put mine in the dog basket," interjects Fran. "Then he chews them and I can't read them."

"I can understand that," I say, nodding. "But you know what, Fran? Once you take those letters out of the dog basket and actually read them, you'll find they're not nearly as bad as you think."

"You really think so?" says Fran tremulously.

"Open each envelope," I suggest, "and write down all the outstanding amounts. Then make a plan to pay them off, even if it's only £5 a week. You can do it."

There's a long pause.

"Fran?" says Emma. "Are you still there?"

"Yes!" says Fran. "Yes, I'm still here—and I'm going

to do it! You've convinced me. Thanks, Becky! I really appreciate your help!"

I beam back at the camera, my confidence restored.

"It's a pleasure," I say. "And you know, Fran, as soon as you turn that corner and wake up to the real world, your life will be transformed."

I make a confident sweeping gesture with my arm, and as I do so, my gaze takes in the whole studio. And . . . oh my God, it's him.

I'm not hallucinating.

It's really him. Standing at the corner of the set, wearing a security badge and sipping something in a polystyrene cup as though he belongs here. Derek Smeath is standing here in the *Morning Coffee* studios, ten yards away from me.

Derek Smeath of Endwich Bank. It doesn't make any sense. What's he doing here?

Oh God, and now he's staring straight at me.

My heart begins to pound, and I swallow hard, trying to keep control of myself.

"Rebecca?" Emma says puzzledly, and I force myself to turn my attention back to the show. But all my confident words are withering on my lips. "So you really think, if she tries, Fran will be able to get her life in order?"

"I . . . that's right," I say, and force a smile. "It's just a question of facing up to it."

I'm trying desperately to stay cool and professional—but all the bits of my life I'd so carefully buried are starting to worm their way out again. Here they come, wriggling into my mind, one piece of dreadful reality after another.

"Well," says Rory. "Let's all hope Fran takes Rebecca's very good advice."

My bank account. Thousands of pounds of debt.

"We're out of time, I'm afraid," says Emma, "but before we go, do you have any last words of advice, Rebecca?"

My VISA card, canceled. My Octagon card, confiscated in front of that whole crowd. God, that was humiliating.

OK, stop it. Concentrate. Concentrate.

"Yes," I say, forcing a confident tone. "I would just say . . . in the same way you might have a medical checkup once a year, do the same with your finances. Don't ignore them until they become a problem!"

My whole terrible, disorganized life. It's all there, isn't it? Waiting for me, like a great big spider. Just waiting to pounce, as soon as this phone-in ends.

"Wise words from our financial expert," says Emma. "Many thanks to Rebecca Bloomwood, and I'm sure we'll all be heeding her advice. Coming up after the break, the results of our makeover in Newcastle and Heaven Sent 7, live in the studio."

There's a frozen pause, then everyone relaxes.

"Right," says Emma, consulting her piece of paper. "Where are we next?"

"Good work, Rebecca," says Rory cheerfully. "Excellent stuff."

"Oh, Zelda!" says Emma, leaping up. "Could I have a quick word? That was fab, Rebecca," she adds. "Really fab."

And suddenly they're both gone. And I'm left alone on the set, exposed and vulnerable. Rebecca Bloomwood, top financial expert, has vanished. All that's left is me, Becky. Shrinking on my seat and frantically trying to avoid Derek Smeath's eye.

I don't have anything to give him. The money from *The Daily World* has got to go straight to Suze. I'm in as much trouble as I ever was. What am I going to do?

Maybe I could slip out at the back.

Maybe I could stick it out here on the sofa. Just sit here until he gets bored and leaves. I mean, he won't dare to come onto the actual set, will he? Or maybe I could *pretend to be someone else*. God yes. I mean, with all this makeup on, I practically look like someone else, anyway. I could just walk quickly past, and if he talks to me, answer in a foreign accent. Or else . . .

And then suddenly I stop, midtrack. It's as though I'm hearing my own thoughts for the first time in my life. And what I hear makes me ashamed of myself.

Who do I think I'm kidding? What exactly will I achieve by dodging Derek Smeath one more time? It's time to grow up, Becky, I tell myself. It's time to stop running away. If Fran from Shrewsbury can do it, then so can Rebecca from London.

I stand up, take a deep breath, and walk slowly across the set to Derek Smeath.

"Hello, Mr. Smeath," I say in polite, calm tones. "What a coincidence to see you here." I hold out my hand for a symbolic, peacemaking handshake, but Derek Smeath doesn't even seem to see it. He's staring at me as though he's seen a goldfish begin to talk.

"*Coincidence?*" he echoes at last, and a technician gestures to us to keep our voices down. Derek Smeath firmly ushers me out of the studio into a foyer area and turns to face me, and I feel a twinge of fear at his expression.

"Miss Bloomwood," he says. "Miss Bloomwood—" He rubs his face with his hand, then looks up. "Do you know quite how long I have been writing letters to you? Do you know how long I've been trying to get you into the bank for a meeting?"

"Ahm . . . I'm not quite—"

"Six months," says Derek Smeath, and pauses. "Six

long months of excuses and prevarication. Now, I'd just like you to think about what that means for me. It means endless letters. Numerous phone calls. Hours of time and effort on my part and that of my assistant, Erica. Resources which, quite frankly, could be better spent elsewhere." He gestures sharply with his polystyrene cup and some coffee slops onto the floor. "Then finally I pin you down to a cast-iron appointment. Finally I think you're taking your situation seriously . . . And you don't turn up. You disappear completely. I telephone your home to find out where you are, and get accused most unpleasantly of being some kind of stalker!"

"Oh yes," I say, and pull an apologetic face. "Sorry about that. It's just my dad, you know. He's a bit weird."

"I'd all but given up on you," says Derek Smeath, his voice rising. "I'd all but given up. And then I'm passing a television shop this morning, and what should I see, on six different screens, but the missing, vanished Rebecca Bloomwood, advising the nation. And what are you advising them on?" He begins to shake with laughter. (At least, I think it's laughter.) "Finance! *You* are advising the British public . . . on finance!"

I stare at him, taken aback. It's not *that* funny.

"Look, I'm very sorry I couldn't make the last meeting," I say, trying to sound businesslike. "Things were a bit difficult for me at that time. But if we could reschedule . . ."

"Reschedule!" cries Derek Smeath, as though I've just cracked a hysterical joke. "Reschedule!"

I gaze at him indignantly. He's not taking me seriously at all, is he? He hasn't shaken my hand, and he's not even listening to what I'm saying. I'm telling him I want to come in for a meeting—I actually *want* to—and he's just treating me like a joke.

And no wonder, interrupts a tiny voice inside me. *Look at the way you've behaved. Look at the way you've treated him. Frankly, it's a wonder he's being civil to you at all.*

I look up at his face, still crinkled in laughter . . . and suddenly feel very chastened.

Because the truth is, he could have been a lot nastier to me than he has been. He could have taken my card away a long time ago. Or sent the bailiffs round. Or had me blacklisted. He's actually been very nice to me, one way or another, and all I've done is lie and wriggle and run away.

"Listen," I say quickly. "Please. Give me another chance. I really want to sort my finances out. I want to repay my overdraft. But I need you to help me. I'm . . ." I swallow. "I'm asking you to help me, Mr. Smeath."

There's a long pause. Derek Smeath looks around for a place to put his coffee cup, takes a white handkerchief out of his pocket, and rubs his brow with it. Then he puts it away and gives me a long look.

"You're serious," he says at last.

"Yes."

"You'll really make an effort?"

"Yes. And—" I bite my lip. "And I'm very grateful for all the allowances you've made for me. I really am."

Suddenly I feel almost tearful. I want to be good. I want to get my life in order. I want him to tell me what to do to make things right.

"All right," says Derek Smeath at last. "Let's see what we can sort out. You come into the office tomorrow, nine-thirty sharp, and we'll have a little chat."

"Thanks," I say, my whole body subsiding in relief. "Thank you so much. I'll be there. I promise."

"You'd better be," he says. "No more excuses." Then a faint smile passes over his features. "By the way," he adds, gesturing to the set. "I thought you did very well up there, with all your advice."

"Oh," I say in surprise. "Well . . . thanks. That's really . . ." I clear my throat. "How did you get into the studio, anyway? I thought they had quite tight security."

"They do," replies Derek Smeath. "But my daughter works in television." He smiles fondly. "She used to work on this very show."

"Really?" I say incredulously.

God, how amazing. Derek Smeath has a daughter. He's probably got a whole family, come to that. A wife, and everything. Who would have thought it?

"I'd better go," he says, and drains his polystyrene cup. "This was a bit of an unscheduled detour." He gives me a severe look. "And I'll see you tomorrow."

"I'll be there," I say quickly, as he walks off toward the exit. "And . . . and thanks. Thanks a lot."

As he disappears, I sink down onto a nearby chair. I can't quite believe I've just had a pleasant, civilized conversation with Derek Smeath. With Derek Smeath! And actually, he seems quite a sweetheart. He's been so nice and kind to me, and his daughter works in television . . . I mean, who knows, maybe I'll get to know her, too. Maybe I'll become friends with the whole family. Wouldn't that be great? I'll start going to dinner at their house, and his wife will give me a warm hug when I arrive, and I'll help her with the salad and stuff . . .

"Rebecca!" comes a voice from behind me, and I turn round to see Zelda approaching, still clutching her clipboard.

"Hi," I say happily. "How's it going?"

"Great," she says, and pulls up a chair. "Now, I want to have a little talk."

"Oh," I say, suddenly nervous. "OK. What about?"

"We thought you did tremendously well today," says Zelda, crossing one jeaned leg over the other. "*Tremendously* well. I've spoken to Emma and Rory and our senior producer"—she pauses for effect—"and they'd all like to see you back on the show."

I stare at her in disbelief. "You mean—"

"Not every week," says Zelda. "But fairly regularly. We thought maybe three times a month. Do you think your work would allow you to do that?"

"I . . . I don't know," I say dazedly. "I expect it would."

"Excellent!" says Zelda. "We could probably plug your magazine as well, keep them happy." She scribbles something on a piece of paper and looks up. "Now, you don't have an agent, do you? So I'll have to talk money directly with you." She pauses, and looks down at her clipboard. "What we're offering, per slot, is—"

Twenty-three

I PUT MY KEY IN THE LOCK and slowly open the door of the flat. It seems like about a million years since I was here last, and I feel like a completely different person. I've grown up. Or changed. Or something.

"Hi," I say cautiously into the silence, and drop my bag onto the floor. "Is anyone—"

"Bex!" gasps Suze, appearing at the door of the sitting room. She's wearing tight black leggings and holding a half-made denim photograph frame in one hand. "Oh my God! Where've you *been*? What have you been doing? I saw you on *Morning Coffee* and I couldn't believe my eyes! I tried to phone in and speak to you, but they said I had to have a financial problem. So I said, OK, how should I invest half a million? but they said that wasn't really . . ." She breaks off. "Bex, what happened?"

I don't reply straight away. My attention has been grabbed by the pile of letters addressed to me on the table. White, official-looking envelopes, brown window envelopes, envelopes marked menacingly "Final Reminder." The scariest pile of letters you've ever seen.

Except somehow . . . they don't seem quite so scary anymore.

"I was at my parents' house," I say, looking up. "And then I was on television."

"But I phoned your parents! They said they didn't know where you were!"

"I know," I say, flushing slightly. "They were . . . protecting me from a stalker." I look up, to see Suze staring at me in utter incomprehension. Which I suppose is fair enough. "Anyway," I add defensively, "I left you a message on the machine, saying not to worry, I was fine."

"I know," wails Suze, "but that's what they always do in films. And it means the baddies have got you and you've got a gun jammed against your head. Honestly, I thought you were dead! I thought you were, like, cut up into a million pieces somewhere."

I look at her face again. She isn't kidding, she really was worried. I feel awful. I should never have vanished like that. It was completely thoughtless and irresponsible and selfish.

"Oh, Suze." On impulse, I hurry forward and hug her tightly. "I'm really sorry. I never meant to worry you."

"It's OK," says Suze, hugging me back. "I was worried for a bit—but then I knew you must be all right when I saw you on the telly. You were fantastic, by the way."

"Really?" I say, a tiny smile flickering round the corners of my mouth. "Did you really think so?"

"Oh yes!" says Suze. "Much better than whatshisface. Luke Brandon. God, he's arrogant."

"Yes," I say after a tiny pause. "Yes, I suppose he is. But he was actually quite nice to me afterward."

"Really?" says Suze indifferently. "Well, you were brilliant, anyway. Do you want some coffee?"

"Love some," I say, and she disappears into the kitchen.

I pick up my letters and bills and begin slowly to leaf through them. Once upon a time, this lot would have sent me into a blind panic. In fact, they would have gone straight into the bin, unread. But you know what? Today I don't feel a flicker of fear. Honestly, how could I have been so silly about my financial affairs? How could I have been so cowardly? This time I'm just going to face up to them properly. I'm going to sit down with my checkbook and my latest bank statements, and sort methodically through the whole mess.

Staring at the clutch of envelopes in my hand, I feel suddenly very grown-up and responsible. Farsighted and sensible. I'm going to sort my life out and keep my finances in order from now on. I've completely and utterly changed my attitude toward money.

Plus . . .

OK, I wasn't actually going to tell you this. But *Morning Coffee* is paying me absolute loads. *Loads*. You won't believe it, but for every single phone-in I do, I'm going to get—

Oh, I'm all embarrassed now. Let's just say it's . . . it's quite a lot!

I just can't stop smiling about it. I've been floating along ever since they told me. So the point is, I'll easily be able to pay all these bills off now. My VISA bill, and my Octagon bill, and the money I owe Suze—and everything! Finally, *finally* my life is going to be sorted.

"So, why did you just disappear like that?" asks Suze, coming back out of the kitchen and making me jump. "What was wrong?"

"I don't really know," I say with a sigh, putting the letters back down on the hall table. "I just had to get away and think. I was all confused."

"Because of Tarquin?" says Suze at once, and I feel myself stiffen apprehensively.

"Partly," I say after a pause, and swallow. "Why? Has he—"

"I know you're not that keen on Tarkie," says Suze wistfully, "but I think he still really likes you. He came round a couple of nights ago and left you this letter."

She gestures to a cream envelope stuck in the mirror. With slightly trembling hands I take it. Oh God, what's he going to say? I hesitate, then rip it open, and a ticket falls onto the floor.

"The opera!" says Suze, picking it up. "Day after tomorrow." She looks up. "God, it's lucky you came back, Bex."

My dear Rebecca, I'm reading incredulously. *Forgive my reticence in contacting you before. But the more I think about it, the more I realize how much I enjoyed our evening together and how much I would like to repeat it.*

I enclose a ticket for Die Meistersinger *at the Opera House. I shall be attending in any case and if you were able to join me, I would be delighted.*

Yours very sincerely,

Tarquin Cleath-Stuart.

"Oh, Bex, you must go!" says Suze, reading over my shoulder. "You've got to go. He'll be devastated if you don't. I really think he likes you."

I look at the ticket, for two nights' time. "Gala Performance," it says, and I feel a sudden excitement. I've never been to an opera gala! I could wear that divine Ghost dress which I've never had a chance to wear, and I could put my hair up, and meet lots of amazing people . . .

And then, abruptly, I stop. However much fun it

would be—it wouldn't be fair or honest to go. I've hurt
Tarquin enough.

"I can't go, Suze," I say, thrusting the letter down.
"I've . . . I've got plans that night."

"But what about poor Tarkie?" says Suze, crestfallen.
"He's so keen on you . . ."

"I know," I say, and take a deep breath. "But I'm not
keen on him. I'm really sorry, Suze . . . but that's the
truth. If I could change the way I felt . . ."

There's a short silence.

"Oh well," says Suze at last. "Never mind. You can't
help it." She disappears into the kitchen and emerges a
minute later with two mugs of coffee. "So," she says,
handing me one, "what are you up to tonight? Shall we
go out together?"

"Sorry, I can't," I say, and clear my throat. "I've got a
business meeting."

"Really?" Suze pulls a face. "What a bummer!" She
sips at her coffee and leans against the door frame.
"Who on earth has business meetings in the evening,
anyway?"

"It's . . . it's with Luke Brandon," I say, trying to
sound unconcerned. But it's no good, I can feel myself
starting to blush.

"Luke Brandon?" says Suze puzzledly. "But what—"
She stares at me, and her expression slowly changes.
"Oh no. Bex! Don't tell me . . ."

"It's just a business meeting," I say, avoiding her eye.
"That's all. Two businesspeople meeting up and talking
about business. In a . . . in a business situation. That's
all."

And I hurry off to my room.

Business meeting. Clothes for a business meeting.
OK, let's have a look.

I pull all my outfits out of the wardrobe and lay them on the bed. Blue suit, black suit, pink suit. Hopeless. Pin-striped suit? Hmm. Maybe overdoing it. Cream suit . . . too weddingy. Green suit . . . isn't that bad luck or something?

"So what are you going to wear?" says Suze, looking in through my open bedroom door. "Are you going to buy something new?" Her face lights up. "Hey, shall we go shopping?"

"Shopping?" I say distractedly. "Ahm . . . maybe."

Somehow today . . . Oh, I don't know. I almost feel too tense to go shopping. Too keyed up. I don't think I'd be able to give it my full attention.

"Bex, did you hear me?" says Suze in surprise. "I said, shall we go shopping?"

"Yes, I know." I glance up at her, then reach for a black top and look at it critically. "Actually, I think I'll take a rain check."

"You mean . . ." Suze pauses. "You mean you *don't* want to go shopping?"

"Exactly."

There's silence, and I look up, to see Suze staring at me.

"I don't understand," she says, and she sounds quite upset. "Why are you being all weird?"

"I'm not being weird!" I give a little shrug. "I just don't feel like shopping."

"Oh God, there's something wrong, isn't there?" wails Suze. "I knew it. Maybe you're really ill." She hurries into the room and reaches for my head. "Have you got a temperature? Does anything hurt?"

"No!" I say, laughing. "Of course not!"

"Have you had a bump on the head?" She wiggles her hand in front of my face. "How many fingers?"

"Suze, I'm fine," I say, thrusting her hand aside. "Honestly. I'm just . . . not in a shopping mood." I hold a gray suit up against myself. "What do you think of this?"

"Honestly, Bex, I'm worried about you," says Suze, shaking her head. "I think you should get yourself checked out. You're so . . . different. It's frightening."

"Yes, well." I reach for a white shirt and smile at her. "Maybe I've changed."

It takes me all afternoon to decide on an outfit. There's a lot of trying on, and mixing and matching, and suddenly remembering things at the back of my wardrobe. (I *must* wear those purple jeans sometime.) But eventually I go for simple and straightforward. My nicest black suit (Jigsaw sale, two years ago), a white T-shirt (M&S), and knee-high black suede boots (Dolce & Gabbana, but I told Mum they were from BHS. Which was a mistake, because then she wanted to get some for herself, and I had to pretend they'd all sold out). I put it all on, screw my hair up into a knot, and stare at myself in the mirror.

"Very nice," says Suze admiringly from the door. "Very sexy."

"Sexy?" I feel a pang of dismay. "I'm not going for sexy! I'm going for businesslike."

"Can't you be both at once?" suggests Suze. "Businesslike *and* sexy?"

"I . . . no," I say after a pause, and look away. "No, I don't want to."

I don't want Luke Brandon to think I've dressed up for him, is what I really mean. I don't want to give him the slightest chance to think I've misconstrued what this meeting is about. Not like last time.

With no warning, a surge of fresh humiliation goes through my body as I remember that awful moment in Harvey Nichols. I shake my head hard, trying to clear it; trying to calm myself. Why the hell did I agree to this bloody dinner, anyway?

"I just want to look as serious and businesslike as possible," I say, and frown sternly at my reflection.

"I know, then," says Suze. "You need some accessories. Some businesswoman-type accessories."

"Like what? A Filofax?"

"Like . . ." Suze pauses thoughtfully. "OK. Wait there—"

I arrive at the Ritz that evening five minutes after our agreed time of seventy-thirty, and as I reach the entrance to the restaurant, I see Luke there already, sitting back looking relaxed and sipping something that looks like a gin and tonic. He's wearing a different suit from the one he was wearing this morning, I can't help noticing, and he's put on a fresh, dark green shirt. He actually looks . . . Well. Quite nice. Quite good-looking.

Not that businessy, in fact.

And, come to think of it, this restaurant isn't very businessy, either. It's all chandeliers and gold garlands and soft pink chairs, and the most beautiful painted ceiling, all clouds and flowers. The whole place is sparkling with light, and it looks . . .

Well, actually, the word that springs to mind is *romantic*.

Oh God. My heart starts thumping with nerves, and I glance quickly at my reflection in a gilded mirror. I'm wearing the black Jigsaw suit and white T-shirt and black suede boots as originally planned. But now I also have a crisp copy of the *Financial Times* under one arm, a pair of tortoiseshell glasses (with clear glass) perched on my head, my clunky executive briefcase in one hand and—Suze's pièce de résistance—an AppleMac laptop in the other.

Maybe I overdid it.

I'm about to back away and see if I can quickly deposit the briefcase in the cloakroom (or, to be honest, just put it down on a chair and walk away), when Luke looks up, sees me, and smiles. Damn. So I'm forced to go forward over the plushy carpet, trying to look as relaxed as possible, even though one arm is clamped tightly to my side, to stop the *FT* from falling on the floor.

"Hello," says Luke as I arrive at the table. He stands up to greet me, and I realize that I can't shake his hand, because I'm holding the laptop. Flustered, I plunk my briefcase on the floor, transfer the laptop to the other side—nearly dropping the *FT* as I do so—and, with as much poise as possible, hold out my hand.

A flicker of amusement passes over Luke's face and he solemnly shakes it. He gestures to a chair, and watches politely as I put the laptop on the tablecloth, all ready for use.

"That's an impressive machine," he says. "Very . . . high tech."

"Yes," I reply, and give him a brief, cool smile. "I often use it to take notes at business meetings."

"Ah," says Luke, nodding. "Very organized of you."

He's obviously waiting for me to switch it on, so experimentally I press the return key. This, according to Suze, should make the screen spring to life. But nothing happens.

Casually I press the key again—and still nothing. I

jab at it, pretending my finger slipped by accident—and *still* nothing. Shit, this is embarrassing. Why do I ever listen to Suze?

"Is there a problem?" says Luke.

"No!" I say at once, and snap the lid shut. "No, I've just—On second thought, I won't use it today." I reach into my bag for a notebook. "I'll jot my notes down in here."

"Good idea," says Luke mildly. "Would you like some champagne?"

"Oh," I say, slightly thrown. "Well . . . OK."

"Excellent," says Luke. "I hoped you would."

He glances up, and a beaming waiter scurries forward with a bottle. Gosh, Krug.

But I'm not going to smile, or look pleased or anything. I'm going to stay thoroughly cool and professional. In fact, I'm only going to have one glass, before moving on to still water. I need to keep a clear head, after all.

While the waiter fills my champagne flute, I write down "Meeting between Rebecca Bloomwood and Luke Brandon" in my notebook. I look at it appraisingly, then underline it twice. There. That looks very efficient.

"So," I say, looking up, and raise my glass. "To business."

"To business," echoes Luke, and gives a wry smile. "Assuming I'm still *in* business, that is . . ."

"Really?" I say anxiously. "You mean—after what you said on *Morning Coffee*? Has it gotten you into trouble?"

He nods and I feel a pang of sympathy for him.

I mean, Suze is right—Luke is pretty arrogant. But I actually thought it was really good of him to stick out his neck like that and say publicly what he really thought about Flagstaff Life. And now, if he's going to be ruined as a result . . . well, it just seems all wrong.

"Have you lost . . . everything?" I say quietly, and Luke laughs.

"I wouldn't go that far. But we've had to do an awful lot of explaining to our other clients this afternoon." He grimaces. "It has to be said, insulting one of your major clients on live television isn't exactly normal PR practice."

"Well, I think they should respect you!" I retort. "For actually saying what you think! I mean, so few people do that these days. It could be like . . . your company motto: 'We tell the truth.' "

I take a gulp of champagne and look up into silence. Luke's gazing at me, a quizzical expression on his face.

"Rebecca, you have the uncanniest knack of hitting the nail right on the head," he says at last. "That's exactly what some of our clients have said. It's as though we've given ourselves a seal of integrity."

"Oh," I say, feeling rather pleased with myself. "Well, that's good. So you're not ruined."

"I'm not ruined," agrees Luke, and gives a little smile. "Just slightly dented."

A waiter appears from nowhere and replenishes my glass, and I take a sip. When I look up, Luke's staring at me again.

"You know, Rebecca, you're an extremely perceptive person," he says. "You see what other people don't."

"Oh well." I wave my champagne glass airily. "Didn't you hear Zelda? I'm 'finance guru meets girl next door.' " I meet his eye and we both start to laugh.

"You're informative meets approachable."

"Knowledgeable meets down-to-earth."

"You're intelligent meets charming, meets bright, meets . . ." Luke tails off, staring down into his drink, then looks up.

"Rebecca, I want to apologize," he says. "I've been

wanting to apologize for a while. That lunch in Harvey Nichols . . . you were right. I didn't treat you with the respect you deserved. The respect you deserve."

He breaks off into silence and I stare down at the tablecloth, feeling hot with indignation. It's all very well for him to say this *now*, I'm thinking furiously. It's all very well for him to book a table at the Ritz and order champagne and expect me to smile and say "Oh, that's OK." But underneath all the bright banter, I still feel wounded by that whole episode.

"My piece in *The Daily World* had nothing to do with that lunch," I say without looking up. "Nothing. And for you to insinuate that it did . . ."

"I know," says Luke, and sighs. "I should never have said that. It was a . . . a defensive, angry remark on a day when, frankly, you had us all on the hop."

"Really?" I can't help a pleased little smile coming to my lips. "I had you all on the hop?"

"Are you joking?" says Luke. "A whole page in *The Daily World* on one of our clients, completely out of the blue?"

Ha. I quite like that idea, actually. The whole of Brandon C thrown into disarray by Janice and Martin Webster.

"Was Alicia on the hop?" I can't resist asking.

"She was hopping as fast as her Pradas would let her," says Luke drily. "Even faster when I discovered she'd actually spoken to you the day before."

Ha!

"Good," I hear myself saying childishly—then wish I hadn't. Top businesswomen don't gloat over their enemies being told off. I should have simply nodded, or said "Ah" meaningfully.

"So, did I have you on the hop, too?" I say, giving a careless little shrug.

There's silence, and after a while I look up. Luke's gazing at me with an unsmiling expression, which makes me feel suddenly light-headed and breathless.

"You've had me on the hop for quite a while, Rebecca," he says quietly. He holds my eyes for a few seconds while I stare back, unable to move—then looks down at his menu. "Shall we order?"

The meal seems to go on all night. We talk and talk and eat, and talk, and eat some more. The food is so delicious I can't say no to anything, and the wine is so delicious I abandon my plan of drinking a businesslike single glass. By the time I'm toying listlessly with chocolate feulliantine, lavender honey ice cream, and caramelized pears, it's about midnight, and my head is starting to droop.

"How's the chocolate thing?" says Luke, finishing a mouthful of cheesecake.

"Nice," I say, and push it toward him. "Not as good as the lemon mousse, though."

That's the other thing—I'm absolutely stuffed to the brim. I couldn't decide between all the scrummy-sounding desserts, so Luke said we should order all the ones we liked the sound of. Which was most of them. So now my stomach feels as though it's the size of a Christmas pudding, and just as heavy.

I honestly feel as if I'll never ever be able to get out of this chair. It's so comfortable, and I'm so warm and cozy, and it's all so pretty, and my head's spinning just enough to make me not want to stand up. Plus . . . I don't want it all to stop. I don't want the evening to end. I've had *such* a good time. The amazing thing is how much Luke makes me laugh. You'd think he'd be all serious and boring and intellectual, but really, he's not. In fact, come to think of it, we haven't talked about that unit trust thingy once.

A waiter comes and clears away all our pudding dishes, and brings us each a cup of coffee. I lean back in my chair, close my eyes, and take a few delicious sips. Oh God, I could stay here forever. I'm actually feeling really sleepy by now—partly because I was so nervous last night about *Morning Coffee*, I hardly slept at all.

"I should go," I say eventually, and force myself to open my eyes. "I should go back to . . ." Where do I live, again? "Fulham. To Fulham."

"Right," says Luke after a pause, and takes a sip of coffee. He puts his cup down and reaches for the milk. And as he does so, his hand brushes against mine—and stops still. At once I feel my whole body stiffen. I can't even blink, in case I break the spell.

OK, I'll admit it—I kind of put my hand in his way.

Just to see what would happen. I mean, he could easily move his hand back if he wanted to, couldn't he? Pour his milk, make a joke, say good-night.

But he doesn't. Very slowly, he closes his hand over mine.

And now I really can't move. His thumb starts to trace patterns on my wrist, and I can feel how warm and dry his skin is. I look up and meet his gaze, and feel a little jolt inside me. I can't tear my eyes away from his. I can't move my hand. I'm completely transfixed.

"That chap I saw you with in Terrazza," he says after a while, his thumb still drawing leisurely pictures on my skin. "Was he anything—"

"Just . . . you know." I try to give a careless laugh, but I'm feeling so nervous it comes out as a squeak. "Some multimillionaire or other."

Luke stares intently at me for a second, then looks away.

"Right," he says, as though closing the subject. "Well. Perhaps we should get you a taxi." I feel a thud of disappointment, and try not to let it show. "Or maybe . . ." He stops.

There's an endless pause. I can't quite breathe. Maybe what? What?

"I know them pretty well here," says Luke at last. "If we wanted to . . ." He meets my eyes. "I expect we could stay."

I feel an electric shock go through my body.

"Would you like to?"

Unable to speak, I nod my head.

"OK, wait here," says Luke. "I'll go and see if I can get rooms." He gets up and I stare after him in a daze, my hand all cold and bereft.

Rooms. Rooms, plural. So he didn't mean—

He doesn't want to—

Oh God. What's *wrong* with me?

We travel up in the lift in silence with a smart porter. I glance a couple of times at Luke's face, but he's staring impassively ahead. In fact, he's barely said a word since he went off to ask about staying. I feel a bit chilly inside—in fact, to be honest, I'm half wishing they hadn't had any spare rooms for us after all. But it turns out there was a big cancellation tonight—and it also turns out that Luke is some big-shot client of the Ritz. When I commented on how nice they were being to us, he shrugged and said he often puts up business contacts here.

Business contacts. So is that what I am? Oh, it doesn't make any sense. I wish I'd gone home after all.

We walk along an opulent corridor in complete silence—then the porter swings open a door and ushers us into a spectacularly beautiful room, furnished with a big double bed and plushy chairs. He places my briefcase and AppleMac on the luggage rail, then Luke gives him a bill and he disappears.

There's an awkward pause.

"Well," says Luke. "Here you are."

"Yes," I say in a voice which doesn't sound like mine. "Thanks . . . thank you. And for dinner." I clear my throat. "It was delicious."

We seem to have turned into complete strangers.

"Well," says Luke again, and glances at his watch. "It's late. You'll probably be wanting to . . ." He stops, and there's a sharp, waiting silence.

My hands are twisted in a nervous knot. I don't dare look at him.

"I'll be off, then," says Luke at last. "I hope you have a—"

"Don't go," I hear myself say, and blush furiously. "Don't go yet. We could just . . ." I swallow. "Talk, or something."

I look up and meet his eyes, and something fearful starts to pound within me. Slowly he walks toward me, until he's standing just in front of me. I can just smell the scent of his aftershave and hear the crisp cotton rustle of his shirt as he moves. My whole body's prickling with anticipation. Oh God, I want to touch him. But I daren't. I daren't move anything.

"We could just talk, or something," he echoes, and slowly lifts his hands until they cup my face.

And then he kisses me.

His mouth is on mine, gently parting my lips, and I feel a white-hot dart of excitement. His hands are running down my back and cupping my bottom, fingering under the hem of my skirt. And then he pulls me tightly toward him, and suddenly I'm finding it hard to breathe.

It's pretty obvious we're not going to do much talking at all.

Twenty-four

Mmm.

Bliss.

Lying in the most comfortable bed in the world, feeling all dreamy and smiley and happy, letting the morning sunlight play on my closed eyelids. Stretching my arms above my head, then collapsing contentedly onto an enormous mound of pillows. Oh, I feel good. I feel . . . sated. Last night was absolutely . . .

Well, let's just say it was . . .

Oh, come on. You don't need to know *that*. Anyway, can't you use your imagination? Of course you can.

I open my eyes, sit up, and reach for my cup of room-service coffee. Luke's in the shower, so it's just me alone with my thoughts. And I don't want to sound all pretentious here—but I do feel this is a pretty significant day in my life.

It's not just Luke—although the whole thing was . . . well, amazing, actually. God, he really knows how to . . .

Anyway. Not the point. The point is, it's not just Luke, and it's not just my new job with *Morning Coffee* (even though every time I remember it, I feel a leap of disbelieving joy).

No, it's more than that. It's that I feel like a completely

new person. I feel as though I'm moving on to a new stage in life—with a different outlook, and different priorities. When I look back at the frivolous way I used to think—well, it makes me want to laugh, really. The new Rebecca is so much more levelheaded. So much more responsible. It's as though the tinted glasses have fallen off—and suddenly I can see what's really important in the world and what's not.

I've even been thinking this morning that I might go into politics or something. Luke and I discussed politics a bit last night, and I have to say, I came up with lots of interesting views. I could be a young, intellectual member of parliament, and be interviewed about lots of important issues on television. I'd probably specialize in health, or education, or something like that. Maybe foreign affairs.

Casually I reach for the remote control and switch on the television, thinking I might watch the news. I flick a few times, trying to find BBC1, but the TV seems stuck on rubbish cable channels. Eventually I give up, leave it on something called QVT or something, and lean back down on my pillows.

The truth, I think, taking a sip of coffee, is that I'm quite a serious-minded person. That's probably why Luke and I get on so well.

Mmm, Luke. Mmm, that's a nice thought. I wonder where he is.

I sit up in bed, and am just considering going into the bathroom to surprise him, when a woman's voice from the television attracts my attention.

". . . offering genuine NK Malone sunglasses, in tortoiseshell, black, and white, with that distinctive NKM logo in brushed chrome."

That's interesting, I think idly. NK Malone sunglasses. I've always quite wanted a pair of those.

"Buy all three pairs . . ." the woman pauses ". . . and pay not £400. Not £300. But £200! A saving of at least 40 percent off the recommended retail price."

I stare at the screen, riveted.

But this is incredible. *Incredible.* Do you know how much NK Malone sunglasses usually cost? At least 140 quid. Each! Which means you're saving . . .

"Send no money now," the woman is saying. "Simply call this number . . ."

Excitedly I scrabble for the notebook on my bedside table and scribble down the number. This is an absolute dream come true. NK Malone sunglasses. I can't quite believe it. And three pairs! I'll never have to buy sunglasses again. People will call me the Girl in the NK Malone Shades. (And those Armani ones I bought last year are all wrong now. Completely out of date.) Oh, this is *such* an investment. With shaking hands I reach for the phone and dial the number.

And then I stop.

Wait just a moment. The new Rebecca has more self-control than this. The new Rebecca isn't even *interested* in fashion.

Slowly I put the phone down. I reach for the remote and zap the TV to a different channel. A nature program. Yes, that's more like it. There's a close-up of a tiny green frog and a sober voice-over talking about the effect of drought on the ecosystem. I turn up the volume and settle back, pleased with myself. This is much more me. I'm not going to give those sunglasses a second thought. I'm going to learn about this tiny frog and the ecosystem, and global warming. Maybe Luke and I will talk about all these important issues, over breakfast.

NK Malone.

Stop it. *Stop* it. Watch the frog, and that tiny red beetle thing . . .

I've wanted NK Malone sunglasses for so long. And £200 is amazing value for three pairs.

I could always give one pair away as a present.

And I deserve a little treat, don't I? After everything I've been though? Just one little final luxury and that's the end. I *promise*.

Grabbing the phone, I redial the number. I give my name and address, thank the woman very much indeed, then put down the receiver, a content smile on my face. This day is turning out perfect. And it's only nine o'clock!

I turn off the nature program, snuggle back down under the covers, and close my eyes. Maybe Luke and I will spend all day here, in this lovely room. Maybe we'll have oysters and champagne sent up. (I hope not, actually, because I hate oysters.) Maybe we'll . . .

Nine o'clock, interrupts a little voice in my mind. I frown for a second, shake my head, then turn over to get rid of it. But it's still there, prodding annoyingly at my thoughts.

Nine o'clock. Nine . . .

And suddenly I sit bolt upright in bed, my eyes wide in dismay. Oh my God.

Nine-thirty.

Derek Smeath.

I promised to be there. I *promised*. And here I am, with half an hour to go, all the way over at the Ritz. Oh God. What am I going to do?

I switch off the TV, bury my head in my hands, and try to think calmly and rationally. OK, if I got going straight away, I might make it. If I got dressed as quickly as possible, and ran downstairs and jumped in a taxi—I might just make it. Fulham's not that far away. And I could be a quarter of an hour late, couldn't I? We could still have the meeting. It could still happen.

In theory, it could still happen.

"Hi," says Luke, putting his head round the bathroom door. He's got a white towel wrapped round his body, and a few drops of water are glistening on his shoulders. I never even noticed his shoulders last night, I think, staring at them. God, they're bloody sexy. In fact, all in all, he's pretty damn . . .

"Rebecca? Is everything OK?"

"Oh," I say, starting slightly. "Yes, everything's great. Lovely! Oh, and guess what? I just bought the most wonderful . . ."

And then for some reason I stop myself midstream.

I'm not exactly sure why.

"Just . . . having breakfast," I say instead, and gesture to the room-service tray. "Delicious."

A faintly puzzled look passes over Luke's face, and he disappears back into the bathroom. OK, quick, I tell myself. What am I doing to do? Am I going to get dressed and go? Am I going to make the meeting?

But my hand's already reaching for my bag as though it's got a will of its own; I'm pulling out a business card and punching a number into the phone.

Because, I mean, we don't actually *need* to have a meeting, do we? I'm going to send him a nice big check.

And I'd probably never make it in time, anyway.

And he probably won't even mind. He's probably got loads of other stuff he'd prefer to be doing instead.

"Hello?" I say into the phone, and feel a tingle of pleasure as Luke comes up behind me and begins to nuzzle my ear. "Hello, yes. I'd . . . I'd like to leave a message for Mr. Smeath."

$\mathscr{F}$INE $\mathscr{F}$RAMES LTD.
The happy home working family

230A BURNSIDE ROAD LEEDS L6 4ST

Ms. Rebecca Bloomwood
Flat 2
4 Burney Rd.
London SW6 8FD

7 April 2000

Dear Rebecca:

I write to acknowledge receipt of 136 completed Fine
Frames ("Sherborne" style—blue). Thank you very much
for your fine work. A check for £272 is enclosed, together
with an application form for your next frame-making pack.

Our quality control manager, Mrs. Sandra Rowbotham, has
asked me to inform you that she was extremely impressed
with the quality of your first batch. Novices rarely come
up to the exacting standards of the Fine Frames Quality
Promise—it is clear you have a natural gift for frame-
making.

I would therefore like to invite you to come and
demonstrate your technique at our next Framemakers'
Convention, to be held in Wilmslow on June 21. This is an
occasion when all the members of the Fine Frames
homeworking family gather under one roof, with a
chance to exchange frame-making tips and anecdotes. It's
a lot of fun, believe me!

We very much look forward to hearing from you.

Happy frame-making!

Malcolm Headley
Managing Director

P.S. Are you the same Rebecca Bloomwood who gives
advice on *Morning Coffee*?

Ms. Rebecca Bloomwood
Flat 2
4 Burney Rd.
London SW6 8FD

10 April 2000

Dear Ms. Bloomwood:

Thank you for your recent deposit of £1,000.

Bearing in mind the relatively healthy state of your current
account at the present time, I suggest that we might
postpone our meeting for the moment.

However, be assured that I shall be keeping a close eye on
the situation and will be in touch, should matters change
in any way.

With best wishes.

Yours sincerely,

Derek Smeath
Manager

P.S. I look forward to your next performance on *Morning
Coffee.*

ACKNOWLEDGMENTS

Warmest thanks to Susan Kamil and Zoë Rice for all their guidance, inspiration, and enthusiasm. Also to Kim Witherspoon and David Forrer, Celia Hayley, Mark Lucas and all at LAW, all at Transworld, Valerie Hoskins and Rebecca Watson and Brian Siberell at CAA.

Special thanks to Samantha Wickham, Sarah Manser, Paul Watts, Chantal Rutherford-Brown, my wonderful family, and especially Gemma, who taught me how to shop.

This book is dedicated to my friend and agent, Araminta Whitley.

ABOUT THE AUTHOR

SOPHIE KINSELLA is a writer and former financial journalist. She is very, very careful with her money and only occasionally finds herself queuing for a sale. Her relationship with her bank manager is excellent.

THE "TREAT YOURSELF" NOVEL OF THE YEAR
FROM THE AUTHOR OF
Confessions of a Shopaholic
Shopaholic
Takes
Manhattan
Because there just
aren't enough shops
in London....
New York Times Bestselling Author
SOPHIE
KINSELLA

Packing light takes on a whole new meaning when Becky Bloomwood (and her credit cards) head across the Atlantic . . .

SHOPAHOLIC
TAKES
MANHATTAN

With her shopping excesses (somewhat) in check and her career as a TV financial guru thriving, Becky's biggest problem seems to be tearing her entrepreneur boyfriend, Luke, away from work for a romantic country weekend. But packing light takes on a whole new meaning when Luke announces he's moving to New York for business—and he asks Becky to go with him! Before you can say "Prada sample sale," Becky has landed in the Big Apple, home of Park Avenue penthouses and luxury boutiques.

Surely it's only a matter of time until she becomes an American TV celebrity, and she and Luke are the toast of Gotham society. Nothing can stand in their way, especially with Becky's bills miles away in London. But then an unexpected disaster threatens her career prospects, her relationship with Luke, and her available credit line! *Shopaholic Takes Manhattan*—but will she have to return it?

On sale in mass market

SOPHIE KINSELLA

New York Times Bestselling Author of
Confessions of a Shopaholic

Shopaholic
Ties the Knot

There's never been a better excuse to buy a new dress (or two) as Becky Bloomwood walks down a whole new aisle in . . .

SHOPAHOLIC
TIES THE
KNOT

Life has been good for Becky Bloomwood: She's become the best personal shopper at Barneys, she and her successful entrepreneurial boyfriend, Luke, are living happily in Manhattan's West Village, and her new next-door neighbor is a fashion designer! But with her best friend, Suze, engaged, how can Becky fail to notice that her own ring finger is bare? Not that she's been thinking of marriage (or diamonds) or anything . . .

Then Luke proposes! Bridal registries dance in Becky's head. Problem is, two other people are planning her wedding: Becky's overjoyed mother has been waiting forever to host a backyard wedding, with the bride resplendent in Mum's frilly old gown, while Luke's high-society mother is insisting on a glamorous, all-expenses-paid affair at the Plaza. Both weddings on the same day. And Becky can't seem to turn down either one. Can everyone's favorite shopaholic tie the knot before everything unravels?

On sale in mass market

Can You Keep a Secret?

a novel

SOPHIE KINSELLA

The New York Times
Bestselling Author
of
Confessions of
a Shopaholic

Now Available in Hardcover

Becky Bloomwood returns for more

hilarious hijinks in a new novel about

married life, best friends, and a long-lost

sister who (gasp!) hates shopping . . .

Shopaholic
& Sister

Shopaholic
& Sister

On sale in hardcover

OK. I CAN do this. No problem.

It's simply a matter of letting my higher self take over, achieving enlightenment, and becoming a radiant being of white light.

Easy-peasy.

Surreptitiously I adjust myself on my yoga mat so I'm facing the sun directly, and push down the spaghetti straps of my top. I don't see why you can't reach ultimate-bliss consciousness and get an even tan at the same time.

I'm sitting on a hillside in the middle of Sri Lanka at the Blue Hills Resort and Spiritual Retreat, and the view is spectacular. Hills and tea plantations stretch ahead, then merge into a deep blue sky. I can see the bright colors of tea pickers in the fields, and if I swivel my head a little, I glimpse a distant elephant padding slowly along between the bushes.

And when I turn my head still further, I can see Luke. My husband. He's the one on the blue yoga mat, in the cut-off linen trousers and tatty old top, sitting cross-legged with his eyes closed.

I know. It's just unbelievable. After ten months of honeymoon, Luke has turned into a totally different person from the man I married. The old corporate Luke has vanished. The suits have disappeared. He's tanned and lean, his hair is long and sun-bleached, and he's still got a few of the little plaits he had put in on Bondi Beach. Round his wrist is a beaded bracelet he bought in India, and in his ear is a tiny silver hoop.

Luke Brandon with an earring! Luke Brandon sitting cross-legged!

As though he can feel my gaze, he opens his eyes and smiles, and I beam back happily. Ten months married. And not a single row.

Well. You know. Only the odd little one.

"*Siddhasana*," says our yoga teacher, Chandra. He's a tall, thin man in baggy white yoga trousers, and always speaks in a soft, patient voice. "Clear your minds of all extraneous thought."

Around me I'm aware of the eight or nine others in the group moving into position on their mats. Obediently I place my right foot on my left thigh.

OK. Clear my mind. Concentrate.

I don't want to boast, but I find clearing my mind pretty easy. I don't quite get why anyone would find it difficult! I mean, not-thinking has to be a lot easier than thinking, doesn't it?

In fact, the truth is, I'm a bit of a natural at yoga. We've only been on this retreat for five days but already I can do the Lotus and everything! I was even thinking I might set up as a yoga teacher when we go back home.

Maybe I could set up a partnership with Trudie Styler, I think in sudden excitement. God yes! And we could launch a range of yoga-wear, too, all soft grays and whites, with a little logo—

"Focus on your breathing," Chandra is saying.

Oh right yes. Breathing.

Breathe in . . . breathe out. Breathe in . . . breathe out. Breathe . . .

God, my nails look fab. I had them done at the spa—little pink butterflies on a white background. And the antennae are little diamonds. They are so sweet. Except one seems to have fallen off. I must get that fixed—

"Becky." Chandra's voice makes me jump. He's standing right there, gazing at me with this look he has. Kind of gentle and all-knowing, like he can see right inside your mind.

"You do very well, Becky," he says. "You have a beautiful spirit."

I feel a sparkle of delight all over. I, Rebecca Brandon, née Bloomwood, have a beautiful spirit! I knew it!

"You have an unworldly soul," he adds in his soft voice, and I stare back, totally mesmerized.

"Material possessions aren't important to me," I say breathlessly. "All that matters to me is yoga."

"You have found your path." Chandra smiles.

There's an odd kind of snorting sound from Luke's direction and I look round, to see him looking over at us in amusement.

I *knew* Luke wasn't taking this seriously.

"This is a private conversation between me and my guru, thank you very much," I say crossly.

Although actually I shouldn't be surprised. We were warned about this on the first day of the yoga course. Apparently when one partner finds higher spiritual enlightenment, the other partner can react with skepticism and even jealousy.

"Soon you will be walking on the hot coals."

Chandra gestures with a smile to the nearby pit of smoldering ashy coals, and a nervous laugh goes round the group. This evening Chandra and some of his top yoga students are going to demonstrate walking on the coals for the rest of us. This is what we're all supposed to be aiming for. Apparently you attain a state of bliss so great, you can't actually feel the coals burning your feet. You're totally pain free!

What I'm secretly hoping is that it'll work when I wear six-inch stilettos, too.

Chandra adjusts my arms and moves on, and I close my eyes, letting the sun warm my face. Sitting here on this hillside in the middle of nowhere, I feel so pure and calm. It's not just Luke who's changed over the last ten months. I have, too. I've grown up. My priorities have altered. In fact, I'm a different person. I mean, look at me now, doing yoga at a spiritual retreat. My old friends probably wouldn't even recognize me!

At Chandra's instruction, we all move into the *Vajrasana* pose. From where I am, I can just see an old Sri Lankan man carrying two old carpet bags approaching Chandra. They have a brief conversation, during which Chandra keeps shaking his head, then the old man trudges away again over the scrubby hillside. When he's out of earshot, Chandra turns to face the group, rolling his eyes.

"This man is a merchant. He asks if any of you are interested in gems. Necklaces, cheap bracelets. I tell him your minds are on higher things."

A few people near me shake their heads as though in disbelief. One woman with long red hair looks affronted.

"Couldn't he see we were in the middle of meditation?" she says.

"He has no understanding of your spiritual devotion." Chandra looks seriously around the group. "It will be the same with many others in the world. They will not understand that meditation is food for your soul. You have no need for . . . sapphire bracelet!"

A few people nod in appreciation.

"Aquamarine pendant with platinum chain," Chandra continues dismissively. "How does this compare to the radiance of inner enlightenment?"

Aquamarine?

Wow. I wonder how much—

I mean, not that I'm interested. Obviously not. It's just that I happened to be looking at aquamarines in a shop window the other day. Just out of an academic interest.

My eye drifts toward the retreating figure of the old man.

"Three-carat setting, five-carat setting, he keeps saying. All half price." Chandra shakes his head. "I tell him, these people are not interested."

Half price? Five-carat aquamarines at half price?

Stop it. Stop it. Chandra's right. Of course I'm not interested in stupid aquamarines. I'm absorbed in spiritual enlightenment.

Anyway, the old man's nearly gone now. He's just a tiny figure on top of the hill. In a minute he'll have disappeared.

"And now." Chandra smiles. "The *Halasana* pose. Becky, will you demonstrate?"

"Absolutely." I smile at Chandra and prepare to get into position on my mat.

But something's wrong. I don't feel contentment. I don't feel tranquility. The oddest feeling is welling up inside me, driving everything else out. It's getting stronger and stronger . . .

And suddenly I can't contain it anymore. Before I know what's happening, I'm running in my bare feet as fast as I can up the hill toward the tiny figure. My lungs are burning, my feet are smarting, and the sun's beating down on my bare head, but I don't stop until I've reached the crest of the hill. I come to a halt and look around, panting.

I don't believe it. He's gone. Where did he vanish to?

I stand for a few moments, regaining my breath, peering in all directions. But I can't see him anywhere.

At last, feeling a little dejected, I turn and make my way back down the hillside to the group. As I get near I realize they're all shouting and waving at me. Oh God. Am I in trouble?

"You did it!" the red-haired woman's yelling. "You did it!"

"Did what?"

"You ran over the hot coals! You did it, Becky!"

What?

I look down at my feet . . . and I don't believe it. They're covered in gray ash! In a daze, I look at the pit of coals—and there's a set of clear footprints running through it.

Oh my God. Oh my *God*! I ran over the coals! I ran over the burning hot smoldering coals! I did it!

"But . . . but I didn't even notice!" I say, bewildered. "My feet aren't even burned!"

"How did you do it?" demands the red-haired woman. "What was in your mind?"

"I can answer." Chandra comes forward, smiling. "Becky has achieved the highest form of karmic bliss. She was concentrating on one goal, one pure image, and this has driven her body to achieve a supernatural state."

Everyone is goggling at me like I'm suddenly the Dalai Lama.

"It was nothing really," I say, with a modest smile. "Just . . . you know. Spiritual enlightenment."

"Can you describe the image?" says the red-haired woman in excitement.

"Was it white?" chimes someone else.

"Not really white . . ." I say.

"Was it a kind of shiny blue-green?" comes Luke's voice from the back. I look up sharply. He's gazing back, totally straight-faced.

"I don't remember," I say with dignity. "The color wasn't important."

"Did it feel like . . ." Luke appears to think hard. "Like the links of a chain were pulling you along?"

"That's a very good image, Luke," chimes in Chandra, pleased.

"No," I say shortly. "It didn't. Actually, I think you probably have to have a higher appreciation of spiritual matters to understand."

"I see." Luke nods gravely.

"Luke, you must be very proud." Chandra beams at Luke. "Is this not the most extraordinary thing you have ever seen your wife do?"

There's a beat of silence. Luke looks from me, to the smoldering coals, to the silent group and back to Chandra's beaming face.

"Chandra," he says. "Take it from me. This is nothing."